Lords of Asylum

By Kevin Wright

Quantum Muse Books

Also By Kevin Wright:

The Clarity of Cold Steel

Monster City

GrimNoir

Swamp Lords

It came in this darkest of years, this winter of bitterest cold, when dire wolves loped marauding through the city, laying drek and slaughter upon man, woman, and child. When finally they retreated, it was believed a miracle from God. It was not.

—*Journal of Sir Myron Chalstain*

Chapter 1.

IN THE COLD dark lands, I dreamt of death and black murder.

> *Bang!*
> *Bang!*
> *Bang!*

"*Jesus Christ*—" I snorted awake to the hammer-slam of a gauntleted fist pounding against the wagon. Fast. Metallic. Urgent. I lurched up from my wagon-bed, groping blind for my sword but smashing my head against one of the stacked crates instead, nearly knocking myself senseless. At first, I thought we were under attack. Again. With my blade fumbled into hand, I poked my head out the rear of the wagon, looked around, trying to focus, and met only cold winter silence.

Wincing, I felt at the ragged stitches along my forehead. Still intact.

Nothing moved in our little camp. The lion's share of snow we'd dug out from the ruins of an old Roman way station built atop a small rise. A thousand years old. A thousand years dead. Only two walls still stood intact, forming a corner eight feet high, the rest just a ghost, a shell. A cozy little camp, except for the carnage, a God damned raven-feast come sunup. Long slashes of black splatter fouled the winter white. Tents lay torn, the ground strewn with arrows and weapons. Bodies lay next to my wagon. Five. All lined up in a neat row. A small cooking fire smoldered by the wall. I made to settle back into my makeshift bed, pull my blanket over my head and die when I noticed him standing there in the dark, a shadow, gazing off east.

Karl.

"What the hell are you doing?" I asked.

"Get up, asshole," Karl rumbled low. Shorter than me by at least a head, he was a squat, grizzled bulldog of a man. The kind of bulldog you hide from the book-men and bettors, so he doesn't screw the odds. Ruin the bets. The one the pit-bear looks at with a kind of fear in his war-weary eyes, knows that maybe this is the one. "We've visitors." He pointed off down the road. "Wolves. The two-legged sort."

The night was old, the air dead, dead and cold and dead. The kind of cold that just sits there and latches on, soaking into your bones, your soul, becoming part of you. Hot soup and grog and August sun might stave it off, but they're far off, long gone. Always. I pushed the crates back into some semblance of order, rubbed my pounding head. I could barely see straight.

"You alright?" Karl peered in. "Reckoned you for a goner."

I shifted. "Nothing broken." Just everything hurt.

"Hrrrm…" He squinted close at my stitched forehead.

"Am I still pretty?"

Karl stifled a chuckle.

"Is it Stephan?" I nodded toward the road.

"Don't know." Karl reached in, setting a bulls-eye lantern on the wagon-bed. "Got it?"

"Yeah." I took up the lantern, my fingers enwrapping the warm tin. Pressed it against my cheek. Let loose a soft groan.

"Maybe I should leave you two alone." Karl pulled out his flask. "Here." He set it atop a crate. "I'll take a gander."

He disappeared into the dark while I scrambled ravenous for his flask. I tore the stopper free, took a pull, relaxed almost instantly, reflexively, and felt it, that delicious burn searing all the way down. But then something went wrong. Nausea. Torqueing my guts. I waited for it to pass, head swirling, pounding, gorge rising. I couldn't hold it and let loose a torrent of puke. Fierce. Prolonged. Homeric.

Dangling half out of the wagon, soiled, senseless, useless, I remained for a piece, the hanged man of some pathetic tarot stack. I blinked. Our horse lay beneath, feathered shafts sticking out of its neck, its flank, its eye. "Fine shot." Beside the horse carcass laid the five human ones. My men. Michael. Riddled with arrows. Aaron, a spear sticking out of his chest, butt-end aimed up at the heavens. The others had been smashed, hacked with axes or swords. It didn't matter. Not now. And not ever again.

"Sorry fellas." Wasn't much else to say. I wiped my mouth on the corner of my cloak and hauled myself back up. Bones creaking like rusted hinges. I collapsed against the stacked boxes of Flanders wool, the best on the continent, and waited for Karl.

That flask, though, glimmered in the lantern-light. And it was still nearly full. "If at first you don't succeed…" I bent it back, feeling the cool smooth against my lips, and drank my venom, my mass, my sacrament. It stayed down this time. *Victory.*

Beyond, the Hellwood lay silent. No wind. No sounds. No nothing. Even the wolves, the four-legged ones dogging our heels the past few days, twin amber moons flashing in the dark, were silent. I reached for my blade, Yolanda, her ugly brass hilt worn, pitted, her ragged sharkskin grip rough but reassuring. Comfortable. Mine. Sheathed, she ain't so pretty, it's true. But you draw her out, all that crucible Damascus steel singing sad and slow, revealing all that's gleaming, cold, and merciless sharp? Beauty incarnate.

I wrestled my mail shirt on, tightened my belt and leaned back, settling in. Pulling my blanket up over my shoulders, I took another swig, felt the warmth from within spread out from my belly, down my arms and legs to my fingers and toes.

Karl came trudging back, mail shirt rustling, weapons clinking, breath steaming heavy. "Riders." He yanked a slender tree branch from out the top of his hobnail boot, tossed it aside with a grimace. "Coming up the road. Some afoot, too."

"See who it is?"

"Naw. Too fucking dark."

"How many?"

"More than two fists. One's leading a draft horse." Karl nodded down at our own draft horse lying dead in the snow. "And there's a woman."

"Oh?" I brushed my hair down and smoothed my goatee reflexively.

Karl muttered profanities unfit to repeat. "Scouts coming up first. On foot. Pair of 'em." He pointed with the head of that thane-axe. "North side of the road. Uphill. Through thick underbrush. Deep snow. We've a moment or two."

"Moving to flank?"

"*Flank?*" A grin split his face, fierce, wicked as a knife. "Well, look at you, using that trove of war-words." He slapped me on the back. I nearly died. Right there. Karl paused, stiffened, sniffed. "You puke?"

"You're standing in it."

"Odin's teeth—" Karl scraped the sole of his boot on the frozen horse carcass. "Rrrg. What in hell's the play?"

I glared down at the dead, all five staring back up at me, all five blue as ice. In my furor, after he'd stitched my wounds, I'd argued with Stephan, my baby brother, telling him it was a waste of time, a fool's errand, him riding off into the old night on some quest to save them, to save me. Somehow. But I'd never stopped him before. So why now? And where the hell was he? "I want to live."

"Run-live? Or fight-live?"

"Too drunk to run-live." I shook my head. "Too sober to fight-live."

"You ain't never been too sober to do nothing."

"I don't know what that means." From between snowdrifts, a section of tiled fresco peeked up from the ground, untouched by fresh murder, a Roman cavalryman in full regalia down on one knee, offering a rose to a red-haired maiden of somber beauty. "Where'd you stash the bad guys?"

"*We're* the bad guys," Karl sneered.

"Right. Where'd you stash those dumb dead fuckers tried killing us?"

Karl grunted, nodding in the direction of a drift of snow where the two intact sections of wall met. The snow was deeper there. What before I'd taken as a gnarled stick I now made out as a hand crippled into a rictus poking out of the snow. "Sick of looking at them."

"Any get away?"

"Yar."

"How many, you hazard?"

"Hrrm," Karl counted on his fingers, "some."

"Great." I crawled like a palsied dog out of the wagon, barely, and managed not to fall, surprisingly. Staggering to the wall for support, I looked out over the Hellwood. Trees lay for leagues every which way except north. North lay the sea. The road paralleled it, west to east. I imagined I could see a glow, coming up it. Far away. Just not far enough. Eleven men. Eleven fighting men. At least. A lady, though? And a draft horse? *Strange.* "Alright." My gears were turning. "You go. Hide. Keep watch, yeah? Take the crossbow. I'll stay. Suss them out. Put this silver tongue to good use."

"Licking boots or arse?"

"Whatever it takes." I nodded to myself. "We ain't losing the goods." My head was clearing, by necessity. "Sound sharp?"

"They ain't coming to dice at hazard, lad."

"It has to be Stephan." Probably true. It was too late for someone to be coming for anything on the level. That was plain. But highwaymen? Twice in one night? Even *my* luck's not that bad. Usually. Or was I wrong? Was it indeed them? Come back to finish us? No. It was a different group. They had a woman with them which was strange enough, and they were coming openly. They knew we were here. Knew we were stuck. "It has to."

"Ain't have to be no one, lad," Karl cautioned.

"They had the wherewithal to bring a draft horse." My decision was made. "I'll signal if I need you."

"How?"

"I'll scream like a little girl."

"And then?" he asked. "Gonna take the rest on yourself?"

"Alright, so maybe we *are* gonna lose the goods," I conceded. "Still, I ain't leaving."

"Your funeral." He hefted his crossbow, loaded it, set it on the wall.

Somewhere to the west, the deep woods, a lone wolf howled, breaking the long silence.

"Always a good omen," I said.

These old woods, a thousand years ago the Romans had come here with their centurions and scorpions. Thousands of them. To conquer. To take. Karl's pagan ancestors had stopped them. The Roman war machine, slaughtered to a man.

"Still can't see shit." I squinted.

"There."

"Yeah." Beyond the skeletal cover of a bare-branched copse of wood, I caught a glimmer of light. Distant. Disappearing. Flickering. A torch. Then another. They slid in and out from behind the trees, glowing, floating, beckoning, will o' the wisps fishing for souls. Lucky me, I pawned mine ages ago.

"Ain't Stephan," Karl spat. "Stephan'd warn us. Knowed he might get shot."

I grunted, noncommittally. "Can you make them out?"

"Naw." Karl watched like a hawk, his eyesight comparable. "Got to be one of them knights. Or a lord. Horses, men, armor, the ruckus and all."

"Hell," I didn't even have to think, "the Cyclops, then."

"Naw, even Stephan wouldn't trust that prick."

"No, he wouldn't." But a sliver of doubt swelled in my rock of resolve. "But he's the only one has a keep between here and the city. Only one that's near." Shit. "Got the men. The means." I white-knuckled Yolanda tight. "Well, I'll find out soon enough." The entourage rounded a bend in the road. "Ain't exactly sneaking. That's a good sign, yeah?"

They came in a line, three astride horses, seven walking, trudging, the last one leading a draft horse. As they neared, I saw the woman, slender, cloaked, poised, an elegant figure upright riding side-saddle. Except for her and the man leading the draft horse, they were all armed.

"Scouts." Karl glared at something beyond the road.

"Best get moving."

Karl hung there for a moment. "Sure a wagon of wool's worth it?"

I clenched a fist to my mouth as a tidal wave of nausea crashed. "It ain't," I took a deep breath, "but this ain't about a wagonload of wool, now is it?"

...too late for such measures to prove effective. The city-guard has been decimated, nay, more than decimated, and food has grown ever scarce in the eastern half of the city. People are starving there, and yet the fools persist in killing one another...
—*Journal of Sir Myron Chalstain*

Chapter 2.

IN THE PULSATING DARK, I crouched by the campfire, adjusting to the forest silence, straining my ears, drawing back layers, reaching, hearing things I hadn't before, the break of waves on shore, the soft rise of wind rustling through fir needles above, the clomp of hooves on the old Roman road. Close.

A shadow emerged from the woods to the crush of dead twigs, the clang of weapon and armor. He oozed like oil across the ruin's north wall, his yellow eyes searching everywhere but somehow still always fixed on me. "Be dropping that sword, mate," he grinned, "if ya know what's good for ya." In his gloved fists, he bore a wicked spear.

"Fuck off." Using the wall on one side and Yolanda on the other, I managed to rise straight and tall, projecting a figure of haughty indifference, in control despite every evidence to the contrary. Breathe slow. Breathe deep. "Where's your lord and master?" I gazed off beyond the Grinner, dismissing him as a horse clomped into camp.

A huge horse.

A giant rider.

I swallowed. Maintained. Ram horns curved down, sprouting from the giant's helm, hiding his face behind a mask of cold iron. A hell-beast conglomerate the two were, steam pouring from the ventail of his helm, orange embers licking off his torch, the black iron chaffron forged skeletal, engulfing the hell-steed's head.

"That's close enough, good sir." I steeled my voice to something approximating a man's, but only just. "Your business. State it or be gone." *Imminent*, a word that sprang to mind.

Dead silent, he just stared past me. Steel scraped, jangled. The warhorse snorted, blowing snot across the fresco, scuffing muck under shod hoof as he and rider circled, gaze focused outward to the surrounding wood.

"Sir, I am under the king's protection." Yolanda hung heavy in my hand.

The giant still said nothing. From the road, seven men loped like a pack of wolves into camp, spreading out. In the flickering torchlight, their armor shone dull brown and grey. They bore long swords. Shields. Spears. The monstrous giant barked in some foreign tongue and two crossbowmen took up position before me, one left and one right, bolts aimed at me. Bookends.

"Gentlemen—" I stuttered to a halt as another rider clomped in from the road. He dismounted smoothly, handing the reins off to one of his men. A lord, no mistaking that, by his fine fur-lined cloak. His craggy face was weathered raw by age, gnarled by life and by death, mangles of scar writhing up across the right half as though some beast had savaged him tooth and claw. His close-cropped beard was as white as his dead left eye.

I stifled a shudder. Fucked. I was that. It was the Cyclops, Lord Raachwald, the Gallows Lord. History, he and I shared a piece. And not the good kind.

"What have we?" Lord Raachwald asked in a near whisper, the sound of a blade drawn deliberately across whetstone.

The giant barked something, gesticulating toward the forest.

"Aye," the lord answered, "see it done," and that white eye, the clouded eye of a long-dead fish, turned back on me. "Which king was it you spoke of?" He cocked his head a mite.

"My lord...?" A bead of freezing sweat rolled down my back.

"You claimed protection under some king." He glanced around in a mockery of search. "I merely wished to ascertain which king it was that offers you this...*supposed* protection?" That word '*supposed*' rang in my mind like a church bell tolling and not the wedding kind.

"Yeah, uh…I might have overplayed my hand there," I admitted.

"Svaldrake is under the jurisdiction of no king." He was old, but not weak, a gnarled tree only hardened by age. "We have no kings. We desire no kings. We *suffer* no kings."

"Then, of course, it is you, my lord, whose aegis shields me." I bowed low, just shy of true groveling by a hair. "Sir Luther Slythe Krait, at your—"

"Enough." Lord Raachwald's good eye gleamed a savage gold. "You know who I am. And I you. Games, I am not over-fond of them." He drew in a long breath. "Did you truly believe it possible I would not know you?" He grasped a log from the woodpile and dropped it into the fire. "You are not presently dead. See that as a pleasant yet uncertain situation."

I swallowed.

The giant growled something ferocious.

"No." The lord glanced over. "That shan't be necessary. Have Old Inglestahd construct another fire, and see to it the lady is brought up. Some hot wine would do. Or cider. Her choice. And bring the wheeler as well." He studied the corpses lined up by the wagon. "You've no small measure of death upon your hands."

"The lads drank a little too much," I deadpanned. "Tripped and fell on their swords."

One of the crossbowmen barked a laugh at that.

Lord Raachwald silenced him with a curious glance. "And what of the dead buried yonder?" He nodded toward the corner.

"Merchants," I answered, as one of Lord Raachwald's men cut a ringed finger from Aaron. "Ahem," he tossed the finger, kept the ring, "interested in procuring our wool. They made an offer. It was low."

"And yet still they paid a price."

"Pardon, my lord," I looked around as armed men took everything in the world that I owned, "are you here to aid me?" It wasn't much, but... "You've a wheeler in tow? How...fortuitous."

"Haefgrim," Lord Raachwald said to his giant, "secure the area. We shall remain as long as necessity demands." The lord scanned the dark forest. "Do what you deem necessary."

The giant growled something, and he and mount disappeared into the darkness, six warriors in tow.

Lord Raachwald turned and bowed woodenly. "The Lady Narcissa Volkendorf."

A lady strolled into the ruins, wrapped in a dark purple cloak dagged at the edges by ravens in flight. Black ermine lined the hood, her face lost in its shadow. My heart pounded. Gliding ethereal, with perfect composure, grace incarnate, she came by the fire, her gloved hand upon the arm of a fierce old codger guiding her.

Lord Raachwald dismissed the codger and waited until the lady sat before he did so himself. That lidless white eye found me again, after a long hungry gaze allotted to his companion. "Sit."

"My lady." I bowed and sat on a log. Lord Raachwald and Lady Volkendorf together...? Their houses were enemies. *Ancestral* enemies.

"Haefgrim says you have a man in the wood." The lord studied me. "This wood is ancient. It is treacherous. It is mine. North to the sea. West to Flanders. East to Asylum. All of it. Your man had best practice caution. Wolves...and far worse than wolves dwell here."

"Your man is mistaken," I lied.

"As I said, I hold no fondness for games." A scar hewn in an age gone long to dust bisected the lord's golden eye, as though he'd been chopped with an axe just shy of hard enough. "One man lived." Yggdrasil, the world tree, his house sigil, splayed out across his chest, black on a field of green, its branches reaching high, claw-like, rending the sky, its roots leviathan long, grasping deep the earth below. "That is truth. We do not deny truth."

"I ordered him off." I shrugged. "I thought you

brigands come back to finish your work."

Shadows slid across his face, the tangle of scar seeming to writhe, to dance. "And do you now *not* believe that?"

"Heh…" I chuffed a forced laugh, playing it off as a jest as my bowels dropped in my gut, through my gut. But it was no jest, no pretext to a jest. Jesus, if ever there was a man who did not jest.

"Haefgrim and his men are fond of the hunt," Lord Raachwald said. "Proficient, they are. What odds on your man?"

"You claimed to dislike games," I retorted reflexively, stupidly.

"A wager?" The edges of his coat-of-plate squealed softly against one another. "Nay. A curiosity. Professional."

I rubbed my hands over the fire. "Then, I imagine I shall have to find another man."

As I spoke, a stocky peasant emerged from the road, huffing, lugging a bulging work bag over his stooped shoulder, leading a draft horse. He knuckled his forehead and bowed then began inspecting the broken wagon wheel.

"What are you, Krait?" Lord Raachwald leaned forward. "A stalwart defender who sent his man off to live whilst he alone faced death?"

"Me?" I stifled a laugh. "Nay. Just a man. And barely that by most reckoning."

"A coward, then? To remain? To offer surrender? To beg clemency?"

"You're getting warmer."

"So swiftly he concedes the point…?" His lips pursed. "You think you're clever? I must warn you, I have always been deaf to silver-gilt tongues. A gamble. You think that cleverness and wit shall win you the day where steel or fear have not? That has not been my experience. I've met my share of clever men. Aye. Soft men." He extended a mailed hand toward the lady. "In a room filled with women and wine they see themselves invincible. Indomitable. Strutting about like peacocks, babbling word-troves. Rattling jewelhilted swords. But I've never known a man to spout cleverness as charred bones were drawn smoking from his blackened feet." My toes scrunched up reflexively within my boots. "Yet I ken a *true* coward would have run or hid."

"I was too drunk to run," I explained. "And as for any success in me hiding—"

"It would have required a hunter devoid of sense of smell," Lady Narcissa hissed.

The fire crackled in response, a log popping, embers jumping, me not daring to move. Or blink. Or breathe.

I dry-swallowed. Finally. "Forgive me, my lady." I reeked of vomit; I could smell it now, again. "My appearance. My manners. I've been traveling for quite some time, and one forgets the niceties of civilized life when long ahorse. If I offend you, please, allow me a moment to clean up."

Behind the lord and lady, the Grinner set to pulling the boots from Michael's feet. They were new boots. Fine boots. From Stettin.

"A moment?" Her voice was harsh, lyrical, beautiful. "A *week* would do little to assuage it."

"Again, my lady proves painfully accurate," I admitted. "Might I inquire—"

The lord raised a hand. The wheeler had concluded his inspection and stood by patiently, gaze averted, crumpled hat clutched between shivering fists.

"Is it salvageable?"

"Aye, milord." The wheeler looked down, away. "Two hours."

Lord Raachwald glared, judging him, weighing his words, his worth. "On your word then, master wheeler."

"Aye, milord." He knuckled his forehead again and was back at the wagon.

"What think you of our knight errant, my lady?" Lord Raachwald asked.

Lady Narcissa settled back. I studied her, trying to garner a glimpse, but she was still hooded. I could smell her perfume, though, taste it, even, a soft flowery scent that put me in mind of a white wine I'd sampled in Troyes, years past, in the company of a young lady who was thankfully quite unladylike.

"Mother of mercy, Pyotr..." she muttered. "Must I?" She waited for an answer, got only dead air and empty silence. "Very well. For your kindness and," she cleared her throat, "generosity of spirit." Her eyes glinted in the shadow of her hood, appraising me. I felt naked. And not in the good way. She started at my muck-covered boots and worked her way up, as though I were a slave at auction. I half expected her to check my teeth. "First off, he looks like a rat. A rat drowned in a cesspit. Filthy, bloody, reeking of sick. A drunkard, no doubt."

I forced a grin. She wasn't wrong.

"And he's stupid," she continued her barrage, "yet doesn't realize it. The worst kind. He labors under the misapprehension that he's intelligent, charming, witty, when it is quite the opposite. He cannot even help himself."

"My lady, please—"

"I thank you, Pyotr." She cut me off, leaned in close to the lord, her hand lighting upon his shoulder. "Thank you for indulging me at such a late hour. But this venture is played out. I must admit, the travails of the past month have made me hopeful, weak. T'was but an idea, a sorrow-laden hope, I see now. There was no savior. There is no savior." She held a hand out toward me. "There is but a vagabond."

"I prefer the term *knight errant*." I dabbed at the stitches across my forehead. "Reminiscent of the old songs. Roland and such."

"Roland was a count and a hero and a martyr." Lady Narcissa drew back her hood. A Gregorian choir of monks chanting had somehow invaded our campsite as raven hair spilled like liquid midnight, and I forgave all the awful things she'd said of me. The dichotomy of flame and shadow caressed her perfect face, a face young and serious and smooth, her vibrant eyes glimmering like twin indigo moons. "For you to draw comparison between the great count and yourself is a miscarriage of taste and culture if not outright justice."

"Well put, my lady—"

"Mother of Mercy," she hissed at the stars. "A fool, a rat, and a sycophant. An unholy triumvirate. Worthless. Witless. Spineless. As I said, I wash my hands of this venture. I am weary. I am cold." Her hand had found the lord's knee, now. "I wish to be warm." Lord Raachwald turned his head, slowly, like some spring-driven automaton. "You say you know of him, Pyotr? Well, then, you judge him. But he possessed not even the wits to flee as his man obviously did. Spare *him*. He might prove some use. But this one? This one would be more suited to mucking latrines."

"I'd gladly muck latrines. But," I raised a hand, "my man did not flee, my lady."

"And what of it?" She raised a perfectly wicked eyebrow.

"You'll forgive me, but I feel it prudent to educate you in the manner of rats. Rats, whom I, you've most correctly noted, bear much in common with. Rats possess many traits worthy of note. They're quick, my lady. Adaptable. And they're cunning, too. Fierce in a pinch. But, above all, they are survivors."

"I've most oft heard of them in reference to sinking ships."

"Hear him." Lord Raachwald laid a hand atop hers. "Speak swiftly, sir."

I nodded. "My point is that even vile men such as myself have some use. My lady, you said to Lord Raachwald that *'he cannot even help himself.'* You said *'he'* would be better suited to cleaning latrines. The implication being that you are in need of some form of service. Service a great man might find beneath him. Well, I am no great man," I knelt on one knee before the two of them, fist over my heart, "and it is a service I would be most keen to provide."

"You would swear an oath without hearing terms?" Her lips curled back in disgust. She was still beautiful.

"Considering the alternative?" I asked.

"What if he orders you to kill a king?" Lady Narcissa crossed her arms.

"Then the queen rejoices already."

"A man of God?"

"I'll send him to that which he prays to daily."

"What," her voice nearly faltered, "what of a *child*?"

"I pray that it's so, my lady." I snatched up a stick from the woodpile. "Much easier to kill a child than a king." I snapped the twig with a sudden jerk, opened my hands, let both halves fall into flame.

She stiffened at the crack and rose, lost, forlorn. "Please," she offered a stilted bow, "excuse me."

"Apologies for my crudeness..." I called after as she strode away.

If she heard, she gave no indication.

"T'is but a small matter." Lord Raachwald waved a hand. "To the meat of it, now. At present, you are wondering why I have come to you in the darkest of woods, in the hours of dead-night. How I knew of you. How I knew you were here and in such straights?"

"No, my lord." I shook my head. "I wonder none of those things. I'll admit I'm selfish. Prideful. Lustful. Hell, even slovenly, but blatantly stupid? That has never been one of my charms, contrary to what the lady may believe. You learned all from my brother, Stephan. It was he who sent you.

"What am I wondering?" I rubbed my stubbled chin. "I'm wondering where he presently resides? How he got there? How he found you? Or you him? I'm wondering why he didn't return with you? But mostly, I'm wondering if he's still alive?"

"None matters but the last," Lord Raachwald said.

"Yeah." I considered it a moment. "And Stephan would not have surrendered the information easily. Not to you. Not to anyone. He's stubborn in such matters. It's a matter of pride for him, one of his legion of faults."

"An impressive young man. Poise and grace tempered by wisdom and character. And nay, indeed, he would not divulge anything, and I was…persuasive. It is not often I am met with failure." He stared into the fire. "The lady, however, proved a different matter."

"Is he alive?" The word *persuasive* echoed in my mind.

Lord Raachwald nodded a mite, vacant, staring after the lady.

"You'll forgive me if I don't believe a twitch of the head." I pounded the log beneath me. "Is my brother *alive*?"

"Aye," Lord Raachwald whispered, "for now."

"Prove it."

"Who are you to question me?" He scowled. "To question my word?"

"The word of a *lord*," I scoffed.

"The word of a lord, aye." His voice didn't rise, but it grew coarser, sharper, rasping, ripping. "Kingdoms rise and fall upon such. Kings are made. Reigns ended. Armies slaughtered." He glanced at the crossbowmen still at the ready. The Grinner, too, slick as oil, Michael's boots on his feet now, Aaron's short-hafted axe in hand, his fingers fluttering on the haft. Aaron kept that axe sharp. They waited on their lord's word, or hoped, rather, hoped for the command that would set them to action, make them forget the cold, at least for a little while.

"Apologies, my lord." I tucked my tail between my legs. Smartly. "Stephan is my youngest brother. I had more than a hand in raising him. He was my page, my squire. I…" My hands quivered. I stilled them, inhaling slow, deep, deliberate. "He's a prisoner to be ransomed then?"

"Aye."

"And what payment do you demand?" I glanced at my broken wagon, what was left of it, the ruin of the camp, a carcass gleaned clean. "What I could offer you already possess, it seems. I could offer my life. That would please you, I'm sure."

"Your life?" Lord Raachwald squinted. "Do I not already possess it?" The crossbowmen took half-steps forward. Yolanda lay across my back now, scabbarded. I made no move for her. Two sticks to the chest would do me no good. "Truth. We have unfinished business, you and I. Bad blood. And I have made something of a study of you, these past years. It has become a passion of mine, doling out coin for scraps about you, whispers, legends. Whores in taverns. Court judgments. Justiciars. Outlaws. And here we are in the dark of the wild. I could murder you in this wood and nary a soul would know. Not your wife. Not your children. No one." His balled fist quivered to a still. "But by the twin face of Hel, tonight my hatred proves your salvation, for I have need of a low man such as you, a man able to hold his head just high enough out of the filth he wallows through to seek his destination. As does the lady, though she may not yet ken it." He turned to Lady Narcissa, staring off into darkness. "We wish you to hunt someone, Krait. We wish you to hunt a murderer."

Chapter 3.

"THEY CLAIM COLDSPIRE is impregnable." I glanced up. Lord, was she beautiful, beautiful and fierce and somber and vulnerable.

"Yes, that is what they claim." Stifling a shiver, Lady Narcissa drew her cloak tight about her, engulfing herself in a trim of soft fur. "The horses were screaming that night. Dying. Freezing in their stalls." She covered her mouth. "For two days we had borne the full brunt of the storm, trapped within Coldspire.

"On the third, one of our guards spied him, a monk, wandering." I glanced at Lord Raachwald, his attention rapt, focused on her words, upon every movement of her lips. "To come amidst such a storm, to come pleading, begging as their kind are so wont to do? A lunatic, no doubt. I told my husband this. He is…*was* a hard man. But even he would not turn away a servant of God in the midst of such a brutal storm. It would have been tantamount to murder, he had said.

"This monk, this man…" She reached out to Lord Raachwald. He took her hand in his. "He bore a look…something was amiss with him. Something even now I am pressed to explain, a feeling, the ghost of a whisper of a feeling. I know not." She shook her head. "My husband. Duty. Honor. Fidelity. What did he know? Would that he had listened. My husband offered food. Shelter." Her chin trembled. "In the morning he was gone. He was gone and my…my boys, they were dead." She dabbed at her eyes with a handkerchief. "My husband as well."

"What were their names?"

Something changed in her eyes at that. For an instant. "Michael and Gilbert. My husband was named Arthur."

"Forgive me, my lady," I said, "but, what was the manner of their deaths?"

The lady looked to the sky, a river of silver trickling down one cheek.

I bowed my head, staring at the fire.

"My son Cain was murdered as well." Lord Raachwald rubbed his hands together, his teeth bared, canines sharp and long and gleaming. "My last son," no emotion crept into his voice, "had been strung up like cattle. Slaughtered. His throat had been slit." He sniffed. "As were Michael's and Gilbert's, their corpses drained of blood."

"You saw this yourself?"

"Aye." Lord Raachwald nodded. "I answered the hue and cry. Lady Narcissa sent her handmaid for me. My men and I arrived at the first light of dawn, just as the storm broke. It was…terrible."

"What do you believe happened?"

"Sorcery. Magic," he took up a stick and broke off the branches one by one, "of the *darkest* sort."

I turned to Lady Narcissa.

"Yes," she whispered.

"Through eternity it has been whispered." Lord Raachwald stared into the fire. "Asylum's history is rife with it. It is older than its people, older than the land, older than the very roots of the mountains."

Black Magic? I'd heard of it, had even maybe seen it once, but if I had a penny for every time someone claimed black magic in conjunction with murder… "What of Lord Volkendorf?"

"He had been beaten to death," Lord Raachwald answered. "Beaten, broken, torn asunder."

"He was a warrior of some repute, was he not?"

"Forgive me, my lady." Lord Raachwald laid a hand upon his breast. "His man Lucien was, aye. His men, too, few though they were. But Volkendorf himself? Nay. Middling at his best. And he had not seen his best in long years. All bluster, all boast, all gone to sot and soft. But then, he and I were no allies."

"No?"

"We hated one another."

"Yet your son was his ward?"

"Ward. Hostage." He jabbed at the fire, growling. "You choose the word. The two meant the same to me."

"And was Volkendorf armed at the time?"

"Yes. Yes, indeed," Lady Narcissa answered. "The great-sword of his father, a fine weapon. The only thing of worth left to him, besides Coldspire itself, and..."

"We found it next to his corpse," Lord Raachwald said. "Smashed all to pieces, shattered, as was he."

"And his men?" I asked. "This man, this Lucien, what of he? Is it possible he was complicit in the murder?"

"Lucien and his men were killed as well," Lady Narcissa explained. "Seven men, all told. They died defending their lord, felled by his side. And they were prepared. It made no difference."

"Barrow-fodder," Lord Raachwald spat.

"A battle?" I sat back.

"Fierce, aye." Lord Raachwald nodded. "Fought in Coldspire's great hall. The bodies, it took some time to match the parts. For the burials, you see?"

I nodded. "What else? Anything strange about it?" What was not strange?

"Some of the body parts were gone," Lord Raachwald said.

"Gone?"

"Aye. Missing. And the great hall door." Lord Raachwald frowned. "It had been smashed in. A stout door. Iron-barred. Reinforced thick oak. It would have taken some doing."

"Why was the door broken, lady?"

"I do not know." The lady looked me in the eye. "I did not witness the battle. My husband sent me away in an effort to save me. And I obeyed."

"An axe?" I asked Lord Raachwald.

"An axe and an hour," he said. "An uninterrupted hour."

"And you hunted this monk, I assume?"

"Hunt?" Lord Raachwald growled beneath his breath. "But, of course. Aye. I formed the *posse comitatus*. Immediately. My men and I. We searched the castle. Scoured the grounds. The island. The city. The lands. We found the boys quickly enough," he glanced at Lady Narcissa, "but we found no trace of this monk. Gone. We search still without fruition."

Wood popped in the fire.

"Did your husband have enemies?"

"What great lord does not?" she answered. "Do you know of Mummer's Isle? Of the five houses? The seat of the five lords of Svaldrake?"

"Yeah." Asylum City was a legitimate city, tens of thousands strong, a center for trade within the Hanseatic League, and it formed a sort of nexus in Svaldrake. Five Lords, five lands, five pieces of a pie cut in a half circle, the shores of the North Sea forming its northern border. Asylum City sat along the shore at the center.

"Then you know of the great game." Her eyes narrowed. "Coldspire, my family's keep, has traditionally been the prize. For centuries, harkening back to Charlemagne himself. Before, even. For two generations my family has held it. But the Five Lords vie ceaselessly, conspiring endlessly to win it back."

"Was this a power grab?"

"I…" Lady Narcissa's eyes flickered toward Lord Raachwald, "I think not."

Tread carefully, you fool, I told myself. "And you're certain the killer was a monk?"

"You question the veracity of my story?"

"Any man might don the robes of another," I said.

She nodded curtly. "Of course. Yes. He was a monk, or a man of God, at least."

"And what color was his cowl, my lady?"

"Brown."

"A Franciscan, then." Dominicans wore black. Now, Franciscan monks don't often commit murder, but wisely I bit my tongue. A Dominican, though, some of them might darken even the devil's doorstep, but a Franciscan monk was something different. Generally. "How are you certain he was a monk?"

"He was a learned man. In repayment for lodging, for food, he insisted on conducting a...a sort of mass for us. He read passages from our family's Bible."

"Yet you did not witness the crimes?"

"No." She rubbed the back of her neck. "I was ill that evening. I retired to my rooms. Early. I emerged later that eve, only to have my husband order me back. He saved my life, it would seem."

"It would seem," I echoed. "Now, if you did not see this man commit these crimes, how do you know that he did?"

"Did I not tell you there was something strange about him?"

"You did, milady. But, might you not add specifics? How old was he? What color hair? Was he a tall man? Did he have a name? Those types of things would prove useful."

"Yes, of course, I see." Lady Narcissa nodded. "He said his name was Brother Gregory. He was a grotesquely large man, larger even than Lord Raachwald's monstrosity. Arms of an ape-like cast. His hair tonsured in that ridiculous manner and of deepest black. Middle-aged, like you. But he wore no beard, nor mustache, and he bore the very countenance of the devil."

"Meaning...?"

The good lady sat simmering in her seat, eyes blazing.

"Very good, milady," I said, breaking off. At least we weren't analyzing my shortcomings or throwing nooses over the branches of trees. "Have you any notion as to where this devil might have fled?"

"That is the task we have set *you* if I am not mistaken," she replied.

* * * *

We reached a crossroads near dawn, grey light rising above the canopy of needled branches as we labored east along the road. There, it forked in twain, one road heading north toward the rocky shores of the North Sea. The other headed east toward Asylum City.

Lord Raachwald's country holdings lay at the terminus of the north road, an old wooden motte and bailey style castle built upon a rocky promontory just kissing the sea. Seagulls wheeled and screeched from afar. Waves pounded, sprayed. A stockade wall of tree trunks, each sharpened at the top, surrounded a bent, dilapidated keep. Stephan was imprisoned somewhere inside that hoary monstrosity, chained up, freezing, alone.

Jesus.

A cold wind blew, carrying with it the stench of low tide and salt, of rotten things dredged from the deep, of things best left there, things best forgotten.

My feet ached. My head pounded worse. My tongue and throat burned dry. I needed to sleep, needed to eat, needed a drink. Many drinks.

Lord Raachwald reigned in his horse as his men continued by, single file, following my wagon, my wares, nearly everything of mine in this world, all trundling on, out of reach forever.

Lord Raachwald waited until his retinue had passed beyond earshot. "A week's time I'll grant you." His voice a slashing whisper. "Seven days to hunt him. Seven days to heel him. Seven days to bring him here, to me, in Dunmire. Dead or alive, though preferably alive." He gazed toward his keep. "And I have yet one more demand in this task I have set you." He cut me off when I opened my mouth. "No one is to know you are working in accordance with me."

"What about them?" I raised an eyebrow conspicuously toward his retinue, trudging onward north.

"They do not know who you are," he answered. "If they did, you would be barrow-fodder."

Yolanda lay sheathed at my back. For an instant, I

saw myself drawing her, cutting the legs out from under the fucker's horse. Stabbing him in the neck. Then it was gone. "My lord, the task would be best accomplished under your seal."

"Do not call me *your* lord."

"Yeah. Right." It didn't sit well with me, either. "And I'll need to get onto the rock."

"I assure you," his horrid face darkened, "the killer is no longer on Mummer's Isle."

"Lord Raachwald, see reason," I implored. "I'll need to see the murder site." I glanced over at the lady, lowered my voice. "I'll need to examine the bodies. Please. Tell them I'm a mercenary in your employ. Tell them I'm a cook. Tell them whatever you damn well please, but I need to get onto that rock if I'm to accomplish this."

"You are on your own, Krait." I could hear his teeth grinding. "When next we meet, you'd best have the murderer heeled, for your own sake, for your brother's sake. Now remove yourself from my path." He snapped the reins.

I darted aside as his steed clomped onward.

The Lady Narcissa sat alone, mounted upright, austere, statuesque, the wind blowing back her hair. A breathtaking sight, truly, and for a moment, she weighed me, looking as though she wished to say something.

"My lady?" Maybe I'd get lucky and she'd just run me down. End all this bullshit.

But she continued on past, mud splashing. "I have heard that the Stone Ruin Ten is still quite a passable establishment." That baleful hiss in her voice had fled, was gone, and with it the haughty demeanor, leaving only a weary look and a heavy burden bowing her back and shoulders.

*One simply cannot fathom the depths of depravity mankind will sink to
in times of struggle, in times of death, in times of dire…*
—*Journal of Sir Myron Chalstain*

Chapter 4.

GRAVE MARKERS STOOD crooked and numerous along
the road, wizzled as an old drunkard's legs. Most stood
nameless, just a pair of sticks strung together with a bit of
twine, of cloth, of whatever lay at hand. They'd be gone
come another month, another week, a stiff wind. Some of
the corpses had been buried, not deep, but buried. Others
lay where they'd died, huddled frozen against trees, crippled
hands clawing at the bark. Like something from a nightmare,
faces peered out from under a thin sheen of snow, eye
sockets empty, staring.

I stopped by a gnarled signpost jabbed upright in
the mud.

"Shit."

Three crows were nailed to the warped sign, and all
three crows were dead. Not surprisingly. You nail something
to a board, and if it's not dead, it soon will be. Just ask Jesus.
White bone, thin, sharp, hollow as a reed, shone through
where black feather had failed, skeletal wings fluttering a
twitching dance in the breeze as though some life yet dwelt
within. The sign read, '*Asylum City.*'

A crude arrow pointed east.

I marched on.

Where to start searching? Usually, I consider a
mystery a tapestry. I probe for loose threads til I find one
then just start pulling, hoping to unravel it. Sometimes it
works. Sometimes it doesn't. Sometimes, you start pulling
and the whole damn thing comes crashing down atop of
you, smothering you.

Last night, I was fair certain that had nearly been the
case. The good Lady Narcissa's story was rife with loose
threads. I could have started pulling at a myriad, for I was
fair certain she'd withheld something, if not veritably

everything, of import. But I held back because of the *Gallows* Lord. Not a name to take lightly. Him watching over her the whole time, emotionless, like he was tallying each word she spoke? He'd not swallowed her story, either. Was he testing me? Her? Searching for inconsistencies? Something. There were only two things I knew for certain. Ten people had been killed, and two more would follow suit if I shit the bed.

I mounted an outcropping overlooking the wide expanse of the Morgrave River, splitting through the valley below. Asylum City lay strewn across the river's mouth and along the coast like the half-eaten carcass of some titanic swine that had just dropped and lay rotting. Spires stood dazed and leaning like gleaned ribs. Towers of ominous smoke spumed up from within, tendrils of filth roiling, climbing, poisoning the sky.

Asylum hadn't changed.

It never changed, not for the better at least.

Church steeples jabbed like daggers at the sky. They were nothing, though, for Saint Hagan's Cathedral dwarfed them all. Beyond the wall, squatting like some pagan god, it loomed over the whole of the city. Except for Mummer's Isle. That fist of rock rose south of the cathedral, entrenched in the current of the Morgrave. Keeps dotted the cliff sides, clinging like beasts, watching from on high. Lady Narcissa's Coldspire clung to the top, perched precariously like some ossified crow, a black obelisk jutting up from its midst. That was where I needed to go.

"Shit…"

For perhaps the hundredth time, I glanced back over my shoulder, up the road. West. Hoping for a glimpse of Karl. The bastard was still alive. I knew it. Lord Raachwald would have gloated if Haefgrim had taken him, would have brought back his head, his hands, something. But he hadn't. He'd been silent on that score, his professional curiosity conspicuously forgotten. I'd not seen fit to remind him. A rare point in favor of sobriety's virtue.

My stomach rumbled. But it was mere hunger. Not siege hunger. Not eat-rats-or-worse hunger. And this wasn't that. My soft underbelly was thirst. I'd finished Karl's flask hours ago, during the predawn march, and it wasn't yet upon me full. But it was hounding me. I could feel it watching, stalking close, sweat-prickles stippling up my neck.

Wooden cages lined the side of the road plunging through the Asylum's outskirts. Bone-wraiths and wizened sticks of desiccated flesh huddled motionless within, frozen, except for fabric tatters wagging in the wind. Frost-rimed ghasts of emaciated black peered out, hands dry-rotted to bars.

I trudged on past.

"Oy…" A dead echo as I passed the last cage. A tilted sign atop it read, '*Murderer.*'

I nodded at the wraith crumpled within. "You didn't happen to murder a lord and his family?"

The living skeleton raised its head, quivering atop its rope-thin neck, sunken eyes straining, unfocused. It had room only to sit, its knees shoved up to its chest. Its nose was frozen black. Man? Or woman? I couldn't tell. Whatever it was, it'd be dead soon. "Nay…" its lipless mouth managed, working, teeth missing. A frost-bit hand reached through the bars, trembling, strength failing. It slumped over in a shambles.

"Well, it was worth a shot…"

Quarking gleefully, a crow lit on the sign above the cage, scattering snow. It regarded me from on high.

I turned my back to it, toward the west, toward the wild.

Karl would come.

But he hadn't.

And he didn't.

The rains came instead, rolling in off the grey North Sea, a cold winter sleet ripping across my face. I considered the crow. "Saw a few of your friends up the road."

Best to get moving.

"Shit…"

Three dead crows meant there was plague in Asylum.

...plague stalks the streets, striking down people at will. They are littered with more bodies than the dead-carts can handle. His Lord Eminence has finally agreed to let the dead burn. I fear the decision too late...

—*Journal of Sir Myron Chalstain*

Chapter 5.

SKULL-LIKE, DEMON-fanged, grinning despite the sleet, the stone gargoyles glared down, twin sentinels set to guard from the tops of the gate towers.

Three guards manned them. One lay asleep in a wagon-bed, legs hanging out the back. The other two stood huddled underneath a makeshift lean-to built against the wall, a crackling fire rippling beneath. They rubbed their hands over its warmth.

I didn't recognize either of them, and I knew quite a few. Or *had* known, at least, once upon a time.

These two wore soiled aketons, cheap linen jacket-armor, and pot helms, all ill-fitted, mismatched, cobbled together. Faded tabards graced their chests, a red ship on field of blue, Asylum's sigil. Each bore a short truncheon at his hip, city guard standard issue. That's what they call it, anyways, when they hand it to you. A truncheon. Most'd call it a stick, a stout one, maybe, but a stick, nonetheless. Great against drunks and thieves. Not so against anything more.

One of the guards, a runt, snatched a billhook leaning against the wall and marched towards me. Lips pursed, chest thrust out, determined. He was young, sixteen or seventeen at most. Light brown hair. Pockmarked face. Ears sticking out to here.

Cannon fire boomed from the east, far off beyond the wall.

"What the—" I started.

"Cannon fire," the Runt drawled.

"No shit," I said. "Whose?"

He shrugged. "Don't know."

"Well, who's fighting?"

"Everybody."

"Right." I gave him the hard glare.

"Lord Bishop and the Isle men." He shrugged. "Old hat."

"Jesus Christ—" I started as another round of cannon fire boomed. "Kline working tonight?"

"Who?" The Runt tilted forward to better hear, though with those ears.

"Kline," I repeated. "Manned this gate last time I came through. Tall fellow. Thin as a rail. Drinks like a man who's not."

"Don't know no Kline, mister."

"Sir," I corrected. "I'm a knight."

"Right." The Runt glanced at his buddy, the Fool. His jaw was long and his teeth, the ones he had, were prominent. "Know any Kline?"

"As a doornail." The Fool nodded, slow and sure. "He's dead."

"Kline's dead," the Runt repeated.

"Thanks," I deadpanned. "Anyone old enough to grow facial hair still around?" The sleeping guard started coughing, a hacking wet cough that probably meant death creeping through his lungs. "Sleeping Beauty, maybe?"

"Naw." The Runt kicked a rock. "Let him sleep."

"Yeah. Sure. Why not?" What the hell did I care? "Plague?"

"Naw. Consumption. Been eating at him over a year. Plague done missed him."

"Lucky guy."

The Runt shot me a glare like maybe he wasn't as stupid as I took him for, or I wasn't as smart. "Rest of the guards are gone. Dead mostly. Those that ain't? Beat-feet once the plague come ripping in." He frowned. "We're it for here."

"And I'm sure Asylum's good citizens sleep well at night knowing it."

"What's your business?" The Fool clomped over, brushing hair from his eyes. He was a little older than the

Runt, a little bigger, a lot dumber.

"I came for the sights."

"It's getting late, mister." The Runt folded his arms across his chest. "We been at post all day. Last night. Yesterday…"

"I'm a caravan guard." I relented.

"Well, where's your caravan?"

"I'm not a very good caravan guard. Can I pass?"

The Runt considered a moment, fingering his lip, "Hell, why not?" and stepped aside.

"Any good inns still standing?" I needed that drink, could hear the beast behind me, galloping, ravenous, gaining. "Or taverns?"

"Well, up north a piece is the Crow's Foot and west is the Angler's Daughter— No, it burned down." The Runt pointed past my head with the billhook one way and then swept toward the other, missing my nose by inches. I nearly broke my teeth grinding them. "Up the point's the Kraken Arm. But I ain't never been to it." He glanced at the Fool. "You?"

The Fool smirked. "Nice place."

"Anywhere I *won't* get my throat slit?" I knew all about the Kraken Arm.

"Outside the wall?" The Runt scrunched up his mug then shook his head. "Naw. Out of luck on that score. Not that inside's much better."

"Direct from the lips of the city-guard," I commented. "Any scuttle on the Stone Ruin Ten?" And there was the crux of my problem. My concern. Was the Lady Narcissa on the level, or was she setting me up? Was there a thread to unravel or a squadron of blackguards looking to slit my throat? Which was the act? The shrew or the grieving mother?

"Hrrmm… Some better, some worse. Still got food and drink, last I heard. And won't give you the shits. Well, maybe." The Runt paused. "You really a knight, mister?"

"Yeah, why?" My great cloak was threadbare, covered in mud, blood, and my clothes underneath were about the same. Rust spotted my mail. I needed a wash, a shave, a week's sleep. I needed whiskey. Ale. A woman. Not necessarily in that order.

The guards glanced at each other sidelong, practically daring one another to crack first.

The Runt adjusted his grip on his billhook, pretty much a glorified pruning hook, his gaze twitching to the sword across my back. Yolanda, the one knightly thing about me undeniable. "Meant no offense, mister."

Smoke poured up in a black column beyond the gates.

"I could use a guide."

"We all could, mister," the Runt answered.

"You misunderstand me."

"I ain't stupid."

"You sure?"

The Fool raised a hand, offering his services. "I'd be—"

"Not you." I waved him off. "Him."

"Ain't for sale, mister," the Runt said.

"Good, cause I ain't looking to buy, just rent." That sounded less jarring in my head.

"Mister…" Warning lit into his voice.

"Relax." I raised a hand. "You're not my type. Just looking for a guide to Stone Ruin Ten." I reached for my coin purse. "I'll pay you up front, yeah?" I always kept a few coins in my boot in the event some threadbare lord and his shitty minions came calling on me in the dead of night, looking to tax. "Provins silver, the real deal. One for a walk and a conversation. Both short. Shit, I'll even buy you dinner. Warm food? Ale? You'll be back at post in under an hour."

The Fool hissed, "Silver—" and shoved the Runt through the gate.

* * * *

It was a scene from the *Inferno*. The heat intense, blaring at us in a gale wind as we made our way through the city square, past pairs of men hurling corpses into the foundation of a razed home. Smoke ripped past, a choking fume. Handkerchiefs covered workers' noses and mouths as they toiled, sweating, burning so close to the pits. The Runt kept his head down as we marched on past, body after body thumping, rolling down the hill of scorched bone.

Cold resettled fast within us as we strode down a dark alley, ramshackle houses rising to either side like waves about to break over us, their roofs almost touching each other overhead, each story up a little wider than the one below. Claustrophobic. Cave-like. Quarantined. As far as the eye could see.

"How'd it come in?" I stepped past a boarded-up door.

"It come in riding the tides, near two months past." The Runt scratched the back of his neck. "A cog out of Genoa. Mercenary ship. Rode in with them greasy dago bastards."

"Dago bastards..." I echoed. "I hate dago bastards." We walked on. "And who's Lord of Asylum now? Heard Volkendorf's moved on."

"*Moved on?*" The Runt shot me a glance. "Rich way to put it." Appraising. He *wasn't* stupid. "It's His Eminence, the Lord Bishop Judas-Peter running the show now."

"Wow."

"Huh?"

"Judas Peter?" I commented. "Now there's a trustworthy name. One denies, the other betrays. Jesus Christ, what happens when you put them together?"

"Yer looking at it, mister." The Runt shouldered through a small flock of nuns. He muttered '*good days*' and '*pardons*' as we worked our way through. They disappeared nearly as soon as they'd appeared. Ghosts. "Like to have met his folks. Takes some stones naming your kid *Judas*-anything. They say he was born the son of some goat-herd. Come up from the southern hills. Thuringia. Swabia, something or other. Name like Judas might not matter if you're a goat-herd out in the sticks. But a bishop? And with a city like Asylum?"

"Rough going, either way, I'd wager," I said. "Think it's a true story, goat-herd and all?"

"How the hell would I know?" The Runt traversed a long springy plank fording an enormous stream that also happened to be the street. "I ain't nothing. He's an ancient old geezer, that's all I know. 'The *Vulture*,' they call him, not to his face, I reckon. Decrepit, some say senile. Well, a lot say senile. But don't think anyone was alive back then to know if the story's level."

"Well, it sounds good, anyway." Arms out, balancing, I followed him across the plank. "And that's more than half of it. A high church official, a lord bishop, especially, should always be the son of a goat-herd, or a shepherd. Preferably. Even if he's really just the pampered fourth-born son of some shit nobleman. Which most are. Better if the masses think the bishop knows what it's like to have to work on an empty belly."

"Funny, you saying that, being a knight and all."

"Oh, we work…occasionally," I admitted. "So what did happen to Volkendorf?"

"He's dead," the Runt drawled. "Died during a blizzard, 'bout a month past. Murdered, they say."

"*They* who?"

The Runt thought about it then just shrugged. "Just *they*."

"So Judas-Peter came to power before Volkendorf was murdered?"

"Yup. Year…year and a half or so."

"Neat trick."

"Nothing neat about it, mister." The Runt stepped aside as a corpse-cart, drawn by four empty specters, lumbered down the road. "Blood in the streets." Bodies stacked close to tumbling filled the cart, arms and legs hanging over the sides, some dangling limp, others stiff, frozen. Another two specters followed the wagon, pushing it from behind. Backbreaking. Disgusting. Like all truly necessary work.

"Know anyone who looked into it?"

"Sure." The Runt nodded. "Lord Bishop himself sent me and my partner up the Rock to investigate. Marched right across the Bastard Bridge and turned Coldspire upside down. Slapped the lords around for tidings. Went like clockwork."

"*Anyone* check it out?"

"Sure. Some knight. And they say he went missing."

"Missing?"

"You sure ask a lot of questions for a caravan guard."

"Well, you're just so fascinating."

Up ahead, lost in the twists and turns of the labyrinthine road, a woman started screaming bloody murder.

"Pardon," the Runt shouldered his billhook, "got to go to work," and sprinted off.

Shit.

At a trot and hanging to the wall, I trailed the Runt, keeping him in sight, but only just so. When I caught up to him, I realized it wasn't a woman. It was a kid, a gutter-rat by the looks of him. In the midst of the street, he and a man struggled, slick-sliding, flailing in the muck, the gutter-rat wriggling like an eel to escape.

The kid, maybe eight-years-old, screamed and kicked and bucked as the man, a big bald fucker, snagged a flailing foot, got a good solid grip and started dragging him wailing and flailing. The bald fucker's head steamed. A slick butcher's apron sat over his big belly. He trudged toward a dark alleyway. Two bruisers stepped from that alleyway, guffawing as the Butcher slipped and fell to a knee in the middle of the street.

A group of men and women hurried by, eyes averted, ignoring the drama.

Smart folk.

The kid kicked, screaming with renewed fury. The Butcher grunted like a bull, snorting as he regained footing, leaned over, and snatched the flailing boy by the throat. "*Up!*"

The Runt marched through the mud and cut the Butcher off from the alley. Jesus. He had the two bruisers at his back now.

"Stop!" the Runt commanded.

"Fucking move, boy." The Butcher turned, keeping a white-knuckled ham-fist round the gutter-rat's throat, and cuffed him across the temple. Hard. Crimson spittle flew. The boy dropped rag-doll limp face-first into the mud, blowing bubbles.

"Back off." The Runt leveled his billhook.

"Shut yer gob." The Butcher pinned the kid's head under the muck.

"*Let. Him. Up.*"

The Butcher snaked a hand round to his back.

The Runt swallowed.

Waiting for the Butcher to act first was a mistake. Another one.

Tightening his grip, the Butcher lifted the bedraggled kid, dangling limp, filth running. "*Happy?*"

The Butcher fixated on the Runt's billhook. With good reason. Billhook's a nasty bit of business with a stabbing blade aimed forwards and a sweeping crescent blade slung back. Good for pruning trees and shrubs. For chopping off legs, too. The Runt grasped the haft, white-knuckled. The Butcher clutched the kid in front of him like a shield, a big butcher blade in his other hand. He glanced past the Runt, at his comrades and nodded almost imperceptibly.

The two bruisers closed in like a pair of rabid wolves.

I'd strode across the street by then, swiftly, quietly, taking their backs after they emerged. Yolanda was still sheathed, but in hand, ready. I snatched a glance down the alley at my back.

Empty. Good.

"Evening, gentlemen!"

Both started. One bore a huge knife, the other a

table leg moonlighting as a mace. "Can't help but notice you've brought a knife and a stick to a swordfight."

The Runt glanced over his shoulder a moment, froze, cussing beneath his breath.

"A scared little boy," the Butcher snarled.

The two bruisers, Slash and Smash, grunted to one another. I slid Yolanda from her scabbard, holding one each in either hand. I had their attention. The two slogged towards me, lumbering through the mud. They had numbers. I had the weapon, the high ground. Mental math, meaningless once the fun starts. And by *fun,* I meant the complete opposite.

Slash moved left, Smash right.

"Let him go, mister." The Runt sounded like a fucking chipmunk. "Won't be saying it again."

"Fuck you," the Butcher growled.

Smash guffawed, glancing over his shoulder. Stupid. I whipped my scabbard end-over-end into Slash then cut at Smash, Yolanda arcing out lighting tight. Stupid Smash, guffawing, glanced back an instant too late, stopping dead as my blade *snicked* an inch from his nose. I felt nothing but heard a roar, and suddenly Smash wasn't holding his truncheon. Wasn't holding anything. He was clutching a stump where his hand had been.

I followed in with a step and a boot to his chest, connecting hard, heel to breastbone, knocking him off his feet. A tidal wave splash. But I didn't see. My focus switched to Slash, backing up reflexively, a broken dog, eyes glued to Smash's hand twitching in the mud. Smash was up then, scrambling down the street. Slash broke, giving chase, mud splattering, disappearing into darkness.

I turned.

On his knees in the street, the Butcher cursed the Runt and his comrades and Jesus and the kid and me all to hell and tried to stand but fell again to his knees. "Fuck." He clutched his big butcher blade. "FUCK!"

"You alright, boy?" the Runt asked. The back swung crescent blade of his billhook was red.

The gutter-rat nodded, eyes as big as the moon. "That was real fast…"

The Runt pushed the boy behind himself.

"What am I, boiled tripe?" I retrieved my scabbard, shook it off.

The Butcher roared, ranted, pounding fist and blade, splashing in the mud. Spittle flew. His huge knife slashed to and fro, still gripped throttling in his fist. Kneeling in red, the Butcher clutched at the back of his leg as blood poured free. Hamstrung, dead, dying, just he didn't know it yet.

"I owe ya, mister." The Runt picked up his pot helm and set it back on his head.

"Damn right you do." I crossed the street. "What's your name?"

"Nils—"

"*Damn you!*" the Butcher hollered, launching himself toward me, diving belly first into the mud.

I kept walking, avoiding the mud, the knife, the asshole.

The Butcher rolled over, wallowing like a swine, half sobbing. "I'll fucking kill you. I'll…" he still clutched his knife, stabbing mindless until he couldn't, and then he didn't, and then he wasn't.

...His Eminence bade me investigate the murders. A tricky piece of puzzle this shall prove. His Lord Eminence is subtle. He believes my history with Lord Raachwald may prove...

—*Journal of Sir Myron Chalstain*

Chapter 6.

TAKING A DEEP, long, glorious breath, I slid into the dim-warmth of Stone Ruin Ten, inhaling the pine scent of rushes, the brew of ale, of whiskey, of crusted baked pike. Music played. A buxom wench slid past, a tankard of ale in each fist, a knowing grin on her lips. There are no words to adequately describe the sensation, especially when you've been on the road over a month. Thirsting. It cleared my senses, absolved me of weariness, stoked the dying embers of my heart. Home. Heaven. What have you. There's just nothing like a good tavern, and this was one.

Flames crackled in the hearth, a shank of meat rotating slowly over it on an iron spit. Men and women sat at tables scattered across the room, a constant lullaby of chattered voices. You'd never know hell lay beyond those front doors.

I had the gutter-rat by the scruff of the neck. He flailed angrily, petulantly, covered in mud and blood. "Easy, kid," I warned. "Don't hit anyone bigger than me."

"Let me go," he whined.

"Can't." I leveraged him tiptoeing forward through the press. Folk parted like a whore's legs as I moved onward with him kicking, swearing, snarling. Nils strode behind, a turtle trying to tuck its head so far into its shell it came out its arse-end.

"Thought you said you were good with kids?" Nils muttered as we reached the bar.

"You see the path I just cleared?"

"Let me go!" the gutter-rat screamed.

"Not yet. Sorry."

"You're *not* sorry!"

"True," I admitted.

"So let me go."

"After we talk to the bartender." I pointed with my thumb over shoulder. "Deal's a deal. Look, I promised Nils I'd get you fed. At the least. Quit kicking, will ya? And take a whiff. Smells good, yeah? You want to eat? 'Course you do. And you can't be left wandering the streets, starving, getting raped and eaten by ham-stranglers and wild dogs and God knows what else."

"Why not?" He thrust his bottom lip out.

"Well…" I tried sussing out a reason. One did not spring immediately to mind.

"We're gonna get you cleaned up, kid." Nils leaned in, consternation brimming in his eyes. "Full belly. Place to sleep. Don't worry, alright?"

The bartender's glare at the flailing gutter-rat turned to a look as though this were the fifth he'd had dragged in kicking and screaming the past hour. Maybe it was. He continued cleaning a tankard, muttering beneath his breath. He perked up at Nil's guard insignia. "Good evening, *Herr* Gentlemen," he offered in a brusque accent. Somewhere from the northeast of the Empire, the Holy Roman.

The kid punched me in the liver, and I stiffened, grabbed his arm, chicken-winged it behind his back.

"Evening," Nils and I said simultaneously.

The bartender took a deep breath. "What is it I can be doing for you?"

"You could get me something strong." The kid squirmed in my grip.

"Whiskey?"

"A hammer," I grumbled, practically drooling at the word, '*whiskey*.' "Ale'd be just fine. Keep it coming til I can't tell you my name. *Then* whiskey." I glared the kid into stilling. "Never drink whiskey on an empty stomach."

The bartender slid a ceramic tankard full of sloshing ale down before me. I took it in hand, a tentative lover at foreplay, licking my lips, savoring the moment. The old ceramic was cold. Smooth. Reassuring. The only way to slug ale. No metallic tin taste when your lips touch it. No fingernail texture of a horn mug, little bits chipping off in your mouth, sticking to your tongue and the back of your throat. And wooden tankards? Need I say more? Eyes closing, I took a long pull, feeling it pour, that blissful burn.

"You alright?" The bartender squinted through one eye.

"Yeah. Fine. Thanks." I wiped my mouth. "Looking for a room for the night, too. A few nights. Just me. But dinner for three. If you're looking to barter...?" I held the kid up, wriggling like a fish. "Any idea what this thing's worth?"

The kid promptly punched me in the side of the head. Mud flew. I offered the bartender my most-winning smile.

"*Nein*. I do not conduct such business, *mein Herr*," the bartender said, trying to suss out if I was funning.

"He don't mean it, mister." Nils leaned in. "I think, anyways."

"Actually," I put the kid down, maintaining my grip, "this fine city-guard's seeking to gain this spirited young lad employment. A bath and meal at the very least. An orphan. Found him on the street, beset by man-eaters trying to stew him." I mussed the kid's hair. "He's a fine, fine lad. Really fine. Thought you might need some help sweeping floors, cleaning tables, dredging cesspits—ouch!" He bit me. "Or maybe you need something to flavor *your* stew?"

"What is being his name?" The bartender was shorter than me but stout, with thick arms, a big belly, discerning brown eyes.

"Doesn't have one," I said. "Too poor."

"His name's, Girard," Nils cut in. "If you could help him out, mister, I'd appreciate it."

"That is so, eh?" The bartender shook his head. "Well-behaved, you claim, *Herr* Guard?" He gave Girard the eye. "He is seeming like more than a bit of trouble."

Girard made to run, and I nearly lost an arm holding

on.

The bartender crossed his arms, doing the math, and it was coming up short. "See here, *mein Herr*—"

"Luther," I offered.

"*Herr* Luther, you are paying for a meal so you three can eat, of course, but I cannot…eh?" He paused, straightening.

A hush descended like the fall of autumn leaves, the men milling about turning as one then parting as an angel strode through, a wave of eyes and surreptitious glances following in her wake. An aroma of rose water preceded her, not strong, just enough, like a whispered-hint of spring on a long cool winter breeze. She was wide where it counted and had that something about her, in those green eyes and that wry smile, like she knew something you didn't, and maybe she lived more than everyone else, just a little maybe, but more. She sidled up to the bar, squeezing past me, taking her time, brushing her red-gold hair from her face.

"You're cute," she said in a husky voice.

"You should see me all cleaned up." She was talking to the kid. I didn't care.

Ignoring me, as all women of discerning taste are wont to do, she bent down, eye to eye with the kid.

"Mother of mercy…" I stared down. Unabashedly.

Nils did, too, but had the wherewithal to fluster and start sweating.

"Sakes alive, you need a bath," she said.

"I am filthy," I admitted.

"I was talking to the boy," she said, pointedly *not* looking my way.

"I wasn't," I said.

Lips pursed, she suppressed an annoyed glare and continued. "What's your name, boy?" She fixed the kid's collar, smoothing it out gently, firmly.

"What's yours?" I asked.

"Girard, ma'am."

"Girard, a fine name." She was a woman who got what she wanted, that was plain. She glanced up at the bartender. "We could use him, Schultz. Hmm? We need a boy to clean the floors and tables. Muck the stalls. If there's ever any horses again. A strong boy." She ruffled his hair. He'd suddenly gone all shy. "A good boy. Are you a good boy, Girard?"

"Yes, ma'am," Girard lied.

"I've the bite marks to prove it." I raised my hand, a ring of teeth marks prominent on my wrist. No one cared.

"Is he willing to work, Lorelai?" Schultz rolled his eyes. He'd already lost, and he knew it. "Willing to listen? I am not needing extra mouths, extra trouble. Barely enough victuals to go around as it is."

"Are you willing to work, Girard?" Lorelai cut the bartender off.

Girard hid behind his hands, peeking out.

"He cannot be biting customers," the bartender warned.

"Of course he won't, you ass." She sounded as though she gargled whiskey, her voice rough and smoky and perfect, and as I stared at her, I realized she was older than I had thought initially. Her eyes glowed with a vitality, but there was a tiredness in there as well. A night's tiredness, a day's, even a week's, maybe. But not yet a lifetime's, though I felt intrinsically she was somehow working on it. "My, what a good boy. What a fine boy. And will you listen to me? The girls? To Schultz?" She glanced up at the bartender. "He is the boss."

"Why is it that I am never feeling like the boss?" Schultz muttered.

"I ain't so good at listening, ma'am." Girard's eyes rose to Lorelai's. "That's what my master always says...said. I'll try to be good." He nodded, staring into those vibrant eyes. "I like you."

"Kid's got good taste," I commented like the boorish arse I am.

"You know," Lorelai whispered sidelong, still ignoring me, her eyes beaming for the kid alone, "I wouldn't trust a boy that always listens. A boy that always listens is a boy without spirit. A boy *should* be partly wild. Means there's something alive in here." She placed a fingertip gently on his chest. "And you are. You aren't broken, aren't cowed. Not like the rest of them." She waved a hand, encompassing the entire world within that flick of her slender wrist.

Girard tugged at the hem of his shirt.

"Send his dinner up to my room," Lorelai said. Schultz grumbled, nodding as she rose regal as a queen, smoothed her skirts, adjusted her bodice then took the kid by the hand. "I'll get him cleaned up and fed and working. Right quick."

"Yes, you shall." Schultz thumped the bar noncommittally, defeated. "Alright." He poured two whiskeys, slid them down my way. "He'll work for room and board only. I cannot be affording to be paying him. And if he is not working out, he is back on the street."

I knocked back the rest of my drink, that prodigal part of my soul returning joyous with but the bend of an elbow. I stepped in Lorelai's path, offering a short sharp bow, enjoying the view all the way down and all the way up. "My lady."

She paused there, glaring me up and down, hands on hips. "Do I look like a '*my lady*?'"

"No, you look like something more." I stepped aside, allowing her to pass. "Forgive my rudeness."

"From before, or is there more yet to come?" The crowd was tight. She slid past close enough to brush up against me. Good lord. "Good night…sir." She drew Girard along by the hand.

I stood there staring as she sauntered on, hips swaying slowly, smoothly, like she practiced at it. The crowd parted before her, men looking the other way somehow sensing her and moving aside, every one of their gazes following after as she strode past, the kid in tow, both disappearing as the press of bodies closed in around them.

...the holes are glaring, legion, obvious. Without a doubt, she is hiding something from me...
—*Journal of Sir Myron Chalstain*

Chapter 7.

TWILIGHT HAD SPAWNED and metastasized into full-blown night by the time I awoke. Yolanda lay cool and slick by my side. The butcher's blade, beneath my pillow, was clutched in my fist. A fine blade. Would've been a shame to leave it to the mud. I rolled over, scratched the back of my leg. Bed-bugs. Not too many. The place was fairly clean.

I got up, naked, checking the door and window. Inns may be lovely, but they aren't safe. I hunted an old couple from London to Edinburgh a few years back. They'd owned a well-to-do inn on the north bank just outside the city. Seems one night some drunk stumbled into their root cellar, found some bodies. And by '*some*,' I meant a shitload.

My door was still locked. A cheap lock, but the burglar-bar still lay in place. A stout kick or a small piece of wire and well-placed hole and it could be beaten. I'd checked for holes, checked the door, had even balanced an upside-down tankard on the knob.

I took a shot of wine. It'd been ale then whiskey then wine. The floor creaked underfoot, floor planks bowing as I walked. Thin. Orange flames flickered from outside the opaque window, lighting the night sky in cascading waves of orange and red.

The plague pits.

Was it already past midnight? Probably. Jesus, I'd already lost a day.

Where to start? No threads had presented themselves at the inn, nor had a squad of blackguards waylaid me in the dark. So Lady Narcissa was still a mystery.

My clothes were cleaned and mostly dry, folded up outside my door. My rusted mail was somewhere still being cleaned, apparently. Maybe they'd scrubbed off all the rust and found nothing left. I got dressed, walked downstairs. I hoped to see Karl, miraculously sitting at one of the tables, but did not.

The tavern was still stifling hot, the singing still fierce, forcefully jovial, tankards waving through the air, sloshing froth and foam as fists pounded tabletops. Men chanted along with the golden-haired jongleur on stage.

Plague does different things to different people. Some pray all day and night, and some go to the local tavern and drink and fuck and spend money til they die. You just never know. I'd seen scribes become hellions and hellions become monks, seen folk go on as if nothing were happening, denying, stepping silently around the rotting dead, slogging off to work day after day, balancing ledgers, carving wood, dyeing cloth, seeing less and less folk, less and less family until one night they lay down in an empty bed in a silent home and pray they never wake back up.

I pulled up a stool at the bar, set Yolanda leaning against it.

Next to me sat an old, worn-out whore. She was working her magic, her limited magic, chatting up some looming corpse-hurler who looked like unto death himself. Her hand rested lightly on his thigh. Smiling. She was smiling like he was the most charming bloke in the world. He was not.

I caught Schultz's eye, raised a hand.

"Meal, *Herr* Luther?" he nearly shouted. The place was loud. Boisterous. Desperately so.

"Yeah, I'm starving," I called back. "My mail shirt?"

Schultz nodded. "To be cleaned by morning."

I nodded, looked around for Lorelai, nowhere to be found. "This place ever slow down?"

"*Nein.*"

"The street-rat working out?" I took in the room.

"Eh?" Schultz thumbed over his shoulder noncommittally. "Lorelai has cleaned him up. He is being somewhere. Running around, most hopefully dragging a broom. You are looking better."

"Thanks." I nodded at a keg. "I could feel even

better."

"But of course." He filled another tankard.

"Mind if I ask you something?"

Schultz wiped his hands on a towel. "Surely."

"Know anything about the monasteries in town?" There were two, Dominican and Franciscan. I figured on visiting them tonight, sussing out the lady's ludicrous tale of murderous monks.

"*Nein, Herr* Luther." He handed me a tankard. "We have the two. *Had*, I should be saying. I am not getting much business from their way, you see? Monks. And the Dominicans are all being dead. Makes some sense."

"Yeah, how so?"

"Well, with the plague coming in from those accursed Jews and all," he replied. "I am hearing some say they poisoned all the wells around Goathead." He thumped the bar. "That is where it began. And their monastery lies up yonder, midway between there and the Point. Anyways. It burned to the ground. Early on."

"How about the Franciscans?"

"Their monastery is yet standing. I am knowing that." Schultz rubbed his chin. "I am hearing they got hit hard, as well, though." He crossed himself. "Show me someone who did not. Aye. I don't know if any are being still alive, though. You take Church Street down until you reach the Borderlands."

"Borderlands?" I remembered generally where the monastery lay but didn't know the '*Borderlands*' reference.

"Ah, yes, be forgiving me. The lords burned down a few blocks. The war, you see? There lies nothing but ruin. The Borderlands they call it. Watch yourself down there, *Herr* Luther. Gangs. Cutthroats. Thieves and such. The monastery lies just inside." I thanked him. "What are you wanting monasteries for?"

"Thinking of taking vows." I took a sip of pure bliss. Golden ale. It stung just right.

"We have a Teutonic hospital, too, by the big bridge. North Bridge. They're monks, too, of a sort. Maybe more to your colors." He raised a hand. "I'll get your meal." Schultz tossed the bar towel over his shoulder and disappeared into the kitchen.

Settling in, taking a proper pull from my ale, I glanced to my right.

The passion-play next to me was deteriorating fast. Miserably. Jesus, it was like my ten years of marriage condensed into seconds but slowed down just enough to highlight the truly loathsome moments.

The corpse-hurler didn't have enough money. Why? Because he was disgusting and she needed to charge him more because of that. He countered that she was a toothless old hag and that she should lower her exorbitant price.

Both presented fair points.

Haggling ensued between the hag and haggard. He didn't use the word *exorbitant*. And she? She had no patience for shitheels light on coin. His rage boiled. She cold-shouldered him, turning her back, started honing in on me, all seductive and coy, whispering in my ear, playing it thick and hard. I refused, almost politely, but it was too late. She'd cuckolded him in front of everyone.

I could hear his steam whistling like a kettle, threatening to blow as whispers and snickers across the room threatened to explode to crowing cacophony.

I told her I had no money, either.

She ignored me, pressed on, doubled down, telling me I was so bloody handsome I didn't need to pay. That was true. She wasn't much, but, well, it'd been a fair stretch on the road, devoid of warmth, and while she sure as shit was no Delilah, she made up for it in poured-on charm.

I could sense the corpse-hurler's shadow engulf me. I turned just as he shoved her off her stool. He thrust a black finger the size of a sausage into my face.

The music screeched to dead silence. Instantaneous. All eyes turned our way.

It went downhill from there, the whore continuing her tirade from her backside, pointing up, castigating as the corpse-hurler snatched up a chair up, holding it overhead like a maul. The whore screamed, a banshee wail, covering her face with wobbly arms. The chair whipped down, just missing her, shattering to pieces against the floor, and only because I'd nudged the bastard off balance.

I raised an open hand. "Easy, mister." Yolanda lay just out of reach.

"Shove your *'easy'* up your arse." He wiped spittle from his chin with the back of his black hand.

I reached for my new blade—

"Knife!" someone cried.

I saw a glint. That's it.

The corpse-hurler lunged, a spike of burnished steel in an oak-knot fist. His calloused paw smashed onto my shoulder, clamping a fistful of shirt, blade shooting up from below. Pivoting and parrying his hand with my own, I seized it with a swipe of my other, leading him off balance. He stuttered a step, and I reached across him, sliding in tight, hip to hip, and blocked his far knee with one hand, levering him toppling over. His head crashed against the floor hard, all his weight behind it.

Stools and folk scattered to all quarters like bowling pins. The whore crab-walked on all fours out of the way. Unattractive. I ripped the butcher's blade from its sheath, icepicking it. But the corpse-hurler didn't move. He just lay there beneath the bar, snoring ragged, gurgling on a puddle of his own blood.

Schultz materialized at my shoulder, club in hand. The crowd pressed. Eager. Heated. Curious. Lorelai appeared in the stairwell. Her eyes were wide, flecks of gold embedded amidst the green. From across the room, across the sea of people, I could see those flecks plain as day. I winked.

Lips pursed, she nodded once. Smiled.

I sheathed the butcher's blade, grabbed Yolanda.

"My lady…" I said as I made my way past Lorelai and through the crowd.

Without a word, she placed a warm hand on my shoulder and squeezed. The harridan on the floor was finally silent. Everyone was silent. But the chatter and music had both recommenced long before I reached the door.

...Suffice it to say, never have I seen a man capable of inflicting such wounds upon another, never mind the ludicrous notion of any man with even a precursory knowledge of Asylum nobility going to the door of the Lord Volkendorf and begging for anything short of a swift boot to the...

—*Journal of Sir Myron Chalstain*

Chapter 8.

LADY NARCISSA'S story was suspect at best, but it was my sole lead. The tally told of a possible killer-monk and a definite kill-site. I'd have preferred scouting the kill-site first, something solid, but I had figured on hazarding that under the light of day. That left the phantom killer-monk. And while I figured the Dominican priory for a waste of time, due diligence was, unfortunately, a necessary evil to any proper investigation, and you have to start somewhere. Eliminate it as a link in the murder chain, move on, maybe find a thread. That was the plan.

As always occurs when it fails to suit me, I was right. The Dominican Priory proved a waste of time, a ruin, a blasted out charnel shell of a ruin. Clear in the moonlight, crazed lines spalled across foundation stone like the web of a mad spider. Scorched skeletons peeked out from amid debris, glazed in ice, the glisten of frost turning them back to white. Lovely. I picked around in the dark, found nothing but corpse and despair.

I returned the way I'd come, headed south from Goathead, stopping at the West Gates and begging Nils for a spare lantern. The moon still glowed bright, but I'd broken mine and counting on Mother Nature for anything short of cruel indifference was a sucker's bet.

I wondered where Stephan was. Probably some lonely cell, huddled in the dark, numb, freezing, starving. Lord Raachwald hadn't been forthcoming with details. Maybe that was for the better.

Houses along the row glowed from within. Most were dark.

I ambled past, cloak clutched tight against the cold as the world abruptly turned to shit. The row just ended, only burnt skeletons beyond. The Borderlands. A pack of mongrels, coats mottled in swathes of mange, watched me from an alleyway, ten shining eyes, growling low. Better the four-legged kind.

The eastern half of the monastery's grounds ran adjacent to the Morgrave River. A sheer drop into darkness. An old Roman wall encircled the other three sides. A massive chain strangled the gates like a constrictor snake, rusted orange, frozen.

I listened to the hollow wind moan.

Desolate, a word that came to mind.

Only the silent fanfare of leering cast-iron cherubim answered. The wall was about ten-feet-high and well built, cleanly cut, the stones flush. But the ornate gate? A work of art, fat cherubs and frozen ivy intertwined, twisting and turning to the top. Very ornate. Very beautiful. Very easy to climb.

I clambered over it and landed on a cobblestone path. Snow-filled gardens lay to the left and right and monk cells ahead, a whole row of them, cold and dark. One of the doors creaked in the wind. I poked my head inside, saw nothing of note, continued on past neighboring cells and barren gardens to the church's front doors. They were modest, not like a public church. And they were open.

Snow began to fall.

Inside, there was nothing but the altar, a monolith of bare wood, and the stench of old death. A thick, caustic fume. No chairs, no pews, no comfort, only bare stone floor. Past the altar, I crept down a long hallway, following the thickening miasma of death. Something sounded from the hall's end. I froze. A clink. A clatter.

I slid the lantern's eye shut and waited, breathless in the gloom.

Nothing.

I moved on.

Keeping to the wall, I made my way as silently as I

could, wincing at every scrape, every scuff, every misstep. My eyes adjusted to the dark. A double door lay at hall's end, one side ajar. Was there a glimmer beyond? Maybe. That noise again. Metallic. Yeah. Someone readying a weapon? Or the clatter of utensils? Best bet on the weapon. My thoughts drifted to my mail shirt.

Watching, waiting, eyes straining, I could see tables beyond. A kitchen or great hall.

I tested the door. It didn't budge. I pushed harder, and it resisted still. Only silence lay beyond. A deep breath and I dropped my shoulder into it, suppressing a grunt, and it spilled open to me clattering into shadow and echo.

It was the great hall. Five long tables, each over thirty-feet long, four lengthwise heading away from me, one widthwise across the hall's end. Beyond, built into the far wall, three huge hearths stared back, empty, cold. But that wasn't all.

Like some lurid scene from Boccaccio's *Decameron*, dark forms filled each table, thirty to each, maybe, hunched carcasses splayed out, reaching for cups and for plates and for whatever else lay set out before them. Some leaned back in their chairs, arms poised in rigor. They wore the brown homespun cloth of their order, and they were dead. They were all dead. Their stench had weight. Taking a step was like moving headlong into a gale wind. Rotting food lay before them in a cornucopia of filth, the reek of soured wine, of vinegar, of fetid corpse.

My eyes watered.

It didn't make any sense.

They'd all died of plague. Presumably. And if they had, what the hell were they doing here? People don't die of plague at the dinner table. Not alone. Not *en masse* at some grand banquet. I wish they did. Wouldn't be so bad going out drinking and feasting alongside friends. But no. They died in bed if they were lucky, festering and fidgeting in an incoherent fever, pissing and shitting and oozing from every orifice, black boils weeping tears of bile from their necks, their armpits, their groins.

I strode along the left wall. Paintings lined it, pastoral scenes, lambs and shepherds, and grassy green knolls. Against the stifling reek, I tried to imagine Lorelai's rosewater scent as I breathed through my mouth. I passed a monk who was nearly a skeleton, then one freshly dead, his grimaced lips blue-black. Someone had placed them all here. Recently.

I turned in a circle. All the windows were shuttered. There was the pair of doors I'd come through and another pair up ahead. Probably the kitchen. I tried them. Locked.

I whipped around as something clattered on the right side of the hall. Wooden. A cup? Then and there, I nearly bolted, fearless knight that I am. Instead, I drew Yolanda and against every grain, every fiber of my being, waited in the heavy silence.

Bravery. It's a fickle thing. To ebb and flow on such whims. As I waited and watched, and watched and waited, it seemed as though the dead monks began to move, minutely at first, some drawing breath, long languorous intakes and exhales, a head shift here, a twitch there, the shrug of a bony shoulder. Some leaned over, whispering to neighbors, confiding secrets only death could confer, others giggling drunkenly as they reached out for more and for more and for more.

"Enough." My voice echoed across the hall, the stone walls vibrating to a ringing halt. "I am not going away." As much as I want to. "I mean you no harm." Maybe. "I wish only to ask questions. I'm here to do God's own work. You should appreciate that.

"A man was killed." I walked on, reaching the three hearths.

Silence. I took a right, the empty voids yawning, drawing me in.

"His men with him."

More silence.

"And his children…" Nothing. "The blame has been laid at the foot of this monastery. I'm looking for a man said to be a monk. A large man. A massive man. He has hair of dark black. Described as having the countenance of the devil. Possibly if you know this man, you know what that means. Others paid with their lives." I waited. "Three lads of eight to ten years each. Murdered. Good lads." Or maybe they were caustic shits.

Corpse after corpse stared back in mute laughter, teeth bared, frozen.

"*You'll go…*" A whispered cackle as though some crow had taken roost. "Heh-heh…"

I nearly shit myself. Right there. Instead, I turned. Tried gauging its origin.

"Yes-yes, you shall…"

"I won't." I still couldn't place it. "A hard truth."

"If you won't, you will, heh-heh."

"Jesus. Riddles? I'll forgive your ignorance for we've only just met, but I despise men who speak in riddles. Are we in a faery tale? Shall I catch you? Demand three wishes?"

"Neither."

"Who are you then?" Keep him talking. Hone in. "A monk?"

"I am he who waits amongst the dead for death to come."

"Jesus." I kicked a cup from my path. "You're no monk. You're a thief. Stealing quotes from Petrarch?"

He cackled again. From the far end? Or near? Definitely far. Cracking the eye of my lantern, it cast light, soft and weak and orange. The hearth-eyes stared. The monks were all moving, dancing now as shadows undulated in concert to the movement of my lantern.

"You, my friend, are an asshole." I passed a monk whose face the rats had gotten to. "And if I have a name, to you, it is *Death*."

"Dear me, look who thinks so highly of himself. Delusions. Nay-nay. I've seen death, as it were, dared him, dined with him. Look around. We dine every day now, and you are not he." I wheeled around. "Heh-heh. Is this the Great Alexander himself, perhaps? You think yourself so high. So mighty. Conqueror of the great East? Chief amongst the Nine Worthies?" Keep jawing. "Come to ransack an empty monastery. Come to threaten a sick, broken man. Heh-heh. I was mistaken. No hero-lord is he, just another buzzard, come to pick us clean."

"Blade. Boot. Bare hands, I ain't picky." I stalked the perimeter, clockwise, toward the right half of the hall. "I'll be your end one way or another if you don't reveal yourself."

"You threaten me with death? Heh. The ultimate cure? The final panacea? Please. Send me to God. To Heaven. I pray that you do. I beg it." His voice lowered then. "You wish to threaten me? Threaten me with life, then. With health, with longevity, with friendship. For that, by far, is the crueler fate."

I found myself back at the entrance doors. With the two doors on the left side of the hall locked, these offered the only escape. I wedged a broken chair leg under the open door and piled chairs in front of both.

"I was the Alpha, and now am the Omega," the voice railed.

"You were the first, and now you're the last?" I strode counterclockwise now, back up the right side wall. I had him.

"Hee-hee-heee! Death shall be a relief!"

"You piece of *repeating* shit," I said. "You live in a monastery. What the hell do *you* know about life? Cloistered? Secreted? Tucked away within a closed world without fear, without pain, devoid of anything that has to do with life."

"We cloister ourselves to protect us from the temptations of the world..."

"The temptations are the only thing worth living for, friend."

"Yes-yes, and yet they find us here still..."

"I'll pass on an explanation."

"We are men of God!"

I was halfway up the last table. He was near. But where?

"Very well." I stopped. "You mocked me with a

riddle. Well, I solved it." I straightened. "You were the first of your brethren to succumb to the plague, but you survived. And now you're the last. You're new to riddles, I'd guess. No sphinx at any rate. Next, you compared me to Alexander. Well, I *am* he, and you are my Gordian knot, and though I cannot untie you—"

With that, I slashed the foot off one of the corpse-monks. It flicked off along with the leg of the chair he was sitting on, the pair tipping in tandem. I moved on to the next one and cut off an arm, licking through bone, shattering a wine bottle. Stepping toward the far wall, I slid Yolanda between the ribs of another monk. I stepped and stabbed, slashed and stepped, keeping the double doorway always in view.

I kicked a skeleton over then backhand chopped another. Yolanda sheered through flesh as though nothing were there.

A shadow bolted past—

I tore on after, snatching him by the scruff of his neck, yanking, stepping, and hurling him arse over tea kettle into the riot of piled chairs. A smash and cascade, an avalanche. Struggling, whining, he flailed, kicking, drowning for the blocked doors but entangled like a rabbit in a huntsman's snare.

...her mourning to be genuine in the loss of her two sons. I have known liars; oft times it seems I am acquainted with none but, and she is obviously one. Despite this, she is plainly distraught, though her grief did at first bear an element of gleeful hysteria which she was initially unable...

—*Journal of Sir Myron Chalstain*

Chapter 9.

STRANGE. To sip tea, spattered in gore, in the dead hours of night alongside a man I had recently threatened to kill. Brother Tomas slurped his barley tea with grey lips, palpating delicately along the brim of his cup like an elephant's wrinkled trunk. The carnage of the great hall was one thing, death, horror, rotting corpses, the devil's delight compared to Brother Tomas's flaccid, glistening lips.

His cell was close, ten by ten at best. Mountains of books surrounded us, some piled near high as I was tall. A small fire crackled in the hearth.

"...and so Brother Justinian was the last to pass into darkness," Brother Tomas finished.

"A sad tale." I wrung my hands. "But, what of the man I seek? A man capable of single-handedly killing seven warriors." I ran my thumb smoothly across my throat. "And murdering three children, to boot."

"Is it not enough to murder men?" Brother Tomas bemoaned the heavens. "Men have sinned. Yes-yes. And shall sin. But children?" He crossed himself. "Was there ever such a man as this?"

"The answer to your question is yes. Yes, and in droves. Piles. Legions. Yes, and one sits before you. Wears your robes. Crowds your streets. Your land. Your home."

His spoon clinked as he hastily stirred his tea. "Your view of mankind is prodigiously dim, Sir Luther."

"On the contrary, it's one of the few things I view with the utmost clarity."

"Bleak, then."

I paused, considered, nodded. "I'll grant you that." I poured a lick of wine into my tea, stirred it with my finger. "Please, brother, was there ever a man of such description here?"

His rheumy eyes regarded me, leaking like a hound's. "No."

"And you've been here how long?"

"Near my whole life."

"What's that, then?" I took a sip. "Fifty? Sixty years?"

"Twenty-one."

"Jesus—" I spluttered, choked, settled. "Sorry." I wiped myself off.

"It has taken its toll," Brother Tomas conceded. "It was enough that I could minister to my brothers, bear them through their last days, shrive them, wash them, dine with them night after night after—"

"Uh—" I raised a hand but then just let it go.

"Heh, heh." He blushed like a shy girl. "I...digging holes...ground frozen...was lonely."

"There are men who collect the dead."

"Nay." He thumped the arm of his chair, eyes blazing, fierce for an instant, and then like the wind it was gone. "My brothers shall be laid to rest each within their own graves, upon these hallowed grounds, afforded proper Christian burials. Headstones, so that I might visit them, talk to them, pray for them." His hand quivered, tea spilling over the rim of his cup. "They shan't be cast into plague-fire and forgotten."

"Fair enough." I ladled parsnip soup into a bowl, handed it to him, did the same for myself. "Warm soup," I took a mouthful, chewed, "makes one hell of a difference."

"Yes-yes." He hefted his bowl. "To...to justice, justice and warm soup!"

"No." I raised my spoon. "There'll be no justice in this affair. I'll toast to heeling the bastard. Running him down. Seeing he gets what's coming to him. Nothing more."

I glanced up, paused, shrugged. "And to warm soup."

"Hear! Hear!"

I raised my bowl to his, and we clacked them together, his horrid face beaming. It was still awful. So awful. He looked like a man whose skin was made too big, his face practically sliding off his skull, his story of plague survival etched plain in withered desiccation. All the teeth on the right side of his mouth had fallen out, leaving only slick black gums. He took a palpating sip, wine dribbling down his chin.

I puked inside my mouth.

"You put me in a mind of, oh, who's the one from the *Iliad*?" Giggling softly to himself, Brother Tomas took another sip of the wine. His fourth cup. He closed his eyes, swaying slightly, a grin upon his lips. He was in a good place, probably the first time in a long while.

"Achilles?"

"No, the other one." He pointed. "Heh-heh. With the ship. The sheep. The Cyclops." Only he slurred, '*shyclopsh.*'

"Odysseus," I said.

"Yes-yes!" He pointed emphatically with his spoon. "Homer? You've read him? You can read?"

"A bit."

"Oh, bless me, a learned man to sup with." Brother Tomas clapped his hands in fervent delight. "A gift from God you are."

"That is a first for me."

"A fitting analogy, no?" His feet were bouncing. "You're far from home, are you not? A stranger in a strange land, amidst its myriad travails, threats, perils."

"What are you?" I rolled my eyes. "A college student composing a thesis?"

"Well, I admit it's not perfect, but you wear a wedding ring upon your finger." He settled back, wheezing. "You have a family somewhere, I presume? A wife? And your accent? Angland? Perhaps you travel back to her?"

"No." I was no Odysseus. He wouldn't be sitting

here in the middle of the night with some shit-house-crazy monk. He'd have stolen into Dunmire and snatched Stephan right out from under Lord Raachwald's blind left eye. Would have blinded the right for good measure, too. "I'm no hero. Not on some stupid quest."

"He was going home."

"Huh?" I looked up.

"He was going home. Returning from war."

"Your point?"

"It wasn't stupid. Returning home is not a stupid quest. It is perhaps the most meaningful."

I grunted, took another mouthful of soup.

"And you? Hah!" He slapped his thigh. "I thought all knights ignorant brutes."

"The best are."

"Yet, it was my thinking that reading and writing were considered...unknightly."

"Oh, certainly. Unknightly. Unmanly. Unconscionable," I explained. "Merely a part of my training."

"Training? I had thought knights trained only at dashing each other's brains out with implements of war."

"Oh, we do. But there are other fields of expertise." I counted on my fingers. "Hunting. Hawking. Torture. Plunder. Debauchery." I held up that one finger. "Particularly debauchery, it's the very foundation on which the whole institution is built."

"But, what of the code of chivalry?" The monk crossed himself. "The pontiff's *Truce of God*? *The Peace of God*?"

"Bells. Whistles." I waved a hand as if dismissing a serf. "Something for the storybooks. For church. For places of light. And light has no place in knighthood. Your *Peace of God*? Your *Truce*? Mindless church babble scripted to placate the masses. Show that they're doing something to protect the ones who feed them, clothe them, support them." I took a sip of wine. "Plague's done its killing, but knights have borne their fair share. You been outside these walls lately?"

"But," his voice went quiet, "you don't seem like them…"

"Disappointing folk is one of my strengths."

"But plunder? *Debauchery*?"

"Trust me." I smiled and then didn't.

"Trust a man who admits he's untrustworthy? I thought you despised men who spoke in riddles?"

"Frequently and furiously, and I'm many things, but no hypocrite. I can swing a sword and skewer with lance, but my fortune was never meant to be forged solely by my arm. Wish it were. So much easier, so much simpler to just go where your lord points. Kill who he bids kill. My father…" I paused. "My father is a hard man. A cruel man, some would say. Most. But my father is a man who sees the truth in people. Cuts to the quick. Fast. Sharp. Clean. And he saw the truth in me."

Brother Tomas's spoon froze halfway to his mouth. "What truth?"

I cradled the warm bowl between my hands. "That I am not a good knight. That I would never *be* a good knight."

"But you are a knight. And I believe—"

"Yes, but a knight is just a word. A word that elevates us above the common folk. You know."

"Pardon?"

"You're nobly born. Or if you're not, your father's a rich man, or well off, yeah?" Brother Tomas twitched a reluctant nod. "You live in a large building with a solid roof over your head. You eat three meals a day. Have an education. The room where you work has walls that block the wind, the rain, the cold of winter."

"Copying texts is not so easy."

"Sure. But it's not digging ditches." I glanced out the window at the snow. "What makes us better than *them* but an accident of birth?"

Brother Tomas swallowed. "A strange notion coming from a knight."

"I told you, I'm not a good one. People can fight without me. Pray without you." I raised a conspiratorial hand to my mouth. "Just don't tell *them* that."

"So, what necessitated your learning to read?"

"My Uncle Charles. He was justiciar in my father's court. A wise old bastard. A right funny one, too." Jesus, I missed him. "But he was second born. And had the misfortune of having a barren wife. Lacking an heir, my father named me his ward and apprentice, in effect. A tedious business, justice."

"Yes-yes, but vital." Brother Tomas nodded emphatically. "Often the sole recourse of the weak and downtrodden."

"Yeah, no." I shook my head slowly. "Justice is important because it's one of the lord's chief incomes." I rubbed my fingers together. "Seizures. Fines. Forfeitures. Very lucrative."

"J-Justice is not a trade." Brother Tomas's lips trembled.

"*Truly*? Who makes out in trade?"

Brother Tomas shrugged. "Trade of what?"

"Trade of anything," I said.

"Surely the poor…?"

"Sure. To some degree. The rich to a greater. But the ones who truly make out are the ones who created the system. The ones who make the laws. Levy taxes. And who's that?"

"The lords."

"Yeah. And who makes out in the courts?"

"It cannot *only* be about money."

"True. That'd be suicidal. The poor would catch on eventually and revolt. And there's a shit-ton more of them than us."

Brother Tomas fumbled his tea, dropping his spoon.

"Your mistake is thinking of justice as a conflict between two parties. There're three. The accuser. The accused. And the court. And the court always gets its pound of flesh. Bet on it. Whoever wins, the lord collects a fine. Seizes a house. Requisitions the wrongdoer's best cow. And sometimes, when a blue moon shines, he just basks in the reflected glory of having done what was truly right." I sat back, holding my hands out open. "So that next time, he can dip his beak in a little deeper, a little longer, and sneak an extra taste."

Brother Tomas's face had fallen. "That sounds…"

"Awful, yeah, I know." I shrugged. "But not compared to the paperwork. And justice is mostly that. Warrants. Writs. Affidavits." Those, I didn't miss. "My uncle taught me to be fair. To never trust the clerks serving beneath me. To read and understand everything myself. So I learned."

"Very good." Pushing himself upright with hands on knees, Brother Tomas stood, teetering there for a moment. "I—whoa." He caught his balance on his chair. "I shall show you now. We shall stride the great hall and gaze upon the visage of each of my brothers so that you might ascertain whether your fiend has met his end." He burped, swayed, and immediately sat back down. "Oof."

"Easy." I waved him off. "Relax. You knew everyone, yeah?"

"That…" His head was swimming. "Excuse me. Yes. I have. I do. Know each man." He hiccoughed, covering his mouth belatedly. "A thousand pardons. *Knew*."

"And you said none fit the description."

"No, Sir Krait. Err… Yes, Luther. Sir."

"Then I see no point in rifling the dead." I kicked my feet up on a stack of bibles. The snow was still raging, but the sky had lightened.

"You…trust me?" Brother Tomas's face peeled back in a toothsome grin. A horrid sight. "Never such a man. Not here. One hundred and forty-seven men…" His jubilant smile withered, black gums consumed behind grey lips. "We came to die, to die as we had lived, as one. A community of brothers. So many. So sick. So fast. Like a black wave, it struck us, swallowing us whole. I, the first to succumb, as you guessed. But…" his voice cracked, tears spilling down his cheeks.

"Could you ladle me some more soup?" I held my

bowl out.

"Eh?" He looked up, "Yes, of course," and ladled in some more. "Forgive me." He wiped his eyes.

"No sweat." I took the bowl. "What of the Dominican monastery?"

"I…I never knew any from the Dominican Abbey, and if there were such a man, he's dead now. Most likely. They were hit as hard by the plague as us, and earlier on. The abbey was razed that same week."

"A quarantine measure?"

"I don't know."

"Townsfolk or lords?"

Brother Tomas shrugged. "Does it matter who? Or why?"

"It'd matter to me if I were one of them. But I'm not. Now, what of the Teutonic Knights?" Brother Tomas sputtered. "You alright?" He waved me off. "I'm told they've a priory here. A hospital, as well." The Teutonic Knights were a brotherhood of knight-monks sworn to fight the pagan menace in the north. "A monk trained in the arts of war would stand a better chance against armed men."

"But against *seven*?" Brother Tomas's face went from ashen to white. "How much better?"

"A little." Jesus, it sounded ridiculous to me, too.

"Now, your murderer," Brother Tomas clutched at the crucifix at his neck, "how is it you know he was a man of God? Truly know?"

"I don't. I have only a lady's word."

"And you trust this lady?"

"No. Not even a little."

Chapter 10.

I QUIT THE MONASTERY to the sound of cannon fire booming far off to the east. Across the river. I headed south on Mill Street. A quick jaunt. Mummer's Isle, stark against the grey morning sky, rose before me from the churning depths of the Morgrave River. The Isle rose some seventy or eighty feet from the rapids until equal with the level of the streets, then continued another eight or nine hundred beyond, a fist of gnarled stone.

Gulls swirled above, wheeling, screaming.

Five castles clung to its sparse cliffs, but only three visible from my vantage.

Lord Raachwald's keep, Old-Oath, sat high upon a cliff, walls peeking above the rim. Lord Hochmund's Gold-Tooth lay south along the Isle. I could just see one of its shining towers cresting the Isle's jagged ridge. And perched atop the Isle's peak, Coldspire leered down bleak as Odin's crow, commanding the land and sea for twenty leagues in all directions.

I spent the morning scouting the Isle from its west side, trying to suss out a lay of the land. In the early afternoon, I took the North Bridge across the Morgrave, into the eastern half of the city. Towards the cannon fire. The bridge was a shambles. Broken weapons lay scattered amongst bits of armor and spalled brick and frozen blood. Men had died here. Recently. Scraggly tinker folk hustled past, gleaning scraps of fallen metal.

Off the North Bridge, I headed south to check out the eastern lay of Mummer's Isle. From there, I could see not only Coldspire but also Solemn Rock of the Taschgarts and Azure-Mist of the Brulerins. The same problems present on the western side were here as well: steep cliffs, raging river, a guarded bridge. The Brulerin Bridge.

I wondered the whole way back why Lord Raachwald had refused me passage onto his shitty rock. He had the right. The power. And although he hated me, and with good reason, his son had been murdered. Why loose a bloodhound on a trail in one breath, only to chain it the next?

The Borderlands were as desolate under light of day as they'd been at night. Maybe more so. Whole neighborhoods had been razed from the river all the way to the city wall. A quarter mile of scorched timber, scorched earth, flooded foundations. Gang sigils covered the walls of those houses still standing. I recognized some. The black unicorn of the Four Horsemen and the double sword of Hughes's Razors. Others, I didn't. Motleyed claws and crows and dragons and cocks and everything in between all slathered in paint across one another in some contest of artistic one-upmanship.

Something skittered across my path.

Asylum. It was anything *but*.

The Bastard Bridge spanned to the western side of Mummer's Isle. A sturdy-looking structure, the straight span had certain touches I could only describe as Romanesque. They reminded me of aqueducts I'd seen in and around Cordoba, structures over a thousand years old, still working, still flowing water, still servicing the lords of that grand city. Except for the five corpses dangling from beneath it, that is. Cordoba's aqueducts hadn't had those.

With only two bridges onto the Isle from the city or a climb up sheer rock, Mummer's Isle itself was a daunting defensive structure alone. Impregnable. Add the five keeps, ballista, cannon, and enough armed men to man them, and it was *really* impregnable. For an army at least.

Where an army met a wall of armor, perhaps a single man might find a chink wide enough to slip a slender dirk through.

The river raged below, white water shooting

through a sluiceway. The grey cliffs beyond looked sheer from my vantage, but an able man might be able to climb them if he knew where to begin. If he were willing to brave the pounding rapids and succeed, an able man, with no shortage of courage, might scale a sheer rise of a thousand feet. Slowly. Meticulously. And topping that, it'd need be accomplished under cover of darkness, in the numbing March cold, fingers bleeding raw from rock and salt, nails digging into cracks, back-breaking, arms screaming. Yeah, a brave man just might scale that stone and pierce the security. But there was just no way in hell it was going to be me.

I continued south along the parapet.

My big plan?

I strolled right up to the Bastard Bridge guard post, little more than a lean-to. Both guards wore the livery of House Hochmund, a red fox on an orange field, and bore short spears and shields. Good mail. Short blades hung from their hips.

Not a sizable defense considering the reputation of the Borderlands.

But across the span, I noticed a guard-shack on the far side, smoke drizzling up from its chimney. The rest of the guards would be in there, watching, waiting.

A stout guard, a short wide fellow, hugged himself against the cold. When he noticed me, he shook it off, trying to cut an at least semi-intimidating figure. He failed. Miserably. Tough to act the hard case when your nose is red, your face streaked with snot, and you're shivering like a newborn calf.

Grit crunched underfoot as I made my way toward them.

Both were at attention now.

"Greetings," I said.

The first guard, the stout chap, watched me, wary. His partner, tall and thin, stood behind, smoking a pipe, watching me from below drooped eyelids. Both were youngish, which made this the shit job of the outfit.

"That's far enough." The stout guard raised a hand.

I stopped just shy of a turnpike set across the bridge's mouth. "You ain't no church-man, are you?"

I glanced below, at the dangling corpses, crosses of blue across their chests. The Lord Bishop's men. "I hope not."

"State yer business, then." He hugged himself against the cold.

"Ought to pace a bit," I offered. "Better than standing in one place. Freezing your arse off."

"Freeze my arse off no matter what," the stout guard grumbled. "Come on now, what's it you want?"

"To speak to Lord Hochmund."

"And I want a hot fireplace and tankard of ale."

"Might be able to help you with one of those."

"No one's allowed on the Isle," the stout guard waved a hand, "and Lord Hochmund ain't taking no messages."

"Yeah? Why not?"

"Cause he ain't."

"Fair enough, but I'm a comrade of his. From way back."

The stout guard frowned. He was considering the possible truth of my statement, factoring in my monk-spattered garb and general dishevelment, and weighing it all against the effort and repercussions of running across the bridge to bother his sergeant. "Sure."

Very politic.

I grumbled internally at the prick but managed to choke it back. I'd have done the same if our roles were reversed, only I'd have been a sight more rude. "Yeah. I'm a little worse for wear, but it's true. I even saved his life once."

It was true that I knew Lord Eustace Hochmund. 'Comrade' might have been a bit strong, but I had, in fact, saved his life. In a whorehouse, though, not the battlefield. We were waiting for ladies of the night to free up—not a classy establishment, obviously, but on the road, one must persevere—eating a hurried dinner, road fare, when he choked on something. A gob of chicken? Pork? Something.

So I pounded his back, slapped him in the face, shook him, yelled. Finally, I punched him in the gut as hard as I could. Which worked.

"Oh yeah?" He glanced at his partner, who shrugged and blew a short-lived smoke ring. "Where?"

"At the battle of *Belle's Ball*." *Belle's Ball* was the name of the whorehouse.

"Never heard of it."

"Your loss." I meant it sincerely.

"Lord Hochmund don't like no beggars," the stout guard said, "and he don't like me telling him about no beggars."

"I'm no beggar." I flipped him a penny. He caught it. "Keep it. And could you tell him? Please."

"Hmmm...?" He studied the coin, turning it over. "You know who else don't like me bothering him?"

"Who?"

"Everyone else up my chain of command."

"And how many's that?"

His face scrunched up as he thought. "Right now?" He counted on his fingers, slowly working it out. "Four. Sometimes three. Today it's four."

"You said you wanted ale. Well, I don't have ale. What I do have is wine." I took a wineskin I'd 'borrowed' from Brother Tomas, held it up, jiggled it a bit. "Not to mention that shiny penny. Now, look. You're freezing. Why not take a walk? I promise not to storm the Isle. And I'm sure your partner and the fellows in the guard-shack can handle me if I change my mind."

"You see that fucking path?" He scowled over his shoulder at the footpath up. A heart-attack special. It switch-backed left then right, back and forth, up across the entire rock-face, hundreds of vertical feet, until it ended in a cliff.

"You're young," I scoffed. "And you'll be warmer. Less bored. And you'll have company." I waggled the wineskin. "Wine in your belly, a nice wintry walk? Not so bad. All you're missing's a sweetheart." I could almost hear his mouth watering, staring at the wine, his cold feet begging for movement, for a moment in that heated shack. "Maybe your sergeant lets you hang around in that cozy shelter while he goes off?" Highly unlikely, but...

He gazed off across the chasm, forlorn, eyes filled with mournful longing for that shack, that shitty little shack with that shitty little chimney, and that shitty little trickle of smoke weeping out. Probably his life's dream to just sit in there all day and do nothing.

"What'd you say your name was?" He eyeballed the wine.

"Didn't. Just tell him about *Belle's Ball*. Fella who saved him."

He grumbled to himself.

"One last chance..." I dangled the wine.

It took but an instant for him to reach out, snatch it, turn. He thumped his partner on the shoulder, "Be right back," and marched on across the bridge, disappearing into the guard-shack. He wasn't inside it a moment before he was slogging head down up the pathway.

I'd dealt with Lord Eustace Hochmund here and there since I was a squire to my uncle. And my uncle never failed to tell me the same thing each time we dealt with him.

"I've three serpents in hand," he'd whispered to me as he brandished three short threads gathered from the hem of his shirt. "Two are poisonous." He separated them. "One harmless. You know the first to be poisonous, the second harmless." He brandished one then the other. "Now, the third. It appears identical to the harmless one but, in truth, is as deadly as the first." He fixed me with a glare. "So, my lad, which is most deadly?"

"The third," I answered without pause.

"Nay. Understand this," he held up a finger, "the first and the third are *equally* deadly. The added danger lies not within the third serpent itself but within you. It is a weakness of *your* perception. *Your* character. 'Tis a weakness within you for not recognizing *his* inherent danger." He rolled the pieces of string between his fingers, let them fall. "Lord Hochmund is the third serpent." Even now I wonder if he told me each time to remind me or to remind himself.

I waited for what I figured an hour before the stout guard returned, huffing, sweating, a menacing glare in his eyes. He tossed the wineskin on the ground before me. Empty. Rude. There he stood for a moment, catching his breath, swaying. His partner leaned against the turnpike, still smoking, still watching, still unimpressed.

"Well?" I asked.

"Said he didn't know nothing about no *Belle's Ball*."

"He's lying," I commented.

"So what?" The guard's gaze flitted to Yolanda's hilt, poking above my shoulder. "He's a bloody lord. And he also told me to tell you something else."

"Yeah? What?"

"He told me to tell you to '*piss off*.'"

...to speak to her handmaiden, but I cannot ascertain her whereabouts.
—*Journal of Sir Myron Chalstain*

Chapter 11.

IT'D BEEN A WASTE of a day, and I didn't have any to burn. Neither did my brother. I hadn't got onto the Isle, and I'd found neither Karl nor sign of him. Backtracking east along the Dunmire Road had proved fruitless. Karl couldn't read or write, but he's fairly blunt with regards to communication. No decapitated horses hanging from trees or Thor's hammers scrawled across the broad sides of barns. He'd be in the city by now, searching for me, looking through taverns. There were more than a few.

I jawed up Nils as I passed back in through the gates. He hadn't seen any pagan murderers skulk through and wished me well. And I him.

I had it in my head I'd make for the Jewish Quarter and meet with Abraham Ben-Ari, my boss. In part. It hadn't been his shipment of wool I'd lost, per say, but I'd been hired on his word, and he had a stake in it, so it was a close thing. I made it to the gates of the Quarter and stopped. A contingent of the Lord Bishop's men were stationed there. Thirty men. Heavily armed. I took it as a sign, a sign that said *'fuck it and head home,'* or what passed for it.

So that's what I did.

My stomach was rumbling, my mouth dry, feet throbbing by the time I got back to the Stone Ruin Ten. The sun had set though I'd not seen her all day, sheathed behind cold grey. I ate. I drank. I staggered upstairs to shut my eyes for an hour or two. Clear my head. Then I'd resume pounding it against the cobblestone streets, trying to unearth some way onto that blasted Isle. How the hell to do it, though? I could try Lord Hochmund again. Sure, the bastard owed me, but he obviously didn't care, and there was no twisting his pudgy arm. Not from my side of the bridge.

So what? Steal a boat? Brave the rapids? Snag a grappling hook and attempt the climb? East or west approach? Jesus.

I pushed open the door to my room, took a long pull of ale, froze.

My short blade was in hand reflexively.

Someone'd been in. I could tell. Ask me to explain it, I couldn't. Maybe a smell? A lingering scent? A dark suspicion beyond conscious thought? Winter twilight had long come and gone, replaced by the flicker of plague fire from far beyond, blossoms of orange frost glistening across the feathered glass. I could barely see, but what I did, confirmed my suspicion. On my bed lay a note, neatly folded, a dab of pressed wax holding it shut. I closed the door, snatched up the letter, held it up to the window. Nothing written on the outside. No seal in the wax. Naturally.

I slit open the seal, unfolded it. In the gloom, the writing was almost legible, tight, spidery, concise. Two lines. Maybe…an address? Too dark to read. I turned at a light knock on my door. I hid the note away, gripped my blade. "Hello?"

"Lonely?" came a husky voice.

I cracked open the door. It was her. Lorelai. Hair spilled across one bare shoulder, the bodice of her dress loosened up top, strings dangling, snowy white chemise peeking out. Quite a sight.

"I'm always lonely." I tucked the blade behind my back.

She drank, or sucked rather, from a small wineskin, tipping it back, gaze fixed hard on me the whole while. Not demure. Nothing subtle or ladylike. She was drinking hard, drinking with purpose, drinking to get drunk fast or make damn sure she stayed that way.

"What're you drinking?"

"They hurt?" She reached forward, running a fingertip gently along the parade of stitches marching across my forehead.

"Not right now."

"Gonna invite me in?" She gave me that look.

Intoxicating. Made you feel like you were someone, something, even when you knew you were nothing. Better than wine. Better than whiskey. Better than anything. I wondered if she had that look for every man. Wondered what it cost her. And if it cost a lot.

I said nothing, though, just stepped aside, sheathed the blade, heart pounding all of a sudden.

Pushing off the wall, she stood up straight, swaying, found her balance, and slipped a length of red-gold hair from her face. She brushed past me inside.

I nodded at her wineskin. "May I?"

"You asking for a taste of this?" She lowered the wine, wiped her mouth. "Or something else?"

"What do you think?"

Her eyes were but twin points of wavering light, flame reflecting, glistening amidst their depths.

"Been waiting long?"

She shrugged. "Maybe."

"Maybe?" I held out a hand for the wine.

She knocked back another mouthful. "You a real knight?"

"Sure."

"Hmm…? Never met one before." She circled me. "Up close. Personal."

"Can't say the same."

"Got a sword?"

I nodded toward Yolanda, leaning against the bed. "Ain't she a beaut?"

"Ain't what I mean." She quit circling and slid up against me, a question in her eyes as she reached down, hand bold, fearless, caressing me below. "Should I call you, *Sir*?"

"Don't care what you call me." I swallowed. "Name's…Luther."

"I know."

"I'll give you an hour to stop that," my ears buzzing, "or I'm calling the watch."

"Why do you think I'm here, Sir Luther?"

"Maybe you heard I'm worth the wait?"

"You the exception to the rule, then?"

"What rule's that?" My head was foggy.

"The rule that most men ain't," she whispered in my ear, her breath warm.

"Hadn't known."

"Cause you're a man."

"Seems fair accurate," I slid my hand around her waist, "in retrospect," drawing her in, "considering."

Crushed against me, she raised a finger to her lips. Good lips. "Shhhh…"

"You ladies play that one close."

"Ain't no lady." Her hand sliding inside the waist of my trousers now, squirming down, grasping firm.

"I might die of thirst…" I nodded at her wine.

"Would anybody care?" She pulled it out of reach.

"No," I answered.

Her hair smelled of spring and rosewater, the rest of her, wine and desire. She relented, offering the wineskin up. I fumbled it to my lips, killed it. Wine. Good wine. I tossed it, inhaled her, ran my fingers through her golden tangle. She unbuttoned my shirt, one by one, deft fingers working. I shivered but was no longer cold. She finished the last button.

"You haven't been doing this too long." I kissed her.

"Hmmmm…" she let loose a throaty sigh, my shirt sliding off my arm, her letting it, "am I doing something wrong?"

"Everything." Gliding my hand up her leg, beneath her dress, feeling along that soft bare expanse, warmer and closer. Closing her eyes, she inhaled long and slow. I felt her, stroking liquid silk, strumming gently with fingertips, smooth and circular. Her breath fast, faster, rolling her hips slowly against my rhythm. I kissed her neck, her lips. She kissed me back, hard, fierce, her tongue sliding against mine.

She stiffened, stifling a moan, nails digging into my chest as she melted into me, just breathing in and out, in and out, in and out…"Just a moment."

"I'm already done."

She straightened back. "Like hell, you are." She thumped me with one hand, pushed me back a step, pulling her slumping bodice back up her naked shoulder. "We ain't even started." She took hold of me again and dragged me toward the bed. "It's cold."

"The bed's heated." I offered minimal resistance.

She smirked that wicked half-smirk.

Near stumbling, she towed me until we both collapsed onto the bed. I pulled her bodice open with a sharp two-fisted tug, pouring her free. "Mother of God…"

I descended, kissing bare flesh.

"The door," she moaned as she shimmied free of her chemise.

"Sure…" I was on my feet and out of my pants in two steps and trips and as many hops, kicking them off as they clung to one boot, stomping across them as I crossed the room. I kicked the door shut, my boots off, dropped the burglar bar, turned.

Breathless, I froze, catching a glimpse of her against the shimmer of plague fire. She shoved the halo of crumpled linen down from her hips. I stared. Swallowed. Thanked God for that plague fire burning, for the light that it cast, for smooth flesh and hourglass curves glowing ethereal. She turned towards me, face lost in shadow. She ran her hands up through her long hair, pulling it up, back, letting it melt liquid through her fingers like coils of shimmering flame, one by one, coil by coil, falling. And there she stood, bare flesh bathed in the rippling glow of the incinerating dead.

"Well, come on, if you're coming," she whispered.

...thrice-damned Gallows Lord said it would have been unseemly for them to remain hanging. I agreed though it stung me so to agree with such a man as he...
—*Journal of Sir Myron Chalstain*

Chapter 12.

HARSH WHITE LIGHT blared in through the window, burning my brain, my eyes. It was late morning. Shit. Lorelai was gone. The pillow and linen still smelled of her. A good smell. I laid back, taking it in, forgetting for a moment, forgetting everything. Until I heard something outside. The sound of reality, cannon fire, again.

I rolled over and out of bed, staggered to the window, opened it. It was coming from the northeast. The Quarter, maybe? From across the river, certainly. I hadn't meant to sleep, not that long. Hadn't meant for a few things to happen. But who does? My undergarments were strewn across the floor in a twirled mess. I pulled them on as I scanned the floor, feet freezing, dancing, as I searched for socks. Trousers. Half under the bed I found the letter. One word was written across the top. '*Coldspire.*' Below were an address and a time, '*39 Crowley Street, Noon,*' written in a concise hand I'd have guessed was a woman's. But what the hell did I know?

I knew I needed a drink.

* * * *

I slipped into the common room past a crowd of men dicing at hazard, rolling the bones against the wall, a simultaneous cheer and jeer inevitable as each pair skittered to a halt.

I took a seat at the bar. Waited. Schultz was wiping down tankards, filling them, handing them off then receiving them back like he did nothing else in life, an automaton sentenced to some sort of never-ending Sisyphean punishment.

The thin gild of merriment was still in full swing. Beneath it lay desperation, seething, rotten, pervasive. It was within the mad lilt of the jongleur's forced laughter, the ragged strum of the minstrel's bleeding fingers raking across lyre strings, the desperate slurp of ale and wine as men raced to death on their own terms, and it was within the deathly silence that exploded in a suffocating blast anytime anyone coughed or sneezed, all glances latching onto him, her, waiting, watching, wondering, until the music and singing cued back up louder and harder and more desperate than before.

The note said noon. So I had time. Figured I'd eat, drink. Might wish I had later. Sleeping and eating, vital. You don't realize it until you're half starving and your eyelids are lead, and you're stumbling around, slurring words, fantasizing hard about sleep like it's a woman, the woman.

Schultz nodded to me, slung a towel over his shoulder, finally taking a moment.

"Good morning, *Herr* Luther."

"Morning."

"I am appreciating your efforts the other night. With *Herr* Bert."

"Who?"

"Yah, the big fella." Schultz held a hand up high. "He is coming in on occasion. Always drunk. Always getting drunker. Walking a razor's edge. I am never knowing which way he is going to plummet, only that he will." He wiped the back of his neck with his towel. "Usually, he is not so bad. But when he is tipping the wrong way, you see? A man of most mercurial character. *Frau* Cora is being alright, too."

"Oh, yeah?" I tapped my fingers on the bar. "Good."

"The boys wanted to thank you, too." Schultz thumbed over his shoulder at a couple of grizzled toughs lounging in the corner, watch-dogging the room. "You saved them from having to deal with him."

"You're welcome." I pulled a penny out and set it on the bar. "So are the boys. Didn't really have much choice.

My armor?"

"Is not being yet ready." He finished filling a tankard and sent it my way. "I am sorry. On the house, along with breakfast."

I hefted the tankard. "Thanks." Took a sip.

Girard came roaring past and disappeared into the kitchen.

"Cease your running!" Schultz hollered after him, raising a hand to cuff him long after he'd gone. "That boy. My Lord. He is wishing to be everywhere at once and doesn't wish to be anywhere in between. Ever."

"Know who was in my room last night?" I glanced up.

Schultz stiffened, caught off guard, took to polishing again, calmly. "It is none of my business who you are entertaining in your room, *Herr* Luther."

"Damn straight." I looked him dead in the eye. "Though, might be a proprietor's business knowing who's in people's rooms when they ain't."

He said nothing, wiped, grunted.

"I'm asking," I said.

He shrugged. "One of the good women?"

"Ain't a guessing game."

"I had heard you and *Frau* Lorelai…"

"Before that."

He paused. "I am no thief." His eyes over my shoulder, a warning glance to one of *the boys*. "And I am not consorting with them, either."

"Not saying you are or do."

"If something is missing…?" One of the serving wenches set a bowl of porridge in front of me, smiled, dipped.

"Nothing missing." I nodded to the woman. "Just wondering if you knew." And if you did, would you tell me?

"It is a large building, with many rooms. I am not knowing all the goings-on in here, not by half, and I am not wishing to know. It makes life smoother. You are understanding?"

"Yeah. I know all about that. Smooth living."

"Yah sure."

"Heard cannon fire again this morning," I said.

"Yah," his eyes wary now, "a rare morning it is when we are not being graced by it." He hocked into the spittoon under the bar. "Plague has not killed enough. Men must take a hand. Always."

"Lord Bishop's not doing so well keeping the peace?"

"Keeping the peace would be presuming there was being peace somewhere to be kept." Schultz shook his head. "That is not being an apt description of Asylum." He slid closer down the bar. "There is being plenty of killing both sides, and the Lord Bishop and his men have had their fair share. You ask around."

"Who's winning?"

"I could not tell you." Schultz leaned over the bar. "What I can tell you is who is not. Me. And everyone else who is standing with two feet on level ground."

"Where's the line drawn?"

"The river, more or less." Schultz pointed off. "Fighting every day. Morning mostly, with the cannons. I am not knowing why. Maybe they have stonemasons chiseling cannon balls all night, and the fine lords cannot be waiting to use them come sunup. Anyways. Men go marching and stomping across the North Bridge one way and then retreating back the other. All broken and bloodied. The hospital is getting stretched thin, I am told."

"Whose side they on, the Teutonics?" The Teutonic Knighthood was part of the church but were beholden officially only to the Pope. "They backing the Lord Bishop?"

"I am not knowing. They are just keeping the bridge open, I am told." When I raised an eyebrow, he explained. "Things are tightening now and people are starving. Even more would be starving should that bridge be closed, and all because a bunch of noblemen cannot be making peace. And so we suffer." He glared at me. "Like ticks on a dog, sucking us dry."

"Yeah, that's us," I said. "So how'd the church come into power? Last time I came through Svaldrake, Volkendorf was the boss."

"A couple years past the English king '*liberated*' us. At least that is the word that was being used."

"Liberate. Conquer." I took a mouthful of porridge.

"Well, the good king was being on one of his cavalcades, tearing up all of France. And then he turned northeast to Svaldrake." Schultz throttled his bar towel. "He needed a good port, I suppose. Lucky for him we have one." Schultz pounded back a slug of ale. "Not so lucky for us. He was laying siege to us for near a month. The city was hurting much, but we held out. Volkendorf and his Isle men led the defense. Every man, woman, and child doing their part, fighting, dying. A proud time."

"Didn't take, though, did it?"

"Well, we were performing a sight better than the liberating king and his besiegers, I'll tell you that. Out there in their camp, starving. An army of scarecrows, ghouls, wraiths."

"So what happened?"

"Someone opened the West Gates." He spoke through gritted teeth. "And this *traitor* allowed the son of a bitch king and his murdering horde in."

"Who opened it?"

"Now that is being the question, yah?" His hands were shaking. "No one is knowing. Or, everyone is. You just ask them. Every lord, every merchant, every pig farmer is having his own belief, his own theory, and each one more fractured than the next. It is all boiling down to one thing…"

"You traded five lords for one king."

"Yah," he spat. "It was making little difference to me who rules. I never cared. Except, one of my sons was killed, and my wife, she…" He went quiet, frowning. "So this English king, I am not remembering his name."

"Edward."

"Yah, that is it." He spat again. "He took Asylum in

one night. A night of burning and plunder, and when dawn's light shone, there were more of the king's men inside the walls than out and more of them than us. What could one do?"

"Swear fealty to the new king?"

"Yah." He pounded his fist on the bar. "The Five Houses, though? Our *great* lord and his vassals? The one's pledged to *fight*? With tails tucked between legs, they all scurried onto Mummer's Isle. *Dogs.*"

"Stalemate?"

"Yah. To this day."

"They come to terms?"

"In a manner of speaking. The English King Edward did, anyways. He continued on home and left us one of his grafs—pardon, earls, in charge. I am not remembering his name, either. Well, he was not lasting over-long. Someone shoved a hot poker down his throat."

"Ouch."

"Yah, I cannot think of a worse *ouch.*"

"Next time he's passing through, ask King Edward how his father went out," I said. "Same hot poker. But took a more southerly approach. That's what they say, anyways."

Schultz whistled through his teeth.

"Did the king appoint another earl?"

"Yah. To a similar result. This time it was being a war-pick through his eye and out the back of his skull. Nothing left between."

"Volkendorf and the other families didn't take kindly to losing the city," I said.

"So it would be seeming. Now since then, they are all stuck on their island, fuming."

"Except Lord Raachwald. He still has his lands. Dunmire."

"Lord Raachwald is strong." Schultz nodded to himself. "Not like the others. He fought to take back what was his." Schultz swelled with pride. "It was he that took back the eastern half of Asylum, I am told. The others...the others are remaining on their Isle, plotting and sharpening daggers in the dark."

"Any different from the usual?"

"Yah, usually they are sharpening them to use on each other."

"Small lords." I shook my head, as though they were different than big lords, or medium lords, or pig farmers, or any other combination of two or more conscious men in possession of sticks or stones and within striking distance of one another.

"They are being big enough for around here," Schultz said. "Two earls they killed, but then King Edward tried a different tactic. He granted the city and the lands to the church. He made the local bishop a *Lord* Bishop. He must have been surmising that perhaps those killing the earls might balk at the killing of a bishop." Schultz set up some more tankards. "He does not know Asylum."

I nodded, my gaze and attention torn away as Lorelai strode past, looking like she hadn't had much sleep last night. She hadn't.

"Marry me?" I called out in her wake.

She continued on, ignoring me.

"She's already married, *Herr* Luther," warned Schultz. "She is wearing that ring on her finger that is saying so."

"Didn't notice the ring."

"Men are not noticing much when she is about."

"Yeah…" I stared after her as she sauntered over to another fellow seated across the room, a fellow with a great black beard. She ran her fingers through it, laughing at something he said. I hated him immediately. I stood up in her path when she came back around. "My lady." I bowed. "You are a vision."

She returned my bow with a curtsy, grasping her skirts in either hand and dipping, head down, playing the blushing maid. "But, oh, my sir knight, this is improper, for you see?" Her left hand was extended before her, her wedding ring a tiny loop of silver.

I took her hand, kissed it. "Divorce him."

"On what grounds?"

"Tell him he has a wicked wench for a wife."

"Why do you think he married me, Sir Lord?" She touched a finger to her lower lip.

"Can't fathom a single reason."

She smiled as though I were charming, grabbed two tankards of ale, turned to leave.

I leaned in, whispered, "Know who was in my room last night?" Over her shoulder, I noticed Blackbeard noticing me, his glare a dark storm on the horizon.

She drew back in mock surprise. "Hath thou forgotten so soon?"

I laid a hand on her shoulder. "I'm likely to forget a lot. But not that. I'm talking before."

All mirth drained from her. "No."

"If you did, would you tell me?"

"Who the fuck are you?" She pushed me back with the heel of her palm.

Ah, my famous charm. "I must be someone."

"Why?" she hissed beneath her breath. "Cause I didn't charge you?"

"I wondered at that."

"Maybe it was thanks for Bert. Not many men take an interest in the health and well-being of whores. Especially the old ones."

"I'm not many men."

"Oh, well aren't you just Sir-*Fucking*-Lancelot?" She tore out of my grasp, marched away.

I smiled, nodded. I was. Am. You catch less diseases if you take an interest in a whore's health, but truth be told, glaring at Blackbeard across the room, glaring daggers back, at that moment, I was more concerned with my own.

Chapter 13.

THE CLEVERLY NAMED North Bridge rose up ahead, an artifact of the Roman Empire, Asylum's most impressive architectural feat barring Saint Hagan's Cathedral. The bridge arched up in a great rainbow curve over the fetid Morgrave, soaring to its midpoint, maybe seventy or eighty feet above the water, its keystone the size of my erstwhile wagon. Crowley Street lay across its expanse, *toward* the cannon fire. Naturally.

Crossing it wasn't going to be easy, not like yesterday.

Across the chasm, on the far side, a contingent of soldiers in bright orange tabards stood at attention, long spears shouldered. I squinted. Something that looked like a wheel was their sigil. Their captain, by his bearing, began stalking amongst them, pointing, shouting, his words lost to the wind and distance. His men jumped to obey, hurriedly forming a shiltron. Shoulder to shoulder, shields up, they clogged the far side of the bridge like a porcupine-quilled dam, the thicket of spear shafts leveled, still, steel points glinting in the morning sun.

There was a commotion as I neared the bridge. A mob had congregated, jostling about, shoving forward, trying to set foot on it. Hollering, rabble-rousing, shaking fists, the usual. A contingent of city guards stood in a tenuous line trying to hold them back. And failing. The line fast deformed from straight to convex, a bubble set to burst, failure a mouse fart away.

I entered the milling fray, cutting through, knifing my way in, forcing past body after body, shouldering through screaming hags and bellowing churls, nearing the front as one of the city guards raised himself above the mob.

Jesus. It was Nils.

"Oy, you daft fucker! Move!" someone hollered. "We've business across yon river!"

"Turn back!" Nils stood with hands held out before him, raising and lowering them in some ill attempt to soothe and quell. "Listen!" His voice barely audible above the din. "There's fighting across the bridge! Heavy! And they're waiting for ya! Teeth bared! Right over yonder!" He pointed, but the shiltron at the far end lay hidden behind the bridge's arch. "Now back up!"

"There's *always* fighting on the east side!" someone called.

"We're starving!"

"They've grain in the east!" another called. "Food!"

"Aren't you listening?" Nils lost his balance, nearly fell, righted himself. What the hell was he standing on? "They're holding the east end of the bridge! A spear-line! Won't let no one cross!"

"We're dying!" a woman wailed along with the child she carried. "How we supposed to eat?"

"Move back!" Nils's face turned red. "Please! Whoa—!"

Nils disappeared as the mob lurched forward, expanding, breaking the line, and I was borne along with it. Men and women pushed and jostled, growling like wolves, savages, shoving others out of the way as they fought onto the bridge, surging up the arched path, folk screaming from the ground, knocked prone in the stampede, their neighbors trampling them in their zeal.

I surged along, afraid to stop. Hell, there was no stopping. I tripped over a screeching woman splayed across the ground, kicking her in the head, fell to a knee and then rose. She rose, too, latched onto me like a leech, nails digging into my neck. I hauled her up, along, staggering, heaving, dragging her kicking and wailing. Her face streamed blood, mouth working oddly, speaking gibberish the whole while. I surged to the left, taking elbows and shoulders from all sides and throwing them back, smashing, ramming, fighting my way toward the bridge's side.

"Come on!"

The leech lady elbowed me in the balls. Tripped me. I coughed, staggered to the edge, hucked her against the parapet, shielding her with my body as best I could. For some reason, some archaic reflex, vestigial honor brought erroneously to the fore. I caught sight of Nils lurching through the surge just ahead. He hoisted himself scrabbling onto the parapet alongside another guard, took a long breath, steadied himself.

The crowd jostled me and the leech lady, pushing us along the parapet until I was under Nils. "Hey!" I swatted his foot, trying to hold my position, and he jerked his billhook up, butt end aimed at me.

"Can you help me with this?" I barked as the leech lady tore loose screaming.

"My baby!" She strained back to enter the fray.

"Jesus Christ!" I almost let her. Instead, I lunged, grabbed hold, hauled her back. A body slammed into me, knocking me breathless. Another followed instantly. I could barely stand and hold her back.

"My baby!"

"Watch your head." Nils hooked the crescent blade of his billhook over the outside edge of the parapet then jumped down fearlessly into the roiling mass, upstream from me. Grunting, he pushed the billhook out at an angle from the wall, forming a protective triangle around me and the leech lady. He braced with his arms and legs, the surge sliding along the haft of the billhook. "Just… Rrrrg… Keep hold."

"Yeah." I held the woman up as best I could, her kicking and screaming and swooning and doing all sorts of useless shit.

Nils had his shoulder down, feet set, and bodies were sliding past but still crushing in. I glanced up at the other guard, Nil's partner, the Fool, still upright on the parapet.

"Give him a hand, you ass!" I hollered.

The Fool's eyes bugged out, incredulous. Then he nodded, clambered tepidly down and set his shoulder into the haft of the billhook, bracing it behind Nils. I could breathe again. Nils stood next to me, teeth gritting, head down as he took blow after blow after blow.

"You seen her kid?" Nils grunted.

"No," I managed.

"Damn."

"Be over in a minute," I hissed. "Find him then."

A war-horn roared behind, echo reverberating off the chasm walls and mill buildings, the streaming mass of human flesh frozen for an instant, every head swiveled back.

"Teutonics." Nils craned his neck. "Cavalry."

"Bloody hell." I could hear it, the clomp and chomp of iron-shod devil across cobblestone. Unmistakable. Unlovely. *Unlovely* because it means you're about to die unless you're the one making it. With shod hooves, a ton under them and a steel-encased madman mounting its back, wielding twenty feet of wood tipped in sharpened steel? Avatars of the old gods. The gods of war. Ares. Mars. Thor. What have you.

The crowd suddenly lessened, abating, passed, and I could stand upright. Breathe. Blood flowed freely down Nils's head, but he climbed back up the parapet, shielding his eyes from the sun glare, scanning the carnage. I held the fair maid, now unconscious, under the arms for a moment then passed her off to the Fool. "Here."

"Wha—?" He juggled her in his arms like she was on fire, him trying to get a grip, her slump sliding like a loose sack of potatoes.

"Jesus Christ," I grumbled, not that I'd done any better.

A contingent of knights on horseback clomped into view, towering like monsters, slowly, inexorably, six Teutonics. A black crucifix on white coat-of-plate armor covered a skin of mail over their chests, legs augmented by steel greaves, plate armor lobstering their joints. Great helms adorned each, all large men, the one at the fore a veritable giant. His huge red warhorse sneered and whinnied, sloughing white drool, its huge black eye blood simple with constrained rage, its shod hooves clip-clopping along like great iron clubs.

"*Krait!*" Nils leapt off the parapet.

"Wait!" I yelled but was at his side in an instant, helping him roll a corpse off a broken doll—no, not a doll. A young boy, limp, bloodied, broken. Nils bent to pick him up as the knights continued toward us.

I turned, stepped in front of them, hands raised. "Whoa!"

The lead knight raised a hand, pulling his mount to a stop. Which was good. Not wholly expected, but good. I took a step back as its hoof flicked out at me, its mad eyes burning haughty, hungry, its teeth chomping as it tried to bite my face. "Whoa, you devil, hold!" the rider commanded, his hollow metal voice echoing from some far off land. The horse obeyed, though it simmered, snorted, trembled, a steam kettle fit to burst.

Nils had the child in his arms and was scurrying aside. Other bodies were on the ground, those conscious trying to drag themselves. They had the right idea.

"Guard!" the knight boomed. "Is the child dead?"

"Uh—" Nils froze.

"No," I answered. "He's hurt. Breathing. Bad, though, I think."

"Bear him to the hospital." The knight tore on the reins, fighting as his mount went berserk, bucking, rearing. "Whoa! Easy, you fucker. Easy." He tore again on the reins, clobbering it across the skull, and the destrier quelled. "I'll see to him after."

Nils nodded. The leech lady was wailing at his shoulder, flailing for the boy. Nils plunked him into her harpy grasp then took her by the shoulders, guiding her off the bridge, half holding her up.

The knight raised the steel mask, revealing a face wracked by war, by carnage. The left half was a twisted mass of scissored scar, like strips of dried beef, teeth sharp, visible all the way to the back. No eyelid. He glared down at me, the visage of the devil himself. "Something amiss?"

I swallowed.

His eyes lit on Yolanda, slung across my back. Registered. His lance lowered until aimed at my throat. Twenty-feet long, and he held it out as firm and level as I might a spoon.

"Watch it." I swatted the lance tip away. "And yeah, something's amiss. There's a shiltron blocking the bridge's far end."

"Why do you think we have come?" He slavered in barely suppressed glee like he was a kid and I'd told him Christmas morning lay just across the span. "Whose is it?"

"Don't know. Men. About thirty. Tabarded in orange. Something like a wheel for a device." Karl would have known. He knew all that heraldry shit.

"Sir Carmichael. Yes, you would be just stupid enough," he grumbled to himself. "I thank you, sir knight." He half bowed in his saddle. "Now, if you would please step aside? We've God's own work to do." A wicked grin split up the unmarred side of his face, flickering tongues of madness lighting the corners of his eyes. Glee. Lunacy. Steed and rider of one mind. One body. One malnourished soul. He dropped his visor.

I stumbled back as another monster tried to bite me.

"On me!" As one, the six started forward, slowly, hooves clomping on stone and bodies of the fallen alike.

"Wait!" I shot my hands up. Idiot.

The lead knight reigned in again. "*What?*"

I pointed up the rise of the bridge. "There are about two hundred men, women, and children stuck on the far end."

"Then they had best move, eh?"

"Through a shiltron?"

"Touching. To worry not only for their safety but barricade yourself between to save them?" He sat back. "A man of God."

"Huh? Yeah—no." I shook my head emphatically.

"You'll never break that shiltron unless you get up to speed. And you won't if you're bogged down smashing through a mob."

"And what is it to you that we succeed?"

"Purely mercenary."

"Then fear not," he sneered. "We shall."

"The shiltron—"

"I am fair to certain they shall deign to move when the moment is upon them." His five compatriots seemed antsy, the thicket of lances wavering against the blue sky, mounts snorting and spitting.

Standing between a shiltron and cavalry charge with the sole escape a leap into a raging river? The king shit of bad choices.

One of the Teutonics banged his shield against his lance, and the other four followed suit. I covered my ears. It stopped as suddenly as it started. The lead knight, the giant, raised his lance to signal the charge but didn't. "You have the time it takes to recite ten repetitions of the Paternoster. Then we come. Best not be caught between."

A hard truth.

I turned and bolted up the rise of the bridge then over it. At the far end, a bulwark of scattered corpse lay splayed out on the ground, red holes gaping in chests, arms, legs. The soldiers in orange stood their ground, lined up two deep, spears leveled forward in an impassible thicket. The mob pressed forward, those at the forefront resisting, fighting, failing, screaming black bloody murder.

"Move back!" I hollered. "Back!" And no one cared, no one listened, no one reacted. I grabbed a man from behind, turned him, hurled him back up the bridge. "Go!" Then a woman. Both met me with sneers. "Run, you fuckers! Cavalry's coming! Teutonics—"

"Fuck off!" hollered the bastard.

Shit. I turned, hollered again. "Everyone off to the sides! Move."

The crowd was peppering the shiltron with rock and insult.

"Forward!" cried the captain.

The shiltron advanced, folk at the forefront screaming in horror as leveled spears jabbed, advanced, killed. Two paces, they moved, two red-screaming paces. "Hold!" A berm lay underfoot, the dead and dying.

The war-horn sounded as the Teutonic Knights crested the apex of the bridge, pinions fluttering, whapping, snapping at the end of their lances. Only their black outlines were visible against a crack of sunlight piercing the clouds. One of the most rousing damned views of impending doom I'd ever beheld.

The crowd as one turned.

The monstrous knight sounded his war-horn again.

"You're in it now, you shits." I clambered up onto the parapet, keenly aware of the precipice. Floes of black ice chunked past, some sixty feet below.

"Forward!" The huge knight started forward at a trot. In unison, his five followed in tight formation, wedged-shaped, knees touching the flanks of the mounts ahead.

"Get out of the way!" I hollered through two hands. "Back up the bridge!" Which in retrospect may not have seemed like the best idea. One way offered spears attached to killers and the other? Longer spears attached to killers seated on monstrous steeds. And those killers had picked up speed now, were moving down the arch, momentum gaining, lances lowering.

The crowd severed ragged down the middle, a crush of bodies surging outwards. Folk screeched like babies. A woman clambered onto the parapet and fell over, a man grabbing for her plummeting as well. More poured over as the mob reacted as a spooked beast.

I danced aside as folk plummeted like lemmings.

"Charge!"

The destriers clomped at full gallop, hooves sparking across stone, pounding, knights angled forward in their saddles, all one together, a massive crashing battering ram.

But the shiltron still held. The men pulled together,

their spears set into the ground by their back foot, aimed, quavering slightly, the captain barking, "Hold the line!" over the din of screams, "Hold!"

A shiltron of long spear could defeat a horse-charge, but only if they stared down the monstrosities, met death eye to eye, and held. A grim business and one wavered, just one. Understandable. Understandable but unforgivable. And like the great plague, the one's weakness swept contagious across the rest. Others wavered. Faltered.

Then as one, they broke.

Those at the edges dove aside. They lived. Those in the middle turned and ran, scattering, paper dolls set against a maelstrom gale. The charge disregarded them as men, as things of substance, of flesh, of skin, of bone. They were nothing before the impetus of tons of galloping flesh and steel, inertia carrying them forth.

Through their bloody wasteland wake, I tore, pounding across cobblestone by the horse-phalanx's concerted turn, slipping through the ruined shiltron, past the stunned, hurdling the broken, the bleeding, the dying, the dead.

...he would not recognize it. Adamantly, he refuses to disinter his son's remains. He states simply that the wounds were consistent with the two Volkendorf lads...
—*Journal of Sir Myron Chalstain*

Chapter 14.

CROWLEY STREET RAN north to south, parallel to the river. Number 39 was a three-story edifice of beaten rock and weathered stone. It sat there creaking, soft and lyrical, teeter totting minutely like some miser, ancient and warped and felled by some stroke or great palsy, forced now to slump on the brink until the end days, crumbling away to nothing.

No one had lived the house for some time, certainly no stone mason. A roof tile tumbled from somewhere on high, shattering on the street as I meandered past the front. The side alleys each continued on about forty feet, ending in a rather abrupt eighty-foot plummet.

Below, the water churned white, bottlenecked gushing by the foot of Mummer's Isle.

Above, on the far side, Coldspire sat upon the peak of the warped rock, another thousand feet up, black against the sky, a pinion fluttering from its highest tower, the obelisk rising from within its midst a dagger aimed at the Lord. I shielded my eyes against the glare; a light seemed to flicker from one of the windows. A trick of the eye?

I started at a noise—

A wagon trundled past in the street, piled high with corpses, drawn by a skeletal mule, plodding on, hooves of lead, head sagging nearly kissing to the ground. No one leading it. How long had it been plodding on, drawing along its morbid cargo, creeping by degree?

Jesus. This bloody city.

The side door was made of sturdy oak, still hale despite its withered facade. And it was locked. If I had an axe I could have had it down in a minute. Maybe two. But it'd be loud.

On tiptoe, I peeked through a shuttered window. Dark inside. Dreary. I didn't have an axe, but what I did have was Yolanda. Sword's a damn useful weapon. The blade's obvious, but there's more to her than that. The pommel's a fine close-quarter's dental extraction device, and the quillons, the pointy things that stick out from the hilt and keep your hands from getting chopped when someone tries to slice your head off, are nearly as deadly as the blade. You strike a knight wearing a helm with the blade, and his ears'll ring. Strike him with the quillons, giving it your best? He might not hear anything ever again.

Short-blading Yolanda, gripping her two-handed by the blade, I used her quillons as a hammer, quick tapping the shutter slats, short little hammer blows, knocking three out quick and neat. *Bang, bang, bang.* I paused and waited, heard nothing, reached inside, unlatching them. I sheathed Yolanda, put the butcher's blade delicately between my teeth and climbed through the window head first, got stuck halfway and had to buck and kick like a spastic horse to finally fall in.

Hopefully, no one was watching.

Mildew, the hearth room reeked of it. A web of cracks marred the plastered wall. Everything was wet. A hole in the ceiling let in a spiral of light. I closed the shutters, latched them, tried to fit the old slats in as best I could, got in two, gave up on the third. I kept the butcher's blade in hand throughout.

The stairwell to the second floor sagged like the back of an old miner. The banister moved freely. Water dripping from on high, never-ending. The house seemed to rock with the wind, wood supports creaking, promising collapse at some future date. *Precarious*, a word that came to mind.

Since I wasn't brave enough to add any sort of load to the upper floors, most especially my own, I searched the ground floor.

It occurred to me, and not for the first time that there was a fair chance someone had left me that note to draw me into an ambush. Lord Raachwald? He had his reasons for hating me. Or the Lady Narcissa? Had she led me by the nose to the Stone Ruin Ten and then on to here? Rotten, abandoned, secluded, a fine place for disappearing someone.

And then what about her murderous monk? The story I'd discounted from the outset? The giant Teutonic of the North Bridge massacre was as close to her killer-monk's description as any man I'd ever met, a large man, the visage of the devil, and a Teutonic monk-knight to boot. The killing edge of a knight coupled with the austere mental discipline of a monk? A man I wanted no part of. But could even he have single-handedly killed seven armed men? Was such a thing even possible? I thought not, but if anyone were capable…

The kitchen offered a lovely view of the cliff face of Mummer's Isle, but not through a window. Through a torrential split where the ceiling met the wall. The whole of the cliff underneath the house must've eroded away. The floor and lower parts of the walls opened downward, hinged like the lower jaw of some huge skull. To step into the kitchen was to hazard a grade whose severity increased with each step until you were staring straight down into the river.

I chose not to set foot within.

I checked the cellar door instead. My fingertips had just lit on the doorknob when I heard the front door rattle. Sharp. Quick. I turned. Wasn't the wind. Back in the hearth room, a shadow slid along beneath the crack of the front door, feet, two pairs. A shadow skirting down the alley told of a third.

I eased open the cellar door and peered down a set of stairs spiraling away into darkness. I could stand here and fight, surprise them. Maybe. Or I could take the stairs and possibly trap myself. Not the king-shit of bad choices from the bridge, but—

Muted voices chattered outside the window I'd broken in through.

Slipping into darkness, I noticed a lock on the

door's cellar side, which was odd. The door was stout. Reinforced. Iron bars covered its inside. The passageway seemed to have been hewn through the rock. Straight through. Straight down. Damp cool kissed me softly. I eased the door shut, wincing at each minuscule squeak, latched it, slid the burglar bar into place.

It was near pitch black on the stone steps, nothing but a blade of sunlight stabbing through from beneath the door. It didn't illuminate far. Right hand pressed against the wall, step by step, I descended into total darkness, forcing myself against instinct to take my time. Breathe slow. A broken ankle here would not be good. Yolanda, sheathed and in hand, I used as a blind man a cane, tapping down and forth, searching for the next step before setting foot on it.

The hair on my neck rose as a crash reverberated from upstairs. They were inside the house. I kept moving slowly, surely, down, down, down. Fighting panic. They were hammering on the cellar door when I reached bottom. But I could see, suddenly, barely. The stairs ended in a passageway, sunlight at its end but a pinprick from here. I could hear rushing water. The floor was wet. I bolted down the passageway, splashing, another crash reverberating from behind, above. They'd broken the cellar door. I ran now, unabashed toward the light and skidded to a halt at the end, barred by an iron gate.

"Locked." I grabbed the bars, shook them. They didn't magically open. "Shit."

I turned toward the echoes of footsteps. Coming. The three men, three at least, pounded down the stairs a hell of a lot faster than I had. Back to the bars. They were thicker than my wrist and set a few inches apart. I shook them again, pushed them, pulled them. "God-damn." Not a creak. The gate was secured to the outside of the passage somehow, out of reach. And the lock? Jesus. Big as my fist.

The river roared outside.

"Whoa!" I started at a shadow materializing beyond the bars, the silhouette of the Virgin Mary suddenly before me, studying me, her face hidden behind a mask of shadow, surrounded by a nimbus of light.

"*Sir Luther...?*" whispered the Virgin Mary.

I could barely hear her above the river-song.

I gripped the bars, thick, strong, permanent. "Yeah."

Behind, the cluff of heavy boots, the clatter of weapons, the dirge of inevitability.

She craned her neck, wide brown eyes straining past me, crosshatched behind a veil of black lace. "Acquaintances?"

"I can assure you they are not."

"Turn around."

"I'd rather you open this—"

"I cannot."

"Well," I deflated, turning toward fate, "that is extremely disheartening." *Shing.* Yolanda sang free. There was nowhere to hide here. No time to waste. "It's been a pleasure, my lady." I started back towards the staircase. That was the move. Darker there. Waylay the three within it. Have what light there was to my back. The glare. Blind them. Somewhat. And if I had to retreat? I'd have space, some, before I didn't. And if I could somehow slip by them? Gain the stairs, the high ground? Me, the eternal optimist. Hell, maybe they'd all be blind cripples, too.

"Wait," the Virgin Mary hissed.

I froze, listening to the boot steps, each one a step closer, eating my ground, shortening my span. *Crucible*, a word that came to mind.

"Take ten paces back."

I'd counted out the ten before she'd finished.

"To your left. Quickly now. A hidden door. There. Yes. Now, push."

"Can't see it." I dropped my shoulder into the wall, pushed, nothing moved. Futile. I turned toward the Virgin Mary, but she was gone. And me? Trapped. The good Lady Narcissa. Compliments of. "Bloody hell."

The boots were pounding, almost to the bottom of the steps.

The wall beneath my palm jumped, a short jump.

Rock scraped on rock. "Rrrg… Help me," came the Virgin Mary's muffled voice, "push."

I dropped my shoulder into the wall, and it scraped open a fraction, then more and more, my feet slipping in the wet as I struggled for purchase. "Rrrrg…" I got my head through. Then shoulders. "Come on." Waist. Finally my legs. I threw my shoulder into it from the other side, forcing it shut. It went smoother that way. Rock scraped as the stomping of boots grew near, and then the door was shut.

I dared not breathe.

The Virgin Mary touched my shoulder, twitched her head, bade me move. Iron bar in hand, she set one end into a divot cut into the floor. Teeth gritting in the half-light, hissing, she laid the other end against the door, into another divot, ever so delicately, bracing it shut.

I finally dared a breath.

The men were arguing now. Steel rang on steel as someone smashed the bars with something heavy. "Bloody bastard."

They started arguing. I couldn't make out what they were saying. Who they were.

The Virgin Mary beckoned me to follow. I did so without hesitation. The men were still chopping at the bars, grunting, feuding, failing. We hurried down a small tunnel out to the river.

"Come." The Virgin Mary pulled back the hood of her cloak, along with her veil. Mourning attire. She was young, younger than me, certainly, perhaps twenty. Her piercing brown eyes were huge in her face. Sunken, sallow, her cheekbones were prominent. She hadn't eaten in some time. A near-walking corpse, but she moved yet with an elfin grace, a birdlike vitality. "Please. We'd best go."

I gripped Yolanda's hilt. "Can they get through?"

Steel against iron chimed out from behind.

"No." Her voice was certain.

"The iron's thick, but the lock?"

"It's not locked."

"You're *not* making me feel any better."

"Listen," she hissed, "it's not locked because there is no lock. It's not a door. It's forged to look like a fortified gate. The only way through it is the passage we took. The bar's set, and it's hidden."

"Alright..." But I kept hold of Yolanda.

"Shhh." She raised a finger to her lips but in her hand's place was a wrought iron hook. The stink of decay. Putrefaction. Rust. She pointed down a side tunnel, bored straight into the wall. "This way."

…pernicious rumors of the boy's parentage are a knot impossible to grasp let alone unravel…
—Journal of Sir Myron Chalstain

Chapter 15.

GASPING. HUFFING. "Jesus… How many more… Are there?" I collapsed against the wall, slid scraping down to cold stone. The steps were infinite. To my left, blessed wall. To my right? An abyss rimmed by stairs spiraling away down to nothing.

The Virgin Mary paused above me, lantern in hand swaying, casting devil shades careening to and fro. "We're nearly there."

"What's your name?" I propped my head against my palm.

"Mary."

I nodded, sniffed, stifling a grim smirk.

"What is it?" Her eyes narrowed.

"Nothing," I waved a hand, "just, back in the tunnel. At the gate. Thought I was seeing things. You with your hood all lit up from behind, the reflection of sunlight off the water, a radiant halo. For a moment, I thought you were the Virgin Mary come to…" I closed my eyes, felt my heart slow. "Forget it."

"Who were those men?"

I cracked an eye. "Was hoping you might know. Who else knows about this passage?"

"As far as I know? Only Lady Narcissa. It was she who revealed it to me."

Shit. They came from my end then. Trailed me from the inn, most likely. But, other than Lady Narcissa and Lord Raachwald, who knew I was even here?

"Are you just going to sit there?" she asked.

I cracked an eye. "That a viable option?"

Mary simply crossed her arms, frowning down at me, a look I was accustomed to, not from her, per say, but from women in general. Her attire had seen better days, the ends of her sleeves frayed, the edges of her black gown soiled and in tatters. Her light brown hair edged out in uneven swathes. Shorn haphazardly. Fashion? No. Some sort of shaming punishment, more likely. For what? By whom? She cleared her throat. "I was given to understand that you were under task to apprehend a murderer, were you not?"

"Hmmm. Maybe he'll just stroll by," I suggested, walking my fingers up the stairs. "Confess. Promise I'll apprehend him forthwith." I placed a hand to my heart. "Knight's honor."

"Have you not a brother in straits?"

"Thanks to your lady friend, I do."

Mary visibly steamed at that. "Get up, you lout."

"You certainly are a lady, aren't you?" I pointedly deigned not to move.

She stiffened, eyes aglow.

"Tone of your voice." I counted on my fingers. "Set of your jaw. Furrow to your brow. The hack-job haircut and pauper's rags can't mask it. Expect the world to jump on command. And stay jumped til you give leave."

"Curious." She straightened. "That same quality in a man is deemed admirable, is it not? An air of command, I should think it's referred to." The muscles at the corner of her jaw twitched. "And yes, I am a lady, if you must know."

"So what's your stake in all this?" I changed tacks, gauging her reaction.

"I was…" Lady Mary worried her hooked hand into the hewn rock wall, her face twisting into a scowl as she scratched along, bits of stone falling. *Terrifying*, a word that came to mind. "I am Lady Narcissa's lady-in-waiting."

"A devoted maid, then?" I scraped a flake of nitre off the wall just to fit in. "She treat you well?"

"What business is it of yours?"

"She did not seem a peach, is all."

"Well, perhaps it's just you."

"You think?"

She fingered the tip of her hook then started scratching again. *Scritch… Scritch…* "I was…am deeply devoted to her. And I shall continue to be so for as long as I draw breath."

"Might not be too long," I muttered at my boots. The stench of corruption wafted toward me morbid-fresh with every move of that hooked stump. "Narcissa's the last of her line, yeah?" I added.

"*Lady* Narcissa," she corrected. "And yes, if you must know."

"Tell me about her. All this shit you're wading through on her behalf. Deep and dark. Suppose she must be some sort of saint?"

"No. She was no saint, is no saint. But there is duty, and there is honor, and there is loyalty, even amongst those of us of the *lesser* sex."

"I never said—" It hit me then. "You were there that night, weren't you?" I snapped my fingers. "Lady Narcissa said *you* raised the hue and cry. Jesus Christ. The handmaid." I paused, salivating. How had I missed that? "You saw it happen then? The killer. The monk. *Everything.*"

"No," she recoiled as though struck. "I…I don't know what in heaven's breadth it was, but…"

"Lady Narcissa lied then?"

"I…" Lady Mary started drifting like a ghost up the stairs. "Perhaps you were mistaken."

I clambered to my feet and gave chase, practically hearing the gears turning in her head as I double-stepped after. "No, she *was* lying. And I—"

"Enough." She halted, turned, brandishing the lantern, light blaring, in my eyes.

"Enough what?" I blocked the blare. "I need to know the truth. Of what happened. Of why she lied. My brother and I are chained to truth like an anchor, and your *good lady* tossed it overboard. Links are playing out fast. And it's a long cold journey down."

"You were drunk, injured. No doubt you misheard."

"I am *no* servant," I growled, resisting the urge to seize her by the throat and hurl her into the abyss. "Just cause you're using your big girl voice doesn't mean I'm going to stop asking questions." Had Lady Narcissa lied? Or told the truth? Or some grade in between? Gauging someone's motivation? Often the most onerous task in all of investigating. Everyone lies, the guilty, the innocent. The victim. And sometimes the guilty spew truth. It's a blank puzzle of scattered pieces, some missing, never to be found, but still, you must form it into something cohesive if not whole. "For whom do you wear the mourning clothes?"

Lady Mary raised her chin. She didn't like me. That spoke well of her.

"Who died?" I pressed.

"Who *didn't?*"

"Jesus, just tell me the truth. Is it so hard?"

"And if you have it, shall you then find this killer?"

"Maybe," I admitted.

"Then someone shall soon wear this same garb on your behalf."

"Unlikely, but thanks. Now, what did you see?"

"I saw a *glimpse,* only. But I'm not certain what."

"What the hell are you saying?"

"I'm saying that whatever killed Lucien, *my husband.*" She paused, composing herself. "Whatever killed him and the others was…" She retreated up. "It was dark, so very, very dark."

"How many were there?" I hounded along at her heels.

"One." She continued to a landing. A door lay beyond.

"Only one?" I grimaced. It couldn't be. "You're absolutely certain?"

"Yes." Her voice was adamant. "Of that alone, I am."

Lady Narcissa and Lord Raachwald both had said that Lady Mary had been there, and talking to her, I believed her. A gut instinct, a feeling. And she believed it was only one. Or she was one hell of a liar.

A ring of keys jangled as Lady Mary unlocked the door. Jagged teeth rasping past rusted tumblers followed by a loud snap as the mechanism turned. A cold wind squealed as she forced open the door and disappeared through.

I followed.

Coldspire's great hall had been laid to waste. Across it, the front door had been burst in, shattered asunder. A drift of snow had snaked in and lay glistening. Broken weapons scattered about on the floor. Shards of glimmering steel spotted to rust. In the wall set high above, a long face described in polygonal jags of stained glass stared down, the portrait of an angelic man dressed in black scale mail, a black raven, wings spread, soared across his chest. Longsword held overhead, he stood poised to strike.

"Lord Volkendorf?" I nodded up.

"Yes." Lady Mary looked paler up here, sicker, filtered through the scintillating lights from above. "The portrait affords him more justice than ever he afforded anyone."

"Quite the dashing figure."

"Yes, his better days, long past." Lady Mary dismissed him, looking away, pointing across the great hall. "This...this is where they fought." Four doors led into the great hall. A weapons rack lay broken against one wall. "And they loved to fight. Yes. They all *loved* to fight." She trembled. "You *all* love to fight."

We don't all love to fight. We all love to *win*, but I said nothing, for she finally was. The numbing cold had already seeped into my feet, up my legs, promising to work its way north. I stomped in place on the hard stone.

"We believed Coldspire under siege," Lady Mary said as I scanned the room. A series of shields ringed three of the four walls, set high, an evolution of heraldic devices, all differing versions, incrementally changing from one to the next, but all of a raven on a solid field. The field was blue at the beginning, purple towards the end. *Purple*, a color usually reserved for kings. Lord Volkendorf had aspirations. Lady Mary continued throughout, "Something was hammering at the front gate. It awakened us from a dead sleep. A battering ram, my husband had said, donning his mail." She shivered from the cold or the memory. I knew not which. "And then something rending the portcullis open. The iron bars screeched like an eagle." She shuddered. "Awful. We could hear it throughout the keep. Above the gale. And then the hammering again, the hammering as it—as *he* broke through the gate."

Still listening, I began to walk the room, starting at the center and spiraling outward. Shattered swords. Broken rings of riveted mail scattered about. They scraped underfoot, rustling like fallen leaves. Interspersed amongst it all lay little bits of rock. Odd… I knelt, picked up a handful of pieces. Some were small jagged pebbles, others as large as chess pieces. I studied one of the larger ones. "Hmm…" Just a rock.

Peering around, I scoured the floor for the source. The flagstones were smooth and worn with age and showed no gashes. And the walls? Nothing. The ceiling, then. Craning my neck, I looked up, squinting, eyes adjusting to the light. The ceiling vaulted high, supported far above by massive timber posts and lintels. Nothing again. At least I was consistent.

I tucked a few rocks into my coin purse and moved on.

Chairs lay everywhere. Scattered. Three great tables were overturned, one smashed in half. It would have taken some doing. Remnants of iron-banded oak hung creaking from the wrecked skeleton of a front door. Slivers of wood as long as my arm littered the ground, inside and out.

I stepped through the doorway, outside, ducking into the mounting wind. The courtyard was covered in waist-deep snow. The black obelisk I'd seen from afar rose from amidst the drifts, a spear jabbing the eye of the sky. Its sides were smooth, unjointed. It looked ancient.

Wending past the foot of the obelisk, I followed a meandering path to the front gate. A formidable barrier, once upon a time. Just like the keep's front door, it'd been smashed in, torn out, ripped and twisted.

The portcullis, too, had met a similar fate. Stout defenses, the front door, the front gate, the portcullis, all broken asunder. A battering ram? No.

"Anyone of the lords have cannon?" I drew my cloak about me, a vain attempt at warding off the cold. I scanned the bare parts of the ground. Nothing of note beyond the wreckage. "Lord Raachwald?"

Lady Mary shook her head. "Instruments of the devil he calls them."

"Well, he would know." I trudged back in the front door, out of the wind, blowing into my cupped hands. "Any of the others?"

"The Brulerin boy possesses four, at least," Lady Mary said. "You hear him every morning, no doubt. Lord Hochmund and the Taschgarts possess them as well. One apiece, last I had heard."

"Hochmund's always liked playing with new toys."

"You're acquainted with him?" She fingered the tip of her hook. In suspicion? Confirmation? Disgust, certainly. She didn't like him; that was plain. Another point in her favor.

"Don't know." I ran my palm along the jamb of the front door, inspecting each individual stone. "You'd have to ask him." Some were loose. Most, in fact. The massive jolt that had shattered the door had dislodged them. Could one man have done that? No. And in a month could one man have broken that outside gate? The iron portcullis? Twisted it back like that? "Did you hear cannon that night?"

"No."

"Lightning? Thunder?"

"It was a winter storm. Snow. Gale winds."

"The smashes you heard, though?" I pressed.

"I have heard cannon. This sounded like a...a battering ram."

I sighed. I'd seen no evidence of cannon, anyways. No giant stone balls lying around, at any rate. No scorch marks. No powder burns. No lingering gunpowder stench. It would have fit better. But it didn't. So, a battering ram? Used by one man? No. Ridiculous. Perhaps a squad of men with a battering ram breached the gates and then…sent one inside to combat seven veteran warriors? I've served under commanders who no doubt would have considered that strategy the apex of military brilliance, but it was unlikely. Bloody hell. "Who do *you* think did it?"

She started, surprised probably that I'd asked her opinion, but she recovered instantly. "Initially? I thought it an army at the gates. Now?" She nodded to herself. "Witchcraft. Sorcery. Black magic. It must have been. To witness it, the killer was cursed with—with a demon's strength." Her eyes lit up. "Like something born of the pit."

Again she'd referred to the killer as '*it*.' "And what did he look like?"

"It was dark," she hesitated, "and I heard his footsteps, great clanking footsteps, but nothing more. I did not see it, did not want to see it.

"One of the men yelled at its approach," her eyes wide, "Colrick, maybe, I cannot be certain. He swore by Odin it wore the cowl of a monk. As it crossed the courtyard, they shot it through the murder holes. Crossbows. Close. They did nothing." She shook her head as though denying her own truth. "And when it entered? When it broke through? It wore no cowl. It was…it was its head. Or," she paused, swallowed, recovered, "or its helm, yes, a wide helm, a great helm, it had to be. But Colrick had said cowl first. And that stuck in my mind. Monks… Later."

"Could you see anything of his features?"

Lady Mary shook her head.

"Of course not." I frowned. "What of his armor?"

"It…it must have been coat-of-plate. That is still the most formidable, yes?"

"Yeah." There'd been advances as of late, steel plates riveted together to form one chest plate, but I was hesitant to say anything, stanching the flow of memory, information, or warping it.

"Then that is what he wore."

"A knight then?"

"I…"

"Armor as formidable as you describe could only be afforded by a knight. A wealthy knight."

"There are no wealthy knights in Asylum."

"He wore no tabard?"

She gave a look as though I were daft.

"Doesn't hurt to ask."

She wasn't sold that it was a knight, that was plain. Hell, as far as I could tell, she wasn't even sold it was a man. And she had more to say, but she didn't want to seem mad. I'd seen it before, could see it in her eyes. She didn't trust me, and I didn't blame her for that. Not for any of it.

"And then the battle…" I prompted.

"Yes. The battle." Her voice lowered. "The knight broke through. A monstrosity. He had to duck to enter."

The top of the door was at least seven and a half feet high. Shades of the Teutonic giant from the bridge flitted through my mind. Then Haefgrim. Two men. Two giants. But neither was that tall.

"And my husband, Lucien. Lucien of Troyes. Have you heard of him?"

"Of course," I lied, throwing a bone to a starving dog, "a man with a name."

Lady Mary smiled faintly at that, finding ephemeral warmth in a cold memory. "He was Volkendorf's castellan and sword master. Did you know? That was why Lord Raachwald sent his boy here, as a ward, to learn sword-craft from my husband."

Lord Raachwald had claimed different, but I kept my mouth shut, only nodding.

"It," she caught herself, "*he* hammered at the door, while Lucien and his men waited within, prepared. When the door shattered, Lucien," Lady Mary took a moment, drawing herself up, "he stepped forth into the breach and challenged the knight to single combat. Without a word, it strode forth. Without a weapon. He was a giant, yes, but, unarmed?" She shook her head slowly. "I recall thinking it would be over so quickly."

"What of the others?"

"They surrounded him."

I glanced around the hall, getting a feel for the combat. Great hall was a misnomer. Coldspire itself commanded an imposing view, had a single, highly defensible approach, but its footprint was limited, and thus everything within it was, too. Truncated. Tight. Built up instead of out. The melee had been a very intimate affair, indeed.

"Lucien greeted him with steel." She was reliving the moment now, acting it out in her mind. "Struck him a blow to the neck that would have felled any man, any, armor or no. I recall relaxing the moment his blade bit, knowing it was over. The men, too, felt it. They exploded, roaring like wild beasts."

"And then?"

"The blow shattered Lucien's blade. Castle-forged steel. Lucien might have struck him with a...a dandelion." She clutched at her throat, tense, rigid, incredulous. A month later and she was still. "Shattered, it just..."

"Did the blow stagger him?"

"It did nothing." She shook her head. "I could feel the shock they all felt. And then I looked, truly looked, and I saw..." Lady Mary swallowed, continued, "Lucien was a tall man, taller than you. He was but a child next to it. A child. And the knight did not stop. As one, the men attacked, and the knight did not die. He was struck so many times, but his armor was strong, impenetrable. At each blow, I thought '*this time*,' as orange sparks cascaded through the night. So beautiful. The fall of molten stars. Yes. But one after the other they fell. All of them. Lucien struck first. He fell last.

"Remember that, would you?" Lady Mary smiled wistfully. Lost. Forlorn. "He died trying to protect *that*, that sot." She frowned up at the stained-glass lord. "Over his broken form, Lucien stood. Even I knew Volkendorf was lost. Good lord, his head," her eyes clamped shut, "but yet he drew breath, slow, labored, rasping." Her voice reached a fever pitch. "There was nothing left, but he stood there despite, my husband, my life, my love, and it simply snatched him up like I might a child and broke him like…"

"I'm sorry," I offered lamely.

"And I did nothing." One length of unshorn hair fluttered across her mouth. She brushed it aside. "I wanted to run, to run for the children, to save them from this…this horror, this thing, but my strength it…" She bowed her head "My legs were gone. Simply gone. And so I knelt, and I closed my eyes, and I prayed."

"And the Lady Narcissa?"

"She?" Her eyes suddenly clear. "She was by my side, praying as well. Throughout."

* * * *

"Jesus." I covered my nose and mouth with my handkerchief. The stench was thick, cloying, horrid. Encased in a stone tomb, his effigy half carved into the lid, Lord Volkendorf lay before me in all his sordid glory. "This was once a man." I pulled back the rest of the burial shroud, white linen soiled brown and black. A mail shirt graced the shoulders of his carcass, a great rent torn open from neck to navel. *What* could do that? Tear steel like cloth? I could almost hear the riveted links popping, one by one in song, arcing through the air like glistening fish struggling upstream as they poured upon the stone, one after the other. An axe or a war pick. Wielded by a strong man. The strongest man.

Lady Mary turned away.

"The lantern, please?" I breathed through my mouth.

She handed it to me.

I passed it over the carcass, peering in, studying, committing the remains to memory, committing the horror. One of Lord Volkendorf's legs was missing. And only *most* of his skull. A helm had been propped in its place. His skull… Jesus, if I crushed a hen's egg in my fist, yolk squeezing through clenched fingers, it would give some inkling to the wounds he'd sustained. Shards of bone lay within the helm, cast like reading stones. I could make out an eye socket, a cheekbone, teeth, but there wasn't enough bone to form a complete skull. Not by half. The bones of his neck simply stopped abruptly above his collar bones, both of which were broken, as were most of his ribs beneath. "What happened to his leg?"

Her gaze wilted away. "Grave robbers?"

"*Grave robbers?*" I reached in and drew a silver pendant from Lord Volkendorf's sunken chest. "What's the market for legs these days?"

Lady Mary studied her shoes.

"Better than silver, I guess." Gold glittered from the fingers of his right hand. "Gold too." I lifted the pendant, a bauble in the shape of a raven, its wings spread as it twirled on the end of a fine chain. "Here." I held it out.

Lady Mary recoiled from it like a vampire from a crucifix.

"He was a shit, yeah?" I jiggled it.

She shook her head, slow, adamant.

"Suit yourself." I shrugged, reached in to put it back, but palmed it instead. And the gold rings? Only one way to protect against grave robbers, so I snatched them, too. I ran a hand through my hair. Jesus. His corpse? His injuries? Catastrophic. A cannonball could have done it, but hadn't. A ballista? Some great siege weapon? Ares? Thor? "Were you drinking that night?"

"No. I...I drank later. After. I-I've hardly stopped since."

"I know the feeling," I said. "What are you drinking tonight?"

She froze, cheeks coloring slightly, then gave in and reached into her cloak. She withdrew a stoppered leather flask, took a pull, offered it.

I tipped it back, closing my eyes, body sighing. "Thanks." I handed it back.

"I wasn't lying," Lady Mary said, "and I wasn't drunk. I know how it sounds. I do, but, you must believe me."

"I believe you, but I need more." I crossed my arms. "What happened to his leg?"

"How should I know? And what does it matter?"

"You claimed the killer was unarmed."

"He was," she said. "Lord Raachwald and his men…"

"Desecrated the body?" I demanded. "He told me parts were missing. Where are they? Where's your husband's for that matter?"

"Lord Raachwald brought him to the plague pits. All of them. One by one, he just cast them in, and," her fist clutching at the edge of her cloak, "forced me to watch."

"Lady Mary," I took her by the shoulders and looked into her eyes, "you have something to say. Know this, please, whatever it is, I *will* believe you. Trust me in that if nothing else."

"Trust you…?" she laughed as though it were some garish joke. "It, the knight, tore them limb from limb with its bare hands." She snatched a quick sip. "Is that what you wanted to know?"

Impossible. But she *wasn't* lying. She believed it. I could see it. Feel it. So what? Had she been drunk? Addled? Fevered? Something. Or was it true? The knight, or whatever the hell it was, had torn Lord Volkendorf limb from limb. He and his six men.

"It's true," she insisted.

I raised an open hand. "I believe you." But it meant little what I believed. I'd seen things drunk I didn't believe come sobriety. And I'd seen things sober I'd never have believed drunk. For the next part, I'd have preferred to be drunk. "Give me another sip of that, would you? Then take me to the others."

Lady Mary picked her way through the necropolis, her iron hook tip *tinking* on stone. I followed close, past dark tunnels yawning, past sarcophagi, long and cold and grey. Winds moaned. Faces worn smooth by age, pitted by decay, stared at us from the past. Lord Volkendorf's father, his grandfather, others. We strode back through time.

"How'd you lose your hand?" I asked.

"I did not *lose* it. It was taken from me."

"By who?"

"Lord Raachwald."

"Trial by fire?"

"No." She bashed her hook hand against the wall. "He simply cut it off. Then he…" She didn't expound. I didn't ask her to. "He said he wanted the truth."

"And did you give it to him?"

"What reason would I have had to withhold it?" Lady Mary just stared as we came to the end of the tunnel, a final sarcophagus sitting on a dais of stone. "But it didn't matter." No effigy graced this tomb. No faces. No names. No dates. It was smooth, blank, unmarred. "Here. They were laid to rest together. Lady Narcissa did it herself."

"She loved them?" I asked carefully.

"More than anything."

"And what of her husband? Did she love *him*?"

"No."

Taking a measured breath, I made the sign of the cross, more because Stephan was my brother and would have frowned had I not. Were he here. I set the iron-crow between lid and lip and raised the mallet. A few strokes and presses and the lid slid back, revealing its goods, though goods was a poor choice of word.

Delicately, I drew back the burial shrouds. Two desiccated bodies lay beneath, twisted and small. They'd been dressed in mail shirts, tabarded lovingly in dark silk, a silver raven in flight across their chests. Scabbarded short swords lay upon them as well. Little knights. Unlike their father's body, these two were complete, which made it all the more terrible. Lush, golden hair spilled out from decomposing heads, beautiful hair attached to dried withered flesh. A length of linen cloth had been wrapped like scarves around each of their necks.

I could see my own children's faces over theirs. I closed my eyes, rubbed them, waited for it to pass. It didn't.

"That's Gilbert." Lady Mary rubbed her throat.

"The big one's Michael."

I gently slid a finger under the linen swathe round Gilbert's neck.

"Must you?"

"Forgive me," I said to Lady Mary as much as to Gilbert as I drew the linen down. I did the same for his brother.

Both their throats had been slit to the bone. A razor? A dagger? It mattered little. Blade marks notched the front of their neck bones, a single deep cut each, precise, determined, confident. Their wounds had been stitched back together with cord, but the flesh had shrunk, tightened, puckering and pulling, leaving a child's rendering of a ragged monster mouth open across their throats. Up and down and up. I covered their necks again with the swathes because looking at them made me sick in a way that Lord Volkendorf, with all his horrific wounds and deformations, never would. Lord Volkendorf would never visit me in the dark. These two boys, though, there would be nights I'd need drink their faces away. No doubt about that. Strange, the things we're certain of, the things we've no doubt about, the few things, always such *horrible* things.

"Eh?" I leaned close over Gilbert, squinting, studying his face in the light. "What the...?" At the inside of his left eye, there was a puncture wound, small, round. The desiccation of skin had pulled it away, revealing it. There was a similar wound to his brother's right eye.

"What is it?" Lady Mary asked.

"I don't know." I swallowed, blinking away the faces of my own boys, both of a similar age. I'd not seen them in over a year, long ago, far away. "They were murdered *after* the men?"

"Yes."

"And Raachwald's boy, Cain? Him, too?"

"My three little scoundrels." Her voice cracked. "That...that's what I called them. They wanted to confront the intruder, join the men, the battle." She nearly choked. "Dear Lord, I had to convince them I needed someone to protect me."

"I'm sorry."

"Don't look at me like that." She recoiled from the coffin. "Damn me. I locked them in their room. Abandoned them, returned to the great hall, the battle. I wanted to...I had thought the intruder had— Oh, lord. I heard it. I heard it walking away. I swear it."

"And after?" I asked quietly.

"I..." She nearly melted across the floor. "I raised the hue and cry." Her voice was a whisper. "I went to Lord Raachwald," she stared at her hook hand, "for help, God save me. I went to Old-Oath."

"And Lady Narcissa through all this?"

"She...she was ill. She was indisposed."

$$* * * *$$

The sun was beginning its descent as I stared out the window of the boys' room, facing north across the city to the sea. Taking a firm handhold on the sill, I peered out, looking straight down a thousand feet, perhaps more, into the raging confluence of the river as it rejoined itself from its parting around the Isle. Vertigo. A man could have a short but very pointed conversation with himself on that whistling trip.

The bedroom ceiling was high with a cross-beam chandelier hanging down. The door's lock had been hacked clean of the door by an axe. The door was otherwise intact. A deck of tarot cards was stacked neatly alongside a chess board and retinue of wooden knights, all set on a small table. Blunted training blades leaned against the wall. The one great bed was made. The cold hearth in the room had been swept clean of ashes. The room, too, had been cleaned, except for a great stain on the floor, a great misshapen cancer of black beneath the chandelier.

"Here?" I asked.

"Yes." She gazed out the window. "Butchered and hanged like...like meat."

I studied the chandelier. It fit with the wounds to the bodies. Strung up by their feet. Throats slit. Drained of blood. Collected? But what about the puncture wounds? "You saw them?"

"A blessing, no." Lady Mary shook her head. "I only saw them after. After they were taken down. Lady Narcissa was having time with them, her time, binding them, dressing them. I...I offered my help. She simply closed the door. Lord Raachwald took me away after that. Back to Old-Oath."

"And Raachwald's boy?" I asked. "He suffered the same?"

"Yes."

"But you didn't see the Volkendorf boys until later. When did you see Cain?"

"No, it was his father who found him. Them. He broke the door in, cut them all down. He had Cain removed immediately." She paused, looked up at me. "I...I never saw him." She crossed herself. "They—one of Lord Raachwald's men—said he had suffered the same."

"Strange that it was Lord Raachwald and not Lady Narcissa who found the bodies," I commented. "You had gone to raise the hue and cry. And while she, too, had survived the attack, she deigned not to check on the welfare of her own children? How long did it take you to return?"

"She was indisposed, I said."

"You had." I strode to the west window. "Forgive me. Cain's buried down there, then?" Lord Raachwald's keep sat hundreds of feet lower on the cliff side, along a flat expanse overlooking the west side of Asylum. "Any of Raachwald's men still in there?"

"They all fled to Dunmire after the plague struck," Lady Mary said.

Good. I could hike down there in less than an hour, work my way into its crypts, examine Cain's corpse. It shouldn't be difficult.

"Yes." She averted her gaze. "Poor boy, nothing like his father. A lovely boy. Lovely. He did not deserve...he did not deserve any of it."

"What of Lady Raachwald?"

"My personal interactions with either of the Raachwalds has been limited to…" She held up her hooked stump. "I've never spoken to her. I hear she's a mouse. I have seen her at court on occasion yet never heard her speak. Some wonder whether she even possesses a voice."

"Did she grieve?"

"I don't know." The wind whipped her hair back in uneven tendrils. "She is his fifth wife. Fifth or sixth? Hmmm. I don't know. His previous wife was barren, they say. She disappeared. The fate of many. Lord Raachwald and Lady Raachwald were wed a short time later. For a time, they tried to conceive a child after his eldest two were killed." She shook her head. "They had difficulties it was said, but then she finally conceived and bore a son. Cain." She seemed to consider something. "It was a matter of some speculation as to whether Lord Raachwald was the true father, or even whether Lady Raachwald was the true mother."

"That's a neat trick."

"I never lend rumors much credence." She took a long breath. "There's slander about all the lords. It is the nature of Mummer's Isle, of the world, but for a time it was spoken of."

"You're certain that Lord Raachwald opened this door?"

"Yes. He and his man, Haefgrim. With an axe."

The door puzzled me. The murderer who had smashed through a portcullis and two oak barriers next leaves this one not only wholly intact but also saw fit to lock it afterward? The killing of the men and boys were different, obviously and totally. Was it the work of two killers? It seemed so. Or was it one killer with separate motives? The boys seemed part of some…ritual. With the men, it seemed blood-simple slaughter.

Motives were tricky. This could all be smoke, haze, by Lord Raachwald, to cover a grab for Coldspire. That made the most sense. Murdering his own son, though? Seeds of ice he'd need for that.

Something else bothered me, though. Jesus, my half-ass theory was already falling apart. I looked out over the courtyard. "Why isn't Raachwald here already? It's empty. Hell, why aren't all the lords scrambling for the front door?"

"Because Lord Raachwald has *her*." Lady Mary shook her head. "For any to take Coldspire, they must possess legitimacy in the eyes of all the others. There are strict rules or formalities, I suppose, you could say, to ascendancy. To legitimacy. If Lady Narcissa had been killed in the attack, it would have been a powder keg sparked. The other lords would have killed each other, all, without a doubt. Lady Narcissa is the key."

I nodded. Lord Raachwald already had her. That solidified his position. All he had to do now was marry her. "So, kill Lord Volkendorf. Kill the heirs. Take the wife. Marry her to achieve legitimacy. Produce an heir. That his play?"

"I could not say."

"Wouldn't want to be Lady Raachwald right now." But, if all that were true, why would he have bid me do this work? And again, why not just kill me that first night?

"Look." Lady Mary pointed.

I followed her outstretched arm down to Old-Oath.

"Jesus Christ."

A retinue of men appeared, clambering up from the cliff side trail. We were far, but I could see Lord Raachwald leading them. He sat astride a horse, his white hair whipping in the wind, the giant Haefgrim riding by his side. The rest came afoot, trudging in single file, lugging goods, weapons, equipment. My brother Stephan came last, hands trussed before him, towed along by a chain round his neck as he stutter-stepped behind that yellow-eyed grinning bastard. The retinue, some forty, all told, disappeared within the edifice's open maw, down its throat, and into its belly. I didn't see Lady Narcissa.

"Lady Mary, do you believe Lord Raachwald capable

of killing his own son in a bid to seize Coldspire?" I asked. "His own flesh and blood, is he *that* cold?"

"You're *all* that cold," Lady Mary answered without hesitation.

Chapter 16.

A SQUAT RAZORBACK of a fortress, Old-Oath loomed ahead, bristling with tusks of jagged stone, spike-tips jutting up from the snow-filled moat, arrow-loop eyes watching on with slitted interest. The walls were only fifteen-feet high but possessed an aura of solidity, of thickness, of invulnerability. Dark stone. Ancient. Rune-worked. If ever there was a fortress that shouted, *"Go away..."*

Yet here I stood, nonetheless, before Lord Raachwald's very gates, disguised in the tabard of his ancestral enemy, to bid him exhume the body of his murdered son. I expected it to go fantastically. But why the hell was he here? The Lady Narcissa was in his grasp. Coldspire's key. And Dunmire was as good a base of operations as Old-Oath. Better, considering plague rampaged still.

I trod across the drawbridge, under a portcullis, and into the barbican's open maw. Murder holes above inquired silently as to which I preferred: boiling water or oil? I stopped shy of a second portcullis. Jesus Christ. A man had been crucified across it. Heart in my throat for an instant, I thought it was Stephan. It wasn't. The poor bastard had been blood-eagled, his back hacked ragged with an axe, chop by bloody chop, lungs torn out through the holes, hanging limp as soiled dishrags. Eyeless sockets stared down.

Drip...

Drip...

Drip...

Behind the corpse, a shadow emerged, stark black against the glare of sunlight beyond.

"A rare breed of crow, you are." The shadow aimed a crossbow through the iron bars. "Thought you was all killed."

"Well, it appears, my good sir, you were misinformed." The stink of fresh death hung low, thick, but there was something else, too. Fire? I saw no charring on the wooden posts, no spalling of the rock. Strange. An old fire? I nodded at the carcass. "Hmmm." Streaks of soot smudged his ruined form. "What'd he do?"

"It's what he didn't." The guard leered through the bars. "What d'ya want?"

"To parley with the Gallows Lord."

Squinting, he leaned back from the iron cage and pulled a lever. The portcullis behind me dropped, crashing to the stone. Somehow, I didn't shit my pants, but it was a near thing, that's for damn sure.

The guard patted the carcass on the shoulder. "Don't you go nowhere."

* * * *

"*You*—" Lord Raachwald stalked towards me, hell blazing in his eye.

I took an involuntary step back, fighting the urge to draw Yolanda, but Old-Oath's great hall was packed with Lord Raachwald's men. A death sentence if I drew.

"You raze my keep." He kept on coming.

"Whoa," I froze, "*what*—?"

I never even felt his mailed fist—I just crumpled.

Next, I was laid out breathless across stone. Gasping. Ears ringing. The gnarly old lord straddled over me, three of the towering bastards wavering, faces torqued in wolf-malice radiating like three-fold moonshine. "Steal what is rightfully mine." He drew a black axe from his belt and clamped a vise-like hand to the back of my neck. "Murder my men." He pulled me close, slavering in a long stream. "Your brother, I'll blood-eagle the fucker before you." He wiped his chin with the back of his hand. "Tear your eyelids off." Madness constricted his humanity to a pinprick in his lone golden eye. "Force you to watch."

Raze his keep?

Oh shit...

Karl.

"Rrrrrg." I struggled up. "Lord Raach—"

SLAM! This time, I felt it, his mailed fist across my face, stars ringing, stitches popping open across my forehead. Lolling back, dazed, blood rolling warm down my face, I stared up at skulls, a silent audience festering across the walls, sneering down, pupils of rusted iron nailed through each socket.

"Cease your chatter." Looking at me as though I were shit smeared across the sole of his boot, Lord Raachwald snatched at the Volkendorf tabard across my chest. "A crude jape, eh, clever boy? You think me the fool?" Axe raised, knee crushing my chest, Lord Raachwald curled down over me like a hoary old buzzard hunkering to feast. "What's your game?"

"Rrrrrg," I spat blood, "no game."

"How did you gain access to my Isle? Which one?"

"Which one *what*?" I gasped.

"Which lord sanctioned you? Whose man are you?" That axe pressed against my throat. "Or was it the bishop?"

"I'm yours still," I grunted, "and no one knows I'm here." I tugged at my tabard. "Discretion, see?" How long my disguise would last, given present circumstances, I dared not mention. "Nothing but an expatriate Volkendorf guard looking for work." I raised both hands. "I know nothing about a fire. Nor any abduction or murder. I swear it."

"And what is your word to me?"

"Not much," I pressed a hand to my torn stitches, "admittedly."

Lord Raachwald's pinpoint pupil expanded as reason eked through madness, but he manfully bore through it. "You claim ignorance? Another jape. I witnessed it myself. Your brother and your man. You were a justiciar once, aye?" I nodded. "What sentence would you levy against such crimes?"

"For what? Arson? Kidnapping? Murder? Hanging."

"Hrrrrm…" He rubbed his stubbly chin. "A loyal one you are."

"But no hypocrite. And I'm here. That ain't nothing. And I've made progress."

"Progress?" Lord Raachwald straightened, that axe blade drawing a whisker back from my neck. I took a deep breath, swallowed. "Speak. Speak swiftly."

"It wasn't a monk that killed Cain."

"By the bloody spear," Lord Raachwald's spat. "You know nothing."

Possibly he was not impressed with my revelation.

"I wouldn't say *nothing*, my Lord."

"I just did." His men thronged him now. Haefgrim, the giant, leaned a massive two-handed falchion across his shoulder. The Grinner, his yellow eyes watching, Aaron's axe in hand, fingers fluttering in ravenous expectation. The fierce old codger, Old Inglestahd, lips pursed, thick arms crossed. Others crowded the hall, hard-looking men, cold-looking men. Swaths of black char covered them head to foot. "Sot?" Lord Raachwald's gaze shifted to his jester. "Did I not just say so?"

"Eh, milord?" Sot cupped his ear. "What?" The wobbly jester, a sad-sack jumble of a man, his face stung half-red by a wine stain, jingled his motley hat in a nod and forced a wet fart. No one laughed. Not even a little. "Apologies, milord, may have overachieved on that one."

Lord Raachwald also failed to see any humor.

"Perhaps," Sot slurred, "yon crow is deaf?" He was as drunk as I was envious of his drunkenness. Trundling over to me, he placed a finger to his double chin then tapped the head of his wooden scepter. "Perhaps a knock about the squash might cure him of such an ailment? Eh? Jar something loose." He reared back, winding up to strike, tottering cross-eyed, tongue between his lips. "Shall I administer a dose, milord?"

"Lord Raachwald, honor our bargain," I hissed as low as I could. Sot jingled around me. I kept an eye his way. A dose from that scepter in the right spot'd be a cure for just about everything.

"Our fruitless bargain…" Lord Raachwald stalked close. "Nay. Fruitless would mean a stalemate. Fruitless would mean I had started and ended with the same. Nay. Not fruitless. You have slashed and burned my orchard. Salted my earth. Poisoned my well."

"No."

"Then why come?" His canine teeth bared sharp.

"I came for my brother, and I came for *your* son." The moment I said it, I knew it for truth. As did he. I read it in his face. Surprise. Shock. Astonishment. That he believed it as well. And though it was perhaps not conscious thought in that instant, he relented, stepping back, lowering that damned axe.

"Tee-hee!" Sot danced in anticipation, a tumescent toad fit to pop. "All this natter of fruits." Sot leaned over, grabbing my feet and examining my crotch. "Ah, milord, fruits would be a compliment. Methinks these but a wizzled twig and pair of shriveled nuts." *Disconcerting*, a word that came to mind.

I yanked a foot in and kicked the other out, scissoring, twisting the jester off balance, then lashed back out, heel to face, my heavy boot smashing his yapping mouth, yellow teeth shattering like teacups cast against stone. He reeled back, clutching his jaw, spitting teeth.

I rose, dusted myself off, offered him a wink. "Say something *funny*."

With crimson bubbling from his crooked maw, Sot glared, eyes narrowed to twin beams of hatred.

"A mighty crow," someone called from amongst the court, "versus the rotund jester. A potent blow landed! And yet the fool still draws breath."

The court mumbled a nervous laugh.

"Be glad to hazard another." I got another half-hearted laugh.

It died straight away when Lord Raachwald turned. "Leave us."

Weapons clanking, his men as one bowed, turned,

exited. Swiftly. A mousy lady garbed in rustic furs stood in the corner, hands muffled in a mink wrap, cool eyes watching. Lady Raachwald? Had to be. She studied me from underneath half-closed lids, a mask of disinterest on her face. Revilement? Curiosity? A mix of both? She nodded once to her husband, turned and left, followed by Sot, limping in jangling half-steps out the door, scepter dragging behind.

Only Old Inglestahd, the Grinner, and Haefgrim remained. With helm upon his head, Haefgrim looked like a demon. Without it, he looked worse. Black eyes stared flat, blank, emotionless. Scars crisscrossed his bald head. Burns. Cuts. Was it a pattern? Intentional? And falchions. More axe than sword, more butcher's cleaver than axe. Its thick blade was wide at the killing end, adding weight to the stroke, damage to the strike. A weapon of war. If an axe and sword rutted and spawned offspring, the falchion it would be.

The door slammed shut.

"Tell me what you know." Lord Raachwald's gaze flickered to that falchion for the briefest of instants, his meaning clear.

"First, I need to know what you know." I drew myself up. "I saw Volkendorf's body. The damage. What could have caused that?"

Lord Raachwald fingered his jaw. "Did I not claim black sorcery from the first?" he asked. "There could be nothing else. Now you."

I nodded. "It's a power grab."

"By who?" Lord Raachwald demanded.

"One of the Five Houses. All the lords, in some way, benefitted from the deaths. If for nothing more than being one step closer to Coldspire." I raised both hands. "I don't know who, and I don't know how," I added quickly, "but I'm getting there."

"You claim *everyone* benefitted?" Lord Raachwald thumbed the edge of his axe.

"I do." I straightened, swallowed, nodded, then barrel-assed on. "And I'd say that *you* benefitted most." I forced myself to slow my breath. "That's truth, the hard kind. Coldspire is nearly yours now, yeah?"

Haefgrim took a step forward, but Lord Raachwald froze him with the raise of a hand.

"But, whatever benefits you garnered were mitigated by the loss of your son." I was treading thin ice, sharks cruising beneath. "I'm sorry for that." In that moment, I had difficulty envisioning him killing his son. Lady Mary claimed him capable, but none of it made sense now. It would have been a mad gamble, severing his own line in the hope of starting a new one with Lady Narcissa. And why? To cover his tracks? "Lord Raachwald, I'll need to see Cain's body."

Lord Raachwald winced as though struck. "My boy sleeps." A strange thing to see of this powerful man, unsure of himself. "I'll...I'll not have him disturbed." He fixed me with his dead eye. "I...perhaps I can offer something, though." He swallowed. "There is a man, Sir Myron Chalstain. Once an Isle man. Long ago." Lord Raachwald looked out the window. "The man has a knack, is an able hunter of men. He engaged in a hunt for the killer. Or attempted to."

"And what'd he find?" I asked.

"I do not know."

Was this the man Nils had mentioned?

"I nearly cast him into the river," he explained, "but I restrained myself."

Magnanimously, no doubt. "And did he cease hunting?"

"No. A difficult man to dissuade from task. I'll grant him that."

"Where can I find him?"

"They say he has gone missing." It *was* him.

"Then what good is he to me?"

"The man was a keen observer." Lord Raachwald ground his teeth together, suppressing some urge, most likely related to punching me in the face again. "Orderly. Precise. Fastidious to a fault. He chronicled everything in a ledger. Always. If you could find him, or his ledger, it might offer insight."

"Alright," I said, "but why threaten him? Why not just accept his aid?"

"Look out that window, Krait." Lord Raachwald pointed with the black axe.

I glanced out the window, taking in the daunting heights of Coldspire above, its black monolith rising. I imagined I could still see Lady Mary standing in the boys' window, alone up there, staring down, surrounded by ghosts.

"All that you see and beyond was once the domain of the Raachwalds. Years, decades, centuries, past. All once my great-grandfather's and his father's before him and on and on back past the Martels, the Merovingians. Back before the Christian God, before the heathen ones, to a time of the Old Ones." His hand closed into a fist. "It was to be mine, and it was taken, but I shall have it back." Stalking the room, he found himself back at the dais. "Chalstain is the Lord Bishop's man. If I were to allow him access to the hunt, allow him to mete out justice, it would offer legitimacy to that damned *Vulture's* rule."

As if to punctuate that, cannon fire erupted somewhere far off.

"That is why we fight." Lord Raachwald sat upon his throne.

"I *will* find the killer," I said.

"Will you? Will you, indeed?" Lord Raachwald leaned forward. "Even when your brother dances the hangman's jig? Eyes bulging? Tongue lolling long and black? Shit dripping down his leg? Even then?"

"Ahem..." I cleared my throat. "I suppose we are at something of an impasse then, my lord. You have my brother and threaten him with death, whilst I hold the only tools to finding your son's killer."

"You possess nothing so far as I see."

"You've had a month to crack this and failed. You need me. I need my brother. An accord must be brokered."

"I could find other impetus to motivate you..."

"No. You can kill me. Or you can unleash me. But it's one or the other. There's no middle ground," I said. "It's true, also, that my brother's crimes are his own. He'd be the first to admit them. Wouldn't shy from the punishment, either. He'd embrace it."

"True…" Lord Raachwald grunted reluctant assent. "He made nary a peep as I put the question to him. No protests, no begging, no debasing himself. Merely a swallow then a nod."

"His crimes are his own." I swallowed my rising gorge. "But there is the panacea to our standoff. Stephan's no murderer. He'd take no part in it."

"And your man?" Lord Raachwald's voice rising. "I suppose he is no murderer as well?"

"No. He's a most excellent murderer."

"Strange. The man I have under lock and fetter is no murderer, yet the one running free, the one no doubt savaging a noblewoman this very instant, is. How often have I heard similar sentiments from family of the condemned?"

"Have I lied to you yet?" I asked.

"Yet…"

"You've spoken with Stephan," I said. "You asked him if I was involved, yeah?"

"Aye."

"And what do you think of him?" I asked. "Of his word?"

"You would trust *my* assessment?" Lord Raachwald's good eye narrowed.

"You seem a hard man. A cold man. A cruel man. But I think you're no liar."

"Whilst your sigil is the serpent. And I think your forked tongue predisposed to the spewing of lies."

"You're not wrong. But a forked tongue'll sometimes spew truth, even as a stopped clock strikes true twice a day. But enough of me. I'm a liar. I admit it. Now tell me of my brother. Do you believe *him* a liar?"

Lord Raachwald's stone lips pressed together, threatening to crack, to fissure, to split. "Nay."

"Then you understand something of his character." I paused. "And so you must take him at his word."

"I have."

I froze. Shit. I'd thought I had him, but I was missing something. *Clearly*.

"He confessed."

"Under torture, men will confess to anything," I countered.

"He was under no torture."

"Fucking idiot." My brother, the saint.

"He absolved you of any wrongdoing, claiming you surely would have taken part had you known, but that you were not party to the crimes."

"What happened, exactly?"

Lord Raachwald studied my face, trying to read the guilt within. God knew there was plenty enough to go around. "What happened was your man snuck into my keep at Dunmire, set a barn ablaze, which took the stables and barracks before razing my keep. He broke your brother free and in the process murdered two of my men. The two then abducted Lady Narcissa. Your man was successful in the endeavor. Your brother was not."

"And when is Stephan to be tried?"

"*Tried?*" Lord Raachwald barked. "He confessed."

"Stephan is clergy," I was scrabbling for something, anything, "he should be tried in an ecclesiastical court. By the church."

Lord Raachwald turned in question to Old Inglestahd.

"Aye." Old Inglestahd offered a quick nod in answer to the unasked question. "'Tis the law, my lord, if what he claims be truth."

"Cede my powers to the church?" Lord Raachwald glared at him dead in the eye for a few very uncomfortable, very long moments. Old Inglestahd felt it, I could see, but he bore the brunt and did not waver. "He confessed. He shall suffer the axe or the noose."

"He confessed in your court, my lord." I turned to Old Inglestahd. "But was he offered what was his *right* by law?"

"Nay," answered Old Inglestahd.

Lord Raachwald's hands flexed open and closed.

"Then mete out punishment according to the church, and I'll consider it justice," I said. Ecclesiastical courts didn't carry death penalties. Stephan would live if Lord Raachwald accepted. A big '*if*.' "Bring in a priest. Any priest. It need not be one of the Lord Bishop's men. Let *him* pass sentence."

Lord Raachwald buried his axe into the arm of his throne. "He. Is. Mine."

"You'd flout the law within your own halls?" I spat. "Old-Oath is this keep's name, is it not? Does a lord not swear an oath to mete out justice and punishment within the confines of the law?" I turned to Old Inglestahd. His eyes warned me I might have trod too far. Fuck it.

"Do you know where your brother now resides?" Lord Raachwald worked his axe free. "Old-Oath's dungeons have teeth. Bitter. Cold. Teeth. Alone, he hunkers in palpable darkness. Its assault is immediate.

"It strikes the moment the cell door slams and the guard disappears, that blessed lantern with him, cradle of light, of life, wraith shadows streaking long across walls. The last image he shall see. Yet, he shall close his eyes and see his family, fields of autumn, his first love, despite the skitter of nail on stone, the harbinger of rats come to feast. Your brother, though, he is a strong man. The darkness shall not break him."

Lord Raachwald circled me.

"The cold comes next, a doom creeping like disease. A caress deepening with each stroke, lightly at first, and then deeper. Shivering, he embraces himself, stomping and pacing in effort to maintain warmth until he is so spent he can nary move, so weak he cannot stand, so tired he collapses against stone, only to have it suck the last vestiges of heat from his soul. The cold may kill him, but it shan't break him, either.

"It is the final assault, the desolation, that breaks *all* men. Every man thinks himself the hero of his own tale, but bristling with lice and sores and rat bites? The soft parts of his body gnawed away, the flesh fostering corruption, decay? A reeking mess? Who is this man who jabbers and cries and whimpers, hovering over a bucket, wincing as he pisses like a woman? He is a stranger unto his own self. He can be no hero. And so the desolation has stripped him of who he is, who he was, who we would be. And what does that now make him?"

Lord Raachwald waited for an answer.

I had none to offer.

"No longer a man? Not yet a corpse? A twilight thing of the in-between. A thing of decay. And even should he someday be released? I say released because he *cannot* escape. For he is marked and shall bear with him that desolation the remainder of his days, upon stooped shoulder, bent back, hobbled knee. Derision and pity from those he once loved. Frustration, humiliation, indignation whilst lying next to his wife, unable to achieve even a measure of consummation." Lord Raachwald laid the head of his axe across my shoulder. "Your brother has yet even to bend, let alone break. My question to you is, do you wish him to?"

I swallowed. "Yes."

"Then our bargain stands." He lifted the axe. "Bring me the murderer's head, and you shall have what you wish. Ecclesiastical justice."

I nodded.

"Your man," he said. "He is no priest."

"No," I managed.

"Then you shall bring me *his* head alongside the killer's."

"Done." If Lord Raachwald was shocked at my swift acquiescence, he didn't show it. "And I wish to see Stephan."

"Are you a student of history, Krait?" Lord Raachwald gazed out over the city, to the forest beyond. "Do you know the story of my people? The story of the Romans who encroached upon our land? The story of the Hellwood?"

"Yeah. The Romans came. The Romans went.

Significantly fewer wenting."

"It was my forefathers who engaged them." Lord Raachwald pointed up. Atop the wall, crowning the cacophony of skulls, a golden eagle perched. It was a Roman legion's standard, hundreds of years old, gleaming still. "The twenty-fifth legion. It was my ancestors, my forefathers, who slaughtered them, forcing them back. The entirety of the Roman war machine halted, embattled, broken. As his men lay slaughtered about him in droves, the Roman Commander Tiberius begged considerations of my ancestors." Lord Raachwald shook his head slowly. "The Romans, the sole boon of their storied existence was the chronicling of their own demise."

"I wish to see my brother."

A sly look. "You wish considerations, Krait?" Lord Raachwald reached under his cloak and tossed something toward me, bouncing haphazard across the floor. "Then consider this."

It was Stephan's right hand.

...is a force of nature, but it is Slade that inflicts upon me the night terrors. I wonder oft whether he is, indeed, even human.

—Journal of Sir Myron Chalstain

Chapter 17.

"STEPHAN..." I peered through the cell window. My stomach was sick, and it wasn't the reek of eons-old piss and shit and unwashed humanity. "It's Luther." I could see nothing in the gloom. I shuddered. To remain down here, blind in the freezing damp, for who knows how long, would break me, and break me quickly. I knew it. Stephan, though? No. Not quickly, anyhow.

The lantern cast a dim cone of orange that muted the dark, caressing it rather than banishing it. I forced my face against the bars, straining for a glimpse, straining to where the light could only whisper, to a scarecrow strewn across the floor, stuffing kicked out.

A rat skittered across stone.

"Stephan, it's Luther."

"Hello...brother." Chains clinked as the scarecrow slid to the pulsating verge of meager twilight. "How... How's your head?"

I touched the gash across my forehead. "It's fine," I lied. "You patched me up good. And your hand?" *Your stump?* I didn't say.

"Bad." Stephan hacked a wet cough, a pneumonia cough, a death-rattle cough. "It's corrupted."

"Can't fix it?" I already knew the answer. Stephan had a gift from God for fixing wounds. I'd seen him do wonders with nothing more than a needle and thread and some prayer, but this was beyond him, beyond anybody. "How bad?"

"Does it matter?" Stephan asked. "Brother, just do what you claim to do best." Encrusted in grime and soot, Stephan clutched his maimed arm to his body, shivering. *'Do what you claim to do best.'* Code. I'd often bragged of it, my ability to outrun trouble, to run fast, to run far, to run long. *'Get the hell out of here,'* that's what he meant. But what he hadn't said, what he'd only implied, was, *'Abandon me,'* and I'd never done that, not to him, anyways.

"No." I throttled the bars.

He started coughing, hacking, and I realized he was laughing.

"Jesus," I growled. "What the fuck were you thinking?"

"I...they could be listening."

Craning my neck, I glanced down the hall, cell after cell disappearing into the long quiet, and saw no one. "They're gone." I tore the cloak off my back and stuffed it through the bars, tossing it as best I could. "Can you reach it?"

A thin, translucent arm reached trembling into the light. "I knew you wouldn't understand."

"Fuck you." I nearly screamed it, but held back, teeth grinding.

"Ten years ago I wouldn't have had to explain it," Stephan said.

"Ten years ago I was a fool."

"You were a hero."

"And you were a child."

"A child can see life with a clarity adults have sullied into opacity. Into blindness. You were a hero. My hero. You always did right, everything, without hesitation, without reservation, without consideration of consequence, of cost, of anything. Only just right. No matter how difficult the path, and there were difficult paths, brother. You were my hero for that."

"And now?"

Stephan strained for my cloak with his one hand, snatched it, drew it around his shoulders. I could see his breath mist. He looked so small, so diminished, so frail.

"And yet still here you stand," Stephan said, "trying to save me."

"You don't understand. You never understand."

"I chose to come with you, didn't I?" His voice lowered. "I left them behind. Our family. I left them all behind."

"You're my brother."

"So are Willie and George. Would you be standing here for either of them?"

"For William?" I swallowed, saying nothing, thinking for a moment about my eldest brother. "No. And George? I don't know. My thoughts on the bonds of blood have become convoluted these past years."

"I'm sorry for putting you in this position," Stephan said, "for what it's worth."

"Dogshit, that's what's worth. You never think. That's your problem."

"No. I think about every facet of every problem, constantly, assiduously. Perhaps I give no heed to the consequences, but there is a difference."

"Jesus. No heed to the consequences? In Paris, they tried to burn you as a fucking heretic."

"For helping treat a dying man. And I was right to do so."

"And the church was wrong?"

"Yes."

"The church is never wrong."

Stephan scoffed. "I was right then. I was right now."

"You're so fucking stupid. The people in power, the church, the lords, the king. Whoever. Whatever. They're not wrong. They're never wrong. You're wrong. You're. Always. Wrong. *Especially* when you're right. So you keep your head down. You keep that stupid fucking tongue tucked between your teeth, and you bite down hard when you want to apprise them of their shortcomings. Then you swallow it. You swallow it, and you live another day. That's how you get on in this world."

"Forgive me, brother, but if things were truly your way, nothing would ever change."

"Good. Change is bad. Change is bloody. Change is death."

"I'm willing to be one of those who die for it."

"Well, I'm not. And I'm not letting you die, either. Not for some headstrong small-lord. Not for the church. Not for anything."

"That's your choice, brother."

"Great. I accept your apology."

"I didn't apologize. I asked forgiveness for putting you in this predicament. Not for what I've done."

"To be clear about what you're not asking forgiveness for, was it the kidnapping? The arson? Or the murder?"

"I won't lie to save my life."

"But you will to sling your neck through a noose?"

"And who says I'm lying?" Stephan asked.

"Me. I do. Jesus. You wouldn't lie to save your own skin. You wouldn't kill to save it, either. You're no murderer. And you wouldn't burn down a castle, not with people in it. You don't have it in you. Hell, you're only still alive because of me and Karl." I shrugged. "Well, mostly Karl."

"I...I aided in the venture."

"You mean Karl killed the two men, yeah? And razed Dunmire."

"I helped," he insisted.

"Did you kill anyone?"

"I was party to it even if I did not wield a blade."

"Jesus."

"Can you not see?"

"No, I can't, so explain it to me. Use small words."

"She needed help." He kept his voice low. It was easy. He could barely breathe. "She just seemed so...so sad."

"The Lady Narcissa?" I grunted.

"Yes."

"*Sad?*"

"Yes."

"She seemed like a cast-iron bitch to me."

"Well. You and I have always had different ways with women."

"Yeah," I conceded. "You've a light touch."

"And yours is lead."

"I prefer to call it gold."

"Well, heavy, then, at any rate."

"Fair enough," I conceded.

"Ponderous, even. Onerous."

"Yeah. Heavy. I got it."

"She came to me that night, the night I went for help." *I did all this to help you*, but he didn't say that. Jesus. He couldn't even be a proper bastard. "The horse was dead, the wagon broken, and I thought you were dying." He paused. "What of the others?"

"Dead. They're all dead."

Stephan muttered prayer then continued. "Lord Raachwald's men waylaid me on the road. They were lying in ambush. How they knew I was coming? I don't know. I told them I was a nobleman, ordained, that I would be worth coin ransomed. Family, the church, either. I begged them for help, something, anything. They took me to Dunmire." He scratched at his ankle. "Lady Narcissa came to me while I languished in chains. She begged me for help. Told me she could save my life and that she could save yours. I told her I didn't care about my life, but I did about yours, about Karl's, about—"

"And as a prisoner, chained in some dungeon, what help could you possibly offer?"

"Offer? Me?" Stephan shook his head. "None of my own, but I could offer yours. I could offer Karl's."

"And what right did you have to offer it?"

"You're my brother. And Karl is Karl."

"So you helped save her?"

"No, it was she who saved me, or tried to at least. She's the one who snuck me out. She stole the keys and led me out through that black maze."

"After you agreed to help her?"

"After I agreed to help her." He nodded. "Yes."

"Then what?"

"Dunmire was burning, but she had horses ready. We escaped in the confusion, well, almost. Karl met us on the road, somehow. I don't know how. It's still not clear. Lord Raachwald caught wise and set men and dogs hot on our heels, a storm of arrows. My horse dropped beneath me, shot dead. Karl was hit, and she—"

"Ended up with him," I finished his sentence.

"At my bidding."

"And Karl agreed?"

"There was no time to argue. I simply turned around, hands raised and started back towards Lord Raachwald's men, an effort to delay them."

"Or target practice?"

"Heh," he chuffed a laugh. "Yes, I suppose, something like that, anyway. Not my most well-thought-out plan, I admit, and Karl had no choice in the matter. He did what I bade him, begged him. He rode off with her, cursing me the whole way."

"Jesus Christ."

"Lou."

"Fuck off!" I said. "You're lucky to be alive. Raachwald abducted her. You didn't. And you didn't kill any of his men, and you didn't burn Dunmire."

"Raachwald doesn't see it that way."

"His view of reality does not ride the prevailing winds." I shook my head. "I'm going to bust you out of here." I ran a hand up the door, along the jamb—solid construction—then the lock. Old, but stoutly made as well. I crouched, glancing for an instant at the door at the end of the hall, then held the lantern up to the keyhole.

"You think the guards'll just sit by?"

I tried to peer inside, get a feel for the mechanism. It was too dark, and I needed a set of picks, a tool, something, anything. The handle of the lantern—

"There's only one way to get me out."

"The hell there is." I worked the wire handle free, bent it. "I'll break in there and knock you out. Drag your sorry arse—"

"How? Smuggle me out? Carry me? I can barely limp. And where? Through Old-Oath? And then what, after you somehow manage to murder the gaolers? And the rest of them? What then? What about when I wake up and start crawling back?"

"I'll hit you in the head again."

"A fine plan."

"I'm starting to like it more and more." I smacked the bars with an open hand. "You're going to let some backwater small-lord pass judgment on you after he imprisons you? Wrongfully."

"I'm past helping, Lou."

"Like hell."

"I am to be beheaded."

"No. From him, that'd be a kindness. But you know what? They call him the Gallows Lord, Stephan. But he's not even going to live up to his name and hang you like a common thief. You know what he's going to do? What he does. He's going to hack the bones from your back and blood-eagle you."

"It's..." he paused, the silence heavy, "it's the same outcome."

"Like hell it is."

"You can't help me. That's why I confessed."

"No. I fixed it, little brother. Like I always do. He's going to allow the church to carry out your sentencing."

Stephan was silent.

"You'll need to prove you're a priest. Read a passage from the Bible or baptize a heathen or something. And then you'll get ten Paternosters and Hail Marys." I slapped my palms together, rubbed them. "And then you're done."

"You truly believe it'll be that simple?"

I paused. It did seem too good to be true.

"Just help her, protect her," Stephan implored. "I gave her my word you would. That's all I have, all I ask."

"Why should I?"

"Because she needs it, Luther."

"So what? Everyone needs it."

"So do it."

"Jesus. Are you in love with her?"

"If I said yes, would you do it?"

"What the hell do you think I'm doing?"

"You're trying to find a way to break me out."

"Exactly." I brandished the bent wire.

"You're not doing what I'm asking you to do."

"I'm trying to save your life."

"I don't care about my life."

"Oh, here we go. Stephan Lollard, martyr-extraordinaire."

"Listen to me! Do what you must, find who killed her children, but protect her, too."

"Did she cast some spell over you?"

"No. She's alone, afraid. Her children are dead. Her husband is dead. Everyone she knows is dead. She has nothing, no one."

"Well, boo-fucking-hoo. Everywhere you look people are alone. Destitute. Dying. I've seen a thousand in this city today alone."

"That's the plague's doing, and there's nothing you can do for it, no help you can offer, but you can do something for her."

"What makes her any better? What makes her warrant help? Protection? At least she has that fine ermine cloak to keep her warm."

"She's trapped. Raachwald needs her. She was his prisoner."

I did a double take. "She admitted that?"

"Yes. She was as much a prisoner as I am now. More so," Stephan said. "Help her, Lou. Just do it, and I'll die in peace."

"Men like us don't die in peace." *We die in pieces* I almost said, but it wasn't as clever as I thought, not by half, and it made me feel sicker than I already did. I swallowed, picturing him blood-eagled out in Lord Raachwald's great hall or crucified across that portcullis. Eyes gouged out. Dripping. Freezing. I'd kill him myself before I'd let that happen.

"I've seen men die."

"And you're not afraid?"

"Of course I'm afraid. I'm afraid my knees will shake and give out, afraid I'll piss myself. Afraid I'll die looking the coward, weak. Afraid father will hear of it one day and not even react, or he will, and it'll just confirm every suspicion he's ever borne about me." He coughed. "Just do it. Help her."

I almost screamed, but I choked it back. "Where is she?"

"I don't know. With Karl."

"With Karl, you assume?"

"Yes, I assume." He waved a hand. "Now, have you uncovered anything about the murders?"

"No, nothing."

"Nothing? Lady Narcissa told me her handmaid would help you."

"Lady Mary," I frowned, "she told me a story. An unbelievable story."

"Is it unbelievable because you can't believe it or because you refuse to?"

"I just assumed she was bat-shit crazy."

"Did she seem bat-shit crazy?"

"Maybe I was just hoping she was."

"But did she?"

"No, Jesus, she didn't. Not even a little. But she posed more questions and gave no answers."

"So find the answers."

"I'm working on it. Ain't easy when everyone's lying. Lies and tall tales and side-talking. A fucking whirlwind of misinformation. Even she was lying to me."

"Is that truly so rare?"

"No." I shook my head. "Damned commonplace, in fact." I pulled out a few of the rocks I'd gathered from the great hall at Coldspire. "I found these," I said lamely, holding them up. "Another unanswered question."

"I can't see."

"They're just…" I shook my head in frustration. "Just rocks. Little chips of rock. The size of chess pieces.

They were littered about Coldspire's great hall. Where they fought. Where they died. Lord Volkendorf and his men. I couldn't ferret out the source. And Lady Mary didn't know." I went on to tell him about the circumstances of that battle, the broken weapons and the bodies, and Lady Mary's story along with her lie about Lady Narcissa's whereabouts the night of the murder. First, she had claimed Lady Narcissa had been by her side throughout, and then later that she had been indisposed. Had the Lady Narcissa even been there that night? And if not, what did that mean? Jesus. Stephan said nothing, like he does. He just hunkered there wrapped in my cloak, listening, quietly absorbing, forming it all in his mind, examining it from all sides like some alchemist conducting an experiment.

"Could I have one of the stones?" Stephan asked.

"Sure." I flicked a few in, rolling across the floor like seer bones.

Chains rasped across rock as he reached with his foot. "Got one. Two." He was examining them by the dim light. "Hmmm…"

"Anything?" I asked.

"Well. They're sharp-edged. Hard. They've some weight. They seem just rocks."

"Yeah." I deflated.

"You know she had to lie," Stephan said. "She told me that."

"She tell you why?"

"We didn't have a great deal of time."

"Probably didn't trust you."

"Yes, that too, I imagine."

"Great. Raachwald may have lied, too, about his son's death," I said. "It's possible Raachwald may have killed him himself. In some bid for Coldspire. I, ahem, alluded to that when I spoke with him."

"How'd that play out?" Stephan asked.

"I'm still alive."

"What'd you get off him?"

"The man's a tough read."

"He is that. But why kill his own boy? To what purpose?"

"There's rumor the boy was a bastard."

Stephan grunted, unconvinced.

"To erase doubt as to his own culpability?" I offered, still unsure. Funny how something can sound so solid in your head and so much like bullshit out loud.

"Hmmm? He's old," Stephan pondered. "His lineage? A huge risk, not to mention the act itself. Why murder his only heir?"

"Maybe cause he figured I was too busy?" I offered.

Stephan's disapproval oozed like a fume.

"Alright," I ceded, "not funny."

"His sole heir, Luther. You know how mad lords are about securing the future, not even considering the father-son bond. Remember how inseparable father and Willie were—sorry, forget it."

"Or—shit." The idea struck me like lightning. "Maybe Cain's still alive somewhere?" No one other than Lord Raachwald had actually seen his boy's body. Lady Narcissa and Lady Mary hadn't. I hadn't. Lord Raachwald's men had, maybe, but they wouldn't talk. Not to me. "Raachwald hits Coldspire. Attacks. Kills the Volkendorf boys. Hides his own." I nodded slowly. "It makes more sense."

"Is it possible?"

"Maybe. I don't know."

"I think you should go back to Abraham."

"Back?" I scoffed.

"What? You *have* gone to Abraham, right? Please tell me you've gone."

"Okay, I've gone," I lied.

"You've been here, how long?" Stephan demanded.

"Two days."

"Land of Goshen," he gasped. "You have to tell him about the shipment. Explain what happened. Does he even know you're in the city?"

"Jesus Christ. No. I've been too busy trying to save

149

your arse to deal with botched wool shipments."

"Forgive me," Stephan said.

"Hell, Stephan, I don't even know if he's still alive. Plague's still ripping out there. The Isle Men are trying to storm the Quarter. Bombarding it all day."

"You need to go to him."

"Sure, I'll just ask them to hold off their siege for a minute or two." I shook my head. "And do you really give a shit about a shipment of wool? Fuck it. Fuck Abraham. Fuck the Quarter. I need to find Karl and help your mistress."

"Lady Narcissa mentioned the tavern you're staying at? Well, Karl will be watching it, right? So, he'll find you."

I considered, gave in, nodded. "Yeah, I suppose."

"And it's more than just the wool shipment or the money. It's our word. You need to see him. You need to talk to him."

"I was hoping to avoid him."

"For how long?"

"Thirty, maybe, forty years."

"Just go. Tell him what happened. He won't like it, but he'll survive. He always does. We'll have to owe him."

"We already owe him."

"Well, we'll just have to owe him more."

"Easy for you to say. You'll be dead in a few days."

"Dear Lord," Stephan muttered beneath his breath. "And when you're there, ask him about the Volkendorfs."

"What about?"

"Ask about any of their business dealings he may know about. Who they dealt with. Borrowed from. When. Figures. Sums."

"What do you know?" I asked.

"Lady Narcissa told me she and her husband were in debt."

"How deep?"

"Deep enough that Coldspire was on the chopping block."

"How?" I snorted. "No Jew's going to muscle a lord out of his ancestral holdings, no matter how much he owes.

And out of Coldspire? Never."

"I don't know." Stephan hesitated. "It does seem a long shot, but that's what Narcissa claimed. She said Lord Volkendorf had borrowed off nearly every stone. She had concerns but was unable to explain precisely. Maybe there's more to it."

"Shit." I thought about it. "The Five Houses've been hammering the Quarter since I got here. The Lord Bishop's protecting them. Hell. Maybe there is more. You believe her?"

"I do. She said Lord Volkendorf couldn't read, so she managed the ledgers of his business dealings."

"Made sure they weren't getting screwed?"

"Oh, no, they were, hand over fist." Chains rasped as he dragged himself closer. I could just make him out, just outside the barred-trapezoid of light my lantern cast through the window. An arm lit on the floor, in the light. An arm ending in a stump.

"Jesus," I hissed. "He didn't even bandage you—"

"Forget it. It's nothing. Focus. Were they legal or not? The loans? I...I don't know. Maybe there's something there. Bad blood? Bad enough to kill over? I can't think, Lou. Maybe not. You have to check."

"She maintained the ledgers," I said. "Shouldn't she know?"

"Ask her when you find her."

"Yeah," I said, still staring at his ragged stump. "So I have to find out who they were in hock to?"

"It might help."

"It might, but you think Abraham's just going to fork that info over on a silver platter?"

"No, you'll just have to do what you truly do best."

"And what's that?"

"Be an asshole."

...for the duty, no desire to intrude, no desire to confront old foes, to open old wounds. Likewise, I bore no desire to be hurled bodily from the high cliffs of Mummer's Isle...
—Journal of Sir Myron Chalstain

Chapter 18.

WITH MY VOLKENDORF tabard rolled up under one arm, I stepped into Abraham's lending house. A storm of activity roiled inside, men bustling about to and fro, carrying papers, pens, and parchment. Some customers stood in line, some leaned over desks, signing documents, while the bankers nodded approvingly.

"*Shalom*, Abraham," I called as I stepped into line, staring in wonderment at Abraham's desk, though calling it a desk was like calling the battle of Crecy a tiff. It was an expansive cut of wood nearly ten-feet long, divided into various sections carved out by the utility of its inhabitants. Glass beakers with strange bird-beak flutes rose and twisted around in one corner. In another lay a series of open books, gorgeously illuminated by both pen and gold leaf lettering and pictures, some beautiful, some gruesome. Abraham Ben-Ari sat in the south quadrant of his desk, surrounded amidst stacks of ledger and parchment.

Abraham raised his one hand as he peered at a thick ledger, his nose and glasses nearly buried into its crease, and casually tossed a "*Shalom*" my way. In the space of five breaths, four young men had bolted in and then out again, stopping for an instant only to drop a document on Abraham's desk and ramble a quick explanation before disappearing out the back door.

I sauntered up to the counter dividing the relative peacefulness of the front quarter of the room from the chaos of the rest. Eyes were on me, guards, each one posted at either end of the counter. One was tall and lanky and bald. The other was of medium height with bushy locks. The Star of David was sewn onto their jackets like almost everyone else in the room. By law. And while Jews were forbidden to possess weapons, and I couldn't see them, I knew they were strapped. They stared me down, unafraid, just shy of brazen, just shy of open challenge.

"Greetings." I grinned at Baldy.

He chose not to return salutation.

"Uh, Abe?" I slapped the counter. "Can I get some service? A nice cut of pork, perhaps? Or a plate of mussels?"

Abraham glanced up, raising his hand, bidding me wait, then froze. "*Oy vey*." For a long while, he just stared, finally nodding to Baldy, who opened a gate-door in the divider. Baldy stepped back, one hand hidden beneath his cloak. Locks, his mirror, stood at attention as well.

"Thanks." I shouldered past Baldy, pulled the chair in front of Abraham's desk out and sat. A cloak hung across the back of it, a yellow Star of David sewn onto it.

"Krait." Abraham studied me.

"Abe," I smiled. "How long has it been?"

Abraham didn't say '*not long enough,*' but I could read it on his face. "I had heard you might be back in the city."

"Oh?" Jesus. So much for discretion.

"And I heard some troubling news." He slashed a quick check in a ledger. "News about highwaymen and murder in the Hellwood." He peered over his glasses at my gashed forehead, bandaged with a swathe cut from my crow tabard. "I could fix you a poultice?"

"It's nothing." I shrugged. "Just some rough and tumble."

"People are people," he sighed, "everywhere."

"You ever hear of a place where people aren't people, let me know."

"I expected the wool shipment yesterday, today at the latest. I started to worry."

"Fear not. I'm here to quell all your worrying."

"All of it?" Behind Abraham, an iron door opened into a small vault. Two men worked in conjunction on the lock mechanism of the door.

"Well, most of it."

"Talk." Abraham moved aside a stack of papers using his left hand. His right arm ended just above the elbow. Stacks of paper piled like stepped ziggurats ranged across his desk. Rocks and paperweights sat upon each, one in particular most interesting, a crude effigy of a man carved in stone. Its eyes shone of polished coal, the glint in them almost alive. The piles went on for days. Apparently having only one arm didn't hold Abraham back from work. "You have the shipment, then?"

"Uh, no."

"Then how is that supposed to quell my worrying?"

"There's no shipment anymore. So what's there to worry about?"

"I've already received the shipment." He pulled off his glasses and rubbed the bridge of his nose. "Yesterday."

"Truly?" I pulled the starred cloak from the back of the chair the instant Abraham's eyes closed and slid it under my own. I was making quite the collection. Volkendorf. Jew. The only sigil I didn't have in my possession was a red serpent on field of black, which happened to be my own. "Then we're square?"

"A man sauntered in yesterday claiming he'd found said shipment abandoned on the Stettin Road, near the old way station."

"That doesn't sound entirely accurate."

Abraham sat back, face reddening.

"And you believed him?" I asked. "This good Samaritan?"

"I paid three times its worth."

"Bad Samaritan, then."

"He had it all right here, all marked, stamped. He even had the trade manifest, signed by you. May I ask why I had to pay three times the shipment's worth to receive it?"

"Poor business acumen?"

"The shipment is where it needs to be. Fear not."

"Oh, I wasn't afraid."

"At considerable cost." Abraham kept writing.

"How do you know it wasn't at considerable cost to

me as well?"

"Because you're still here, and you're still quipping like a petulant child."

"Well, I'm just more than a little surprised at you. Paying *three times* its worth."

"It was one of Lord Raachwald's men. He didn't say it, but I know of him. Thin fellow. Yellow eyes." Abraham stifled a shudder. "That man makes my skin crawl, something *unnatural* about him, but I paid him, which makes it *good* business acumen, considering I'm still physically able to conduct business."

"Maybe you should have bought insurance?"

"*You* were the insurance."

"Better insurance?"

"He took the horses and cart as well, I trust?"

"The horses died. One around Stettin. The other that night. Old Yellow-Eyes had the foresight, along with his lord, to bring their own. Fortuitous."

Abraham wrestled another ledger in front of him and opened it, spine creaking, to a white page mark. "Ten crates of wool. Two horses. One wagon." He dipped a pen in red ink and marked a column.

"Red ink?" I peered over the tome.

Abraham ran a finger along a column, made another mark.

"Is red ink good?"

"It signifies hemorrhaging."

"That'd be a '*no*' then."

He set the pen down. "Is this a game to you? Because it's my life, my family's lives, my workers' lives. And if I may ask an indelicate question?"

I nodded.

"Where is Hyram's man?"

"Hyram?" I tapped my finger against my pursed lips.

"The man who hired you." His jaw clenched nearly shut. "The man to whom I vouched for you. The man for whom I paid three times as much as they were worth to secure his goods. The man who pays you. Where is his man currently?"

"Oh, that Hyram."

"Yes. That Hyram. And his man, Albert, I believe." Abraham snatched a contract and squinted at it at arm's length. "Yes. Albert Saint John."

I shook my head. "He was anything but saintly, Abe."

"Don't call me, Abe, please."

"Right. Anyways. I did him a favor."

"Albert? Or Hyram?"

"Both."

"Why am I assuming you did quite the opposite?"

"Well, old Albert never had much in common with any saints. Except now."

"He's dead, isn't he?"

"Most saints are. Sort of a requirement, you see?"

Abraham took a long breath, let it out through pursed lips as he dipped a new pen in black ink. "When did he die?"

"Mid-February-ish." I closed my eyes, trying to remember. "The fifteenth. Sixteenth or so."

"And where did he die?"

"The road to Stettin."

"Remind me not to go to Stettin." Abraham started scribbling. "Is there any chance it was an accidental death? Or plague? Natural causes, perhaps?"

"Sure."

He scanned the contract then wrote something in the same column.

"We're in the black again?" I smiled. "That's good."

"A man died."

"Old Albert had no family so no payout."

"Memorial costs. Heriot, death taxes."

"Ah. The Lord Bishop wants his cut."

Abraham nodded as he finished writing. "Hyram will not take this lightly."

"Lucky I'm still around."

"Lucky for whom?"

"Me, mostly. Hyram, too, though. Tell him Albert was stealing. He's not anymore."

"You tell him."

"You're the middle-man. That's our arrangement. The less I talk to people the better."

"I cannot argue with that line of thought."

"Tell him Albert was a rotten thief."

"That's what you always claim when things of this nature occur."

"Well, I never catch the adroit thieves."

"Your people might take it ill, your killing one of your own in the service of a Jew."

"I didn't do it for a Jew."

"Hyram's a Jew. I'm a Jew."

"And here I thought Hyram and Abraham were good Irish names."

Abraham's eyebrows knitted together nearly into one. "You do realize *thou shall not kill* is a maxim universal to both Jew *and* Christian. You seem to flout it with alarming regularity."

"As do most Christians. So I'm in good company. Or bad. Anyways. Christianity is very limiting. How's a guard supposed to turn the other cheek? He wouldn't be a guard for very long. And anyways, I don't do the right thing simply on principle. Sets a bad precedent. People might start having expectations of me."

"I have little fear of that occurring."

"I'll just have to buy an indulgence."

"You have money, then?"

"Not much." I raised my coin purse and jiggled it.

Abraham cocked his head. "Rocks?" His eyes lit upon the stone figure on his papers. Muttering beneath his breath, he reached forward, snatched it from its pile, and shoved it in a drawer.

"Mostly." I reached into my coin purse, dug through the rocks and drew out the second of Lord Volkendorf's golden rings. I'd had to bribe the Lord Bishop's guards with the other ring, a nondescript one, to allow me through the

Quarter's gates, so I had the one left. It was gold, with the Volkendorf crest prominent on it. "Here." I slid it across the table. "Recompense for the shipment."

Abraham leaned forward, adjusting his glasses. Recognition blossomed in conjunction with horror, his face blanching as he thrust it back. "By the—" he hissed. "Put that away. If you were found here? With *that*?" He peered around the room. Business was transacting, and no one seemed to care. The two guards were still eyeing me. I expected that might not stop. "I asked about money. Do you have any?"

"A few coins. The yellow-eyed bastard who fleeced you robbed me."

"Hyram had misgivings about hiring you. I vouched for you despite your reputation," Abraham shook his head, "despite my better judgement, and I do not take the killing of a man lightly, as you seem to. I shall need to revisit our business arrangement."

"Albert was stealing," I repeated. "And I didn't do it for Hyram, as I said."

"He pays you."

"Yes. Amongst many others, he pays me. To guard wares. And believe me, I'm no prude. A little wool from each crate's always going to pad every trader's profit. Can't be helped. The cost of doing business."

"So, you commit murder and advocate theft, just murder that is justified and theft within reason?"

"Sounds about right."

"And you presume to judge others? The Greeks would accuse you of *hubris*."

"Any around?" I glanced over my shoulder, didn't see any, wiped my forehead. "Whew, that was close…"

He shook his head. "What other commandments have you broken?"

"Today? Jesus-fucking-Christ, Abe, not a single one. Look," I shoved papers out of the way, leaned forward, "everyone's going to shave a little. Albert was shaving a lot."

"*Oy Vey.* So you killed him?"

"You want it that simply? Then yes. But I didn't do it for Hyram. You think I give a shit about Hyram?"

"I am beginning to believe that you don't care about anything. What an empty existence you must lead."

"An empty existence, maybe, but not an empty belly. And a guard who lets the wares he's hired to protect get stolen doesn't often have a full belly. Are we done?"

"I lost a lot of money and a lot of credibility on this venture. I was forced to deal with Lord Raachwald," Abraham swallowed, "a lord known not to suffer fools, or Jews, or anyone, gladly. And his predilection for murder is fairly well known."

"That's one way to put it," I muttered.

"*Hubris*, Krait, I understand your deficiencies." He shook his head. "But, Stephan, a cooler head, a level head. Where was he during this transaction? I cannot believe he advocated this."

"You trust Stephan more than me?"

"I trust Karl more than you. I trusted the horses more than you, but yes, I trust Stephan as much as I can trust anyone, Christian or Jew. He's the only reason I vouched for you. I thought him capable of keeping you in check."

"A tall order, but surprise-surprise, Stephan's the one that pulled the trigger."

Abraham looked over his glasses. "Could you clarify that?"

"Stephan's the one who confronted Albert."

"I ask again. Stephan advocated the killing of this man?"

"Stephan confronted him, and things got heated. Stephan caught him in the act. Red-handed. Red, just like your ink. And no. You know Stephan. He doesn't advocate the killing of anyone. For anything. He wanted Albert brought before the local lord and tried in a court of law."

"And you interceded for the path of violence." His lips pursed. "And you were once a bailiff. Tsk. Tsk."

"I prefer justiciar." I nearly punched him in the head

when he made that '*Tsk*' noise, but I restrained myself, heroically. "Bailiff sounds like a paper-pusher. No offense."

"Semantics aside, have you not even a rudimentary understanding of the law?"

"That's generally frowned upon in the justiciar business."

"Stephan was correct. He should have been brought to court, tried," Abraham said. "The court documents might have proven useful in recouping the loss."

"Don't look at me like that, Abe. We're on the road, fifty leagues from anywhere that doesn't use cow-shit for currency. Everyone's rough. Everyone's ragged. A man's stealing. Gets caught. Red-handed. Lies." I threw my hands up. "Things got heated. They tend to when you catch someone in the act. People get defensive. Then they get offensive. Stephan *was* level-headed, even, infuriatingly fair, but Albert wasn't. And you know Stephan. When he knows he's in the right? Yeah. A real pain in the arse. A pain in the arse who refuses to go strapped. So now I can sit back and watch Albert murder my brother, or I can do something."

"And what exactly did you do?"

"Me? Well, nothing, actually. I could barely stand, let alone hold a sword. Bad food. Or good wine. A combination of both?" I shrugged, unsure. "It was Karl actually killed him. Quick. Like he does. No fuss. Albert didn't suffer if that's any consolation."

"None whatsoever." He jotted something down. "You claim it was Stephan that confronted him initially?"

"Yes."

"I'd like to hear it from him."

"Well, that ain't going to happen."

Abraham held my gaze, saw something, shook his head. "*Oy gevalt*. Forgive me. You said at *considerable* cost. My wroth clouded my judgement. I did not hear. Your brother? Is he alright? And Karl? The others? What happened with Lord Raachwald?"

"The others are all dead. Dead defending Hyram's wool." Well, actually, themselves, but it sounded better this way. "Karl was alive last I saw him."

Abraham closed his eyes as though steeling himself. "And poor Stephan?"

I raised a hand. "He's not dead. Raachwald's got him in his dungeons. Languishing. First Dunmire. Now the Isle. Raachwald cut his hand off. He's dying, Abe."

"He's back in the city?" Abraham murmured to himself, scrambling for a sheaf of parchment. "How much do you require?" His pen was poised.

"Require for what?"

He held the parchment up, a promissory note. "What is Lord Raachwald demanding for the ransom?"

"Fifty," I said offhand.

"Fifty what?"

"Uh…crowns."

Abraham sucked in between his teeth, held it, then released, nodding to himself. "Fifty." He scribbled the sum.

"Just like that?" I asked.

Abraham waved off the question.

"What if it were me being held and Stephan here?" I asked. "What would you offer then?"

"My condolences."

"Yeah. Well. Jesus, you're a prick."

Abraham smacked his pen down. "*You* are lying."

"What?"

"Honestly." He slammed the book shut. "Trying to profit off your brother's hardship is repellant even for you."

"Yeah," I shrugged, "I guess so."

"Fah!" His finger was waggling in my face as though he were my grandmother scolding me for stealing cookies. "How I ever vouched for you is beyond me. I must have been sick, sick in the mind. Money. It's always money with men like you." He pointed at the door. "Please, leave and do not return."

"Yeah. Alright. I lied. But about the sum. Not about Stephan. Not about his predicament. I need your help."

"Not my problem."

"He needs your help. Raachwald's going to execute

161

him if he's not dead before."

"Did he give a sum?" He stared into my eyes, trying to read them. "He must have given a sum." I shook my head. He murmured something beneath his breath, and his face went white again. "What…what is it he wants?"

"He wants the murderer of his son brought to him on a silver platter."

"The murderer of his son?" Abraham sat back, wind stolen from him. "And he has chosen you for this?"

"As you said. I was a justiciar. So yeah. He chose me. Serendipity's delight. For Stephan to have any chance at seeing the light of day, I have to do this. I have four days. We need your help."

"But not coin?" Abraham pulled a handkerchief and polished his glasses.

"No." I shook my head. "Information."

"I would prefer coin."

"So would I."

He took a deep breath, his expression that of a man about to step onto a sheet of ice of unknown thickness. "Brokering information is a dangerous activity."

"So's rotting in Raachwald's dungeon."

Abraham hazarded a step out onto the ice. "What is it you require?"

"Do you know what happened?"

"No." Abraham was taken aback. "Of course not. How would I? But always, you hear things, rumor, innuendo. Lord Raachwald's son was murdered along with others."

"Yeah. Lord Volkendorf and his boys. I just visited them."

"The ring," Abraham muttered to himself. "Yes. I had heard this. Everyone had heard, but the past month, with the plague and so many taken, such a…a terrible thing. And these murders. What is it I can do to help you? To help Stephan?"

"I need to know about Lord Volkendorf."

He murmured something beneath his breath. "What is it you need to know?"

"I need to know if he had any outstanding debts. I need to know how much and to whom. I need to know if the ownership of Coldspire was in jeopardy. I'm told it might have been. His business dealings, anything you can get me."

"Records of that nature are generally confidential."

"It's for Stephan, Abe, not for me. And I know they're generally confidential. But I need to know."

"I never lent to the man."

"He came here at some point. To this street. And talked to one of the moneylenders. Took out a loan. Probably many loans."

"I'm not the only money house in the quarter."

"But you are one of the biggest. One of the oldest. You know the others. You're all part of the Hanseatic. You could ask a few questions. Quietly. The crow's dead. It won't ruffle his feathers."

"It's not him I'm worried about," Abraham whispered. "I correspond with a number of men throughout the kingdoms, the empire, one as far as Novgorod in the east, Jerusalem in the Holy Land. Many men, widespread across the land, and I have heard stories of other cities. Of Strasbourg. Mainz. Esselheim. Massacres. Pograms. Holocausts. Have you heard these same stories?"

I nodded. "Yeah."

"And these stories, they are true?"

"Some." I nodded. "Most probably."

"I had held out hope that they were confabulation, but in my heart, I knew them for truth. I had hoped the times of the past were simply that, but some of those men I was telling you about? They have ceased correspondence. I know not whether they are dead. Many wrote warning of the scapegoating transpiring, laying the blame upon my community for the widespread hardship, as though we were not suffering, too. It is as it always has been, as it always shall be, I fear. Tell me something, Krait."

"What is it?"

"You travel much. Have you witnessed these atrocities?"

"Yeah." I'd seen them too much.

"Always, there have been attacks against my people. It is part of who we are, I suppose." He shook his head in despair. "It has happened throughout our history. It has happened everywhere, but those atrocities have never been so abundant, so frequent, so near."

"I understand your concern."

"I wonder truly if you do."

"Plague's outside, Abe. It could hit anyone. Everyone. I've walked through ghost cities. Not even a half-starved dog to chase rats. Bodies in the streets. Christian and Jew. All gone. Show me someone who hasn't lost. Who isn't lost."

"The plague is Shaitan's work. I speak of the work of men. I speak of things that might be averted."

"Averted?"

"Your brother has always been good to me, Krait. A better Christian I have never known, truly, but if the death of Lord Volkendorf and his brood were somehow connected, however tenuously, to my people, it would prove our end. Your people would descend upon us with fire and vengeance."

"Well, let's hope there's no connection then, however tenuous."

"This is no jest," Abraham hissed. "You must promise me, swear to me that you will use the utmost discretion. Swear it by whatever you hold most holy."

"I swear on Stephan's soul and the souls of my children."

Abraham fidgeted for a moment. "Then I...I shall ask your questions, discreetly, for Stephan's sake, but I can promise you nothing. Come back later. Tonight. A few hours hence. Just, I beg of you, use the utmost caution. Times are bad for my people, Krait."

"Times are bad for everybody's people, Abe. You been outside lately?"

"Yes, and I have borne my share of loss, but as bad as times are for you and yours, they are always worse for me and mine."

Chapter 19.

"I AM BEING so very sorry, *Herr* Krait." Schultz wrung his bar towel between meaty fists.

"It's fair to say then," I placed both hands on the bar, "that my room and meals'll be on the house for the foreseeable future, yeah?" It seemed my mail shirt had gone missing. Schultz didn't know how. Didn't know when. Didn't know who. It was just gone. He shrugged apologetically then set a bowl of unseasoned lentil soup in front of me.

I ate.

I had nothing going but to wait on Abraham, pray he dredged up a thread to pull. I'd track down the knight, Sir Myron Chalstain, after I met with Abraham, after I'd eaten, after I'd tipped back a drink, settled my soul. I was halfway through dinner at the Stone Ruin Ten by the time Lorelai finally appeared. I'd been hoping it'd be Karl who appeared, but it was tough to argue with her.

But she was hanging off the arm of that same black-bearded bastard, roaring his head off with laughter as she clutched her gut, nearly crying herself merry.

I gagged down another mouthful of the soup. It was warm, and there was plenty of it, which about summed up its good points. But I've had worse, and I've had none. So I wasn't complaining.

The lovely pair staggered past, Blackbeard slapping some yokel on the back and saying something that made beer shoot out of his nose. All the maids and whores guffawed, all the men around, too. The yokel wiped his face and pounded the table, plates, and wares jumping, and ordered a round for the house. Blackbeard roared.

I was grumbling to my lentils when Schultz set a tankard down in front of me, filled sloshing to the brim with golden brown ale. Cold. Pungent. I took a moment to think about God in all his glory, corners of my jaw tingling as I salivated, taking a deep breath and inhaling. I licked my lips, savoring pre-coital bliss, and then the conception as the smooth enameled tankard pressed cool against my lips as I tilted my head back, eyes closed, all the merriment in the tavern numbed to blurred silence, the golden brown wetting my lips and mouth then sliding down as smooth as Jesus Christ in velvet pants.

Setting the tankard down, I wiped my chin with the back of my hand. "Amen."

Lorelai appeared next to me, leaning against the bar, smirking. Her hair was swept over to one side and hung down loose. Disheveled. Her pupils were dilated. She looked content. Drunk. She ran a hand through my hair then pinched my cheek, suppressing a giggle.

"Hey there." Her smile lit up the room.

"Greetings, my lady."

She pivoted on her stool, resting her elbows on the bar as she leaned back, legs splayed out wide before her. She rolled her head back, looking up at the ceiling then over her shoulder, finally settling her gaze on me. "Hey there."

"Hey there, yourself."

She nodded to Schultz, raised a hand, two fingers extended.

"You're in a good place," I said.

She shook her head and laughed. "Could think of a few better."

"Same here."

"How was your errand?" She took the pair of tankards Schultz set out and slid one my way. She sucked hers down, tilting it back, watching me over the tipped brim with those green eyes.

"Thanks." I took my new brew in hand. "My errand?" I took a pull.

"You were headed to…" She pressed a finger against her lower lip and shrugged. "I don't know."

"It went splendidly."

"I waited for you."

"Well, here I am."

She leaned in close, hand brushing against the roughness of my cheek. Her other hand discreetly found my thigh beneath the bar; then it found something else, not so discreetly, just as the sound of boots clomping penetrated through my mounting haze of lust and booze.

Lorelai jumped to her feet and began fumbling with her hair, pushing it back, smoothing out her dress.

I shoveled the last spoonful of my lentils in, hand near my dagger. "How many?" I asked, mouth full, still chewing.

"Eight," she whispered, a rictus frozen on her face. "The Lord Bishop's man, a priest, Father Paul."

"Well," I took a hard pull, "I am overdue for confession."

"Love to hear that tale."

"Watch. His ears'll start bleeding."

Lorelai turned. "Hello. Father Paul, isn't it?"

I turned. Smooth. Slow.

A tall stately priest stood ringed by armed men. "Yes." Taking Lorelai's hand in his, he bowed deep, low, gracefully. He might have been a courtier. His robes were immaculate white and moved like rippling liquid. His hair was a deep brown, grey just starting to play at his temples. His eyes were clear as blue sky. "A pleasure to meet you, milady. Please forgive the late-hour intrusion."

"It's never late here, Father," I said.

"I've heard your sermons," Lorelai interjected, blushing. She curtsied like a little girl. "They're wonderfully moving, and I do believe you. You'll fix this city."

"Thank you for that, my lady," he beamed, releasing her hand, "but it is *we* who shall fix it. Together."

I almost puked in my mouth.

"Are you hungry, Father?" Lorelai thumbed over her shoulder. "I know it doesn't look it, and times are tight, but I could scare up a dish worth eating."

"Relax, he's a priest." Not that that often mattered.

"Regrettably, no, my dear lady," Father Paul said, either not hearing me or ignoring. He was about as tall as me, slender, had a well-trimmed mustache and beard. "I am here on other business. More, ah, important business." His eyes lit upon me. He bowed, not as low as he had for Lorelai, but lower than custom dictated. "Sir Luther Slythe Krait, I presume?"

"You presume right, Father." Shit. So someone had told them who I was, where I was, when I was. I smiled, stood, put out a hand. "Pleased to meet you," I lied.

Father Paul shook my hand firmly. "You must forgive me as well, but I humbly request you accompany me for an audience with His Eminence, the Lord Bishop."

"I was about to hit the hay, father."

He cleared his throat, smiled. "It is at His Eminence's *specific* request, Sir Luther."

"An audience?"

"Yes."

"As honored guest?" I raised my eyebrows at Lorelai.

Father Paul continued smiling but having the good graces to loosen his collar with one finger while he did so. "Ah, something to that effect." He was a terrible liar.

I glanced at the armed guards, fanned out, weapons sheathed, hands by them, clenching, unclenching. "Do I have a choice, father?"

"You always have a choice, my son."

"Like asking which side of the blade I'd like to be cut with?"

"I am but a humble messenger," Father Paul said.

"You arresting me?"

"Forgive me," Father Paul said. "This is out of the ordinary, I know. You are not being arrested…"

"But?" I waited.

"But you are coming." The squad's captain stepped forward, past his men, past the priest. He was shorter than me but broader, solid looking. He spoke with a muted lisp, and I could see he had a slight hare-lip hidden beneath his mustache. His eyes were serious. The azure cross of Saint Hagan's Cathedral was slathered across his armored chest.

"This is Captain Thorne." Father Paul extended a hand. "Commander of the Lord Bishop's men."

"Might I inquire as to the reason for this, er, audience?" I looked to Father Paul. "That's what you called it, yeah?"

"No, you may not." Captain Thorne stepped aside, raising a hand toward the exit. "This way. Smartly now, sir." His men parted before him like the Red Sea, leaving me a clear shot to the door. The gauntlet. The room had gone quiet. All eyes. Captain Thorne offered a stiff bow, his eyes never leaving mine. "Please."

"Then, I humbly acquiesce to his Lord's request." I returned his bow like my dear mother taught me. Real gracious-like. "My lady." I turned to Lorelai, took her hand in mine, holding it as I might a bird, little heart twittering within my fingers. I pecked it gently then let said bird fly yonder. "Another time."

...be described as genial terms, but I parleyed nonetheless with Hughes, perfunctory leader of the Razors, a gang of thieves that infests Asylum's western half. He was willing to parley in order to absolve his people of...
—*Journal of Sir Myron Chalstain*

Chapter 20.

THE MAN STOOD as best he could considering his condition, beaten, broken, his right shoulder slumped at such a severe angle it had to be shattered. But he stood proud. Defiant. Nonetheless. A once orange tabard clung round his shoulders, now brown, red, black, in tatters. The device of a wheel was on it, near unrecognizable. Grimacing, he adjusted his hanging arm, drawing it across his abdomen with his good hand, shifting uncomfortably every few seconds, trying to hold back a grimace, doing a fair job. Better than I'd have done.

Captain Thorne's escort had grown from eight to about forty, along with a crowd of two hundred or so, come to stand out on a blisteringly raw March night to watch the festivities. Folk do *so love* a good hanging, so long as it ain't their own.

A gallows tree sprouted from the top of the hill, a great bent gnarly old thing with branches thicker than my waist clawing off up into the sky. Yggdrasil. The World Tree incarnate. Torches flickered in the strong breeze. A noose hung nearly to the ground.

Father Paul stood next to me, hands folded. "Apparently, Sir Carmichael took it upon himself to attack the Jewish Quarter this morning. When the Lord Bishop's men fought off him and his men, Sir Carmichael decided to barricade the bridge." He leaned toward me as he spoke, lips barely moving, nearly a ventriloquist act. "All in an effort to upset trade, foment strife, make His Eminence appear indecisive, weak. It garnered opposite results. Sir Carmichael now refuses to relinquish the names of his compatriots, his backers, though, undoubtedly it is through an affiliation with the Isle Men, Lord Raachwald, most likely. Sir Carmichael is an outsider, a sell-sword, you see?"

Nodding, I just watched Sir Carmichael standing there, pale, wavering in the cold. His eyes never abandoned that noose. Captain Thorne, by his side, placed a hand on his shoulder and whispered something in his ear. Sir Carmichael closed his eyes, listening, then nodded once, took a deep breath, opened his eyes. He seemed stronger then. Fuller. He let go of his broken arm, let it hang, and stood up straight. I couldn't hear what he said, but could see him mouth the words, "*My thanks.*"

One of the Lord Bishop's men finished reading Sir Carmichael's sentence. I couldn't hear any of it. Father Paul was still jawing in my ear, "…a contingent of John Gaunt's Teutonics broke them, slaughtered them all, except for Carmichael."

Sidelong, I glanced at Father Paul.

His Eminence, the Lord Bishop of Asylum City, Judas Peter, sat upon the crown of Gallows Hill, holding court out of the arse end of an ornate wagon. Crooked and slumped he sat, heavy furs cast over his shoulders, his frame spare. His crozier, the staff of his office, stood upright before him. Behind and at attention two guards stood, armed, as tall and straight as His Eminence was not. He slurped and twitched a nod to Captain Thorne.

The hillside stretched down and away from the Lord Bishop, ending in a cemetery which stretched all the way to the walls surrounding Saint Hagan's. Beyond, the cathedral rose monstrous.

"The sentence is death," Captain Thorne belted out in a clarion call that pierced the wind, "to be carried out immediately." He nodded to the hooded executioner, placed something in his hand, stepped back. "Have you any last words, Sir Carmichael?"

"Aye." Sir Carmichael coughed. "Forgive me father, for…for I have sinned." He glanced up in question to the stone-faced captain. "T'was Lord Raachwald who hired me. He that set me to do the…the work." Sir Carmichael swallowed.

Captain Thorne offered a nod, an almost imperceptible twitch, and Sir Carmichael hobbled forward and eased himself down, laboriously, one knee at a time, to the hard earth. Before him stood a wooden block. A basket sat next to it. He took a deep breath and leaned forward, his Adam's apple touching the bare hardness of the wood. Poised, eyes closed, he knelt there, waiting.

"The axe, not the noose?" I muttered.

"He confessed," Father Paul said. "A small token of His Eminence's generosity of spirit, I suppose you might say."

"You might," I grunted. "To me, generosity'd mean he walks out of here on two legs, head still attached."

Father Paul crossed himself. "Indeed."

"How's the axe-man?" I'd witnessed executions gone awry. Far too many. Two chops. Five chops, once with a particularly thick-necked squire who'd lacked the proper resources to bribe his sanctioned killer. Poor lad. The last money you'll spend but worth every penny.

"As good as you pay him to be." Father Paul watched, eyes rapt. "I'm told you were on the bridge this morning."

"Busy day."

"Daring heroics, they say," Father Paul commented.

"They say a lot." I shrugged.

"May I ask what you were doing on the east side?"

"Business," I answered.

"The Jewish Quarter, then, I presume?"

I raised an eyebrow.

"A busy bee you are. Might I ask how you circumvented the guards?"

"I bribed them," I answered.

He nodded succinctly. "And what was your business there?"

"I'm just a caravan guard," I grunted.

"They say you are conducting an investigation."

Captain Thorne nodded succinctly to the

executioner, who stepped forward, that monstrous, wide-bladed axe poised at his shoulder. Teeth bared, he snatched at his hood as a sudden gust almost tore it from his head. It passed after a moment. The crowd let out a mock-cheer. Adjusting his hood, the executioner grinned, offering a half bow. They ate it up. Captain Thorne leaned in, whispering something, "*Get the fuck on with it,*" most likely. Nodding, the executioner placed the wide axe head on the floor, spat in one palm and then clapped them both together, rubbing them.

The crowd cheered again, laughing this time. Guffawing.

Captain Thorne was seething.

"And what's it to *them*?" I asked.

"I am merely trying to apprise you of the fact that the Lord Bishop is ignorant of neither your existence nor movements within Asylum. A warning, I suppose." He raised a hand to the scene before us. "And example. The Lord Bishop does not molly-coddle with regards to justice, nor the meting out of justice, and if you are conducting an investigation, you would seem to be meting out justice, no?"

I shrugged, grunted, eloquently.

"You were a bailiff, yes?"

"Yeah." *Justiciar*, but I didn't want to quibble at present. "A long time ago."

"Ahem." Father Paul cleared his throat. "You would seem to be carrying out justice for the Lord Bishop's enemies, then."

"Lord Bishop afraid he won't get his cut?"

"In a manner of speaking, no, and in another, yes."

I smirked. Sourly.

Father Paul gave pause. "The money itself is inconsequential, you understand?" He raised a finger as though lecturing a classroom. "But it is a symbol, and symbols bear power, would you not agree?"

"Sure."

"And the lord of any fief should, of course, receive any windfall associated with any justice dispensed within it.

That is the law. And so, extrapolating from that, the very act of your dispensation of justice under his enemy's aegis within this city, his city, is unacceptable. Treasonous, even. That is how he sees it. You must understand that."

"Mummer's Isle is under the Lord Bishop's control?" I asked. "How about the whole east side?"

"Nominally, yes." Father Paul cocked his head to the side. "In actuality?" He raised his hands. "As I said before, I am but a legate, a messenger in this particular instance, and I am offering you a warning. Arguing perceptions, real or imagined, with men in power, lords, this one, in particular, is not an activity that promises a healthy span."

"Fair enough."

"A man in power remains so because people believe him a strong leader, a strong man. Once that belief is fractured... Well, you understand?"

I glanced over at the Lord Bishop as his miter hat slumped over on his head, sliding across that liver-spotted orb, stopping just shy of plummeting by the grace of God alone. "Never seen one stronger."

"Yes, well, I meant not *physically*, of course," came Father Paul's lame reply.

"I know what you meant."

The executioner hefted axe to shoulder and adjusted his grip, taking his time, finding those grooves that spoke to his hands, telling him all was adjusted accordingly, precisely. His shoulders were loose. His fingers opened and closed on the haft, steam rolling out from his masked face, smooth, even, measured. *Focused*, a word that came to mind. That was good. For Sir Carmichael. At this point.

"What is it you want?" I asked.

"I'll spare you the Samaritan speech."

"Many thanks."

"The Lord Bishop has an interest in finding someone."

"Someone who?"

"Your predecessor, with regards to the murder

you're investigating. A Sir Myron Chalstain."

"Is he missing?"

"Yes, in a manner of speaking." He swallowed then glanced to either side of him. "He disappeared near a month past, not long after the Isle murders. It has been kept under wraps. No one was to know. A matter of propriety, you understand? The disappearance of the chief investigative officer of the Lord Bishop? A most unseemly business. We suspect Lord Raachwald. It's common knowledge he threatened to hurl Sir Myron from the Bastard's Bridge." Father Paul rolled his crucifix between gloved fingers. "I should appreciate it greatly if you would be willing to share any information you might garner through your current investigation. The two crimes, in my mind, seem inextricably linked."

"How do you know Chalstain's disappearance was a crime?"

"Sir Myron was operating under great duress, that was clear, telling and clear. He met with numerous obstacles, roadblocks, and the Lord Bishop has moved on to other things it seems, things of higher import."

"Like waging a street war?"

"Ugly, but yes. But men in power must do what they must to preserve order. And it was not he who struck the first blow. In any case, no one seems to be gaining any ground with regards to the locating of Sir Myron. No one seems to be doing much of anything, except, perhaps you. Perhaps you might find something useful? You have something of a reputation as a sleuth, I'm told."

"Sleuth?"

He nodded, patiently.

"By who?" I asked.

"Whom."

"What?"

"Never mind. By 'They.' The same 'They' who know everybody, and on top of that, I merely wished to warn you of the Lord Bishop. He will not take kindly to you serving Lord Raachwald in any capacity, least of all this. His

Eminence takes it as a personal insult, in point of fact, so you will be starting off the game behind."

"Same place I usually finish."

"I pray not. I pray you accomplish your task, and I pray you do not lie to His Eminence. He is more aware than he seems."

I glanced over at the Lord Bishop, practically snoring upright in his chair. "He'd have to be."

"He is no fool, despite appearances. I beg you not treat him as such, or in so doing, you shall find yourself in Sir Carmichael's company, and swiftly."

The executioner swung the axe from over his head and down onto the chopping block, a precision cut, strong, connected, directed. The blade chunked into the wood, and Sir Carmichael's head hit the bottom of the basket with a *thunk*, a thing of blessed-beauty considering the alternative. The crowd erupted in cheers. The executioner began taking bows.

The Lord Bishop's mean little eyes were already awake and aware and upon me the instant Sir Carmichael's head plopped into the basket. They locked on, terrier strong, watching, and did not waver. Greedy little eyes.

"Come. Best not keep His Eminence waiting." Father Paul held out a hand to guide me. Together we strode up to the Lord Bishop, Captain Thorne marching up from the chopping block, the head-basket clutched in his hands, dripping from below. Father Paul continued beneath his breath, "His Eminence has grown testy in his many years. He is hard of hearing though loathe to admit it, so speak strongly, and allot him ample time to speak, to reply. Patience. He suffered a stroke last year and struggles yet with the reality of his disabilities. Also he…"

"What?"

"I shouldn't be telling you this," Father Paul crossed himself, "but they call him the Vulture. His countenance favors…" He waved a hand. "Forgive me. Forget I mentioned anything. I do not know if you are already aware of the moniker, but best you not refer to him as such. He does not relish it."

"Right."

Captain Thorne fell in behind us a few strides from the Vulture's—shit—the *Lord Bishop's* makeshift throne. I glanced into the basket. Sir Carmichael was still dead.

Father Paul knelt, grunting as his knees touched earth, and bade me do likewise, which I did. Captain Thorne bowed stiffly from the waist then brought the basket to His Eminence, tilting it for the old bird to inspect. His Eminence offered a half-glance then waved, rings glinting like far-off stars, dismissing Captain Thorne as though he were offering a vintage of wine not quite to his liking. His frown deepened as he studied me through rheumy eyes, glinting within the shadow of his ridiculous hat, rendered even more so by its precarious position, perched as though cliff side and contemplating suicide.

I chose to withhold comment. A rare moment of clarity.

The Vulture grimaced, and Father Paul cleared his throat, nudging me with an elbow. The wind blew cold. I swallowed, rose, approached.

Close up, the Lord Bishop did look like the weathered carrion bird that was his namesake, his furs over robes of office giving him a hunched appearance, like great wings folded behind. And with his scaly neck gawking forward, neck waddle loose and jiggling, wrinkled face hairless and grim, I could imagine him gnashing his teeth and worrying flesh from some long rotting corpse. The Lord Bishop sniffed, wiped his nose with his sleeve then reached out, palsied hand rising, episcopal ring prominent and shaking like a leaf in the wind.

"You may, *heh*," he spoke as though half of his mouth were sewn shut, "make your obeisance."

Kneeling, I took his hand, that sallow, liver-spotted claw, vessels squiggling like tumescent worms beneath its surface, joints swollen near to burst, and I kissed it. Long. Hard. Enthusiastically. "Forgive me, father, for I have sinned." The words hadn't helped Sir Carmichael, but maybe they were due.

Behind, whetstone rang on steel as the executioner began sharpening his axe.

Shing...

Shing...

Shing...

"Arise, my son, Sir Luther Slythe, *heh*, Krait." The Vulture's voice was a strangled, wheezing cough. "Your name is not unknown to me."

I remained on knee a moment then swallowed and stood. "Your Eminence." Saint Hagan's rose behind him like a mountain sculpted to the will of God, a halo of torch and stone.

The Vulture repositioned himself, leaning forward, hunger gleaming in his carrion-bird eyes. "I'm told you are snatching what is mine, snatching and then offering it to another." He grimaced, showing brown teeth. "And that *other* is my nemesis. This I was told. It is conjecture. I give you leave to refute it. I give you leave to beg for your life. For, *heh*, that is law."

"Your Eminence, I thought this a simple summons?"

The old man slammed a fist on the armrest of his chair. "Did you not look in the basket?" His face twitched and contorted as he fought to speak. "A Gypsy's crystal, foretelling your future?" He cocked his head at such a horrible angle I feared it might topple off. It didn't. Unfortunately. "Or I could have you hanged like a common thief, Krait. Not even offering you the honor of the axe. Captain Thorne," his eyes moved past me, "perhaps he thinks me soft?"

Captain Thorne chose to withhold comment.

"Your Eminence," I raised my hands, "forgive me. What you accuse me of is true. I'll not deny it. I cannot. But my actions were performed under duress. Simply put, I was forced into this role. I desire no part of it."

"Forced by who?"

"By Lord Raachwald and the Lady of Coldspire,

Narcissa Volkendorf."

"*Raachwald.*" The old man seethed at the name, squirming in his seat like a steam kettle set to burst. "The man's an apostate, a pagan, a worshipper of things unclean." He stretched his neck, vertebrae creaking like desiccated leather. "I am the rule in Asylum, and it falls to me to dispense justice within its borders." He crossed himself, his eyes never leaving mine. "And yet you seek to do so without warrant issued by my own hand."

"Again, apologies, your Eminence." I dropped back to a penitent knee. "Forgive me. Your statement is accurate. I meant not to intrude or overstep bounds or impinge on your authority."

"Despite this, *heh*, you have."

"Lord Raachwald—"

"*Lord?*" He reared back. "Raachwald is no lord. Master of a few bricks, a few stones, crumbled mortar and biting wind. The lowborn rock." The *whole* eastern half of the city, but I didn't say that. "A stubborn one. Refusing to cede to his betters. Clinging to the old ways. Mummer's Isle. A fitting name for a farce it is, indeed. Well, he can have it. But the rest, *heh,* the rest is mine. A poor choice to rule your thoughts and deeds, my son."

"My deeds, your Eminence, only my deeds."

The Vulture squinted. "Do I sense a smatter of treason? Have you the traitor's heart, Krait? They say there are three in the lowest ring of hell. Brutus, Cassius, and…another. Chewed upon by Lucifer himself. And they were traitors, traitors all."

"Raachwald captured my brother and holds him imprisoned," I explained. "I was forced to cede to his will. I owe him no loyalty. No fealty. There was no choice other than condemn my brother to torment and execution. Raachwald has maimed him already."

"*Maimed,* you say?" The Vulture perked up at that, that pale tongue nestled like a yellow viper between those withered lips. "What, tell me, *heh*, what agonies has he wrought?"

"His right hand, your Eminence." I swallowed. "He's cut it off."

"Bah!" He spat. "Hands."

"My brother is dear to me. A most pious man, your Eminence." I withheld mention of Stephan's heresy trial in Paris. "A soul akin to your own."

"You should have come to me." He massaged the loose waddle of skin beneath his chin. "You should have come to me first. I could have aided you. I would have, *heh*, helped you."

"Raachwald ambushed me in the Hellwood." I tried not to stare at his neck. "I had no escape. No other option but cede to his demands. Stephan had been abducted by then. My actions, I take no pride in them. I have been stupid. Ignorant. A dichotomy of grossest afflictions."

"A riddle you are, my son." The Vulture settled back, breath wheezing. "Tell me, *heh*, why it is that Raachwald demands the services of one so ignorant and inept as you? Why entrust a quest of such importance to an admitted fool? Has Raachwald's dyspeptic jester passed on? Perhaps you shall don the jangles and jape for him instead?"

"I fear it's what I do now, your Eminence. I was trained as a justiciar for my father's court. I hunted men. Heeled them. Brought them to justice. That is why Raachwald exploits me."

"You dispensed justice, *heh*, at the behest of English lords? The English king?"

"Others as well." I nodded. "Though, I've not done so for some years."

"You are well known, then? As a hunter of men?"

"No. Not well known. Known within a select circle, perhaps. Mostly other justiciars. Bailiffs. Judges. Some would call on me for aid when met with an impasse. Dead ends. Or needed a fresh pair of eyes."

"And yet Raachwald knew of you well enough to lie in wait and ensnare your brother?" He was a sharp old bird. "And bind you to his will. How could he know you were upon the road that very night? Have you considered that?"

"No… I hadn't." How indeed? I'd assumed it all coincidence. Bad luck. But, in retrospect, how *could* Lord Raachwald have known? Unless someone tipped him. Hyram or Abraham? Or perhaps Lord Raachwald had men watching the road every night? With the roads bad? Plague raging? No trade moving? No, Lord Raachwald knew we were on the road that night. Somehow. He knew we were coming. Knew I was coming. And he had been waiting. "We have history, Raachwald and I."

"*Heh*, history?" Licking his dry lips, the Vulture squinted, his head quivering slightly. "Oh? Oh!" He sat back, waggling a finger, recognition sparking along with crippled delight. "Yes. *That* Krait." A sly grin oozed wide. "I heard of you, long ago, a flutter on the wind, a spider tickling through my brain. Some ten years past, was it?" I nodded. "Yes, I remember. You are the Serpent Knight."

"Yeah," I fidgeted under his newfound appreciation, "that's me."

"Tell me," he balled his fist in glee, "how did they die?"

"With great difficulty," I answered truthfully.

"And yet Raachwald did not kill you?" His frown deepened. "He vowed to. Yes. Before his whole court, he swore a blood oath. The crimson hand oath, sacrificing his blood to some derelict god." He squinted. "Were you not aware? We were not enemies then. But, *heh*, he broke his oath if what you say is true." He stroked his jaw. "So, how is it you still have legs under you, my son? Lungs in your chest? Life within your body?"

"He desires his son's killer found. And he has met a dead end. With all of his options exhausted, he hazards I'll have better fortune. If I succeed, he wins his son Cain's killer. If I fail? He'll kill my brother. And no doubt take a run at me. He made no bones about that. But I think he means to milk the cow before he sends it to the butcher if you catch my drift?"

"Yes," the Vulture slurped drool, "have you, *heh*, much to milk, Krait?"

"Uh…?" I fought to not recoil.

"And would you offer your milk to me?" The Vulture gazed past, as though upon some distant vista.

I cocked my head. "Are you asking me to work for you?" I hoped. "As an investigator?" I added for clarification.

"Perhaps." His hat teetered further to the side of his bald head. It must have been tied in place, or God was just throwing miracles out the window. The Vulture hunkered on his perch. I half expected him to launch up into the night sky amidst a cascade of feathers. "You are a Jew-lover, is this not true?"

I froze. A loaded question. Jews, a divisive factor throughout history. You're either for them or against them. The question was, *what was the Lord Bishop?* "Not precisely, your Eminence."

The Vulture's eyes gleamed. "You traffic with them, though, do you not?"

"The price of business," I answered.

The Vulture's claw hand throttled his crozier. "You conducted business on the east side of the river today." He glared at Father Paul. "In the Quarter, mayhap?"

I nodded curtly. Why lie? No doubt, Father Paul was aping my nod two feet behind.

"What sort of business, I wonder?"

"Correcting a debt I owed."

He fingered his chin. "A debt to whom?"

"Abraham Ben-Ari. He was shorted on the wool shipment I was guarding. Raachwald and his men absconded with it. I felt it prudent to make amends."

"Abraham Ben-Ari?" He sniffed. "And so you were not in the Quarter on Raachwald's behalf?" He waggled a finger. "I warn you, they are a gentled folk, and they are mine. They require no trouble from interlopers. You, *heh*, were not stirring up trouble?"

"No, your Eminence," I lied.

"Jews, they require a firm hand, yes. A firm hand, indeed. Know that I consider the Jews of Asylum City part of my flock." To be shorn regularly and eaten on occasion, no doubt. "And I am their shepherd. I watch over them, protecting them from wolves. Are you a wolf, Krait?"

I straightened, sniffed, nodded. "I am, your Eminence, but I am *your* wolf."

The Vulture seemed taken aback, feathers ruffled, then oozed back into comfort. "Father Paul begged my leave to allow you to continue under my aegis in just such a manner. I wonder, though, if I can trust you?"

"The enemy of my enemy, your Eminence."

The Vulture fingered his jaw.

"And I would, of course, share any information I found concerning Sir Myron Chalstain."

"Oh, you have heard of him?" the Vulture asked.

"Only recently. I heard he went missing."

"Yes, well, *heh*, he has been found," the Vulture announced.

"Oh? Might I have leave to speak to him?"

"No, you may not."

"Pardon, your Eminence," I quickly bowed, "I've not even received official leave to conduct the investigation, and here I am—"

"Alas," he shook his head in sorrow, "Sir Myron was snatched away by the will of God."

"Plague, then, I suppose." Damn.

"No. His head was found in an alley." The Vulture pointed off northwest somewhere. "Near the Point. It had been, *heh*, torn from his body. Pulled in some manner. His body, though, has yet to be recovered. It is apparent that Sir Myron's killer was also that of Coldspire's famed killings."

I said nothing. If what he said were true, the same modus operandi, the same impossible wounds, it likely was the same killer. Except for the children...

"How intent are you upon finding this, *heh*, killer?" The Vulture smirked, one corner of his mouth rising, trembling, a maze of creased wrinkles erupting.

"Intent," I answered.

"And how attached are you to that head of *yours*?"

184

Chapter 21.

THE MOON HAD risen above the clutter of homes when I reached Abraham's money-house, fourth one up on the left on Lender's Row. Buildings rose against the night sky, all dark inside. Yet, within Abraham's money-house, light shone through the windows, and the door was ajar.

I slid inside and froze, except for my hand—instantly on Yolanda's hilt, fixed to draw. Six faces locked on me. Instantaneously. A wave of silence. *Intruder*, it called out. I'd walked into some sort of standoff. Five against one.

"I am begging you, most strenuously, reconsider," the lone man said in a thick dago accent. He stood at the counter, body angled so that he could see everyone in the room. A short man, he wore his black hair slicked back and tied off in a ponytail, a shock of white running through it to the end.

I knew him.

The five stood on the counter's far side, Abraham amongst them, his arm raised as he tried to calm his men. Two were clerks, just boys, really. The other two were the guards. Baldy and Locks. Both stood, eyes glaring, hands on hilts, hungry to draw. All of the five wore the Star of David on their chests. The one did not. He pivoted, stepped back, keeping me in his peripheral.

I raised an eyebrow at Abraham.

He shook his head minutely.

The dago glanced back my way a mite, glared me up and down, eyes lighting first on Yolanda. "He is being closed." His gaze shifted, recognition crystalizing into frigid grin. "Krait?" His eyes lit mirthlessly on the Star of David on my *'appropriated'* cloak.

"I converted," I explained.

"Eh? Most are being converted the other way."

"He's so crazy, what'll he do next?" I wondered. "Door was open."

"Fuck off." The dago smiled joyously. "As I say, they are being closed."

"Though, there is literally a whole tribe of Jews standing behind the counter, waiting with bated breath to speak to me," I said, adding after, "you greasy dago bastard."

"And I have missed you, too." He smoothed his hair back with one hand. "What is it you are wanting?"

"Just looking to take out a loan."

"So sad," he lamented, "a Jew with no money."

"It is sad," I admitted.

"You are looking for money or for work?" He rubbed his thumb and forefinger together. "Both, neh?"

"Always the money, Lon." His name was Alonzo Casagrande, and he was a shit. On his good days. "Not so much the work."

"Eh?" He waggled a finger. "Same old Krait."

"Same old me." I smiled ruthlessly.

"I could use you."

"I'm being used already." I held a hand up conspiratorially. "Overused, truth be told."

"A pity."

"I concur. You're a long way from Genoa."

"Aye. Yes. It is cold here. It does not suit my humors."

"You have no humor, let alone humors. But it does suit your temperament."

"And you are being a long way from whatever rotting hole spawned you."

"Easy, my mother's a saint."

"Eh?" He bowed, a hand to his heart. "Be forgiving me. This insulting of mothers is not...how you say? *Nice.*" Hidden beneath his cloak, the gleam of two hilts, one at either hip, caught my eye. I'd seen him use those blades. He knew how.

I pivoted off to my right, offering full access to the

door. Not smart to put a nervous man on death ground, and Casagrande was that. He just hid it well. "Hate interrupting business, Lon." I put my hands up. "Carry on."

"Loan, eh?" Casagrande tapped quick fingers against the counter. "You are looking to get fucked in the arse, then, is more like it."

"Oh? You devil." I waggled a finger at Abraham. "Offering exciting new services? And beyond just the *standard* fucking? Why am I always the last to know?"

Casagrande had already turned back to Abraham, my wit wasted. "This Daniel was saying—"

"Daniel does not run *my* house." Abraham adjusted his glasses. "I think I have made that inimitably clear. I run it. I make the decisions, all of them, and I have given you my answer for the last time. I wish no part of this. Please convey that sentiment to your employer, whoever it is he may be."

"Forty percent." Casagrande grinned, a gold tooth gleaming, his hands open wide, spread out before him.

"I am not bargaining," Abraham said.

"Then I think you just need to be thinking on it a teensy while longer." Casagrande edged back, hand on a hilt, winking as he slid out the door. "Farewell, Krait."

"Fuck off, Lon."

Everyone watched him go.

No one moved but me.

"A friend of yours?" Abraham asked.

"We used to knit together."

"Why am I not surprised?"

"You're not surprised I have friends?" I said in mock surprise. "Finally, I'm moving up in your estimation."

"That, sadly, is the only path available." His brow furrowed at the Star of David on my chest. "And, I'm not surprised a man such as he would be amongst them if you did."

"I ain't the one doing business with him."

"Nor am I." Abraham straightened.

"He's negotiating."

"No. Our nonexistent business has reached its conclusion."

"He doesn't think so. And if he thinks that, he won't be done, not by a long shot, not til the bodies start piling up."

"Such men," Abraham scoffed, placing a hand on one of Baldy's arms, easing his sword hand down, sheathing the half-drawn blade.

"I know. Dagos, yeah? Less scruples than Frogs, even. Butcher our people. Our language. Take our money. And the greasy little fucks'll eat anything smaller and slower than them." I grinned. "It's true. I've seen it. There was this squashed porcupine once in the middle of the road. Wagon track valleyed right through it—*skwoosh* —" All five men just stared at me. Mute. "Forget it. And just to clarify, Casagrande's no friend of mine. More of a professional acquaintance. From days of yore."

"He's a—"

"I know what he is, Abe." I took in the room, the others in it, one by one. "I don't think any of you do."

"I—"

"You only *think* you know what he is." I placed an open hand to my heart. "And as a side note, I'm offended you didn't come to me when you needed a scumbag mercenary for brutal hire."

Abraham placed his hand on Locks's shoulder. "You won't need that."

Locks nodded, eyes wide, still locked on mine as he let go of his sword hilt. *Reluctant*, a word that came to mind.

"Best watch your back, Abe. With a man like Casagrande, you might start sprouting knives in it. Hell, your front, too. I know he looks like a runty little buffoon. Well, he knows it, too. Acts it. Plays it up. He gets paid a lot of money cause he's good at what he does. He here alone or with his company?" He ran a company of crossbowmen. A tight crew out of Genoa. Expensive.

"His company's here, too," the older boy said.

Locks shot him a dagger glare.

I nodded. "Noticed a few fellows in an alley outside, trying not to be noticed."

Abraham swallowed.

"Wonder how they got past the gates?" I pondered aloud. "And who he's working for?"

"He didn't say," Abraham said.

"He one of Raachwald's?"

"I *don't* know," Abraham reiterated through pursed lips.

"What's he want forty percent of, then?" I asked, expecting the same answer. I got a different one, entirely.

Five burning glares and two drawn short blades were my answer. "Sorry." I raised my hands. "Just trying to help." I considered the two armed guards. "Hope you fellas know how to use those."

"We do, *goyim*," Baldy said. "And keep your fucking trap shut. This is none of your business."

"Damn straight," I said. "My business is staying alive, and if you're dealing with Casagrande, yours ain't." I shifted my focus. "Abe, a word, if you please? In private."

"*Oy vey.*" Abraham cleared his throat. "Have you fully recouped the losses on the wool shipment?" Jesus. You can always tell an honest man. Can't lie for shit.

"Absolutely," I lied flawlessly.

"A quick word then should suffice? Emphasis on quick," Abraham said. "Good. Yes." He glanced up at the taller of the two boys. "Take your brother and go home, please." Abraham took off his glasses and set them on his gargantuan desk. He pointed with his one hand to the back door. "Go. Now. Please. Isaac, tell your mother I'll be along if she's still awake. Use the back door." The older boy took his brother by the arm and pulled him out.

Abraham turned to his two guards, hackles on their backs tickling the ceiling. "See them home safely, please."

Baldy eyed me up and down. "The *pisher's* armed."

"Enough of that." Abraham gripped the bridge of his nose between thumb and forefinger and squeezed. "I am not blind, and I am not helpless. Just follow my boys. Do what I ask. Make sure they get home safely. Please. I shall lock up."

"Daniel said—"

Abraham rose to his full height, striking his desk with an open palm. "This is my house. And you work in my employ, yes? Not his. Is that clear? Good. Now go."

Eyeing me balefully, the two guards slunk out, Abraham watching them go. He collapsed into his chair the instant the door shut. "*Oy vey...*" Wearily, as though his arm were made of lead, he pointed toward the front door. "Would you be so good as to lock that, please?"

"Sure." I did then grabbed a seat at his desk.

It looked the same as before, in broad strokes, mountains, peaks, valleys, though now there were three little stone-men perched on high. Watching. Abraham noticed me noticing them.

"What's Lon want?" I asked.

"What does every man want?" He seemed suddenly weary, old. "Just another satisfied customer."

"Yeah." One of the stone-men caught my eye. "Jesus. You're infested. One of your sons make them?"

"In a manner of speaking." Abraham followed my gaze.

"The eyes, what are they?" I peered close. "Coal? Chips of coal?"

"Obsidian." Abraham grimaced. "I don't suppose my losses have truly been recouped?"

"Ah, no. I figured that for subterfuge. I still have Volkendorf's ring?" I started reaching for my coin purse, but Abraham begged me off. "Hope it's not a huge disappointment."

"Sadly no. I tend to keep my expectations realistic when dealing with you."

"And by realistic you mean '*low*.'"

"What is it you want?"

"Volkendorf," I kept my voice low, "any word?"

"Ahem, yes." Abraham glanced over his shoulder. "I

gently queried a few of my colleagues and competitors. Most were not forthcoming, as you might imagine, but then Volkendorf was not popular in the Quarter." He fingered his lip. "Let us say he was less loved than most of our gentile customers, so some talked, whispered. It seems Lord Volkendorf had had his debts, some rather sizeable, and at more than a few lenders, but they had been settled, for the greater part."

"The greater part?"

"Precisely." Abraham took a deep breath. "Sir Luther, I think it best that you and I cease any and all future arrangements, business and otherwise. I think it best if you do not return. I think it best for all concerned."

"And my debt?"

"Pay at your leisure." Abraham closed a ledger with a *thwomp*. "Or not. Now, please go."

"Abe," I stood, turned to leave but paused, "just one more thing."

"What?"

"What if a client doesn't pay back? And it's at a bank that doesn't have a *pay at your leisure* policy? What measures could a moneylender then take?"

"Besides storming a nobleman's keep and demanding payment?"

"Yeah. Besides suicide."

"Hmm… Retroactively raising interest rates."

"That's legal?"

"If it's in the contract."

"And what are the rates at?"

"Presently?" Abraham shifted in his seat. "About seventy."

I leaned forward, cupping a hand to my ear. "Seventeen?"

"Seventy," he replied, his visage stone.

"We talking percentages?"

"Yes."

"My arithmetic isn't great. But that seems a bit high."

"It covers risk."

"Your risk?"

He nodded. "The lender's risk."

"What else could you do?"

He placed a finger to his lips. "Refuse future loans. Refuse to conduct *any* further business. Censure them."

"Like with me?"

"Yes," he nodded, "like with you."

"Hmm? Outright refusal? How would that go over?"

"Not well, I would imagine. It could happen in theory. But a lender would need the strong hand of his lord at his back."

"And not in the traditional sense of the lord's hand holding a dagger?"

"Did you know? It's not illegal in most cities to murder a Jew if you're a Christian. In some cases, your pope's promised absolution if they do. *Infidels*, they call us. They think we poison wells, steal babies, consort with the darkness. How? How can they believe such stories?"

"People are stupid." I shrugged. "Now, what if none of that worked? What if the lord wouldn't back you?"

"I've been tempted to try begging. And praying?"

"And when that fails?"

"As I said, the Lord would have to back the lender. And strongly."

"The Lord Bishop, in this case."

"Yes," Abraham said. "One would need his favor."

"And he just loves you guys."

"*Love* may be a bit strong."

"But not with regards to your money."

"Of course, no one abhors our money. They abhor only us."

Chapter 22.

MORNING CAME SOONER than I'd wished. But here it was, and I had to get out, get going. Do something. Anything. Patience had never been my strong suit. It's a sour brew I've knocked back from time to time. Goes down like ragged glass and hot turpentine. And with each dose, I either puke it back up or let it stew awhile til it comes out the other end. My disgusting point? It never sticks.

I needed to talk to Lady Narcissa. I needed to talk to Karl. I needed to see Cain Raachwald's corpse, verify he was truly dead, find out who was lying to me. I suspected everyone. Jesus. I still had nothing but was caught up in a crossfire. Nothing to go on and the surest way to rendezvous with Karl or Lady Narcissa was to sit tight. Wait for her to contact me. She had to.

I slid through the crowd at the Stone Ruin Ten.

Blackbeard was there again, sitting in a chair, leaning back on two legs against the wall, laughing, a whore wriggling on his lap. He saw me. He saw that I saw, eyes shifting, following me an instant before resuming their duty of staring at the whore's cleavage. I kept moving, sliding through the labyrinth of chairs and tables, bodies pressed tight. Music played. Lorelai was nowhere in sight, but I was pleasantly surprised to see Nils sitting at the bar, jawing up Girard.

I nodded. "Hey, shithead."

Nils turned, nodded. "Morning."

I thumbed over to the corner. "Follow me."

"Huh?"

I slid past a few wilted drunks, toward one of the two stools open in the corner. They were adjacent to the wall and offered a view of the whole room.

"What?" Nils followed.

"You've got to start thinking," I said over the din.

"What are you jawing about?"

"You're in the city watch now."

"Yah." He bobbed his head. "So?"

"You make a lot of friends stalking around, telling people what to do, righting wrongs?"

"Well…"

"Don't ever sit with your back to the room." I pointed toward the doors. "Never know who's gonna come slinking in. Who's gonna see you. Recognize you. You want that butcher's two asshole buddies stomping in and recognizing you before you them?" I held a finger up to Schultz as he disappeared out back. "Bad day. Got it?"

Nils nodded slowly. "I got it."

"Good. Have a seat." I pounded the bar. "Hey, you lack-wit little shit!" I hollered after Girard. "Fetch me a plate of grub!"

Girard chucked me the finger and ducked into the kitchen.

"Little shit."

"He's doing good." Nils grinned.

"Well, he ain't covered in mud and shit anymore."

Girard scurried up and plopped a plate down in front of me.

"What the hell's this?" I glared down at my trencher full of…something.

"Gruel." The boy smiled innocently. Almost.

"Gruel?"

"Yup."

"Looks like gruel," Nils added, leaning over.

"You want some breakfast, Mister Nils?" Girard asked.

"Sure, kid." He placed a penny on the bar. "Thanks."

Girard took it and scurried off.

"Ain't covered in shit anymore, but he's serving it!" I hollered. I took a tentative spoonful, chewed, pulled a bone out of my mouth.

"How is it?" Nils glanced at it askance.

"A tad...bony." I fished another out, flicked it aside. But I was hungry. "I'd share but—"

Nils waved a hand. Girard came back, bearing a small pastry, glistening warm and brown on a plate. He placed it in front of Nils then turned, but I caught him by the back of his collar.

"What the hell's that?"

"Baked pike."

"Well, shit, I'd have liked some baked pike."

"So what?" He slipped my grasp and took off.

I poked my gruel with my wooden spoon as Nils cut into his pastry, steam erupting in a gout of warmth and spice from within. My mouth watered.

Nils huddled protectively over his plate.

"Fuck you," I muttered, pulling another bone from my tepid mess. "Hello?"

Lorelai entered the room, and I swear the lamps glowed brighter.

She staggered a bit, caught herself on the wall, fixed her hair, looked to see if anyone had noticed. I had. Our eyes met, and I smirked. She smirked back, fixing her dress while starting my way. Then she froze. Turned. To Blackbeard. He was pounding his hand on his table, laughing, calling out her name. He launched the whore squealing off his lap then slapped his thigh. "Kept your seat warm!" She glanced my way again, shrugged, turned away.

"Well, shit."

"Well, shit, *what?*" asked Nils, still slaying his pike.

"Nothing. Just seems my luck's holding up. Or down. Steady at any rate."

"Oh?" He took another mouthful, closed his eyes, apparently suppressing an orgasm. "That's good..."

"Absolutely." I ate more gruel and glanced away as Blackbeard fondled one of Lorelai's breasts.

"Reason I came," Nils said between mouthfuls, "a dead guy was found last night. Sergeant's sending me out to collect him. Put me in mind of you."

"Your sergeant?"

"No, the dead guy."

"What's so special about him?" I asked. "Was he devilishly handsome?"

"Don't know."

Schultz stopped by, delivered me a brew, tipped an imaginary hat, moved on.

"Ugly then?"

"Can't rightly say, but," Nils leaned forward, whispering, "seems his head's missing."

I nearly dropped my spoon.

"And he was dressed well," Nils continued, "for a dead guy. Ragged, worn, but finery, supposedly. And fair decent armor, too."

"Know who he is…was?"

"Don't know." Nils lifted his fork. "Not for certain. But remember that fella I told you about? One asking questions? One gone missing?"

"Yeah."

"Think it might be him. Fella's wearing a tabard or something."

"Yeah? What's on it?"

"Too faded to know, supposedly."

"Anyone else know?" I asked.

"Fella that found him, I suppose. His wife, my sergeant."

"His wife is your sergeant?" I asked.

"Huh?"

"Forget it." I nodded, inhaled my gruel, slugged back the last of my ale. "Where?"

"Goathead. Up by the Point. Near the watchtower."

Goathead was a peninsula west of the city, just outside the walls. It used to be its own village, but Asylum had grown beyond its own walls and consumed it, voraciously, decades past. It was mostly fishermen living there along with a small community of Jews. "Ready?" I asked.

Nils nodded, rose, chewing the last of his pike.

I turned to stand, and Lorelai's bosom was in my face. I froze. Admired. My gaze rose, thoughtfully, gracefully, incrementally.

"Up here." Lorelai crossed her arms, waiting.

I raised a hand. "One moment."

"Should write the gospel on them, least I'd feel I was accomplishing something."

"Oh, you are."

"Not that." Our eyes met. Finally. "Who's your friend?"

"No one." I shoved Nils aside.

"He's cute," she commented.

"In a stunted, runtish sort of way, no doubt." I interposed myself between them. "Besides, he's not fond of women."

"Hey—!"

Smirking, Lorelai appraised Nils, his arms crossed, the wounded look on his face. "Leaving so soon?"

"Important business," I said.

"Oh?" She sidled in close, a hand nuzzling up under my shirt, fingertips sliding behind the waist of my trousers.

"Uh…" I said eloquently. "I have to go?"

"Was that a question?" She suppressed a giggle.

"No…?"

"So soon?" She stepped in closer, her hand sliding down deeper.

I grabbed onto the bar.

"Then come on," she whispered, nodding her head towards the stairs.

"Hey, we got to go." Nils snatched my arm, leaned in, whispered. "You know people. Word's gonna spread, fast, and Goathead's small. So if you're coming, you're coming now." He pointed with his thumb over his shoulder. "Wagon's out back."

Feeling the warmth of Lorelai's breast against my arm, and her hand, elsewhere, I sighed. "Any chance you want to take a ride?"

Lorelai withdrew her breast, her hand, her expression stating plainly that she, indeed, did not.

"I was just hoping—"

"You were just hoping I was the kind of woman who'd lay you in the back of a moving wagon?" Her voice was low, nearly a growl, hands balling into fists. I don't remember anything after that.

…cannot prove who employed the scoundrels, yet I possess an inkling.

—*Journal of Sir Myron Chalstain*

Chapter 23.

WE ROLLED THROUGH the West Gates, the ancient wagon creaking ominously, the ancient horse, too. Nils nodded to his watch buddies as we turned north through the streets. It was a fairly straight shot north to Goathead.

"You truly believe that even if they could call down a plague, they'd hang around to be consumed by it?" I asked.

"Eh?" Nils shrugged. "Suppose not."

"When I first met you, you told me the plague had come in on a cog out of Genoa," I said. "When'd it come in, anyways?"

Nils held the reins in his hands. "Don't know."

"Before the plague?"

He shook his head, unsure. "Maybe."

"Remember its name?"

He shook his head. "Naw."

"And you said it was hauling mercenaries, yeah?" I asked.

He nodded, spat over the side.

"Know anything about them? They crossbowmen?"

"Hmm, don't rightly know," Nils said. "I'd assume they were, cause dago mercs ain't good for nothing 'sides dropping points." Nils glanced at me sidelong. "Least, that's what I hear."

"Hear anything about their captain?"

"Of the ship?"

"No, the company."

Nils let out a long breath, thinking. "Naw. Ain't heard much about them. Above my pay grade. Though, I seem to recollect someone jawing on about their captain being a little fella. A little fella with a big name."

"You remember it?"

"Naw. You know how dago names are. Lotta parts.

Can't say them, let alone remember them."

I nodded. A little fella with a big name. Not a bad description of Alonzo Casagrande. "Know who they're working for?"

"Naw."

"Seen any around?"

"Nope."

"Probably all on the east side, then," I said. Nils would have seen someone, sometime, somehow, him watching the West Gates and all. "So, most likely not the Lord Bishop." The Lord Bishop wouldn't have sent a man like Casagrande to treat with his prized cows, not unless he was looking to make steaks, anyways. So he was working for the Isle Men, most likely. But who on the Isle could afford to hire an entire Genoese mercenary company? Big money. Did Lord Raachwald have the scratch for that? Hochmund always had money, a little, anyways. I didn't know about the Taschgarts or Brulerins, though. Was there a third possibility?

"All's I was saying," Nils continued on, "was they found a king-rat in the Jewish Quarter. Right smack dab in the middle of the square. Fifteen rats all tied squirming by the tail into one squealing beast, snapping and biting at folk. Monstrous. Some rat-catcher fella supposedly bagged the entire thing. Dried it. Probably has it nailed to a wall in his house now."

"Sure his wife loves that." I checked my blades. "Hughs still run the docks?" Michael Hughes was a thief and a murderer I'd had some dealings with in the past. Him and his gang the Razors. Odds were he'd know who Casagrande was working for. I had a thread, not necessarily the one I wanted, but one I'd pull anyways.

"Naw, skinny was, he met a razor of his own and got a Stettin necktie." He pulled a thumb across his neck and stuck out his tongue. "Or the plague, depending on who you ask. Some fella named Red Tom's running the waterfront now, from what I hear."

"Damn. Where he's based out of?"

"Little tavern called the Fool's Hand, on the waterfront." The wagon trundled to a stop. "Gang goes by the same name. We're here."

I glanced up. A watchtower leered over us, some fifty-feet high, marking the western bank of the mouth of the Morgrave. The surf pounded against the rocky coast. The sun had finally come peeking out through the clouds, sending shafts of light down in miraculous patterns across the water, turning it a deep green where it lit. For once it wasn't horrible.

* * * *

"You keep the barn door locked?" I asked the man.

"Errr, yes, sir. I do." His hat was clutched in his hands, his head bowed to near groveling status as he spoke, even to Nils. The Star of David was plain on his chest, so he had to.

"How long's the door been broken?"

"Don't know." The man stared at the opening.

I slid my hand along the rough wood. The door jamb bowed outward like something had forced it apart. It was a strong door, well built, which was why it was still semi-intact, but it had given.

I stood at the threshold. The barn was empty. Sometimes you can just feel it. Whether there's something alive. Something dead. Sometimes you just know. And I'm not talking sounds or smells. It's something different. Like the building's a hole, a quiet yawning hole, and it's drawing you and everything around you in, pulling, real gentle-like, but definitely there, whispering, enticing. And death lay inside. I could feel its hollow pull yearning.

"That's it." The Jew pointed in.

I squinted. A black heap lay in the shadows. "Help me with the doors, yeah? Need more light."

Nils and I dropped our shoulders into one door and managed to force it open. "Now, the other."

As the second creaked wide, a yellow blade of

201

sunlight slid incrementally across the floor, reaching, reaching, reaching, until it illuminated the heap.

It was a corpse. The corpse.

"Stay here." I stepped inside.

The corpse's head was missing, so was one arm up to the shoulder. Carefully, I walked a circle around the body. Except for the stab of sunlight, it was gloomy inside, dust hanging motionless in the air despite the fresh sea breeze. The ceiling vaulted into cathedral dark. Lofts lay above and to either side. Silent. No animals braying. The floor was hard-packed earth. No footprints. Just scattered hay. The dead man had no weapons on him, though he was dressed like a knight. A hedge knight. His tabard was nigh unreadable due to wear and grime, but I could make out a blue cross on a field of white. Or a faded grey cross on a field of slightly lighter field of grey. A riveted mail shirt, rusted practically into one piece, lay beneath. His clothes were filthy. He stunk. Rotting stunk. He lay face up, well, chest up, as he had no face, no head. One leg was folded back beneath him.

"C'mon in," I said. "What's your name?"

"Jacob."

"Jacob, you ever see this man before?"

"He has no head."

"Right." I nodded. "You talk to anyone about this?"

"No." He wiped his palms on his trousers. "My wife knows, sir."

"Good thing they don't blab." I smirked. "He's been here a few days. At least."

Jacob nodded. "I hadn't been in here for near a month. I…my animals all died." He looked up like I'd just caught him fucking my wife. "I—I got a," he screwed his eyes shut, fighting to recall the word, "a *special dispensation* from the Lord Bishop to own them. I wasn't sneaking them, I swear."

I waved a hand.

"How'd you find the dead guy if there was no reason to come in?" I asked.

"My wife." He took a breath. "She thought she smelled something."

"Well, she did." I stared down. If his home hadn't been right on the water, I might have called him a liar. With all the stink and death in the city, how would you differentiate between the stink of death emanating from your own barn and the stink of death choking civilization? And the term *'civilization'* I used loosely. But here, right on the coast, the surf pounding so near? The only clean air in the city. And I've found that women often have keener senses of smell than men, which was unfortunate…for them.

Jacob started again, "I came—"

I raised a hand, stopped him short. "You can go. Many thanks, Jacob."

He froze, nodded, half bowed and slid out.

I looked to Nils. "Help me with his shirt."

"This is the guy." Nils's eyes went wide, reading the tabard. I thought he might start jumping up and down. "Look— The Lord Bishop's blue cross. Chalstain, holy shit, we found him."

"Easy, let's not start sucking each other's dicks just yet," I said.

The two of us managed to wrestle him out of his mail. Missing one arm and his head, it wasn't such a chore.

"Jesus—" Nils sprung back as the mail shed off like lizard skin. "Urhh!"

"Just his guts," I said as ropes of black pulled like tendrils of seaweed from within, hooked somehow to the inside of the mail. "Watch your feet." I dropped the mail, guts still attached, stepped around the slithering snake orgy and knelt in a relatively clean spot. "Ow. Jesus." I brushed aside the straw strewn across the floor and found a rock, then another. The same as Coldspire. I looked around for the source. Nothing. I put one in my coin purse. "Come here."

"What's it?" Nils peered over my shoulder.

I held one up between thumb and forefinger. "What's that look like to you?"

Nils shrugged. "A rock?"

"Shit." I started back in on the corpse.

"What're you looking for?"

"Never know til I find it."

Nils stood equally entranced and horrified by the corpse.

"What is it?" I glanced up.

"Holy shit, it's like…" He pulled his collar up to cover his nose and mouth.

"It's like someone tore his head and arm off." I peered close. "Not clean, like blade work. See? You can see where the flesh pulled, twisted, tore. The bone here, too. All spiraled. Broken, like when you splinter a stick by twisting it."

Nils fought to not look away. "Tearing it off like that…"

"Would take some doing." The man's skin was green, soft, rotting. I placed a hand on his chest then checked him head to toe. Well, sort of. "Here. Put your hand on his chest."

"I'd rather—"

"Just do it."

Reluctantly, he laid his hand on it. It's one thing to look at a dead body, another thing to touch it.

"Now push around a bit." I waited while Nils tepidly pawed at it like a dog thinking twice about stepping into cold water. "You *could* try doing it like a man?" I put my hand on his and pushed down, moved around. "Don't worry. He won't mind."

Nils turned green.

"Feel it?"

Nils dry heaved.

"Like a sack full of broken glass," I said. "Feel all that scraping and shifting going on inside? Yeah? All his ribs are shattered on his right side. Both his collarbones, too. Left side is damaged, just not quite as much. Skin isn't broken, though." I adjusted position. "Here. Help me turn him. Wait. Grab that horse blanket." Nils reached over, handed it to me. "Thanks." I took the blanket and laid it out next to the corpse then grabbed the body by the trousers. "A hand, please?" Looking away and holding his breath, Nils hooked the corpse's armpit with one hand. "Alright." Together, we rolled the body over onto the blanket. "Less times we move him the better. For my back, anyways. Now let's get a look at his."

Nils took a deep breath through his mouth. "I think I'm gonna puke." But he stayed.

"Just do it outside." I slid a hand along the corpse's back, palpating, pushing hard all along, starting from the shoulders and on down to his arse, then his arm and legs, feeling the bones, pushing hard, feeling for breaks. Sensing with my fingers, I felt for the telltale scrape of bone on bone I'd found all through the right side of his chest and part of the left. Crepitus.

Nils was breathing real slow.

"His back's fucked, too." I wiped my hands with a handful of straw. "Spine's twisted. Bad. The shoulder bones feel intact but out of place."

"You ever seen anything like this?"

"Yeah." I got up, started walking the rest of the barn. "Coldspire." The barn was average-sized for a barn, which is to say big. "Follow me." I inspected the stall by the door and worked my way systematically around, clockwise. "Same M.O."

"Huh?"

"*Modus operandi.*" I searched another stall. "Latin. Fancy way of saying a method of doing something. In this case murder."

"Why Latin?"

"You speak Latin?"

"No."

"That's why. Gives us lawmen our own secret language. Separates us. Elevates us. Like Mass. Makes us seem more important. And keeps you common folk in the dark."

Nils nodded, following, watching.

"Scuff your feet on the ground behind me," I said. "See if you find anything underneath the hay." I wished Stephan were here. He had the keenest pair of eyes of anyone I knew. And he'd work stuff out I never could. It was a big part of the reason why I'd been so successful hunting down outlaws. Even as a kid, he'd be unraveling knots while I was still trying to find loose ends. It was like he could put himself in the mind of the killer, the killed, and work out what had happened, starting from the death and working his way back. Reading signs was as clear as reading a book for him. The other half of the equation was Karl, but that was for when we found the killer. Jesus. Where was he? Three days now and nothing. He should've been watching the Stone Ruin Ten. Should've found me. Which begged the question…

In the far corner, I found it. Where the dead guy had been living. A small camp was against the south wall of the barn, where the sun would hit it all day, warm it a bit. A small nest of blankets lay scattered about as though someone had been sleeping and then woke up. Suddenly. Tossed them aside. Scrambled to his feet in the dark. I hadn't found any weapon. I rooted around again, even though I knew I hadn't missed one. Nothing. A knight on the run. Weaponless? Shit. Maybe his sword was still attached to his arm, wherever the hell it was.

Up in one of the lofts, hidden between two rafters, I found a small book. A ledger. "Let's get the hell out of here."

* * * *

We trundled along south out of Goathead. The drizzle had started again, cold and slow and straight and miserable. Nils glanced aside, holding the reins in case the horse suddenly woke up and decided to do something horse-ish, like actually pull the wagon. "What's it say?"

"Don't know," I answered, head down, thumbing through it.

"You can't read?"

"Can you?"

"No. But I'm not some big-shot knight."

"Blow me," I said. "I can't read it cause it's coded in cipher." I thumbed through more pages, using the hood of my cloak to protect it. "Hang on. Some of it's written normal. Let's see." I ran my finger along the page. "It is Chalstain's. Jesus. The man's penmanship. Atrocious." The script was nearly illegible, the pages sullied with finger marks and grime. I was fair sure the brown ink was blood, but I didn't tell Nils. He was still looking green. "Hmm…" I read some of it aloud, "*I have seen battle. Five major engagements in my time. I have seen bones cracked, shattered. Yet the bones of these men had been crushed, injuries akin to someone who had been tortured to death on the wheel…*"

Nils turned silently toward the corpse in the back of the wagon.

I thumbed through a few more pages then closed it. Best to stay alert. Get the body back to the Lord Bishop. See what the hell Chalstain was doing living in a barn in Goathead. See why he was weaponless. See if he'd turned into some maniacal hermit. I wondered if he had a wife? Children? Where his missing arm was? Where Volkendorf's leg was? I wondered a lot of things I'm sure Stephan would have had the presence of mind to have asked a lot sooner. "Do me a favor," I tucked the book in my shirt, "not a word about the book to anyone, yeah? I'll see you get the credit. Your sergeant, too. But I need to know what it says before I surrender it."

"A man was murdered." Nils cocked his head. "You think I give a damn about credit?"

"You damn well should," I said. "Might save your life someday, having that crazy old geezer's blessing. Feather in your cap." Nils gave me a look. "What? You too proud to bow and scrape for supper? Try going to bed a few nights with an empty belly and then talk to me."

"I have. I do. I will."

"Alright, Jesus in the desert. You can shove that

baked pike right up your ass."

"Alright, grandpa."

"Wha—" Something zipped stinging across my face—

"Fuck!" Nils screamed.

I half-cartwheeled out of my seat, graceless, flopping into the mud before I could process. Another bolt buried into my seat. Slipping, sliding, I dove underneath the wagon.

Nils screamed above.

"Get down!" I growled.

Beyond, two men crouched on a rooftop. One finished reloading a crossbow while the other knelt, holding his hand over his eyes as a visor against the rain.

"I'm stuck," Nils growled. He sat wriggling-pinned to his seat. His face was white, back hunched. Spittle flew from his mouth in his effort to move. "Fish in a *fucking* barrel."

I snatched a glance. A crossbow bolt had pierced his right flank, punched through his abdomen and come out above his groin, continuing on into his left leg and into the seat of the wagon. He was literally nailed to his seat.

The sharpshooter beyond lifted his crossbow and took aim. I launched, snagging Nils two-handed by the collar of his leather coat and snarled, "Grab the bolt—" before I yanked, arching back in a wrestler's throw, pulling with everything I had.

Wood splintered.

Nils swore, cursing me as he flipped over, another bolt—*thunk!*—burying into his seat. We crashed splashing in the mud, him atop me, wriggling, his left leg folded up to his abdomen, twitching like a dog with a shattered back.

The assassins cursed and presumably were reloading.

The wagon gave cover, but sitting in the mud in the middle of the street wasn't a successful long-term strategy. Already, the assassins were moving for a better vantage. I dragged Nils under the wagon, snatched his billhook from the mud, and used it to hook the fallen reins.

"Go," Nils growled like a trapped animal, trying to straighten his leg, "leave me."

"Shut up." I snapped the reins as best I could. "Move, you stupid fucking animal!"

"I'm gut shot," Nils gasped. "Go!"

The horse seemed unaware of our despair, or anything else, and decided, at that very moment, to shit. "Fucking move!" I roared, prodding it in the arse with the billhook. It tossed its tail, whinnied, and deigned finally to move.

"Rrrg…" I dragged Nils scuttling along crabwise after. "Bolt's pulled back in."

Scrabbling, I dragged him behind me through the mud, keeping beneath the creeping wagon until I heard the *thunk* of a crossbow bolt into horseflesh followed by rearing and screaming, an awful noise. It bolted off, wagon trundling along behind. I rolled, ripping Nils aside with me, avoiding the wheels churning past. The mad horse slammed screaming into a house and continued on, free of its harness, bolt feathers deep in its haunches, blood streaming down its flank, one leg limp and flipping like a strip of uncooked bacon.

The instant the wagon took off, we were turtles without shells. A bolt stuck into the mud an inch from my face.

"Let me go," Nils grunted behind.

Deaf, dumb, defiant, I scrambled for the wagon wreck. One wheel still spinning, it'd punched a hole in a house. I could hear the horse dying somewhere up the street as I dropped behind the wagon again. Huffing. I looked up. The front door of the house offered a perfect vantage to the assassins. The windows were boarded up, but the walls were wattle and daub, which meant sticks and mud, and the hole the wagon had made was considerable. I kicked it wider, grabbed Nils and dragged him through. I slipped on mud and sticks and wet and water, righted, fell again, and yanked Nils further in.

Outside, boots pounded through muck.

"Any more bolts?" I spat. I checked myself. Didn't find a one. Good. Strange, but sometimes you don't feel them, not right away.

Nils swore as I dragged him further from the opening and left him there. I looked around, strode over to a table, hurled it onto its side by the hole. I grabbed another table and tossed it on its side in front of Nils. It wasn't much. "Put pressure on it."

The place reeked. Someone coughed behind, and I turned. A man in a flea-infested bed lay contorted, wide eyes staring jaundiced yellow back. A black bubo was raised at his neck, twitching like a slick black beetle burrowed beneath his skin. Wrapped in his arms like some holy reliquary was a full chamber pot. "Apologies." I turned back towards the hole.

"D-don't matter," the man mumbled back, shivering, feverish. "Don't matter... Don't matter... Don't..."

I waited.

I didn't wait long.

Shadows broke an instant before the assassins burst in, kicking the table aside. I hurled the chamber pot, excrement arcing in a putrid rainbow, bouncing off the wall and splattering both. Then I charged screaming. I skewered the first, bull-rushing on, shoulder dropped, slamming him against the wall. I twisted Yolanda, tore her free and slashed again, his ugly head cascading through the dark. Turning, I slipped again as his compatriot fired a bolt—sparks flew as it glanced off Yolanda's blade. Jesus. Eyes wide in disbelief, the assassin hurled his crossbow at me then scuttled out the hole, groping at his belt for a mace.

Blood streaming down my face, I stalked out after him, pausing at the threshold for a clipped instant. His mace missed me by a nose. He swung again, but I'd already moved, attacked, deflected in one strike, sending mace and fingers flying.

He sucked red stumps as he backed up. Confused. I stalked after, kicking a mud puddle at him as he scrambled backward through the furrows left by the wagon, tripped, and crawled on, suddenly finding Nils's billhook in hand. Awkwardly, he pulled it around with one good hand and one shit.

"I'll let you live if you answer one question." It was a question I wanted answered, but Nils was dying. I lowered Yolanda, her tip nearly touching the mud.

The man swallowed. "What?"

"Who sent you?"

As he grinned that crimson grin that said, "*Fuck you,*" I lunged in and off-line as the billhook stabbed past, Yolanda darting forth quick as a snake-strike, not powerful, a jab really, but it was fast and Yolanda sharp and the assassin's neck unarmored, and it only took about two inches of steel to open his neck. He got about fifteen.

...has set a permanent guard at the gates to the Quarter, at my behest. This mystery is a tree with roots both myriad and deep. They swirl down through the darkness, tapping into the many power structures of this city, from high to...
—Journal of Sir Myron Chalstain

Chapter 24.

"I SAW HIM upon the bridge yesterday," the big man grunted. *Big?* No, not big. "He acquitted himself well." He was huge. "For a peasant." Monstrous. His wide shoulders seemed to absorb all of the space in the small room. "More light, please," he said to one of his assistants. He glanced up. "You, I saw as well."

"You led the charge," I said. My thoughts honed to Lady Narcissa's horseshit story. Here was a man who fit her description. A man capable of killing seven in cold battle, if any man was. His face, too, a thing of beauty. Across half of it lay a crisscrossed contour of cut and scar. A knotted hole in his left cheek revealing teeth back nearly to his throat. He possessed that same air of danger I'd known all dangerous men to possess. Not something quantifiable. I'd never had it but never erred in its judging.

"Charge?" Blood splatters painted him hand to elbow. Nils's blood. The big man peered closer to his work, which happened to be the bolt skewering Nils. "Mere rabble."

"It was a shiltron."

"Shiltron?" The big man scoffed. "Move your hand, please," he bade one assistant. The giant tightened a wooden clamp, almost exactly like a carpenter's clamp, on the spot his assistant had been holding.

He leaned forward and sniffed the wound as one might a glass of fine wine. He grunted. Good? Bad? Who the hell knew? He sat back, inspecting the wound through one eye as though checking the levelness of a door he was about to plane. "Clamp." One of his assistants slapped another clamp into it. "Leg or abdomen?"

"Abdomen," an assistant answered.

"Why?"

"He'd be dead of the leg wound were the great vessel punctured or severed. It will keep now if he keeps."

"Good," the giant said. "The leg is nothing." Nils, if he could speak, might have begged differently. The giant ran his finger along the bolt and traced its wooden course. "We'll spoon it out later if he survives the initial extraction."

The giant glanced up at me. "You look green, all of a sudden."

I gulped. Arrow-spoons. The only thing worse than getting shot with an arrow was having some surgeon prodding around inside the wound, trying to slip a damn arrow-spoon over the barbed head to draw it out. Well, I guess pulling the head, barbs and all, *without* a spoon'd be worse, but it was a close thing.

"Olaf," the giant said to one assistant. "Here." He pointed. "And here." Olaf stepped in and applied two more clamps. The giant wiped his hands on a stained apron.

"Reginald, please cut the bolt," the giant said. "The saw, not the cutters." With a scalpel, he notched the bolt midway between where it emerged from Nils's abdomen and plunged into this left thigh. "Here. Swiftly now. Nay." He held up a hand. "The saw with the fine teeth. Aye. That one. Smoothly now. Smartly. I'll hold him steady."

Reginald set to cutting the bolt with clean swift strokes.

"Olaf, the wine?"

"Boiling, brother."

"The silk?"

"Same."

"Reginald?"

"Done." Reginald laid down the saw. The bolt was severed and Nils's leg no longer pinned to his abdomen.

"Easy." The big man laid Nils's leg down, a gentleness belying his great size. "Olaf, extractor."

"Here." Olaf handed him a strange duck-billed contraption.

The giant slid the extractor over the end of the bolt emerging from Nils's lower abdomen and twisted a metal flange, the duck bills closing, snugging. "The silk is secured?"

"Aye," Olaf grunted.

"Bandages and dressings?"

Another grunt of assent.

The butt end of the bolt had a sheaf of silk tied to it, coiled, floating in a bowl of boiled wine. "We are ready?" The two men nodded and stepped forward, big men both, yet dwarfed still by their leader. One slipped a flat metal disk with a hole in it around the bolt coming from Nils's abdomen. The other took hold of the butt end.

"Krait." The giant was readying other apparatuses, arranging them on a table adjacent to the one Nils lay upon. He was ghost white. "Reg, grease the end of the bolt." Then to me, "Krait is your name, aye?"

Reginald greased the still-protruding tail end of the bolt with animal fat.

"You have me at a disadvantage." I swallowed my gorge. Making wounds is a hell of a lot easier to watch than the fixing of them.

"You're known. Not well perhaps, but known." The giant twisted the extractor minutely. "Good. T'was God's own mercy he passed out."

God's blessing, loss of blood, the sudden onset of death...

"Ready?" The big man widened his stance as though making ready to wrestle a bull. Big as he was, he might win. "Now secure him." His two men aped the big man's stance and readied themselves as though for a tug-of-war, which to my untrained eyes is exactly what it was. "Now." Grimacing, the big man's teeth shown jagged white in the firelight, canines dagger sharp, his whole body tensing as he drew on the crossbow bolt, his huge hand wrapped around the extractor, drawing it free of Nils's abdomen slowly, like drawing a cork from a wine bottle, twisting it minutely when met with resistance. Silk was drawn out of the tub and into the entrance wound as the butt end of the bolt sunk into flesh.

"There." The big man drew the final inch of bolt shaft free, the silk drawn clean through the wound. "Pressure now." Reginald placed dressings over the entrance and exit wound. The exit wound was bleeding again. "Why not allow the bleeding to cleanse the wound? Why the silk and the wine?"

"A last drink before he visits Jesus?" I muttered.

The big man's brow furrowed above an acid glare.

I shut my mouth.

Reginald cleared his throat. "His injury is old. Almost an hour. Had it just happened, bleeding would cleanse the wound. Hopefully removing debris, preventing suppuration. Yet, he has bled too much. More bleeding would kill him, most assuredly. The silk shall sweep the wound clean. We pray."

"Aye. And why the wine and not the water?" He glared as though daring me to speak. I looked at Nils, young, dying, old, his skin the white of new-fallen snow. I couldn't tell if he was breathing.

"Wine...works better?" Olaf ventured.

"Aye. It does," the big man said.

I couldn't agree with him more.

"And if we possessed no wine?"

"Boiled water."

"Good," the big man said. "Now we force more wine into the wound. Use the clyster." Olaf took the clyster, a metal cylinder with a hollow tube on one end, and a plunger on the other, and stuck the tube into the entrance wound. "Quickly now." He pressed the plunger down, and wine started leaking out the exit wound. He continued until it stopped; the big man covered the wound. "You have a question you wish to ask me." He didn't even look at me. He was busy with needle and thread, sewing up Nils's side. "You wish to know how I know your name."

"The thought had crossed my mind."

"A fellow monk mentioned you."

"Don't know any monks."

"I think you do."

"You calling me a liar?" Reginald and Olaf both looked up, like deer, or not like deer, not at all. Like bears, big fucking bears leering over a bloody dead carcass.

"Aye."

"Well…" I shrugged. I'd been called worse. "I am that."

"My name is Gaunt. John Gaunt. Now you know two monks."

"One," I said.

"You already confessed you're a liar. Brother Tomas spoke at length of your travails."

"Who?"

"Brother Tomas, of the Franciscan order. I thought him dead." He wiped his forehead with his forearm. "I thought them all dead."

"Said I've never heard of him."

"Of course," he said. "Draw the silk through now. Then finish sewing the hole. And pressure throughout." The big man began inspecting the wound in Nils's thigh. "The spoons." Reginald placed a case of spoons on the table, a series of flat kite-shaped pieces of metal on metal sticks, the kite's top edges knurled back. Reginald selected one and handed it to Gaunt. He measured it against the wound then selected another one, a smaller one. "Did you get a look at the head of the bolt?"

"Yeah, it had Nils's name written all over it."

Gaunt said nothing; he just stared, or glared, really.

I relented purely for Nils's sake. "A flesh-head. Not a bodkin. The breadth of two fingers." I peered at the open case, at all of the copper spoons laid out by size. I spied an arrow-spoon I guessed of similar size to the bolt head. "That one." I pointed.

Gaunt cursed silently then chose the arrow-spoon I'd indicated. He held it beside the wound, nodding silently to himself, then handed it to Reginald. "Smooth, easy." He checked the clamps his assistant had set. "Brother Tomas told me you had a problem."

"Brother Tomas is half-mad."

"Yet you claim not to know him."

"If he claims to know me, he must be half-mad."

"Brother Tomas may, indeed, be *fully* mad."

"And if he is, what interest am I to you?"

"A storm of discord has been kicked up in this city. Chaos, Krait." He prodded the arrow wound with two metal forks then gripped the red edges and eased them apart. "You may have noticed." He nodded to Reginald. "Use the bolt shaft to guide you. And go between the arrow and the bone. The extraction shall go smoother. Generally. If you meet resistance, work it around minutely until it passes." Reginald winced, hissing like he'd burned his fingers as he inserted the arrow-spoon into the wound. "Aye. Just follow the bolt." The big man watched on with hawk eyes. "Now push it beyond the head. Do you feel it? Resistance? Yes. Good. Now work the spoon over the head until you feel you've captured it." He waited while Reginald worked, nervous, unsure. "Yes? You have it?" Reginald nodded. "Here." Gaunt took both spoon and bolt in hand, tested them. "Good. Now with your free hand, gently pull on the shaft as you pull up on the spoon. Pull from before and behind." Blood seeped drizzling from the wound. "That is the reasoning behind the arrow-spoon. If the head is glued to the shaft, then you may withdraw the arrow without the spoon. Some fletchers, however, use beeswax rather than glue to secure the head. Pull on a beeswax-fixed arrow and you pull the shaft out and nothing more. Bandages, Olaf."

Gaunt steadied Nils's leg as Reginald, letting out a pent-up breath, withdrew the bolt, shaft, barbed head and all. Olaf was on the wound with a fistful of white dressings in an instant. "I'm always interested in chaos, Krait, as it concerns me, God, the people of Asylum. Good, Reg. Olaf, flush it with the wine. Then sew it shut. And pressure. Always pressure."

Olaf inserted the clyster into the leg wound and forced wine in.

"Can you get drunk that way?" A whole new realm

of possibility was opening before my very eyes.

Gaunt glared. At me. Again.

"And this chaos, is my fault, how?" I asked.

"I never claimed it was your fault."

"Then?"

"I didn't claim it wasn't, either," Gaunt said.

"Chaos and discord? Welcome to the world. I know you're a cloistered lot, but what about the plague? Plague's a hellstorm in and of itself. And what of the civil war?"

"You have a guilty conscience, Krait. Regarding your reputation, I can understand why."

"What the hell do you want?" I demanded.

"I'm not accusing you of precipitating Asylum's demise. To lay blame's sum total upon the shoulders of one man would be foolish. Hastening, though? Perhaps. We all have a hand in it. It is never just one man."

"Doesn't mean it doesn't happen."

"Scapegoating, aye, Asylum has had its share. And fools we have as well, a surplus, indeed. But plague? Plague is plague. Men die and another steps up to take the place. I'm talking of the war that's been kicked up." Gaunt placed a dressing then wound a bandage around it. "This city shall not survive it."

"Like I said, I just arrived."

"I know."

"Whose side are you on?" I asked.

"My own."

"Neutral? Those were Raachwald's men you smashed."

"Aye."

"Yet you claim no side? Why not the Lord Bishop's? You're both for the church."

"We Teutonics are beholden only to the pope himself," Gaunt said. "The Lord Bishop has taken liberties in the past. Broken trust. I'll not expound. Thus, we brother-knights have remained neutral in this debate."

"*Debate*? That's like saying that at Sluys a few Frenchmen took a dip in the river."

"You have a gift for undervaluing the lives of men far better than yourself."

"And just because you haven't picked a side in this little war doesn't mean you're neutral."

"I've been tasked with maintaining some form of order in Asylum. Restriction of the people's will is not just. Not in any times, more so in these. And restricting the bridge is restricting their will, their movement, their ability to survive. They're starving in the east. And the city is dying, but it must survive." His gaze set upon me. "Those who hasten its demise shall suffer."

"What the hell's this got to do with me?"

"You like to play games, Krait."

"Does the deer being hunted consider it sport? Jesus. Someone wants me dead. I don't consider it a game. I consider it survival."

"Understandable for a man in your predicament, a man on stage."

"On stage?"

"Aye. They've taken an interest in you."

"They who?" I said.

"Everyone," Gaunt said. "Everyone of consequence."

"You'd think everyone of consequence'd have greater worries than me."

"This city writhes in its death throes, Krait. A dying thing kicking about, lashing out at everything within reach. For weeks, men and women have been scurrying from it like rats from a burning building. Rats are stupid, but they know how to survive. And whilst all the rats are piling out, along comes this one scurrying in. Would that not draw your notice?"

"Might not." Jesus, why the hell was everyone comparing me to rats? "I'm fairly stupid myself."

"It seems so."

"And what of the men who remain?" I asked. "Who do nothing? How smart are they?"

"Oh, come now, Krait. You claim to be a knight. You must have met one or two in your time, men of vision, of ambition, that foul elixir drunk by men who wish to rise. And a plague-ridden city at war? Men of every stratum dying in droves? The nobleman's delight."

"I prefer wine and whores," I said.

"Because you're a man of limited vision."

"Are you calling me stupid…again?"

Gaunt deigned not to answer.

"Well then," I said, "your point?"

"Four lords have died of plague in the past month. Four." He counted on his fingers. "Eight ladies. Fifteen knights. Thirty squires. Countless lesser nobles. Countless clergy. And where space opens, men seek to fill it, rising through the ranks through the mere act of survival. Imagine how high a man of means and will might rise were he to take an active part in it all? If he were to do more than merely survive?"

"By helping along the natural process?" I said.

"By aiding death, aye."

"He might rise far."

"He might, indeed. And he might not appreciate anyone hampering his designs."

"You mean me?"

Gaunt nodded. "What is one to make of our lone rat scurrying in?"

"He's obviously mad, and thus, beneath notice."

"But what if he that came scurrying in were the justiciar of a king? Might that not garner your interest?"

"How do you know all this?"

"Does it matter?"

"Maybe. But you're speaking in the realm of imagination. Invention. This solitary man is but a caravan guard. Nothing more."

"So you say. But once the servant of a king, always a servant, aye? Are you ever a former from that particular duty? Out of favor? Exiled? Ostracized? Aye, you might be all of those things, I know not. But if your king called on you, needed you, you would obey. You would obey like a neutered dog, tongue lolling, wagging your tail, begging for scraps."

"You've a high opinion of my loyalty, assuming I have *any*."

"I have a high opinion of your self-interest."

"Then why am I here?"

"That's what I'd like to know."

I didn't realize my hand was on my sword. I left it there.

Gaunt continued his duties upon Nils, his attendants, too. "Lord Volkendorf's wife goes missing the day after you saunter into town."

"Are you insinuating I took her?"

"Rumor has it some savage took her, murdering ten of Raachwald's men in the effort." Gaunt studied me. "Rumor has it that he is your man, that he and your brother abducted the lady. That they burned Dunmire to the ground. This has been confirmed by my own eyes. So, no, I'm not insinuating. I don't insinuate. Women and eunuchs insinuate. I'm saying so. You took her."

"I did not. And my brother wasn't involved."

"So you say." He rose up, eclipsing the light. "But he's being held. Was tried. I've heard he's to be executed."

I nodded. "You heard right."

"He is involved then."

"Yeah."

"And your man is involved, so you're involved, whether you desire it or not."

"Of course, I'm involved. But I'm just trying to tread water here. My brother? Forget about my brother. He was trying to help Narcissa. And my man was trying to help him. And it all got fucked. Fucked by her. Fucked by him. Fucked."

"A coarse way to put it," he said.

"I'm a coarse man."

"So, Brother Tomas, the monk, you know him now?" Gaunt asked.

"I do." I glanced up at him, way up. "Strange, he didn't mention you."

"Strange, or not so strange." Gaunt crossed his arms. "Perhaps because I match the description of your killer?"

"Now that you mention it."

"And you've come here, to my home."

"You're missing one thing."

"Oh?"

"The lady's story is horseshit."

"Horseshit, yet here you stand. A mere day after seeing me upon the bridge?"

"Are you confessing?" I asked.

"Are you asking me if I'm a murderer?"

"Oh, I'm sure you're a murderer. You're a knight, and a Teutonic one at that. Murder is your business. Your bread and butter. But are you *the* murderer?"

"Perhaps you've come here under the guise of a man in need of aid to assess his prey? To catch him unawares?"

"You're implying I shot Nils in some mummer's farce to come here and suss you out? You give me too much credit."

"How? For ruthlessness? Or cleverness?"

"The second one," I deadpanned.

"A slick bastard you are."

"A slick bastard wouldn't be in my boots. A slick bastard wouldn't be stuck in Asylum-*fucking*-City during plague season. Wouldn't be tangled in this maelstrom."

"Most men would be dead by now, and the rest would be running."

"Stupid, remember?" I tapped a finger to my temple.

"I think not."

"First clever? And now brave?" I shook my head. "I don't think I've ever met a worse judge of character. That whole cloistered thing, again?"

"We see enough. Enough to make friends. Foes."

"Anyone I might know?"

"Take your pick."

"Volkendorf?" I asked.

"Aye."

"You've a history, then?" I asked.

"Aye," Gaunt said. "Volkendorf and all the other nobles in this city. A long history. A bloody history."

"Why tell me this?"

"Because I'm not in the habit of hiding. By any manner, shape, or method."

"What did you have against Volkendorf?"

"He caused problems, let us say."

"Care to elaborate?"

"No."

"Well, all that '*no hiding*' shit just went out the window."

"Indeed."

"Then what did he have against you?"

"The same hatred the rest of them bear against me and mine."

I considered. "A standing army in their city? A standing army those in power don't control, unswayed by local politics, with no overriding love of money? Only for the glory of God and the conquering of land? I imagine none of the nobles of Asylum enjoy your presence. Though, strange it is, that the city did finally end in the hands of God." I watched his eyes. "You have a hand in that?"

"Of course," Gaunt answered.

"For the Pope?"

"The Lord Bishop is a representative of the Pope."

"But you don't back him now?"

"As I said, I am neutral. For the time being. I have chosen to side the priory with neither of the aggressors. We shall let them hash it out. We serve to protect the people until this nonsense concludes."

"Fair enough. Let murder take its course. But what's your point in all this?"

"Simply that I did not kill Volkendorf."

"*Oh?*" I brushed my hands off. "Well, I'm glad that's settled."

"I say this because you'd have found out about me eventually. And you'd have found out I hated Volkendorf. And you'd have found out he hated me. To save you time. To save me the bother, and so that in the end I'm not forced to kill you before you complete your task."

"You're like a saint," I said in awe.

"And also to tell you I am no liar."

"Then you're a rarity. You realize I'd be an even worse justiciar than I am, were I to believe you?"

"In time you might, though. I tell you I didn't kill him because I didn't. I tell you though I might have. Perhaps I should have? I did not kill his men, though I could have. And I did not kill his children because I would not have."

"Jesus must be so proud."

Gaunt said nothing, though I had the distinct impression he was growling, hackles risen.

"Well, then, that's settled." I stepped back.

"Is it?" His gaze flickered to Yolanda, my hand on her. "I have an aversion to knives at my back."

"And ones at your front?" I asked.

"Have never posed a problem for me."

"Well, then. What do you want me to say? I'm not here to kill you? Or capture you? The truth? I came for Nils. That's all."

"And so seeing you yesterday was coincidence?"

"Coincidence?" I nodded. "Yeah."

"I don't believe in coincidence."

"The will of God, then, perhaps? I can assure you I wish only to find the children's killer, release my brother, and be done with this shit-hole."

"And the lady?" Gaunt loomed forward.

"I don't give a damn about the lady."

"Not true."

I thought about it. "Her fate does concern me," I conceded. "We're intertwined but only from the standpoint of my brother's fate."

"Then where is she?"

"I don't know."

"Why should I believe you?"

"Because I was honest with you. I told you I was a liar."

"You're a fool." He scowled. "You should know. Is she even alive? You'd best pray so. Everything you do is incumbent upon that one piece of knowledge. Your life. Your man's. Your brother's."

I said nothing.

"Lord Raachwald is remarkable amongst his kind for only one thing," Gaunt said. "The man hates."

"And what does he hate, besides me?" I asked.

"What all men of power hate."

"Anyone with more," I said.

"And anyone with less. And all shades between. The man is known by many names, all appropriate." Gaunt paused for a moment. "They call him the Cyclops for his one eye. They call him the Lord of Gallows, also. Nomenclature of another one-eyed being, for another reason, Odin, of the old gods. One born with one eye, one crippled by his own choosing. For a cost. The two have little in common. One is little more than a beast. The other? The wisest of the pagan gods. A god and a giant. Enemies from birth to death and beyond. The only thing the two bear in common? Both are dangerous. And he is dangerous, your Lord Raachwald."

"Any man can be dangerous," I said.

"Any man, every man, aye, but he, especially. A man of determination coupled with resources. Power. He hates like they did in the old days, blood-oath hate, pagan hate, tearing-lungs-from-his-foe's-back hate. A hate so deep-seated as to be an inextricable part of his very soul. Perhaps it is its sum total?"

"I know the feeling," I quipped.

"Do you?" The big man just looked at me. I got the feeling he knew how to hate as well, and I was fair sure he was exercising it. "Then you must know that if Lady

Narcissa is dead, so are you, and so is your brother. That one piece of knowledge is the keystone to your whole existence. It is the king amongst pawns. The rest are nothing. Every action. Every reaction. If you're not working towards a conclusion, a checkmate, you're doing only one thing. You're wasting your brother's time. And if she is dead, you are wasting yours."

"Like I said. I don't know where she is."

"But your man has her."

"Or she has him. Or a little bit of both, most likely."

"And they have both gone to ground. For your sake, I hope he proves equal to the task."

"If anyone is, it's him."

Chapter 25.

SHADOWS FELL once again upon the world, another day lost, while I trudged on through the mud and cobblestone, through a world of twilight horror, watching the rooftops of the ramshackle homes for shadow wraiths, silent assassins, for the revenants surely trailing me, hunting me, the quick prick of a bolt skewering me through the throat.

A woman wailed somewhere.

A chill rolled through me as a wide-brimmed figure stepped from an alleyway, staring me down with glistening insect eyes. Death incarnate. My heart jumped. But no. His eyes merely watched as I edged past, inhuman, a long-beaked mask of tooled leather covering his face, breathing in slurping rasps, long stick in hand. A plague doctor. He turned from me and slopped a long crimson slash across a door.

Grasping at crumbling brick, I turned down a claustrophobic alley, delving into the deeper shadows, skirting garbage, watching over my shoulder. Shadows moved. Danced. Plague fire burned to the north. To the south. The east. Everywhere. Death stalked the streets tonight. I could feel it. Taste it. I pushed Stephan, maimed, freezing in the dark, and Nils pale and limp, barely breathing, both out of my mind. Both because of me.

Light. I needed light and some dry quiet to pour through Chalstain's journal, what little of it I might. A stone's throw from the Stone Ruin Ten, I was accosted from an alley, a hand grabbing at my belt. My dagger was skinned in an instant. I let out a long breath. It was Girard, struggling and kicking as I gripped a fistful of his hair, pressing the blade to his throat.

"Fine way to lose your head, kid," I grumbled, my

heart galloping as I shoved him back, sheathed my blade.

"Thought you'd seen me, sir." The boy rose from the mud.

"Well, I—" I gave him an eye-full of murder. "What the hell's with the *sir*?"

Sulking, Girard rubbed his head.

"Sorry about that," I said. "Wound a little tight."

Girard swallowed. "The girl, uh…"

"Lorelai?"

He nodded.

"Don't nod, say it aloud." I crossed my arms. "Say it aloud, and you're more likely to remember it."

"Lorelai," the boy repeated.

"Good," I said. "Forget it at your own peril. Might serve you in good stead some day."

"How?"

"In your case?" I rubbed my chin. "Maybe she's got some winsome lass for a daughter about your age? You never know."

"What's winsome?" he asked.

"Winsome's what they're not after you finally decide to marry them. Now, what does she want?"

"She wants you to go to her house." The boy pointed toward the northeast.

I bowed and held a hand out. "Lead on, good sir."

* * * *

"*This* is a carpenter's house?" I looked up dubiously. The house was two-stories high and leaning noticeably to the left. The rear of the building abutted the old Roman wall surrounding the Jewish Quarter. The wall rose twenty feet, the masonry still straight as an arrow. Its square construction and all the rest of the houses on Carpenter Street made Lorelai's all the more skewed by contrast.

"Don't know." Girard glared suspiciously up at the bent walls of the house. "But this is it."

"She say why?" The house had been boarded up. A

red mark had been slashed across the front door. I checked the alleyways. Nothing of note.

"No, sir." The boy shrugged. "Said you'd give me a crown, though."

"A crown?"

"A crown." He said it with determination.

"A *crown*?" I deadpanned. "Life lesson number two involves the injection of truth into lies. You want it to go down smooth, like amber brown."

"What's amber brown?"

"Lass I knew, long time ago." I checked the front door. "Forget it." It was unlocked. "It was Lorelai *herself* that asked me to come?"

"Uh huh." Girard nodded, eyes wide as he fingered his lip.

"You know what an ambush is?"

"Huh?"

I stepped to the side, drew the butcher's blade and pushed Girard behind me.

"Wait there." I pointed to an alley across the street. "Keep an ear out. You hear me screaming or the clash of swords—"

"I'll run for help."

"No. You run your bony little legs in here and save my arse."

Lorelai's house was like most of the houses and establishments on the street, barring the right angles and the impending aura of collapse. A couple of windows were out front with a collapsible shelf in front to display wares.

I clutched the butcher blade as I stepped through the front door. The front room was small and had once served as a shop. I crept through the door to the back. A hooded form sat huddled in a chair amongst a stable of saw horses and barrels of nails. Tools hung from the wall, coils of rope from the joists above, sinister in their silent inertia.

I approached.

Whoever it was didn't move. I heard light snoring and saw mist forming as the someone breathed.

"Lorelai?"

The form didn't move. I could smell wine. Strong.

I flipped the hood back. An arched eyebrow and a lascivious smirk met me. Lorelai glanced down at my blade. "Not the weapon I had in mind."

"Jesus." I let out a bated breath. "And what weapon was it?"

"One not so sharp." She held my gaze as her hand met mine and gently pushed my blade down, away. "Nor nearly so long."

I smirked, shaking my head, sheathing the blade.

"Mmmmm…" She sat up forward in her chair, stretching her neck, her back, grabbing her wrist and lifting her arms overhead. Catlike. I watched in silent admiration. Not many women can make a homespun cloak alluring. Lorelai could. Did. Was. "I've been here for hours." She yawned, covering her mouth. "Long night. Restless day. Couldn't sleep. Couldn't…anything." She nodded to a bottle of wine on a table. "Thirsty?"

"Always." I took the wine and nailed back a shot, thoughts of Blackbeard on my mind. "Must be tough." I handed it to her. "On your back all day and night."

"Just because I'm on my back don't mean it ain't work." She took a long pull off the bottle, upending it, her throat working, eyes closed, swallowing til she finished. She wiped her mouth. Held it back out to me. "Or pleasant."

"Never?" I took another sip.

"Never."

"So, what's so important?" As I spoke, I stalked around the room, glancing out boarded up windows, listening for the sound of footsteps upstairs. Stacks of lumber lay cluttered in a corner, a matching set of chairs, a headboard.

"Heard you were dead," Lorelai murmured, her husky voice still full of sleep and sorrow, "then I heard you weren't."

"And how many tears would you weep for me, sweet Lorelai?" I glanced up the stairs.

"Hmmm? Me?" She put a finger to her lip. "Oh, none."

"Spiteful wench."

"My husband might, though."

"Oh? My, my. A forward-thinking man. Weeping for his wife's paramour."

"Paramour?" She brushed her hair from eyes. "You mistake me. He'd weep, but over the loss of income. You pay in Provins silver. Richer than the tin-thin shit around here. Thirty percent silver, he used to say."

"But I didn't pay," I reminded her.

She smiled sadly, taking a drink. "We all pay."

"Your husband knows his silver, though." I picked up a hatchet from the workbench. "Mind if I borrow a few things?" She waved a hand. I tucked it in my belt along with a few other items. "A man after my own heart. I like him already."

"As do I." Lorelai watched me.

"Like?" I glanced at her sidelong.

"Love."

"A loving wife?" I cocked my head to the side. "A true rarity in this world. I might find a unicorn in here next."

"As rare as a faithful husband?"

"We were speaking of rare, not nonexistent. But, oh? Is your husband unfaithful?"

"Don't ask me about him."

"You brought him up."

She looked down, away.

"Oh, do tell. Where is the scoundrel?" I looked around. "I'll have words with him. Fisticuffs. Is he a large man?" Lorelai nodded, smiling, almost. "Swords, it is then."

"Oh, my gentle knight," she deadpanned, "ever at the ready to murder men less well-armed and trained than he."

I thumped my inflated rooster's chest then burst out laughing.

Lorelai just watched, placid, half smiling in the darkness, swirling the bottle of wine.

"Now what is it?" I asked.

"It's…it's just nice to hear someone laughing. Deeply. Truly. It's been such a long time. I've missed it. Hadn't known til I heard yours the day past. It's like a memory of, oh, I don't know, of summer. Of childhood. Of another world." She waved her hand. "I ain't a poet. But warm days strolling along a brook, hand in hand with," she took a deep breath, "just laughing."

"It's a pleasure to please you, milady." I swept a hand sidewise, dropping into a bow, taking her hand in mine, offering a chaste peck.

Eyes glistening, she watched me and didn't pull away.

"What is it, milady?" I snapped out a handkerchief.

"I wonder, Sir Luther, why it is that you're not desperate?" She took the handkerchief and dabbed it at her eye.

"Oh, but I am, Milady." *For you*, I almost added but held back because, well, I don't know.

"Not like the people in the tavern. The patrons. The singers. The workers. Everyone. It's like some desperate orgy to live. To sell. To buy." She brushed a strand of stubborn hair back. "To do whatever they think will see them through another day. And if they don't, it's still the same. Desperation. Fear. They're either numb or maniacs or something in between."

"Can you blame them?"

"No, for God's sake, I'm one of them," she admitted. "But you? You seem not to be either, is all. You talk as though you've not a care in the world. Act as though you're on holiday. And it makes me wonder…"

I picked up the wine, brandishing it with a smile. "Maybe I'm just a better actor than the rest?" Viciously, I drank away the image of Stephan's hand bouncing across stone that flickered through my mind. A cut stump in the half-light of a cell. Bodies burning in the night. I swallowed the wine, set it down, pushed it away, forcing a rakish grin. Lorelai didn't reciprocate. "Milady disapproves?"

"Enough. Enough, with the *miladies*." She waved a defeated hand. "Please. I'm a whore. A tavern wench. No, I'm not embarrassed by what I do. I want no pity, but I am that. I am that and nothing more, nothing less. Don't try to elevate me with false flattery. Don't reduce me. Don't—" she took a breath. "Just call me Lorelai. Pay me, fuck me, buy me a drink, leave me alone. I don't care. But do it and be done with it, Sir Luther."

"Fine." I straightened. "But you're more *Milady* than I am *Sir*. I don't know much, but I know that. So if I must call you Lorelai, and it is a beautiful name, then you must call me Luther. We'll meet in the middle, yeah?"

Nodding, a tear rolled down her cheek.

"What's wrong?"

"What's not wrong?"

"Everything going on may have bent you, but you didn't break. You're not broken."

"Jesus. Don't try to *not* be a shit. Not now." She rubbed the back of her neck. "We were speaking of faithful husbands."

"We were. In jest, I had thought."

"What of you, Sir Luther?"

"Just Luther, Lorelai. You must follow the rules. They're your own."

"What of you, then, Luther?"

"What of me?"

"You claimed that faithful husbands are nonexistent."

"What are you asking me?"

"What am I asking you?" She took a drink.

"Are you asking me if I'm faithful to my wife? Or are you trying to start a row? You already know the answer to the first. And I'm an old hand at rows begun by ambiguous questions cast with reckless abandon by beautiful women."

"You wear her ring still." She glanced down at my left hand. "I'm asking why you're not faithful to her."

"Ah. It is a *row* you desire. And what right is it of a

whore to question her patron's faithlessness?" Acid burned in my voice, perhaps too much. "What would she do without it?"

"Starve," she conceded. "I only thought…" She shook her head. "You suppose I should thank you?"

"No," I answered. "A good moral Christian gives alms to the poor and asks no thanks. It's his duty."

"You've strange notions of morality."

"You're very good, Lorelai," I placed a hand over my heart, patting my chest, "but there's nothing in here you can touch."

"Your wife, is she beautiful?"

"Very."

"Of course she is. And am I?"

"You know you are."

"Then why?"

"Why what?"

"Why is *she* not enough?"

"What do you want me to say?" I dropped to one knee, the consummate actor, the consummate liar. "Oh, Lorelai, my wife was taken by the plague, and now I yearn for the warmth of a woman's touch to quell my broken heart!"

"Don't mock me," she spat.

"Apologies, milady." I rose from my knee. "I don't know why I said that." I shook my head. "No. I do. I was reminded of it recently. Once upon a time, I was the best. The best sort of husband. The best sort of man. I worked at it, but truth be told, it came natural to me. And she, my wife, was the best sort of wife. We were simply not best for each other, I suppose. We tried after a fashion. We lived. We fought. We changed. Me mostly." I swallowed. "And we had children, *have* children." I looked up. "Do you have any?"

Lorelai nodded.

"Well then, you know. They say you never know how hard you can love someone until you have a child. You love them so much it hurts your skin, your heart, your soul. Well. It isn't true. Not that I don't love mine. I did. I do. But

I loved my wife like that from the first day I saw her. I was ten-years-old. She was nine. Early to be loving in any manner, but I loved her more, more than anything. And still do." I looked out a window at the descending dark. "But, there's more to it, love and hate, you know? So far apart they're nearly one."

"You love her, but you fuck whores." She took a swig.

"Only the most beautiful." I smiled wanly.

"How many others have you lain with?"

"No." I snatched back the wine. Did what I do. "I've told you enough for tonight. Enough for a lifetime. You asked me here for a reason. So tell it. You say you thought I was dead. How? Why?"

"There…there was a rumor of an attack. Up on Quail Street. Four men killed. Everyone at the tavern was talking of it. Caused quite a ruckus."

I shook my head. "Two killed. Maybe three. The rest of the tale, though? True."

"Who?"

"Don't know."

"But you lived."

"I was lucky." Another swig. "Nils wasn't."

"He's dead, then?" Lorelai pursed her lips. "He seemed…he seemed a good sort."

"That's what got him shot." I turned toward the door. "I've business tonight."

"Wait—"

I stopped, my hand on the doorknob, waiting, saying nothing.

"I…" Her hands curled into fists. "It's not that."

"You've obviously something of importance to tell me." I ran a hand through my hair. "Someone tried to kill me today. And failed. An illness that promises a short remission. Promises return. Tonight, most likely. Tomorrow, most definitely. The day after? I don't make plans that far out." I opened the door, scanned the street. Nothing. "And I've not made many friends in this city. Enemies?" I nodded in earnest. "Well, now, that's never been a difficulty for me. And these'll keep coming at me and coming at me, and they won't stop til I'm dead." I held up a hand when she tried to speak. "I understand your concern. I've been spending time around you. Putting you at risk. You're worried my condition might prove contagious. And your worries are just. But you still need money, yeah? Still need to survive."

"Something," she bowed her head, nodding, "something like that."

"I understand. I have to make one last stop at the inn. Tonight. Pick something up from my room. And then you'll never have to see me again. I won't even take offense if you ignore me, yeah?" I took her chin in hand, raised her gaze to my own, pressing Volkendorf's silver raven pendant into her hand. I closed her fingers around it and kissed her soft lips. "Best have it melted down."

She swallowed, nodded. "Where are you going?"

"You don't want to know."

Chapter 26.

I STARED DOWN at Sir Myron Chalstain's corpse, laid out full in its coffin. His head had been reattached, thick bandages circling his neck. His hair was brown, and a full beard and mustache covered his upper lip and chin, all of it looking warped, distorted, wrong, as though his skull had shattered and only the drawn flesh upon it held everything together. The sleeve of his right arm had been stuffed, probably with straw, a glove sewn onto the end. The azure cross of Saint Hagan's lay tabarded across his chest. He looked whole, somewhat, but death always diminishes, even in cases less extreme. "How'd you find him?" I asked.

"Eh?" Father Paul laid a glimmering blade atop Sir Myron's chest, delicately adjusting it until it met the view in his mind's eye. A fine bit of steel. "Oh? Sir Luther." He took up a great helm and paused, unsure of what to do next. "I was just..." He fixed me a glance, unsure. "Helm, or no helm?"

"Helm," I answered without hesitation.

He nodded slowly then fixed the helm atop Chalstain's mashed head. "Yes."

"I came to report to the Lord Bishop. Captain Thorne sent me down here. To you."

"Yes, yes, my doing." He waved a hand absently. "I was just attempting to fix things."

"And how's that going for you, Father?"

"Forgive me." He dabbed at his eye with a handkerchief. "I misspoke. Truly, I don't know what it is I'm doing. This all came as something of a shock, you understand? I had hoped he would turn up. Somehow. Somewhere." He pursed his lips. "Nay, forgive me. I spoke untrue. I'm not *fixing* anything. I am merely saying goodbye to an old friend, perhaps wallowing in my own grief somewhat as well." He looked around at the eons of skulls embedded in the walls, staring down, an infinity of black hollows watching. "The necropolis seems a fitting place."

"It does indeed."

Stone effigies packed Saint Hagan's necropolis like patrons at a full-bore tavern, some standing, some sitting, some laid out upon their backs staring at the dark above. Columns of stacked bone reached the arched ceiling. And Jesus was everywhere. Effigies. Crucifixes. Bas reliefs. Father Paul adjusted Chalstain's arms, setting the gloved hands atop the hilt.

"You knew him well?"

"Yes," Father Paul smiled wanly, "of course." He waved a hand at the two guards standing at attention. "Leave us, gentlemen, please." They saluted, marched off into the shadowed recesses of Saint Hagan's crypt-infinite. We watched them go, an orb of flickering torchlight following them off. "I came to Asylum City five years ago, knowing not a soul. Such is life in the church. You go where commanded when commanded. Chalstain and I, we worked side by side those years. A good man. A man of character. I've not known many of his cast." He paused for a moment, considering. "None in fact."

I nodded.

"He was the eldest heir to House Taschgart, were you aware of that?" Father Paul asked. "Yes. The eldest of five. Solemn Rock, the Taschgart keep, his for the taking. All of it, and all he needed do was wait."

"Impatient?"

"Nay. Not him." Using the edge of his sleeve, he polished a smudge from the great helm. "He simply bore no desire for it, and he could not abide the vagaries of the Great Game."

"And by *vagaries*, you mean?"

"The deceit. The power-mongering. The knives in the dark. Lord," he scoffed, "the knives in the light as well. He desired nothing to do with it, any of it. He begged a simpler life."

"And now the good Lord Emile Taschgart has no heirs, is that right?" I asked.

Father Paul nodded. "Five sons. One turned away from him, denying him. The rest...the rest all died in the war, Poitiers, Sluys, Rotburg. His hope died along with them. Some say Lord Taschgart is cursed. Some say that whole damn Isle is cursed. This whole city. Sodom. Gomorrah." He flipped a hand, exhausted, dejected, disgusted. "What have you."

"Very biblical, father."

"Yes, quite." Father Paul cleared his throat. "Asylum was once a great city, a center for trade, and it could be again, but these imbeciles, fighting over plots of stone. Coldspire. Solemn Rock. Grand names to such inconsequential things." He crossed himself and rose. "Bits of rock upon a bit of rock. And five foolish Neros, gallivanting whilst Rome burns. If they could only forgive, forget, live in peace. Forgive me. It is an old story, a bent story, a broken story oft repeated."

"What happened to Sir Myron after he left Solemn Rock?"

"Sir Myron married the Lady Irene Chalstain, which, I'm told was another bone of contention with Lord Taschgart. The Chalstains were poor, Irene's father but a lowly knight. Lord Taschgart did not consider her house worthy of merging with his own. And Irene, Lord forgive me, she was no great beauty, so there was even no carnal reason he could cite for the union." Father Paul shook his head, chuffed a laugh. "But Sir Myron loved her just the same. He took her hand, and after he took her hand, he took her name. He became lord of her family's fief, little more than a farmhouse and fallow plot by the sea. Not that Myron ever cared for such things."

"And how did he come to labor for the church?"

"Sir Myron always possessed a reputation for character, honor. Even after the break with his father, perhaps especially after." Father Paul shrugged. "It enhanced his reputation, in point of fact, turning away from all that. A man untouchable by the vices common to so many. The rarest commodity in the city. Yet, his financial situation was ever at straits, a sad reality, and so I offered him a place here as the Lord Bishop's bailiff. A natural decision. It was a small stipend, a bit of coin, enough, but he was grateful for it and performed his duty with honor and skill, as I knew he would."

"How did you find his body?" I asked.

"Reports from Tanner Street. He was found dismembered in a cart. And his head? I still don't know where it was found. His Eminence has not been forthcoming and, the crows and dogs had..." He stifled a shudder. "His arm?" He looked up hopefully. "Did you chance to find it?"

"Sorry."

"A pity. I would have preferred him whole for the funerary services." He sniffed. "Not that it makes any difference, truly, but a thing broken must be made whole, no? It must be bent back to its nature, sewn, glued, reforged, for that is its nature, my nature as well. To fix things. Does that make any sense?"

"Everyone's got their crosses to bear, Father."

"And what is yours, Sir Luther? What cross bends your back and burdens your shoulders?"

"A brother with morals and me with none."

"I think that hyperbolic."

"Hyper *what*?"

Father Paul stared at me a moment, trying to discern whether I was joking. "I'm told we have you to thank for discovering the remains. Where was it you found him?"

"Along the coast. Up north. Goathead. An old empty barn next to the watchtower. Looked like he'd been hiding out there for a few days at the least. Don't know for sure. Living like an urban hermit. I found some blankets. A bit of food. Any idea why he'd be hiding there?"

Father Paul rubbed his chin. "No."

"And you mentioned that he'd been met with obstructions?" I said. "What sort?"

"Besides the Raachwald incident?" Father Paul said.

"It seemed to me that he lacked the backing of the Lord Bishop with regards to certain facets of his investigation. His Eminence was reluctant to grant access with regards to the Quarter."

"Any idea why he didn't come here?" I asked. "Saint Hagan's seems a mite more secure than some Jew's cowshed on the water. Nice view, but…"

Father Paul glanced aside, ashamed. "Forgive me, Sir Luther." He lowered his voice, glancing this way and that. "Men such as Chalstain are rare, rare for their drive, rare for their honor, but those qualities come at a price. That price is inflexibility, obstinacy."

Sounded like Stephan, always letting his damned morals guide him. Never giving an inch. Never backing down.

"Yes. A man of morals and uncompromising in their application. Thus, he was not well-liked by many." He glanced over his shoulder, his voice hushed. "You understand?" I nodded. "And His Eminence was chief amongst them. I'm afraid the two did not see eye-to-eye on a myriad of subjects. I advised him to go through me for his work so that he might not be placed in a position that would compromise his…" He left the end of the sentence unsaid. "But compromise and justice he felt were two ideals ever at cross purposes."

"I understand." You'd think the highest ranking men of the church'd be the most pious, the best, the brightest, but like any power chain, the top was often held by the most ruthless, the hardest, the worst.

"He should have come to me." Father Paul clenched a fist. "He should have…"

"Someone was after him," I said.

"Perhaps."

"*Perhaps?*" I cocked my head. "Any idea who?"

"As I said, Lord Raachwald had threatened him. That much I know. Not a man to make idle threats, that one. But though it would not surprise me that Raachwald had a hand in this, I could not say with certitude, you understand?

But I think it the most likely of possibilities. The two had a history."

"Yeah? What?"

"Sir Myron served as Lord Raachwald's squire in his younger days. It was Lord Raachwald himself who knighted him. That was the reason His Eminence sent him to investigate, on some forlorn whim that Lord Raachwald might honor their past and allow Chalstain to act as justiciar."

"But Raachwald wouldn't have it."

Father Paul shook his head. "Nay."

"Anyone else who would want him dead?" I asked.

"Sir Myron had no dearth of enemies in Asylum," Father Paul said. "Many men had their lives ended by the noose or the axe for his diligence. Isle Men, common criminals, the gangs, many of those men left behind brothers, fathers, friends." Father Paul adjusted his robe. "And of course, the one who murdered Volkendorf, naturally. Of course, I think it a juncture with our former topic of discussion."

"You think Raachwald fits the writ?" I asked.

"It seems the most likely solution. Lord Raachwald is capable of anything. Though I am no investigator, and proof, evidence, headway, admittedly, were all difficulties for Sir Myron. He confided in me so himself. I see it with you as well."

"The burden of proof," I lamented.

"Truly amazing, is it not? The man disappears for weeks. And the man is a good man, a strong man, sound of both mind and body and soul, an uncompromising man, uncompromising where it counts, with his principles, with his thoughts, his every action. He disappears. Vanishes. Every man available searches for him and finds nothing. He only manages to find his way back to the house of his lord *after* he has been murdered, and he is discovered by you, a man in the city but days."

"Actually, it was one of the city-watchmen that caught wind of it," I admitted. "He's the one told me. I went with him. He ought to get the credit, him and his sergeant, if there's credit due."

"This is the guard caught in the ambush?"

"Yeah."

"The Lord Bishop has men searching even now for the assassins," he said. "And the guard, he will be provided for and in the event of his death, his family's heriot will be waived."

"They'll be overjoyed."

Father Paul's eyes narrowed. "You are a strange man, Sir Luther. You tread the line of being insufferable and seem the opposite of Sir Myron, yet you are not wholly unlike him either, in some inscrutable manner, if you don't mind me saying."

"Not at all." I glanced down at the corpse in the box. Hopefully, our similarities ended there.

"Many would have taken the credit themselves."

"Only credit I'm interested in is the money-kind. Was there a reward?"

"Is gratitude a reward?"

"It can be, depending on whose it is."

Father Paul placed a hand to his chest, offering a slight bow. "Mine."

"You're sure there's no gold? Silver?"

"Was anything else found with Sir Myron?" Father Paul asked.

"A few blankets," I answered, the rocks in my coin purse and the ledger I'd secreted away in a nearby vacant house, standing foremost in my mind. "Some food, as I said. A spoon. Nothing more. The strangest part? For a man on the run, a *knight* on the run, I found no weapons. I turned the place upside down searching."

"Yes, indeed," Father Paul said. "You found nothing else, you're certain?"

"Yeah."

"Well," he clasped his hands together, "I thank you for your efforts and your reporting this directly. I took liberties, but thought perhaps you might wish to deal with me rather than His Eminence."

I nodded. "He taking a nap?"

Father Paul smirked despite himself.

"What of it all, though?" I asked.

"Excuse me?"

"His injuries, Father."

"Horrific." Father Paul shook his head.

"Know anything in the neighborhood that could cause them?"

"In the neighborhood?"

"On the earth, then?"

"I…I couldn't possibly imagine."

"Maybe someone hurled him from a trebuchet into a war hammer emporium?" I stared down at the body. "How about his wife?"

"His wife?" Father Paul rubbed his throat, staring at me like he wasn't sure he liked what he saw. "Lady Chalstain, Irene, is not well. One of her sons, her youngest, was murdered in an attempt on her life. She was placed in Saint Edna's soon after. An asylum for lunatics and the mentally feeble, the same asylum the city takes its name from. A few weeks past, following Sir Myron's disappearance, Lady Chalstain went mad with grief at his loss. Apparently. She was in a…a state. *Catatonic* is the word, I'm told. She hasn't spoken a word since she's been there."

"Hmmm. How many children did they have?"

"Six," he answered. "Six scattered to the winds. Children? Nay, most are grown. No doubt word has not even reached them yet. I sent letters concerning his disappearance, weeks past. I shall have to send more. Lord, his eldest is fighting in the east, Samuel, with the Teutonics, for seasoning. In Novgorod, or thereabouts. He'll be returning no doubt, once word reaches him. The others? One is a priest. Two are but squires at far-flung castles, I believe. His daughters? One is married to a graf. Another is in Florence."

"I've been in Florence. Breathtaking."

"I sadly have never been to Italy."

"Who's talking about Italy?"

"I...*what?*" Father Paul stammered.

"I'd like to speak to Lady Chalstain."

"Well," he pressed steepled fingers against his lips, took a deep breath and then nodded, "I can't see what good it would do, but I can't see what ill, either."

"All this cost him his life. He was a man trudging through hell. A son murdered. His wife felled, infirm. Enemies engaging in force. On the run. Cast out from his home, from his Lord. What drove the man?"

"What drives all good men of faith and character, I should suppose," Father Paul answered.

"And what's that, Father?" I asked

"I haven't the faintest."

...write this by candlelight in my den. The moon is full tonight, and I imagine I can see someone creep outside my home, casting dim moon-shadows upon the shutters as he skulks...
—Journal of Sir Myron Chalstain

Chapter 27.

"Tea?" the sister asked.

"No, thank you." I was parched but it wasn't tea would quench it.

Fresh rushes lay spread across the floor, and the room had a pungent just-cleaned scent like maybe they'd recently scrubbed the floors and walls. Impressive, as far as asylums go. I'd been in some where the only thing on the floors was shit. Of course, Lady Chalstain was a lady, and that was worth something. The mattress of her bed curved like an eroded mountain, smooth and crescent and lofty. It was well made, both in structure and furnishings.

Out the tiny window was a picturesque view of the city, stretching west along the coast to the bay and across, the watchtower on Goathead far off, just barely visible, its flame atop it rippling silent across the sound.

Lady Chalstain sat slouched in a chair against the wall, her dark hair tied in a loose bun atop her head, vines of it snaking down across her pale face, so pale as to be almost translucent. Beads of sweat glistened on her forehead as she aimlessly chewed whatever it was that the sister had spooned into her mouth. The sister crooned a soft melody as she worked slowly, purposefully, beaming when she was able to get a full spoonful in.

"Forgive me the late hour," I said.

Lady Chalstain said nothing as porridge slid down her chin.

"There, there, milady." The sister spooned up the porridge and reintroduced it to Lady Chalstain's mouth as though she were a baby. "Good. Good. Now swallow. Yes. There. Now another." With never-ending patience, she eased another spoonful into the lady's slack, open mouth. "You need your strength, milady."

Lady Chalstain's head was cocked to the side as she stared at the flame of the watchtower, her eyes unfocused, blank, empty. The sister dabbed at the corner of her lip with a napkin.

"Lady Chalstain…" Leaning forward, I waved a hand in front of her face. No reaction. I snapped my fingers like a complete asshole, right by her ear. Again, nothing. The sister gave me a stern glare, and I withdrew, fearful she might skin a ruler and rap my knuckles. "How long's she been like this?"

The sister frowned. "A few weeks." She was a robust older woman, and even when frowning, there was a round joviality to her that I'm sure served her in good stead. "Poor, poor lady." She held a hand up in front of her mouth as though to share a secret. "I heard they found her husband today." She glanced at Lady Chalstain. "This very morn, it's said."

"How is he?" News did travel fast.

"*Dead*," she mouthed.

I shook my head. "And what happened to her?"

"Grief." Her hands clasped at her breast. "Oh, a grief so powerful it plowed a furrow right through her very soul, I think." She made the sign of the cross on her ample bosom. "It was just too much for the dear. Sadly, we see it here too often. Like a bridge bearing too much weight, something must give." She sighed. "Tragic. The dear just couldn't take her husband's…well, she just couldn't. And to have lost a son that very week? Murdered, they say." Her voice was a whisper again. "Would have lain anyone in a stupor."

"Do they ever come out of it?"

"Aye." The sister smiled half-heartedly. "Sometimes."

"Do you think she will?"

"The Lord works in mysterious ways." She clucked to herself, then undid the bun of hair atop Lady Chalstain's head.

"He sure does." I thought for a moment. "When did her husband disappear?"

"Oh? Hmm…" She gathered the lady's hair up in two hands. "Seems near a month ago, a few weeks at any rate, after the plague. He just up and disappeared." She glanced at Lady Chalstain sidelong and lowered her voice. "Though, for weeks people have claimed seeing him."

"Yeah? Whereabouts?"

"Oh?" She adroitly tied the lady's hair in place with a length of blue ribbon. "Here and there, I suppose. I heard some brewer claimed seeing some knight in his loft. Blue cross on his chest. Very polite, Sir Chalstain was."

"He never showed up to see her?"

"Not that I know of," the sister answered, putting the final touches on the bun. "There."

"Did anyone ever visit?"

"Father Paul." She shook her head in admiration. "He came here himself and sat by her side for quite some time, just sitting with her, talking with her, reading to her. She never said a thing back, of course, but…"

"What's your name, milady?"

"Sister Milicent, milord." She wagged a finger at me, blushing.

"Sister Milicent. A beautiful name. Very alliterative," I said. "Does Lady Chalstain ever speak?"

"Oh, no, milord. She just sits here, staring out the window, gazing off toward the ocean. She does love it so. She grew up by it." She pointed out the window. "And the watchtower, she loves to gaze at its rippling flames, all night sometimes. A thing of beauty amidst all this grey."

"That it is," I said.

She nodded.

"And she's been this way since she came here?" I asked.

"She was grief-stricken, it's true." Sister Milicent patted the lady's hand. "But she had her wits. At first. They were dragged through the mud and addled, maybe, but she had them. No, t'was a few days after she came here. A few days of hysteria, and then like a gale wind it passed, passed into this. Peace."

I stood and offered a bow. "Well, this has been most help…" I froze mid-bow. A tear had welled up in the inner corner of Lady Chalstain's eye, glistening there as it grew until it trickled down her cheek. I said nothing, just staring as Sister Milicent shushed her like a newborn and wiped the tear clean with a handkerchief.

Lady Chalstain was weeping blood.

...privy to ancient tomes describing dark rites and occult mysteries of the old country...
—Journal of Sir Myron Chalstain

Chapter 28.

THE JOINT FELL silent before I even closed the door. Gazes turned my way, slowly, synchronously, eyebrows furrowing, backs straightening. Eight men. None of them looked particularly friendly. A hushed conversation was the only sound but for the break of ocean waves not far off, the whistle of wind, the creaking of worm-infested ships.

The Fool's Hand. A shithole. At best.

Settled amidst the warehouses and storage dumps, the claustrophobic tavern was nearly impossible to find. I'd circled the same block, passed the same rotting docks, the same packs of homeless derelicts, wondering all the while when some assassin was going to take another crack at me. Fifth time around, I saw the motleyed hand scrawled by the front door. Upright slats of hoary gray board, splintery, scaled in runnels of white salt. Calling it a shack would have been unkind to the whole grand tradition of shackdom.

"You lost, mister?" The bartender reached under the bar.

"No." I brushed some snow off my shoulders. "This is the Fool's Hand, yeah?"

The bartender glanced to his right, to a long lanky fellow sitting with his feet up, watching me from under the hood of his cloak. He itched his red beard, the only thing I could make out on him. Everyone was watching me, pins and needles head to toe and back again. *Eggshells*, a word that came to mind. Redbeard, with his feet up, a book splayed open on his lap, twitched a nod the bartender's way.

"Yah," the bartender answered. "What's it you want?"

I shrugged. "Heard the crab cakes were to die for."

Redbeard chuckled to himself, licked a finger, turned a page.

The bartender swallowed.

"Ale?" I asked.

The bartender's gaze twitched back to Redbeard.

"Ale?" I turned to Redbeard.

"Runnin' low." Redbeard shook his head, minutely. "Have a seat." He swung his feet down, pulled his hood back. His bald pate shined red from too much sun or too much wind or too much drink. Maybe all three. The glint at his ear was a golden hoop. He kicked a chair my way and placed his book on the table. He kept reading.

"Thanks." I pulled the chair round and sat. With the wall to my back and the rest to my front, I could relax, relatively. Six men, all taking an interest, all perched between me and the front door. Six men. Six thieves. I saw stumped hands, facial brands, grim glares. Redbeard took a drink.

My stomach groaned. "What're you reading?"

He pulled the book up, showing the cover. The Bible.

"Be careful with that one," I warned.

He licked a finger, turned a page, kept reading.

"I know you, mister?" he asked without looking up.

"No," I said. "Name's Luther."

"Don't think I want to know you."

"I get that a lot."

"*Sir* Luther…" His eyes still in the Bible. "I can smell the airs on you, nearly taste 'em. Can see that high hat o' yours near brushing the rafters."

"I *am* grand," I admitted.

"Don't get many '*sirs*' walking in here," Redbeard said, "even less walking out." He glanced up from his Bible studies as though to punctuate his statement with a, "*You catch my drift?*"

"Fair enough." I pulled my baldric over my head and set Yolanda on the floor, leaning against me.

Redbeard nodded her way. "Only gear you're lugging?"

I sat back, pulled open my cloak, offering a quick gander of steel, steel, and more steel, then drew it closed.

"Busy, busy," Redbeard grunted. "You come looking for trouble, all of that's gonna amount to all this." He snapped the Bible shut, glanced around the room, taking in the rest of the men, his men. That was plain. They were on the edges of their seats, waiting on his word. Harp strings strung fit to break. I was waiting on the *twang*. "You a praying man, Sir Luther?"

"Not especially."

"Might want to start reconsidering that stance."

"You Red Tom?"

"What do you want?" he asked. "You mention crab cakes again, you won't mention nothing else. Never."

"I'm a justiciar. Looking to ask a few questions."

"Looking to stir up trouble's more like."

"With any luck, no."

"You don't seem to me a man with any luck."

"Whilst you appear to be overflowing," I said.

The corner of his lip twitched, a near-smirk, a dark one, but genuine. "Gonna be a damn shame when I give the word."

"Damn shame for you, too." I shrugged. "All of them. Soon as the Lord Bishop catches wind. And he knows I'm here. Waiting on bated breath for my timely return."

"But you first, though," Redbeard said.

"Fair enough. Can we not agree, however, that it would be mutually beneficial if I weren't slaughtered here tonight?"

"I can always move digs."

"Shave the beard, don a wig, join the gypsies? Can see you belly dancing right now."

He chuffed another laugh despite himself. "Yeah, I'm Red Tom. What the fuck do you want?"

"Just a few questions. On the Lord Bishop's behalf."

"Already answered a few questions on his behalf."

"Oh?" My eyes narrowed. "Who was the lucky fella?"

"Sir," he glanced over his shoulder at the bartender,

"what's his name?"

"Chalstain," the bartender hazarded.

"That's the one." Red Tom snapped his fingers. "Him that gone all disappeared and such."

"Well, he's reappeared. Parts, anyways."

"We jawed. Pleasant-like. For the greater piece."

"What'd he ask about?"

Red Tom stroked a finger across his jaw.

I kept my breathing slow, even.

"Was asking about plenty," Red Tom said. "Mostly about Jews."

My stomach roiled as he took a drink. "And what'd you say?"

"Said I ain't one. So how's I to know nothing?" He scratched his beard. "Course, he mentioned we'd been leaning on them for quite some time, and so I says we ain't been leaning on them. As of late. So I truly didn't know nothing concerning them."

"As of late?" I repeated. "And why's that?"

Red Tom grinned, revealing yellow teeth, some missing. "Cause them bastards started leaning back. Escalation of force. And old Hughes weren't up to snuff. Imagine that? Har. Jews leaning back? And leaning hard-like. You ken that?" He looked around the room, slapped the table with an open palm. "Ain't that right, boys?" He was met with a cold-cocked silence. "Bunch of yellow bastards."

"That why Hughes was voted down?" I asked.

"Heh. Aye, that's it. *Voted.*" He sniffed, wiped his nose. "Only took one. Things is gonna change, though, and soon. Be back proper, right enough. But don't you nor yer bishop be worrying. We got no airs."

"They were leaning back, you say? How?"

"How?" His eyes narrowed. "You daft? How's it always go?" He hunkered forward across the good book as he leered, his long rawboned arm all muscle and sinew and bone. "Men get ahold of steel. Men decide to use it," he sat back, "men die. They got more men."

"How many more?"

"*More.*"

"They come straight at you?"

He looked me in the eye. "No. Didn't come at us at all, truth be told. But when we crossed that line into the Quarter." He shook his head. "Bold fuckers. Killing in the open. Daylight. Dagger-men rushing in, stabbing, disappearing afore… We couldn't get no foothold again once they'd ousted us."

"Really?"

"Calling me a liar?" He cocked his head a mite.

"No, just, you don't hear it much is all."

"Aye. They usually just take it, take it and like it, tip o' the cap, but things is changed." He thumped the Bible. "But like I said, they gonna change back."

"Know any of the names of the men you been dealing with? The name *Daniel* ring any bells?"

"Daniel? Naw." He shook his head a mite, barely a twitch. "Been hearing of a group calling themselves the Masada, though. Whispers and such. No one's talking outright, even with persuasion. Ken they's the ones fighting back, but we ain't exactly on terms I'd call *speaking*."

"The Masada?" I asked. "Know what it means?"

"No." He shook his head. "Lord knows attempts were made to right the scales."

"You poured it on?"

"Poured it on? Aye. Sure. We poured it on." He grinned. "And they poured back."

"That it with the Jews?" I asked. "Nothing more?"

"Sure," he answered.

"Nothing out of the ordinary?"

"What you getting at?"

"If you knew, it wouldn't need asking."

He frowned. "Sure there's more. There's always more, ain't there?"

"Any of your dead men get snuffed in a strange way?"

"Like how?"

"Like maybe they had a warhorse boot them in the

chest and knock them off the roof of the highest building you know?"

A reptile glare, cold, appraising. "What of it?"

"Sound familiar?"

"Sure. Couple chaps making a run at some Quarter merchant got turned near inside out. Bone twisted like rope. Something to see. Washed up ashore a few weeks back."

"Know anything about it?"

"Know I wish the fella done it was working fer me."

"Any means to address it?"

Red Tom grinned. "Cannon?"

"What else you tell Chalstain?"

The muscles at his jaw clenched. "He come asking about killers. Hired an all. Looking to connect someone to all the Isle Men mayhem."

"And what'd you tell him?"

"Told him I know plenty. Told him none of the men I knew'd have the grit to pull a job like he was asking on. Told him no man did, and if he did, no one could afford him."

"And then?"

"And then nothing. He up and left. He was seen after he left if that's what yer driving at. Seen alive, that is."

"No. That's not what I'm thinking. Just wondering what *he* was thinking."

"Har. I told him he was barking up the wrong tree. Thinking some shit-heel thieves like us was gonna go jumping in the Lords' pool? Might dip in a toe from time to time, but..." His glance slid slowly, evenly toward the door. "Now if that's all?"

"One last thing." I stood slowly, Yolanda in hand. "Know anything about a Genoese cog that docked here about a month ago? Don't know the name."

"Am I the fucking harbormaster now?"

"Close enough."

"Lot of ships come in and out."

"And you don't ever take any notice of them, yeah?" I glanced toward the door. "Nor their cargo." About twenty feet away. Seemed a long way. My hands were starting to shake a bit. I could feel the pale shivers coming on. "The cog brought in a company of mercs. Crossbowmen, most like. Genoese."

"Dagos."

"That's the one."

"Aye, I know the boat." Red Tom rubbed his chin. "Some says they brought the plague with them."

"Yeah. I heard that. Heard it was a king-rat, too. Or the Jews. Or some plague cult up the point. Maybe all together. But this merc cog, know anything about it? The company's captain? A little shit, but makes a big stink. Goes by Casagrande. Does work on the side not entirely unlike yourself."

Red Tom stared at me long and hard. "You don't want to be asking nothing about that one."

"You're right, but here I am, asking away."

"Here you are."

"You know him?"

"I'm still breathing, so maybe I don't. But I know who you're talking of."

"Who's he working for?" I slid the last of Lord Volkendorf's golden rings across the table.

Red Tom raised an eyebrow as he took the ring in hand, glancing at it. Then both eyebrows raised.

"Who's he working for?" I repeated.

"Ain't working for me." He tossed the ring to the bartender, who almost caught it. "Have Sorril melt it down. Now. Don't want no crows *kawing* in here." Red Tom stared across the table at me for a while. "You looking for dago mercs in Asylum, only one place you'll find them." He nodded east out the window and across the river. "The Quarter."

Chapter 29.

A HUMID BLAST of humanity-infused air engulfed me as I stepped into the Stone Ruin Ten. The air burned stifling with the stink of humanity. Sweat. Nausea. Desperate song jangled on, ragged, half to the rhythm. Drunken, forced jocularity. Mule guffaws. A horrid dwarf in motley tumbled across the bar, coming back to his feet with a tankard of ale spilling in each hand, howling.

It's different when you know you're being hunted, and by '*it*,' I mean everything. Your current existence. The now. All painted with the muted colors of fear, the strokes of stark panic bound near to breaking, all slathered across a canvas of doom impending.

Cutting through the crowd, knifing past bodies, plunging through conversation after conversation, I searched for the faces of the men come to kill me. Leering faces. Horrid faces. But they wouldn't be leering or horrid.

Sweat beaded the back of my neck.

I didn't see them. Or maybe I did. Maybe they were right next to me. For an instant, I longed for the naked display of threat back at the Fool's Hand. No guessing games there, only bare menace. But when they're hidden in plain sight? Every glance thrown my way was an assassin's appraisal, every bump, every shoulder as I jostled my way through the press, a prelude to murder.

And they were here. I could feel it. But maybe so was Karl.

I kept to the walls til I made the bar.

Schultz noticed me, nodded, worked his way over.

"*Herr* Luther." He nodded filling a tankard.

My thirst, forced down and away, restrained, slavering, suppressed, released suddenly, springing to full bore as tankard touched bar.

"Thanks." I swiped the tankard, slugged it back, and almost gagged it back up. "Small beer?"

"Apologies, my barrels are dry. And no stock is being left in the city. None I can be finding. No wine. No ale. Just the small beer."

I nearly hurled the tankard at his head.

Withering, he blanched, turned, slunk down the bar.

I took another sip and shuddered. Small beer: beer cut with dog piss. Or was it the other way around? Either way, it wouldn't touch me. Leaning against the wall, I propped up my head on my hand and watched. A bored affectation. If they were here, and they were, and they were watching, and they were, they knew the instant I stepped through the door. Thoughts of Red Tom's dagger-men rolled through my mind. Stabbing a man in a crowd's a slick method. A tight pack like this? Can't see anything below shoulder height. Stabs to the gut? Chest? Not many'd see, if any at all. And those that did? Who'd stick their neck out on my account?

A pair of minstrels in blood-red velvet flitted to and fro upon a small dim stage, singing a trilling song of Roland's heroic stand against the Saracen horde. It didn't end well for him.

Schultz edged back my way, serving his swill to a throng of patrons.

"Any more rooms open?" I asked him.

"Yours is being still." Schultz cocked his head in confusion.

"I need another. Room twelve."

"Someone is already renting—"

"Move them. Now."

"I cannot be—"

"Move them, and we're square for my armor," I said.

That did it. Schultz nodded, strolled to a rack of keys and pulled one off. He held it out, just shy of my grasp. "We are being square then?"

I nodded, snatched the key.

Lorelai entered the common room, plying her trade across the way, finding a seat in the lap of that big swarthy fuck, Blackbeard. Again. The shaggy bastard barked a gap-toothed guffaw and slapped Lorelai on the arse. His hand remained there, clutching, gripping as he drained his tankard in one prolonged gulp, then slammed it down, hollering for more.

Lorelai extricated herself from his arms then kissed the bastard before gathering all his empties and making her way to the bar. She wove through the crowd, placed the fistful of tankards down, freezing the instant our eyes met. She recovered then curtsied with a grin, a wicked grin, though her eyes still told that first tale.

"You're looking well," I said.

She shut me up with a finger buttoning my lips. "Are you stupid or just fucking crazy?" She hissed low, her breath hot in my ear.

"Can't I be both?"

"Sake's alive, you setting up shop?" She glared down at my full tankard. "Thought you said it was to be quick? Thought men were coming to kill you?"

"I'm waiting for a friend."

"You got no friends."

"Says who?" Frowning, I leaned past her, glaring down Blackbeard, still rollicking along. "*You,* on the contrary, seem to have plenty."

"Huh?"

"Thick as thieves you two are," I said above the din. "Thicker."

"Well, I'm very good." She set the empties on the bar.

"You are that. Hell, you might be the goodest."

"Jealousy doesn't become you."

"Yeah, but sometimes it's all I've got," I answered. "Relax." I put a hand on her forearm. She was trembling.

"Care to join me upstairs?"

"Thought you were occupied." I nodded at the empties.

"I suppose I could fit you in."

I smirked. "Can't say the offer's not tempting."

Sidling up close to me, she glanced down at her hand, lighting on my cock, feeling me through my pants. "I can tell."

"Whoa, easy," I stammered. "Won't be able to walk."

"Don't like it?" She harrumphed. "Maybe I should go back to my friend?"

"Oh, no you don't." I snaked an arm around her waist, pulled her back, constricting her onto my lap. "You're mine."

"You going to dry hump me all night?" she asked over her shoulder.

"You shouldn't," I said, getting a grip. She couldn't get caught in this because of me.

"I don't like games, Sir Luther." She leaned back into me, her hair smelling of lilac.

"Just Luther. Rules, remember? You shouldn't because I'm expecting someone. Upstairs."

"Oh?" A hand to her bosom, offended. "Your friend? Thought I was the only one you desired?"

"It's not that. I'm expecting men."

"Well, if that's the way you're leaning?"

"The men who ambushed me. They'll try again." I took in the room. "They'll try here."

"Then why?"

"Why what?"

"Why'd you come back?" She hissed.

"Like you said. I'm crazy. Stupid. Both."

"What are you going to do?"

"First off?" I took a long breath, feeling her body pressed warm against mine, soft and at the same time firm, smelling wine on her, the hot swirling air, her long red-gold hair tickling my neck, the lacquered wood of the bar under my arm. Smooth. Cool. Not a bad moment, not bad at all, except for the small beer. "You've got to go." I pushed her up from me, but she caught the bar, resisting.

"No," she said. "If they're going to kill you upstairs, don't go. Sakes alive. Go somewhere else."

"Where?" I asked.

"Anywhere."

I shoved her off me, stood, and offered a sweeping bow before I strode off for the stairwell.

I was upstairs and at my door moments later, unlocking it when I felt eyes on me. Instantly, I exhaled, clearing my head, forcing back the butterflies, willing my body relaxed, gripping my dagger beneath my cloak. I glanced over my shoulder, let out a long sigh.

It was Lorelai.

I deflated. "Leave."

She slid up to me, was on me, a predator enveloping me, a grasping tangle, one hand sliding up my shirt, across my chest, the other working my belt.

"Jesus," I groaned, kicking the door open and sliding in, dragging her after. I nearly hurled her onto the bed as I was closing the door and stripping my cloak off and failing at both.

Lorelai leered, leaning back on her elbows, easing one of her shoes off with the toe of her other. *Thud*. It clomped on the floor followed by the other. *Thud*. She untied her blouse, pulling blessed strings, one by one.

"Well shit," I said as she continued, little by little, corner of her mouth upturned in that wicked smirk.

I closed the door, locked it, slid the burglar bar in place. Both were sorry devices. Adding the door's ramshackle make and frame to the duo made the holy trinity of poor security. One good kick, maybe two…from a crippled leper. "You need to go."

"Why?" She pulled open her bodice and slid shimmying free.

"You know why." I tried not to stare. Failed.

Humming to herself, she raised a knee, started working down her stockings.

"They're going to kill you, too, if you stay." I swallowed, my mouth dry, head buzzing.

"Maybe I don't care."

"Maybe there's already enough blood on my hands without adding yours."

"You practically threw me on the bloody bed."

"In my defense, you were stroking my cock." I was past her and at the window an instant later, tilting the shutters for a quick look-see. "Tends to cloud my judgement." Rooftops and chimneys and smoke were bathed in the orange glow of plague pits. I thought I could make out a form, a black spot against a black sky, hunkered against a tilted chimney. Maybe. Maybe not. "And my judgement's not tip-top to start with."

"Maybe you're just paranoid?" She leaned back on the bed, one long leg rising slow as the sun through the mangle of her dress.

I wilted back. "Stay away from the window."

"Maybe you're wrong?"

"God knows I am often enough," I muttered. "Just usually not about the bad stuff." I closed my eyes, saw the future. "They'll do it in here. Either before or after." I laid a hand to her cheek. "It'll be fast. A few men at least. Say three. Four. Overwhelm us. Stab anything that moves."

Lorelai blanched.

"Now you know," I said.

She blinked, stared off somewhere quiet, somewhere dark.

"Liberating, isn't it?" I lied. "To know you're going to die?" It's not. It's like being stuffed in a musty coffin two sizes too small, wide awake as dirt's piled on top, shovel by shovel, each thump shuddering through your flesh, your body, your soul.

"I don't care," she said.

"There's still time. Leave."

"No."

"Go back to your husband."

"He's dead," she mouthed woodenly.

"Your children then," I said.

"No." She glanced at the door. "Let them come."

"And what about our boy?" I asked, casting my last trump card.

"Who?"

"Girard."

"*Our* boy?" she scoffed. "And what of him?"

"They'll kill him, too."

Lorelai's eyes snapped into focus, the caul of inertia finally torn. She shook her head, and I could see it had crept in there, her eyes, uncertainty, doubt, fear. Not a lovely sight for all her beauty.

"I brought him in." I knelt, taking her hands in mine. "Got him work. He's hung around you and me both. They know that by now. They've been watching me. Following me. Girard's a loose end. And maybe they figure he knows something."

"Where is he?" Lorelai started up for the door.

"Easy." I intercepted her, rising, catching her by the shoulders, stopping her as she tried to plow through me. "Get dressed." I glanced down. "Or not."

"*Where is he?*" she was on the verge, her voice a tremulous squeal.

"Who?" I scratched my head.

"You're an ass." She was gathering her things, pulling them on.

"Yeah, but a consistent one." I twitched my head toward the window. "Girard's holing up in the abandoned house across from yours. I told him to stay there til morning, keep a watch for you."

"Good." She closed her eyes, took a breath, nodded. "Thank you." Then she opened them. "You're going to fight them?"

"No," I laid out the tools I'd borrowed, "not if I can help it." A pair of hatchets, crowbar, rope. I touched a finger to my temple. "Got a plan."

Lorelai stared with disdain at the tools. "What is it?"

"Gonna snatch one."

"Snatch one *what?*" Her eyes screamed.

"One of them."

"*Them?* As in, a full-grown man? What, are they pies cooling on a fucking sill?"

"Didn't say it was a good plan," I conceded. "Need to know who's coming at me. Get a glimpse, at least. Then get out of here on the sly. So I can return the favor. That sound better?"

"Everything you say sounds worse, *always only worse*."

"My family motto." I proceeded to pull the bed across the floor, wincing at every squeal. "Please. Go."

Arms crossed, she sat on the bed.

"I could throw you out."

"I could scream."

"Shit. Alright. Give me a hand, then." I grabbed the bed frame, and she took the other side. "Ready? Lift." Together we slid and carried it, buttressing it against the door. "Buy us some time."

"Why do you trust me?" Lorelai asked.

"Huh?" I shrugged. "Don't know. You just either do or you don't with a person, yeah? Don't give it much thought. Only weight."

"And you do?"

"Yeah." I knelt by the tools, the floor creaking under my weight.

"Aren't you afraid?"

"I'm afraid of everything, Lorelai, except maybe that." You either carry that fear or you don't. Simple, right? Make a choice and wait to see if you get burned. I'd been burned before. But not by her. I slid the sharp end of the crowbar between the ends of two floorboards, wadded the striking end in my cloak and raised the hatchet. "I'll need a distraction."

"A what?"

"A noise. To cover this. For them. If they're listening." I spoke in a whisper. "They'll expect us to be…" I cocked my head toward the bed. "Can you handle that?"

Rubbing her upper arms, she nodded.

I glanced up.

Her feet were still firmly on the floor as she started

bouncing up and down on the edge of the bed. Slowly at first, rhythmically. Then she started feigning the sounds of sex. I was frozen, entranced, transfixed, until she hucked the rope at me, jogging me from my reverie. I nodded, swallowed, struck the crowbar with the flat end of the hatchet and drove it between the two boards, working it deeper and deeper into the crevice, back and forth, trying to get a bite. I did and forced the crowbar torquing over. The end of the floorboard rose an inch and then another. I shoved the hatchet under to wedge it open before I slid the crowbar down and repeated with the other hatchet until the board groaned free. I repeated on the adjacent board. Sideways, I could just squeeze through the hole.

Lorelai paused, offering a long drawn out moan. "What if someone's down there?"

"Room twelve." I worked the nails out. "Mine for the evening. You ready?"

Lorelai closed her eyes, calculated, nodded.

"Come on." I held out a hand. "I'll lower you."

Gathering her skirts, she hunkered down by the hole and inserted one leg in then the other.

"Shhhhh." Bracing my feet to either side of the hole, I took her hands in mine and lowered her. She hung there dangling an instant then dropped into the abyss. "You alright?"

"Yes," she whispered up. "I landed on the bed."

"Perfect." Sitting with my legs dangling in, I tucked the hatchets into my belt, edged forward then dropped down next to her. Reaching up through the hole, I slid the floorboards back in place. Somewhat. Lorelai's soft strong hands steadied me.

"Here," I stepped off the bed, "take my hand."

I pulled her across the room, my hand fishing for the doorknob. Finding it, I slid the key into the lock, wincing as the tumblers jumped. I turned the key, feeling resistance, then nothing as it turned.

"Now, we wait." I pulled my hood up and opened the door a crack.

The hall was empty.

Smash! The sound of an axe on wood crashed from above. Wood cracked, splintered.

Lorelai's nails dug into my neck.

Smash!

The door above gave in. The bed screeched, stuttering across the floor. Feet pounded, clomping, reverberating. Terse voices hissed and growled. Footsteps stumbled above. Grumbles. Swears. Shouting. They slammed open the shutters.

I stepped out into the hall. Empty. Lorelai followed, and I pulled her in front of me, staying close, matching her gait, half-crouching behind, knife in hand. As we rounded the corner, we were at the stairwell, two flights, one up, one down.

Lorelai froze.

A hooded man, a small crossbow clutched in his hands, stood on the landing, his attention fixed upwards, but he turned toward Lorelai, jaw dropping as I stepped neatly past, my blade point pressing to his throat.

"Quiet," I hissed, peeling the crossbow from his hands then forcing him down the stairs ahead of me. "Hands where I can see them."

He stumbled down as stiff-legged as a marionette, my grip on the scruff of his neck the only thing keeping him upright. At the bottom, I yanked him back into the gloom under the stairs. "Stand there." Lorelai nodded, gathered her skirts and stepped in front of us, blocking us as a pair of drunks opened the stairwell door, guffawing their way up, giving her an eyeful the whole way.

"Who's your boss?" I had him by the throat. Shit. He was practically just a kid.

His eyes pleaded, tears welling up. "Please mister…" As I dug the blade into his neck.

"*Who?*"

"Lori, please?" He begged.

I froze. "You know him?" He did look familiar. Somehow.

She nodded, eyes wide. "He's a…a customer."

A voice called from upstairs. "Zak," a dead chill voice, "see anything?"

I pressed the dagger point into his throat. "This way," I said, dragging him toward the door.

"Zak?" It came again, insistent. Footsteps pounded, three men. At least.

"*Zeke, help*—" He blurted the first half out, but not the second cause my dagger slid through his throat as I clamped a hand over his mouth, slamming his head into the wall. His bucking knocked my aim off, my blade careening off his spine, blood spurting past. I hurled him headfirst past, crashing into the other wall, slipped the knife beneath my cloak, and grabbed Lorelai by the arm. I thrust her ahead of me as feet pounded down the hall then down the stairs.

"ZAK! Where are you?!"

"FIRE!" I roared at the top of my lungs as Lorelai and I exploded into the common room, bowling into a swathe of bodies, knocking folk back, aside. "THERE'S A FIRE UPSTAIRS!" I pointed towards the stairs as I slashed on through, screaming like a madman. "RUN! FIRE!"

Folk screamed and started for the front door, lurching, fighting, trampling over one another to escape. Tables overturned. Chairs were hurled, kicked aside. Glass shattered. A void formed in the middle of the room; the mad herd tore instinctively for the front, bottlenecking the door, bodies crushing, fighting for escape. Pushing Lorelai ahead of me, we vaulted the bar, slid out back into the kitchen.

"What the hell is going on?" Schultz screamed as we rushed passed him.

"Someone's screaming about a fire upstairs," I yelled.

"Where?!" He grabbed a sand bucket, and then we were outside, breath steaming, cold biting, lungs burning, running, splashing through the mud.

"Just keep running." I had Lorelai by the wrist, drawing her along through the crowd.

Two blocks south we stumbled, hanging close to the

buildings on our right, then west for a block. I yanked her to a stop, dragged her into an alley, clambered my way through garbage to the end and peeked out. I melted to a crouch, huffing, blood pounding in my ears. The tavern front was filled with patrons milling about, shivering, chattering, some laughing by now, some swearing, some just happy to not be caught in an inferno. Others lay on the ground, exhausted, trampled maybe. Someone'd taken the initiative to start playing an instrument. Poorly.

"Wait here," I said.

"No." Eyes wide with animal panic, she blinked, shook her head, swallowed. "We're too close."

"I need to see them."

Putting an arm out to the wall, Lorelai hunched over, kneeling in the mud and snow, retching, her hair hanging like tangles of damp seaweed. The stink of bile and wine filled the alley, fanning the flames of my own nausea. I bit it down. My head was pounding. "You alright?"

She sniffed, pointed at my head. "Y-You're bleeding."

"It's nothing." I waved her off, though I had no idea if it were true. Wounds happen so fast that sometimes you feel only impact, pressure, not the penetration and retraction of a blade. Sometimes you feel nothing. I had a friend of mine, at Crecy, stabbed through the heart, blade popping out his back like some misplaced tail. Died only after it was drawn free, his face all quizzical, confused, as life started draining from his face, from pink to pale to skull. Might have gone on living with that damned spike through his chest. You never know.

"Sakes alive." She stifled another retch with a fist to her mouth. "Blood. You're covered."

"Not mine," I grunted, unsure.

"You sure?"

"Yeah."

"Here." Lorelai wadded up a handkerchief and put it to my head, then wilted, retching again.

I pressed the cloth to my head, continued watching

the street.

Blackbeard was out along with three others, dragging Zak amongst them, Blackbeard glaring every which way.

"You knew him?" I asked.

She nodded, tears welling. "Practically just a boy." She wiped her eyes, her mouth.

"Friend of Blackbeard?"

"Black...*who?*" She paused, nodded, wiped her eye with her dress. "Yes."

The crowd parted, everyone staring at Blackbeard and his crew. Like a hammock, Zak hung limp and ragged amongst them. Something was wrapped around his neck, a scarf, a bandage, a red bandage.

Cries of, "*Murder!*" filled the night.

"Who was he?"

"No one." She turned to me, a pale ghost in the moonlight. "Do you think he's dead?"

"Barring a miracle." And miracles were in short order in Asylum.

Blackbeard stopped, held up a hand, staring up at the roof of the house across the street from the tavern. He screamed something up. There *had* been a shooter up on the roof. Had he seen us? Blackbeard waited, nodded, looked down the street my way then the other. I could see him thinking. So no. Too much confusion.

"Think I'd be used to death by now," Lorelai murmured aimlessly.

"What do you know about Blackbeard?" I asked.

"Him? I...? Nothing."

"Must know something. What's his name?"

"He...he calls himself Devon. He's a patron. Just a patron, like I said."

Blackbeard snatched one of his men by the back of the neck and pulled him in close, snarling in his ear, then hurled him stumbling off north. The man regained his balance and continued on into a sprint.

"How many patrons you got?" I asked.

"Plenty."

"Fair enough. How long's *he* been one?"

"Two days. Maybe three."

"The others?"

She thought a moment. "About the same."

"Never seen any of them before that? They just showed up, after I did?"

She nodded.

"Last names?" I asked.

"No."

"Distinguishing marks?" I asked. "Tattoos? Scars? Anything at all?" She shook her head. "A street? A house? Place of business? Anything?"

"No." She rubbed her throat. "We never did much talking, just drinking and…"

"Yeah." I waved a hand, begging her off. "Sure."

A man toting a crossbow slid into the street and leaned close into Blackbeard, him still staring off my way. He shook his head, barked something, leaned down and grabbed one of Zak's legs, lifting along with the others.

"I'm sorry," Lorelai muttered.

"For what?" I rose from my crouch, dusting off my trousers, swallowing my rising gorge. "Got any money?"

"You ain't fixed to—"

"Here." Taking her by the arm, I pressed my coin purse into her hand, closed her fingers around it. "Some rocks in there, but silver, too. And don't come here again. Ever." Blackbeard started trotting off north. "They know where you live?"

Lorelai shook her head. "I…I don't think so."

"Then go back to your crooked home. Get Girard. Then just get lost. Get so lost you don't even know where you are."

"And then what?"

"Start over somewhere."

She glanced at me sidelong and groaned, her head collapsing into her hands. I put a hand on her shoulder, pulled her in tight.

"Don't do this," she pleaded.

"I gotta."

She clutched my arm as I started out into the street. "You said there was enough blood on your hands already. You *said* that."

"I lied."

Chapter 30.

FREEZING RAIN PELTED me as I stalked Blackbeard and his men north up Mill Street, the sleet excoriating, raking across my face in razor sheets, freezing, burning. Visibility was practically nil which was both blessing and curse. The mud had frozen, crusting over, but still sucked at my boots as I broke through.

Wind ripped.

Past massive stone mills, I crept along. I crouched. Cringed. Needles of awareness swarmed across my body, reining me in when I pursued too aggressively, when they stopped by a Statue of Saint George, when Blackbeard turned, his face lost in darkness. Who was he, besides the man sent to kill me? Who were they, besides comrades of the assassins who'd taken down Nils? Why'd they want me dead? They didn't know me personally, but that didn't mean it wasn't personal. Killing's *always* personal. And were they the ones who'd killed Chalstain? I figured they were, figured they had to be, figured them for the ones who killed Volkendorf and his men, too.

But the same damned questions reared again. Could Blackbeard rip the head off a man? Tear open a portcullis? Cause those crush injuries? No. So, maybe Lady Narcissa's monk *did* exist after all and *had* ripped Chalstain's head off? The pendulum swings. Was the monk Haefgrim or Gaunt? Gaunt had claimed otherwise, but that meant nothing. Was it some other player in the game? And still, what about the three kids? My mind was as muddled and opaque as the stormy night sky.

Blackbeard turned, followed his squad, leaving Saint George all by his lonesome.

Kneeling in gutter filth, I waited, my nausea waxing

to a head; I turned aside and puked in a gutter, then rose, continued.

Jesus, I needed a drink.

You'd think trailing people'd be easier in the dark of night. It isn't. During the day you can blend in with other foot traffic. Hang back further. Let your eyes do the work. At night your eyes are shit. You have to stay close, closer than you'd like, and you have to rely on your other senses. Sound, mostly. All while trying to keep quiet yourself. Try to not knock over that pile of garbage or step on that cat, to tip your hand, to slit your own throat.

Through tight alleyways and main thoroughfares, Blackbeard and his squad slogged on. Up Mill Street, then down Black Alley and onto Oakside Lane, heading north, always north.

Their pace slackened considerably about twenty blocks onward, fatigue setting in. The kid hadn't looked heavy, but lugging a corpse through slick muddy streets in blinding weather wasn't easy. Not even for four men. For a moment, I thought maybe he wasn't dead, that they were headed for the hospital.

I was wrong. Nigh upon it, they turned east.

They were crossing the North Bridge.

As the others started across, Blackbeard hung back, watching, waiting a long while, standing still as Saint George before turning abruptly and stomping on after them up. Had he seen me? Heard me? Maybe I'd gotten too close? Blackbeard crested the rise of the bridge, disappearing on the far side. Shivering, I slogged through trash and muck as I reached the alley's end then loped on after.

The bridge. Another blessing. Another curse. Tail someone onto a bridge and there are only three places you can go, and down is not generally an option, rather than an outcome. Upside was I knew where they were going, at least for now. The downside? Bridges are damn fine places for an ambush, especially in the dead of night, amidst a winter storm. I glanced over the parapet. Water rushed below, far below, but it was too dark to see.

I was over the apex and heading down, treading over the same ground I'd trod the day before. Echoes of phantom hoofbeats pounded through my skull. The screams of women, the wails of children. Ice floes cracked and caromed off the chasm walls below. Not a preponderance of warm memories.

Sliding along at a crouch, along the parapet, I hustled on quicker to close the gap, catching a glimpse as they set foot off the bridge. They headed north. Again.

When I made bridge's end, I waited, watching as Blackbeard's form disappeared into the murk, north up Long Street. Rising, taking a step, I froze, sensing rather than seeing. A gut instinct—I'd been made.

The rains poured, sheets and sheets rolling on the wind with the tenacity of a cracking whip.

Someone was out there. Watching. I could feel it.

I dropped to the ground just as a crossbow bolt exploded against the parapet, steel sparking on stone. Couldn't make out where it'd come from. Footsteps pounded now, splashing, cracking across cobbles. I peeked over the wall as two black shapes emerged from the hissing rain. Steel glinted. One of them, the slope-shouldered form of Blackbeard, I recognized. And one of the others from outside the tavern, a tall fellow with long shanks. And somewhere in the dark was the shooter, loading his crossbow. Watching. Waiting.

Keeping low, I crawled back up the bridge.

"Oy, there!" Blackbeard called out across the chasm, his grim reaper form stalking along, nigh on the bridge approach. "Rough night for a stroll, ain't it?" His voice didn't echo in the thick air. It just died. "Nothing to say?"

I kept silent, low, still backing up, cloak wrapped around me, searching the dark for the shooter. If I couldn't see him, maybe he couldn't see me. I should've just run, but he was reloaded by now, waiting for me to do just that.

"Maybe killing ain't to your taste all of a sudden?" he called out. "You didn't hold that view back at the tavern.

Not when you were slitting the lad's throat." Blackbeard clashed two short blades together then tapped them together, *tink, tink, tink.* Longshanks strode along at his back. "Come on, Krait."

I could only retreat up the bridge, but to retreat, I'd have to break cover. *Where was that damned shooter?*

"I can see you, crouching there," Blackbeard called out. *Could he?* "Stand up. Like a bloody man."

Eyes straining, searching the shadows. I stayed put. Where was he? Where?

"You're a big knight, ain't ya?" Blackbeard stopped, stood all nonchalant, pointing with a sword as he spoke, gesticulating like we were old friends in a bar jawing over ale. "What're you hiding for?" He turned to Longshanks. "We're nothing, ain't that right?"

How far up the bridge? I squinted. Could I beat them? And once I made the far side? What then? Find an alley, make them come at me one at a time. Run. Hide. Retaliate.

"Hah!" Blackbeard turned to Longshanks. "Yellow fucker, ain't he?"

"He is that," Longshanks replied.

I drew my legs up, set a heel.

"C'mon, Krait." Blackbeard and Longshanks reached the end of the bridge, Blackbeard just standing there, peering, his thick arms crossed. "My man here's faster than a courser. And you ain't no hare. He'll heel you."

I gripped one of the hatchets.

"About forty feet, eh?" Blackbeard straightened a mite, a buck who'd caught a scent. "Jacob...?" He called over his shoulder as Longshanks' head exploded in a gout of blood and bone. Throwing up an arm, Blackbeard scuttled blind as another crossbow bolt zipped past. Boots clomped on stone as he disappeared down an alleyway.

I almost made to get up but didn't as a squat form shambled out of the darkness, a wolf pelt slung across his shoulder, a crossbow in hand, haft of his thane axe clicking against the ground with each step. I oozed back against the wall, slid almost to the ground in relief.

It was Karl.

I'd have kissed him if I wasn't crouched cowering, if my legs hadn't seized up from the cold, if he wasn't so short and ugly and frightfully troll-like.

Longshanks twitched a bit then lay still.

"You missed one." I squinted up.

Karl spat on Longshanks' corpse, crossbow bolt jutting from his forehead like some hell-spawned unicorn. Stepping his booted foot onto Longshanks's head, Karl leaned over onerously, grunting, and drew the bolt scraping free. He whipped it once, flicking off the gore, then tucked it away. "Didn't miss this one. Or his friend." I knew somewhere off in the dark, the shooter lay dead, too.

"Fair enough." I raised my hands. "I surrender."

"Hrrm, the famous Krait-family battle cry."

"Yeah." I grinned, nodding at the wolf pelt over his shoulder. "New pet?"

"Yar. Found her in the Hellwood. Call her Bitey."

"Forget to feed her?"

"Brave lass." He pulled the pelt tighter around his neck, trying to ward off the cold rain. "Bravest of her pack. 'Course it don't never pay being bravest."

"Amen to that," I said, scrambling to get up but ending up slipping and falling back on my arse. I held up a hand.

Karl grinned down at me.

"I *am* getting better," I insisted.

"You've only one way to go." Karl squinted at my outstretched hand. "Got the shakes, lad."

"Cold."

"How long's it been?"

"Long." I looked up at the sky, feeling the sleet against my face.

"Yar." Karl reached behind his back. "You're in deep this time. Deep since Stettin. Here." Karl pulled a flask from under his cloak, wiggled it. "Take it. Can't be stopping now."

I snagged it, took a pull, felt the surge of burn down my throat. Long. Warm. Reviving. I ignored the numbing rain, the cold, the wet, felt calming warmth spreading out from my belly, reaching out to the rest of me, felt it working.

"Hair of the dog," Karl rumbled.

"Salvation." Wincing, I offered it back.

"Keep it." Karl waved me off.

"Sure you can do without?" I asked.

"Sure you can't."

"Fair enough." I took another swig, nodding to myself, my argument drowning.

"Make it last, lad."

"So," I lowered the flask, "what took you so long?"

"Been off gallivanting," Karl picked his teeth with a crossbow bolt, hopefully a clean one, "with whores."

"Only way to gallivant."

"Har," Karl shook his head, "glad to see all those years of fight-training's paid off."

"I learned from the best."

"That you did, lad." He took my hand in his iron grip and hauled me to my feet. "Don't seem it took, though."

...Lord Bishop has been less than forthcoming with aid in any form. It seems as though the man cares nothing for that which I seek to accomplish, and it was he who set me this task.
—Journal of Sir Myron Chalstain

Chapter 31.

THE STREET WAS DARK and wet and did nothing to allay my misery, but I didn't care. I was alive. Thanks to Karl. Just another in a long list of debts accrued over the years. I took a sip from his flask, swished it in my mouth, savoring it long before I swallowed. We headed north along the river, the same direction Blackbeard had been headed. Karl's hunched gait slogged on, never flagging, never waning, never ceasing, until now. In the yawn of a silent alley, he collapsed against a brick wall and just breathed, slow and ragged, eyes closed.

"Want me to lug that?" I nodded at his crossbow.

He cast a sidelong glare.

"Just trying to be polite."

He pushed himself off the wall and recommenced trudging.

"What the fuck's wrong with you?" I asked. "You're hobbling around like my grandmother."

"Yer grandmother's dead."

"Then you're doing quite well, I suppose."

"Been lugging your dead weight around for years." He glared me up and down. "Must be all caught up with me."

I snatched the crossbow from off his shoulder, met his glare, matched his step.

"Fuck your face," he said.

"I'll pass," I said. "Speaking of fucking faces, though, tell me you've seen the Lady Narcissa."

"Using the term *'lady'* kinda loosely, ain't ya?"

"I always hope most everything involving ladies is loose."

"Don't ken your meaning."

"Morals, I meant," I said, trailing off. "Off my game tonight."

"There ever been a time you been '*on your game*?'" He pointed across the river. "And, yar, I got her. Over there. West. South of the Point."

"In that case, I can't help noticing we're headed north."

"Yar. You're a real noticer."

"Where we headed?" The walls of the Quarter loomed high and foreboding. "Jewtown?"

"Yar." Karl plugged along.

"Any particular reason?"

"Them fellas set about killing you? Jews."

"You sure?"

"Fair sure."

Karl knelt at the corner of a house and pointed. Ahead lay the gates into the Jewish Quarter. A quartet of torches sputtered outside it, along with a contingent of the Lord Bishop's men. Atop the towers to either side of the gate, guards watched.

"Think they'll let us stroll on past?" I asked.

"I wouldn't."

I still had my Star of David cloak tucked in my belt, but I was fair certain Karl was right. No chance in hell they'd let us pass. Not this late. Not looking like we did. Armed like a two-man crusade to Outremer. I waited. Karl, a man who sees to the heart of a problem. In life. On a battlefield. Anywhere. He'll see the weakness in the enemy lines and most advantageous point of attack before I have time to consider the best avenues of retreat. And then he's off, and I'm following mostly because horses are stupid and if one's running one way they all want to be.

"C'mon." Karl pointed with his axe.

I followed him down an alley. The buildings stanched the wind and rain and sleet, and we trudged through the urban brick cavern in silence until we hit a house built right up against the Quarter's wall. The house sat brooding in the dark, glaring back with inexplicable menace.

Karl put a finger to his lips, pointed, brandished a long black skeleton key. "There's a tunnel through the wall. In the basement."

I raised an eyebrow.

Karl took a deep breath, nodded. "Followed one of them lads come tearing out of your tavern. All covered in blood. Tearing out like a banshee. And that black-bearded fella, too, come following. Sent him off running. Didn't see you. Figured I'd follow him. So's I did."

"And where'd he go?" I asked.

"Odin's eye, you're a slow fuck." Karl glanced over up at the house.

"I was giving you your moment."

"What the fuck you talking about?" Karl rang out his beard, water drizzling.

"Forget it." I took another sip, tried to clear my head. "Where'd you get the key?"

"Inside. Fella dropped it. Was in quite a state."

"Guards?"

"Don't know. Weren't none before." Karl made to move on toward the front door, but I grabbed him by the shoulder.

"I'll go," I said.

Karl didn't argue, which was strange. He just stepped aside and plunked down on a step, head hanging limp between his knees, beard tickling the ground, breaths coming in rasps.

I donned my Star of David cloak. Might buy me a second or two. Yolanda, I left with Karl. I carried the butcher blade in one hand and hatchet in the other. They hid under the cloak nicely, better than a bastard sword or crossbow. I made my way to the door, feeling naked, exposed. A fine target, an easy shot from any of the shuttered windows. I walked square, open, relaxed, like maybe I belonged.

No one shot me.

That was good.

The door was locked. I gave the alley a quick once

over, didn't see anyone, said fuck it, and slid the skeleton key in. It went in, and when I turned it, the lock gave way. The door creaked open slowly, revealing nothing but deeper dark. "Oy…?"

Karl was at my shoulder an instant later, pressing Yolanda back in my hand.

"No one," he grumbled.

I nodded, feeling his unease as he shouldered past, disappearing inside. I followed him, one hand on his bunched shoulder as he navigated the mirk to a stairwell down. The house's northern foundation wall was the Quarter's wall, and there was a hole cut through it. Water dripped in the dark, but we heard nothing else.

* * * *

The manor was three-stories high, stone construction, four gables, each facing one of the cardinal directions. Like everything else in Jew-town, it was built square, built well, built strong. A wall the Romans might have been proud of surrounded the manor, eight-feet tall, spikes poking out the top every few inches. A stout wrought-iron gate stood in the front.

"This the place?" I asked.

"Yar."

"What street's this?"

"Temple Row. Temple Street. Temple *something*." He pointed down the road; in the dark stood the quarter's temple, rising above the other buildings.

"Who lives here?"

"I ain't exactly hobnobbing with the high-hats of Jewtown."

"Good thing, too. I'd probably end up owing you money."

"You already owe me money," Karl grumbled.

"More money." I studied the manor. "Solid. Secure. Barred windows."

Karl shrugged. "Most of the houses on this street

have barred windows."

"Fashionable, perhaps?"

"Worried about getting killed more like."

I glanced at Karl. He was shivering and looking like he might keel over and die. "Come on. We'll find out who owns it in the morning. Stake it out. Too fucking wet and cold to be standing out here."

* * * *

"How far?" I asked.

We were back on the west side of the river, out past the West Gates, trudging through a labyrinth of quarantined homes. The ocean pounded, not far to the north. A gale wind blew, cold and raw, whipping the flames of the Goathead watchtower, and I knew that far off to the east, Lady Chalstain was watching it, weeping crimson.

"Not far." Karl hobbled along now like an arthritic old bear.

"Maybe you should tell me where we're going in case you die?"

Karl chuffed a laugh.

"Right." I just walked alongside. "And I got in, by the way. Talked to Stephan."

"Your fucking brother," Karl grumbled. "Raachwald didn't kill him, eh? Well, that's something then, ain't it?"

"Yeah." I glanced sidelong. "Took his right hand, though. And set on taking more."

"Fuck." He stopped.

The rain poured down.

"Yeah," I said. "He wants *your* head, too."

"And what'd you say to that?"

"I politely asked where and when and how. Silver platter or no?"

"Can't say that's surprising." He spat. "You're welcome to it anytime."

"I'll pass." Karl's surname is Skullsplitter. The progeny of a long line of men and women whom, presumably, were not long on debate or patience or prevarication.

"How long we got?"

"What day's it?" I asked.

"Hrrrmmm? Saturday. Just. I think."

"Two days, then."

Karl tripped over something, used his axe to stay upright.

"How'd you manage to break Stephan out?" I asked.

"Huh?" Karl scratched his shaggy beard. "It weren't me. She did. The lady."

"Yeah." I nodded. "He said that. But how'd you coordinate with her?"

"Coordinate?"

"Yeah. She snuck him out of the dungeon while you burned the place to the ground. Killed the jailers."

"Humph. I didn't kill nobody. And I didn't set no fire to nothing, neither."

I stopped. "Yeah?"

"Yar. Think I'm daft enough to go on a kill-jag or torch-party when Stephan's still sporting iron bracelets?" He leaned on that axe. "I was stuck slogging through the woods a day and a half, trying to suss out a way to crack that nut. Place's a shit-sty. Old style motte and bailey, fucking earthworks, even, but that Raachwald fronts a tight crew. None of them too drunk. I'd have sussed a gap, but it weren't going to be no sticks and stones plan." Karl picked something from his eye. "So I'm casing the fort, trying to suss out the best way in, when I see smoke rising. Thick, black. Pouring. Roaring. So's I start hauling ass. Just in time, I see Dunmire's roof fucking collapse, *foom!*" He threw up his hands. "Odin's eye. So I tear out for the main road. Just as the gates burst, out comes Stephan and the lady, tearing arse through. One of them guards wings a lucky shot and Stephan's in the mud and his horse? Good as dead.

"And on his arse in the mud, he tells me to go on with her." Karl shook his head, scowling. "Tells me to protect her. So, I tell him, '*She can go fuck herself.*' And what's he do? Just smiles. Just fucking smiles, shaking that empty head of his. All the while hell's pouring down. Men coming. Arrows flying. Dogs of war. And he uses that fucking voice he uses to soothe horses and folk dying and what not. That voice that makes hard men close their eyes and accept the whims of your almighty. Asks me to watch the lady. Protect her. Asks me to ask you to do the same. Then he runs off. Back. Drawing them off. Odin's breath, he get dropped on his head when he was a boy?"

"Yeah, mostly by me." I whistled low between my teeth. "So it was *her*. Jesus. She set the blaze. Killed the guards."

"Dangerous lady." Karl echoed my sentiment. "You and yours all keep them in dresses. Finery. Silverware." He spat. "Don't mean nothing." Karl leaned over like he was going to puke. "Rrrrg…" He didn't, but for a while, he just stayed there.

I kept an eye on him the rest of the way, jawing in his ear about everything that'd happened since we'd parted, starting with my conversation with the good Lady Narcissa and the less good Lord Raachwald. Karl listened then spat again, wiped his beard, grinning in triumph, that wolf-grin, all teeth and black murder. He nodded up. "We're here. Upstairs."

I looked at a three-story monstrosity, a slash of red across its front door. "Lovely."

"So what's our play?" Karl started up a rickety set of stairs, pushing off his right knee with each step. I trailed, half expecting him to collapse and roll down the stairs, taking me with him. At the top, he bulled open a door, flickering orange pouring out from within. A few high-backed chairs half-ringed the fire in the hearth.

"Hunt down the murderer." I followed him into the room, stripping off my sopping cloak, looking up as a lithe form rose from one of the high-backed chairs. It was Lady Narcissa, cloaked in rippling gloom, a glass of wine sparkling in her hand.

…was Lord Raachwald's son truly a bastard, as the rumors claim?
—*Journal of Sir Myron Chalstain*

Chapter 32.

THE LADY NARCISSA'S violet eyes simmered. She was poised, perfect, a svelte statue sculpted meticulously of pristine hubris, some ancient goddess brought to life, fierce, haughty, proud to a fault, past a fault, a league past.

"You look worse," she commented. "And you were in quite a state *then*."

"Worse than what?" I asked.

"Not you." She waved a hand to stifle me. "Has it reopened?"

"Has what re—"

Karl collapsed into a wooden chair and poured himself a long drink. He raised his flagon, nodded, took a pull, tossed the wineskin to me. In the flickering firelight, I could see a tourniquet wrapped round his thigh, crimson soaking dark through his trousers. He was pale. The water puddling beneath him was pink.

"Fuck." I was kneeling by his side at once. "Why didn't you say something?"

"What were you going to do," he sucked in a deep breath, "surgery?"

"Unlikely," I admitted.

"Carry me?"

"Shit no."

"Faint?"

"Now you're talking." I drew my blade. "Jesus. Maybe I'd have dragged your arse to the hospital?"

"Like I'd let those shit-fuckers lay their damned hands on me. Fuck them. Fuck their hospitals. Fuck them twice."

"Sure is a lot of fucking," I said. "Well then, I might've recited some rousing poetry to aid your flagging spirits."

"Glad I kept my trap shut then."

"Where?" I scanned his leg.

"Here." He pointed, just above his right knee. "Bastard winged me." Stephan had told me that. I remembered it now. "Through and through."

"Let me see."

"See it then." Karl collapsed back.

I wiped my blade on my pant leg.

"Careful with that," Karl rumbled. "You and blades. Rrrrr. I pulled it out. Whole. No splinters, I think."

"You hope." I pulled his boot off then slit a hole in his trousers. "Where's the bolt?"

"Don't know. Fuck. My new trousers…"

"Shut up." The wound was just above his knee, the tourniquet wound tight above it.

"There's a lady present," Karl grunted as I gave a good two-handed tug on either side of the slit, splitting it almost to his crotch.

"You talking about me or her?" I muttered. "Besides, there's nothing she hasn't seen before, or you haven't tried showing her."

Karl took another slug of wine.

"Winged?" I whistled. The wound was a jagged puncture, wide, entrance and exit both. "Jesus." It had puckered white around the edges from the soaking he'd taken in the rain. "Good thing he didn't hit you square."

"Ain't bleeding no more." He'd stitched the two wounds shut, but the stitches had pulled through.

"Will once the tourniquet comes off."

"Leave it on, then."

"You'll lose the leg."

"Naw. It's right there…"

"Great. When it finally drops off, I'll hang it on a lanyard, dangling rotten-green round your neck." I turned to Lady Narcissa. "Might start a new trend, yeah? I can see the women of Paris even now…" If I'd farted, I might have received a better response. "Find some rags. Linen. Something. Please."

Arms crossed beneath her perfect bosom, Lady

Narcissa's gaze flickered to Karl's corpse-pale leg. Lips pursed, she nodded, imperceptibly, almost.

While I cut the rest of his pant leg off, she started cutting the bedsheets and tearing them into lengths. She tore about five, left some wide squares, handed them to me. I slit Karl's ruined stitches, pulled them out, folded two lengths of bedsheet over and over until they were thick, passable dressings. Karl was about to take another sip of wine when I snatched it from his hand and took a drink myself. He was pale. I was green. We both were sweating, shaking, me more than him. I levered him up and half dragged him across the room, gimping along to the bed. The man was made of lead. "Lie down."

"I was using that." Karl pawed for the wineskin.

"Sorry." I looked up. "This might hurt." I shoved the spout of the wineskin into his wound, lifted the back end, squeezed. Karl stiffened. I squeezed the bag as much as I was squeezing my eyes shut. I didn't want to look, not at Karl, not at his leg, not at anything. Nothing happened for a moment, then came the splatter of the wine on the floor, drizzling first in a red trickle then pouring out as I squeezed.

"What, *the fuck*, are you doing?" Karl grunted.

"Just shut up."

"You're wasting a shit ton of wine."

"I know." My mouth was watering, stomach dropping, simultaneously.

The wineskin went flaccid. I stopped squeezing, yanked it free, applied a dressing front and back then bandaged it snug. Karl didn't seem any worse. Well, he still looked like death warmed over, but he'd barely winced when I shoved the wineskin spout into his wound. Which was good, or...maybe it was bad?

"Can't feel nothing," Karl wiped his mouth. "leg's drunk."

"I'm gonna loosen the tourniquet." I pressed a few more dressings and wrapped them, too. They were a gleaming white bulky mess in the dark until I loosened the tourniquet, gingerly first, untwisting the spoon he'd used as a windlass. The white bandages blossomed red like summer roses, growing, unfurling, a red so deep they were nearly black. I circled my hands around Karl's leg and squeezed on the bandages.

Lady Narcissa hovered over my shoulder, watching with dispassionate interest. "Mother of mercy, what are you doing?"

"Pretending his leg's your neck," I grunted, throttling down, trying to stanch the flow. Adjusting my grip to that of a headlock, I used the crook of my elbow and shoulder to squeeze it, awkward, a little too close to Karl's crotch for comfort, but effective. I hoped. Then for I don't know how long, I knelt there holding his leg up, squeezing it for all I was worth.

* * * *

It was still dark when it stopped, the bleeding stanched, the hearth fire burned down to grey-white ember. My arms were shaking, my neck sore, legs, the rest of my body. Spent. Soaked. Bedraggled. Clotted blood encrusted my arms and shoulders. Wine and gore stained the floor. A murder scene. I wound another length of bandage around his thigh, elevated it with a stack of blankets. He'd passed out a while back and looked as comfortable as an absinthe-addled corpse. But he was breathing.

Lady Narcissa sat upright perched in a chair, perusing Sir Myron's journal, a finger at her cheek.

"It's done, then?" She glanced up.

I said nothing, wiping blood crusted thick from my hands using a spare bandage, wrapping it around each finger before giving it a pull.

"We must go now." Lady Narcissa rose stately, prim, elegant. She inserted the journal into a rucksack and started for the door, offering me an annoyed glare when she saw I hadn't moved. "You've done what you can for him, made him comfortable, a most admirable effort."

"*We?*"

"He's dying."

"You don't know Karl." Glaring, I strode over, tore into the rucksack, ripped out the journal. "Karl doesn't die."

"Yet, I fear there's nothing to be done, Sir Luther." Her delicate hand lit on my shoulder as she said it, nearly a whisper, squeezing ever so gently as she slid it down my arm to my hand, clasping it, entwining fingers. Those violet eyes. "Come." She drew on my arm as she made for the door. "Please."

I backhanded her across the face.

She staggered, stumbling back, wheeling, and caught herself on the mantle, pawing dumbly at her face for an instant in disbelief. Then she mastered it and rose. Defiant. Blood trickled in a thin line from the corner of her perfect lips. Her eyes gleamed fierce and full of hate, and also with a certain satisfaction, as though I'd just confirmed everything she'd ever suspected about me. Probably I had.

She marched for the door.

I let her.

Willed her to.

I looked down at my hand, red, throbbing, pulsating, stinging from the rain, from the blood, from the blow. It hadn't made me feel any better. It made me feel like shit, but it needed doing. And not because of her. Because of me, because I was so God-damned weak. She'd almost had me there, tipping the scales. I'd felt myself sliding, resolve crumbling, withering, acquiescence growing like a brandy-warmth through my gut, spreading like weeds. Almost. "You can rot for all I fucking care." Yet that lasted all of a minute because I was lying to myself, and I knew it even as I was saying it. That had felt good, but I did need her, and Stephan needed her, and so I gave chase.

Her hair was plastered across her face in tendrils, all slathered down to her purpling lips as the mix of snow and rain poured down. Already, her cheek blazed red where I'd struck her. She simply stared at me with those almond-shaped eyes, quivering mad, a blade tucked in a trembling fist to her bosom.

"Thinking of killing yourself?"

"No," she spat blood, "only you."

I said nothing, just listened to the whispered hush of snow careening. "I'm sorry." I stepped aside, offering a pathetic bow. "Come in. Please."

The rain and snow fell.

Her turn to say nothing.

"My Lady, I—" I cleared my throat. "It was poorly done. I apologize."

She sniffed, stared, ice water trickling down her face.

"Please," I implored. "I promised I'd help you. Allow me to fulfill it. And I apologize again, for what little good that does."

"It does none, but I cannot say it shocks me." She squeezed the hilt of the blade. "This is the only thing men such as you understand."

"You're not wrong, lady."

She drew herself up. "I would prefer to wait out here."

"For what?"

"For you to beg."

"Lady," now I drew myself up, "while I'll admit that it does indeed appear that hell's freezing over—"

"No matter," she said. "I shall wait. I shall stand here and—"

Quick as an adder, I snatched her by the upper arm and yanked her in, stepping aside, my other hand controlling her wrist, launching her past me. I slammed the door shut after. "You'll catch cold out there, milady," I said, catching up the burglar bar in one hand, keeping an eye to her knife, waiting for her to move, to lunge, to anything.

"And in here I'll catch my death," she said.

"No."

"Words a woman would be a fool to believe. Any girl of six in this life should know better." Her gaze lowered, focusing on the ring on my left hand. "Oh, the lucky lady who married you."

"You'd like her. Hates me more than you."

"I don't think it possible." The lady's gaze went toward Karl. "You and he are so much alike."

"He saved you. Respect that."

"The mechanics perhaps. The brutal actions of a blunt object."

"Does sound like Karl."

"But then, his kind are merely instruments," she mused. "Servants. Lackeys. Oh, don't look at me like that."

"I'm not. I agree. He is an instrument. Just so happens, he's one could kill me in the blink of an eye. With just his little finger. So, I try to appreciate that during my rare moments of clarity. Perhaps you should as well."

"You expect me to believe a man as callow as yourself holds any regard for those beneath him? Does the dog care for the excrement he treads through?"

"You lost me," I said. "Am I the dog? Or the excrement?"

"Base sentimentality."

"I may be a poor knight, lady. A knight who strikes women, who smothers himself with whores, drinks himself daily from the realms of excess and on into the shining nirvana of gluttony, a mercenary hedge knight whose loyalty goes to the highest…" I rubbed my chin. "Err, did I have a point?"

"Have you ever?"

"Do you truly care who killed your husband?"

She sat down, eyes wide, a doe that just heard a twig snap. It was gone an instant later. "No, I don't. *That* he died. *How* he died. My husband was a beast, an animal, a bully, a fool, all congealed together into one." She looked down at her fine delicate hands, once prim, demure, now cracked raw and red from the cold. The knife was gone. No. Hidden. "I was but a prize mare paired to him in effort to correct moldering debts.

"But my sons? They…I do care very much about. Very much, indeed." A tear formed at her eye and she slashed it away, crushing it out, rolling it between thumb and forefinger like an ant. "I know they're dead, know I shan't ever see them again, but I still expect to. Even now. Around every corner. Through every door. I expect to see them sitting there, smiling, waiting…waiting for me. I forget every instant, only to remember the next. Wounded afresh. How two things so good and pure could have come from…"

I held a handkerchief out.

"No," her hate returned, bulling back the sorrow, "I shall accept no kindness from you. No matter how inconsequential."

"Even finding your sons' killer? Drawing him from the shadows? Bringing him to justice?"

"It is no kindness. You owe me."

"Oh?" I crossed my arms.

"You believe it coincidence that Pyotr was watching the road that night? Hmm?" She sat back in her chair. "Coincidence that you were attacked? Coincidence that we later arrived? Coincidence that you still draw breath?"

"No." Again, I wondered who it was who had sold me out. Enemies, the sole commodity I bore no dearth of.

"Yet, survive you did," Lady Narcissa said, "and your brother as well. And a fine lad, he is. I pity him, truly." She nodded. "Pyotr knew you were coming. His men had lain in wait night after night for near a week."

"And how did he know?"

"A letter received some time ago forewarned of your coming."

"From who?"

"An Albert Saint John," she answered. "He claimed to be traveling in your company. He was to receive recompense following the attack."

"He got paid in advance."

"I had heard of you, of course," she continued. "Many have, though few dare speak your name in Pyotr's presence. I dared, and in so doing persuaded him to utilize you, to break his oath. It was no small feat, I assure you. Indeed, you would hang blood-eagled from Dunmire's walls, your head decorating a rusting spike, were it not for me. So this is no kindness, indeed. It is a reckoning."

"If that's true, why lie about the murders?"

Her lips pursed.

"I assure you, Lady, I've a keen nose for the lie. A farmer knows crops, even those he's not personally sown. So tell me the truth, for once. Were you truly there the night of the murders?"

"I was."

"Then tell me who the monk was."

"I saw something…"

"Jesus Christ," I snarled, nearly pouncing on her. "I need a straight answer. Were you drunk?"

"You think I'm chained to a bottle like you?"

"Were you blind?"

"Do not mock me. I was…indisposed."

"Yeah. That's right. Indisposed." I nodded. "The good Lady Mary used that same word. She claimed two stories, in truth, though she may not have realized it. *She* lied to me, too."

"Mary?" A look of forlorn hope glimmered far off in her eyes. "How fares she?"

"Raachwald hacked her hand off," I responded abruptly, cavalierly. "It was suppurating. She'll die as soon as the poison reaches her heart." Her look of hope died stillborn. "Am I wrong?"

"Who are you to question me?"

"The only one who can solve this damned riddle. Now tell me about '*indisposed*.' It occurs to me that '*indisposed*' is a word women use when they wish to tell men to fuck off. Politely. An elusive word. An ephemeral word. Were you with child? Or was it some other womanly complication? I'm not too cultured to forgo more invasive questioning, I assure you."

"I was ill."

"You weren't there."

"I told you I was."

"Ill?" I snorted. "Funny. My grandmother was a cripple."

"You hail from such an *impressive* line."

"She fell in her dotage one night." I stifled the lady with a glance. "Broke her hip. Amazingly, she recovered. Well, '*recovered*' is perhaps not quite appropriate. She lived. She was mobile, to a lesser degree than before. And she was slow and old to begin with. This was after nearly a year of work with the bonesetter and doctor. So she could walk. Amble. *Shuffle*, a word that comes to mind. One of our carpenters constructed a wood frame for her to lug about. Some type of light, strong wood, I don't know. But she could manage with it. Walk. Not stairs. Flat ground, but she could manage."

"A wonderful story."

"Please, indulge me just a moment." I scratched at my temple. "You see, one day my grandmother was hobbling along with Stephan, my lovely, younger, dumber brother. Two peas in a pod, for he was a cripple, too, or cripplish, at the very least. He couldn't walk until he was about five, and even then it took him years to learn a stride that wasn't mocked behind his back. Or in front of it, really. But never mind. One day the two of them were hobbling along like the cripples they were. In the yard, of course. My father wouldn't allow them outside the walls. Wolves, brigands, stiff winds. Well, one of the mastiffs we kept in the pen had been ill. No one had noticed, or no one had said anything. Certainly, no one had done anything about it. Mad, he was, gloriously, horribly foaming-at-the-mouth mad. He should have been put down, destroyed, but, the master of hounds was away, on a hunt, or a worthless drunk, I can't remember which.

"Long story short. The mastiff broke free and set upon them. Stephan and my grandmother. I remember hearing it as I was working at the pell. The barking. The screams. Like a hellhound, that barking, followed by a slurred burning gurgle. Short. Choppy. Horrible. Stephan. It was him screaming. Do you know who didn't scream?"

Lady Narcissa just stared haughtily, disinterested, not playing my game.

"My grandmother. She didn't scream. My hundred-

294

and-fifty-year-old grandmother fought off a fifteen-stone demon mastiff. This dog could break a wolf's neck. Shake it like a fucking rat. Literally. Well, I guess *'fought off'* is a mite strong, but she fought him. She used that wooden frame at first, but the mastiff just shattered the thing. Stephan remembers. You should see his eyes when he tells the story. They glow like the moon. He tells it far better than me. But then, he was there. Saw it with his own eyes. Saw my crippled grandmother, whose bones were about as hard as stale bread, take on a monster twice her size with her bare hands. I wouldn't believe it if I hadn't seen the aftermath. Her splayed out on the ground, hands wrapped around its thick neck. Blood everywhere."

"She killed it?" Lady Narcissa asked, despite herself.

"God no. Jesus. It tore her apart. Ripped her fucking throat out. Shattered her body. Take your pick. One of the guards killed it. Speared the fucker. Ten or eleven times it took." I nodded. "Stephan told us how the mastiff went for him, but she wouldn't let it. Hobbling around as she did, getting between the two of them. Somehow. Jesus. How? My grandmother? Bravest person I've ever met. Hands down. And she was terrified of dogs, too. Did I mention that? She hated them. Absolutely. Wouldn't go near them. Hated the barking, the slobbering, the teeth, the smell. Hated it all."

"I don't follow." Lady Narcissa crossed her arms. "Are you insinuating I wasn't there because my story lacks what? Details?"

"No." I raised a hand. "I think you weren't there because you're here. You have some of my grandmother in you. The iron. And if you'd been with your children the day of the demon-mastiff, you'd have done the same as she. You'd have fought tooth and nail until it killed you or you it. Same with your *supposed* killer-monk. But you didn't. Cause you're here. Alive. If you'd been there, indisposed or not, ill or not, your sons either wouldn't be dead, or you would be, too."

Lady Narcissa bowed her head, whispering

something I couldn't hear, a prayer, a hiss, a curse.

I simply waited.

"I tread a fine line, Krait." She licked her lips.

"We all do, lady. Only a lord can afford to rip a ragged course."

"With Pyotr, I mean. Here is a man who takes his vows most gravely. Old-Oath, his keep is named, passed down through generations, second in antiquity only to Coldspire. And he keeps his word, he always has. It's life and death to him. And he holds others to a similar standard. *Others*…? Everyone. From lord to serf, and should you break your word? You are nothing."

"A tryst." As soon as I said it, I knew it for truth. "You were with someone that night."

She drew herself up. "As I understand it, you're famous for your *whoring*."

"Well, my prices are quite reasonable."

"But then, you're a man, and there is a double standard for such things."

"As we make all the rules, we thought it wise."

"You jest, yet you understand. You're not quite so stupid as you seem on first impression."

"The lady showers me with such compliments," I said to Karl, drooling in bed.

"I was detained that night, yes."

"Where?"

"Does it matter?"

I considered for a moment then shook my head. "No. Not yet, at any rate."

"Not Coldspire, then, let us say."

"Fair enough."

"In knowing this, you know I was not lying to you. I was lying to Pyotr."

"Raachwald."

"Yes. You were only there for the retelling. That night…that cursed night I returned to Coldspire just prior to dawn. After the attack. After my boys were—but before Pyotr arrived. Mary returned with him, mad with grief. She grasped at me, babbling a tale in bits and chunks. I could not tell what Pyotr knew. I…I concocted a story, utilizing the bits garnered from Mary. Cobbled it together. It…it was not a cogent story, I admit, but I was forced to maintain consistency, a foolish consistency, but a consistency nonetheless."

"But why lie to Lord Raachwald? Why not tell him you were indisposed? He and your husband hated each other."

"You have no idea what it is to be a woman."

"All sunshine and roses?"

"Impressive," she murmured. "It is impressive what a woman in this life can become inured to. The pain. The degradations. The…"

"There are others have it worse."

"Oh? Is suffering a contest?" She glanced up. "If so, then, yes, I concede. No blue ribbons to boast of are pinned to my breast. There are others worse off, indeed, of course. I had a roof, a sated belly. I had a bed. Servants. I also had a man who…treated me ill."

"Ill?" I echoed, not wondering at the true meaning behind the simple word. Knowing. "Your husband." It was not a question.

"Perhaps you are correct." Acid dripped from her tongue. "Perhaps the life of a noblewoman is all sunshine and roses. Perhaps I am just *fickle*."

"You killed two of Raachwald's guards, yeah?"

She glanced up, caught off guard. She didn't deny it.

"So why not off your husband?"

"You say it as though it were some small thing," Lady Narcissa murmured. "The taking of a life. I grew up the daughter of a lord, and so have seen my share of death, of justice, injustice, murder, even. They don't call it that when they take the head of some dolt peasant for killing deer, but that is what it is. I never thought it right. I found it unsettling, and never believed myself capable of such barbarity. I was a patron of the church. I heeded my commandments. I knelt. I prayed. I suffered in silence.

Sometimes not so silent, admittedly, but that was what I was taught. The day Dunmire burned, I learned a new lesson, many new lessons. Would only that I had steeled myself to them sooner."

"If you wanted my help from the start, why turn your back on me in the Hellwood?"

"With a man like Pyotr?" Lady Narcissa shook her head. "The surest way to ensure your death would have been to beg for your life. You understand? Pyotr is the sort of man who does not take to others' ideas with alacrity. He is wont to do the opposite of whatever idea someone puts forth, even if that idea shows merit. He is contrary by nature, and thus I offered the opposite, knowing that only by that path there lay some chance."

I knew men like that. Hell, most were, never wanting to take another's advice even if it was built square. "Raachwald needs to marry you to obtain Coldspire, yeah? So why not say '*no*?'"

"And what do you suppose would occur then? He murders his wives. You think he would hesitate to do so to me?" She fingered her lip. "Perhaps if my house were intact. Perhaps if I commanded thirty swords. Twenty, even, in these dismal days. If '*perhaps*' were a flower I would possess a garden. But my house is stricken, my line sundered. I had to bide my time. I am but a prize mare. Yet a prize mare has worth so long as those vying for her see her as such. If Pyotr saw me as a breaker of the marriage oath, he would see me as something other than a prize mare. He would see me as nothing, and I assure you he would treat me accordingly."

I nodded.

"Stephan spoke so highly of you," she said. "He was so convincing. I could hardly believe it, yet I knew I must hazard a chance, my sole chance to escape, to regroup, to rebuild," her eyes blazed, "to reclaim."

"You want Coldspire back?"

"You think only men possess ambition?" Her lips curled back over even, white teeth. "It is cramped. It is cold. It is hell, but it is my hell. *Mine*." She pounded a fist. "I'll be damned if I let it fall from my grasp."

"Tell me what happened that night."

She drew in a long breath, held it, then proceeded, "It was nigh on dawn when I returned to Coldspire. No one was there, no one but corpses."

"You had no fear of your husband finding out?"

"When my husband drinks—drank, he was on a mission. To oblivion. If for some reason he hadn't been that night, I would not have left, but he was. There was no chance of him waking, short of being dragged bodily out of bed."

"How long after you arrived did Lady Mary and Raachwald arrive?"

"Moments. I was in the great hall, picking my way through the carnage, fearing...I didn't yet know about my sons. I prayed they had escaped, somehow, prayed I'd not find them amidst the..."

"What then?"

"Pyotr arrived, bidding us remain in the great hall while he searched out the confines of Coldspire, to ensure the killer had truly fled as Mary had claimed. I protested, and we argued, but Pyotr brooked no argument. He put us under guard, and in my own hall." Her nails dug quivering into the armrests. "And so I waited in the long silence for word of my dead sons, Mary by my side, staring at the broken body of her husband the whole while. Poor Mary.

"Pyotr had my boys borne to Old-Oath. I...I cleaned them there, mended them, stitched their wounds." Her eyes were clamped shut as she spoke, a woman lost in a dark wood. "Then I dressed them. I sat with them for...for I don't know how long. He had a priest called in to offer them their last rites, bless them, shrive them. I laid them to rest in the crypts below Coldspire the very next day."

"Did you ever see Raachwald's son?"

"Cain?" She looked up, considering. "No. Pyotr's men bore him to Old-Oath."

"What about his funeral?"

"There was a ceremony, yes, but I was not in

attendance."

I nodded. I still had no witnesses to the boy's death. "Tell me about the finances of Coldspire. Stephan told me you were in debt."

"Debt?" She laughed a short strangled snarl. "Nay. A cautionary tale, rather. A survey course in how not to manage a house, how to spin your gold away to nothing, to beggar yourself blind, to clip a raven's wings."

"So, yes?"

"For Christ's sake."

"But you managed the finances of the house, yeah? Why allow it?"

"*Allow?*" she scoffed. "I kept track of the family finances as best I could. I begged for scraps, rumor of his spending. I tallied losses, stanched bleeding. I made no decisions, only estimates, and mostly blind at that. Yes, I tried to squirrel away coin, to spin gold from straw, to balance my husband's wants and lusts and idiocy against some semblance of business acumen."

"A losing battle?"

"Calling it such would be the utmost of generosity."

"How bad, truly? A number?"

"We were so deep in debt that I do not believe the full worth of Coldspire itself could have dug us out."

"You believe Coldspire was in danger of being taken?"

Lady Narcissa straightened haughtily. "No, the ones we owed could never have managed that, could never have touched us. Jews, all of them, according to my husband, but we were very deep indeed."

"Did he say which houses he borrowed from?"

She shook her head. "My husband was not forthcoming with information."

Damn. "What did your husband spend it on?"

"Whatever he desired. He bore no intention of repaying, and so he saw no need to curb his desires. Horses. Whores. Weapons. Armor. Gambling. How should I know? He would never tell me. He would only tell me when and how much and only on occasion."

"Control." I nodded. "And you're certain it wasn't paid back?"

She just glared. "If you think this amusing?"

"Was *any* of it paid back?"

"They had sent letter after letter gently imploring my husband to pay his debts, begging, pleading. This persisted for months, years."

"And what did your husband do?"

"He laughed. He burned them. He wiped his arse with them."

"Was any recourse taken?"

"Publicly?" She considered. "No. What could a Jew possibly do? And against a lord? I'm told various lenders approached the Lord Bishop, but his word would have only strengthened my husband's resolve against reimbursement."

"What would you say if I told you most of the loans had been paid off?"

Her eyes narrowed. "Are you indeed telling me this?"

"I've it on good authority."

"Impossible." She shook her head. "There was nothing left. Nothing. Whoever it was that told you this lied."

Abraham? No. Not unless he was the most adept of liars, and I was fair sure he wasn't. Had someone else paid it off? But who? Who could afford to?

"Men have gone missing over the past year and a half or so, Jews and my husband's men. I was never privy to what was transpiring. No one ever spoke of it, not openly, but there were killings."

"Who?"

"Both sides. Christian and Jew."

Was this shades of Red Tom's Masada?

"A war in the shadows, so to speak," she continued. "My husband had championed a cleansing of the Jews in Asylum City."

"You make them sound like laundry."

"My husband was never strong enough to rally a force capable of doing so." She shook her head in disgust. "He only railed about it in his drunken foolery, picked at them from his high tower. He lacked the sand of Pyotr. I'll say that. Pyotr gives no heed. He fights. He takes, openly, but my husband? Nay, it was his undoing."

"Are there any amongst your husband's friends who you could call on for help?"

"Friends?" she said, incredulous. "He had nothing of the sort."

"Is there anyone still in his debt?"

She shook her head.

"What about you?"

"Mary, but she has sacrificed so much already." Lady Narcissa leaned forth toward the fire, peering into its depths. "I have no allies, but an accord might be bought."

...persisted for two days now. My wife remains yet unaware, and I bear no wish to alarm her; therefore I sit here waiting and watching and...
—Journal of Sir Myron Chalstain

Chapter 33.

"A THOUGHT had occurred to me after you left." Brother Tomas slurped tepidly at his parsnip soup. Some color had returned to his face in my absence. And though yellow was perhaps not the color one would wish to acquire, it beat the hell out of grey. "The three boys were killed with a blade." Mouth full, chewing, he pointed with the spoon for emphasis. "Their throats were slit, yes-yes?"

"That's the story." I sipped at my own spoonful of soup. It was bland and thin and piping hot. It was my second. I planned on a third.

"The method of killing seems in line with the Jewish preparation of food stock." Brother Tomas reached forward, finger sliding down along the bindings of a stack of books. "Hmm? The *Book of Leviticus.* Yes-yes. Old Testament." There seemed even more books stacked in his cramped cell than the day before. He withdrew a book from the stack and began carefully turning through its pages. "Hmm... It involves a single cut across the throat and the subsequent draining of all the blood." He angled the book so I could see an illumination of a man slaughtering a calf. "A Jewish rite."

"The blood libel, you mean?"

"Oh, no-no, forgive me, of course not." Brother Tomas seemed repulsed, embarrassed. "I was merely making a comparison between...if you were an ignorant person—"

"I'll work real hard to wear that hat a moment."

"If you were an ignorant person, and you were trying to lay a false trail, trying to make it appear as though someone else, Jews, in this case, had committed a crime of murder, might that not be an adroit tactic? Inflame the ire of men not known for their cool heads. Playing upon long-imbedded prejudices. The well of hatred for the Jews has seldom run dry."

"Sure." Thoughts raced through my head. The bodies. The impossible, no, the *improbable* wounds. There were connections. Red Tom had confirmed his men'd been killed fighting the Jews. Their wounds were consistent with Volkendorf and Chalstain. And the children had been slain in a manner in line with Jewish ritual. But there were the eye socket puncture wounds... I took a long breath. There were threads, but they were long, tenuous, difficult to see, to grasp. "Say for the moment it were true?"

Brother Tomas stirred the soup. "If what?"

"Black magic," I said. "Blood magic? What if it were?"

"Oh dear me, yes-yes, or the appearance—"

"No," I waved a hand. "Not the appearance. The real thing."

"The real thing?" Brother Tomas crossed himself. "Well, most everyone knows the blood libel stories. Wretched scapegoating incidents to some, holy gospel to others."

"Jewish cabal shit. Yeah. Murdering for blood. But if it were true, what would they use it for?"

"I'm afraid I haven't the faintest. And there's a dearth of Jewish texts outside the Hebraic communities." Hand to his chin, he considered. "Yes-yes. Here." Scrabbling from his chair, he nimbly slid through the perilous stacks. "Just the thing." On hands and knees, he searched until he arose grasping another book. "*Malediction of the Upright.* By Yurin the Crow. A seventh-century Norwegian monk. A treatise on various magics. It encompasses many religions." He flipped through the book. "Pagan. Hmmm. Otherwise. Here. The chapter on blood magics. Christianity, the sacrifice of the Lord's son, Roman burnt offerings, Thuringian sacrificial... Ah here, Judaism." He scanned the page, his finger trailing along as he read. "Hmmm. Yes-yes. The blood could be used in the binding of *shedim* and *malachim*. Ah. Demons and angels, respectively. Another use is the animation of unliving matter, in effigy, so to speak, of God's own creation of Adam."

"Binding demons and creating men?"

Brother Tomas reread a passage, nodding as he did so. "Yes-yes. Yurin, unfortunately, fails to delve into deeper detail. His research is pervasive but fails to penetrate the skin, so to speak." Brother Tomas's lips moved as he skimmed the text. "Was blood harvested?"

"Don't know." In my mind's eye, black blood pooled, creeping across that floor, a thing alive, growing, consuming like cancer, back in that room, back in that castle. "There was a lot, I'm told. But then, I'm told a lot of things."

"Precisely. Listen, you also claimed it was a monk that committed the murder."

"No." I waved a hand. "I spoke to Narcissa. Finally. Her story's bullshit, just like I thought. Wasn't a monk. Don't know who it was. Don't know what." Theories of blood-bound demons started careening through my head, keening, slavering, beating bat wings.

"Oh," Brother Tomas said, crestfallen.

"Speaking of monks," I added carefully, "what about your *giant* friend?"

Brother Tomas blanched, taking a sudden and overwhelming interest in the floor.

A word sprang to mind, *dodgy*.

"Brother Gaunt?" I held a hand up over my head. "About yay tall. Big scary fucker who reasonably fits the killer's description. And by *reasonably*, I mean, exactly."

Brother Tomas giggled, shaking his head to himself, muttering to his soup as he stirred it. His soup said nothing in return.

"Master of the Teutonic Knights of Asylum City?"

"No, no." Brother Tomas shook his head.

"Horribly scarred? Hulkingly titanic? Carries a *zwiehander* longer than I am tall?"

Brother Tomas shrugged.

"Nothing? No memory?"

"I...I," Brother Tomas stammered.

I leaned in closer, forcing him to look me in the eye. "You know him, yeah?"

"Yes, b-but he is no killer."

"I'm afraid that's all he is."

"Oh, no-no." Brother Tomas shook his head as he looked down, away. "John would not harm a child."

"Yeah. Sure," I said, just to be agreeable, "but he'd murder the child's mother and father then let father-winter draw life's breath from *it*. Or starvation. Or wolves."

"He would not."

"He's a monk, but he's also a knight. And I know knights. That's what we do. That's *all* we do."

Brother Tomas stammered.

"Relax." I held up a hand. "He's your friend?"

Brother Tomas nodded a quick twitch, nothing more. "Yes."

"You sought to protect a friend, then?"

"Yes." Brother Tomas swallowed. "Fruitless, obviously. I fear I am an improficient liar. Even those by omission. You have my sincerest apologies. You were kind to me in my hour of need, and I have repaid you in the sin of salted earth."

"Eh?"

"I have urinated in your well, I have—"

"Easy. Relax. We just met. You were protecting a friend. I get that. I just wanted to know for sure. Needed to know, in fact. I keep running into him. Just yesterday. The day before. A delightful chap."

"Oh, yes," Brother Tomas said. "He's promised to visit tonight. That's why I made so much soup." He leaned in, placing a hand alongside his mouth, conspiratorially. "He eats as much as a horse."

"*Apologies, brother,*" a deep voice rumbled from the doorway.

I burst from my seat, Yolanda whipped clean and quivering point forward at the massive wraith that emerged like mist from the darkness, darker than the darkness, seeming to spread higher, wider, like giant bat wings. "*Jesus-fucking-Christ,*" I hissed. "How's someone big as you move like a ghost?"

"With men like you, so entranced by the sound of their own voice?" He closed the door behind him.

"Melodious, though, is it not?" My breath steamed down the length of my blade.

The wraith stepped into the light and past me as though I weren't brandishing a length of castle-forged death-dealing crucible steel aimed in his specific vicinity. He took a seat by Brother Tomas's side, armor scraping, and selected a bowl, then ladled himself a portion. "My thanks, Brother Tomas."

"You're welcome, Brother John." Brother Tomas nodded. "You are always welcome."

Gaunt threw back his hood, revealing that awful face. "You can lower the blade, Krait."

"You granting permission?"

"There's simply no need for it. I'm not going to kill you. Here."

"And who says I'm not going to kill you?"

Gaunt spooned a mouthful in, closing his eyes, and chewed, teeth working, visible through the ragged jags ripped through his face, drool leaking continuously.

"Anyone can be got to, Gaunt."

"Aye." He wiped the leaked wet from his jaw. "You don't look so good, Krait."

"Having a rough night."

Gaunt didn't take the bait, but Brother Tomas swallowed it whole and ran with it. "What happened?"

"Five men tried to kill me."

Gaunt scowled. "You're not very popular."

"Oh, I am. Just with the wrong people."

"Another ambush?" Gaunt asked.

"Yeah, but this time I saw it. And I caught it."

"What was your plan?"

"Didn't have one." I shrugged.

"There's the heart of your difficulties." Gaunt pointed with his spoon.

"And I'm pretty sure I know yours."

"Well, from chaos came order," Brother Tomas

giggled, leaning forward, pouring himself a lick of drink. "*Book of Genesis*, creation, all from nothing. A lesson to learn there, no? More soup, John? Krait? Anyone?"

"My thanks." Gaunt held his bowl out while Brother Tomas ladled some in.

"Yeah." I lowered Yolanda. "You know, the northmen have their own creation story, too. Says everything in the world was carved from the corpse of a rotting titan. I was thinking Asylum City might be its asshole." I cocked my head toward Gaunt. "What's that make you?"

Gaunt's glare darkened.

"Ain't my story." I shrugged. "It just is. And if you have a problem with that you can shove this up your arse." I patted Yolanda. "I hear monks favor that sort of sport. No offense, Tomas."

"None taken." Brother Tomas shrank into his chair.

Gaunt bristled like a bear set to charge.

"Gentlemen," Brother Tomas said. "Gentlemen, please. Krait. Brother John. To each his own." Brother Tomas raised a cup, offering it to Gaunt, to me, to anyone. "Cheers. Cheers…?"

"Wine?" I asked without looking.

"Help yourself."

"Thanks." I snatched the cup from Brother Tomas and knocked it back. It was good. Damn good.

Gaunt waved off Brother Tomas's offer.

"Your brother?" Brother Tomas asked me, tapping a finger against his cup. "Has he turned up?"

"Yeah. Most of him."

Gaunt chuffed, short and sharp, shaking his head.

Brother Tomas blinked, quizzical.

"What Krait means is Raachwald is taking him in part," Gaunt said, "before the sum total." He glanced over my way. "*Fingers?*"

"No. His hand," I said. "His right hand."

"Oh, oh my word," Brother Tomas sputtered.

"He's to be executed the day after tomorrow," Gaunt said.

"Yeah. I'm working on that."

"But, is that legal?" Brother Tomas asked. "In this day and age?"

"Sure." I took another swig of wine. "Anything a lord does under his own roof's legal. Besides. Stephan confessed to abduction. Stealing a woman against her will. That's Raachwald's reasoning. Penalty for thievery's the loss of a hand."

"Then he should be set free!" Brother Tomas announced. "He's served his sentence."

"There's also the small matter of Raachwald's two dead men, not to mention the razing of Dunmire."

Frowning, Brother Tomas pushed his bowl away.

"Have you found the lady?" Gaunt leaned in.

"No," I lied. *Fuck off.*

Brother Tomas shuddered, eyes widening.

I ignored him. "And what of Nils?"

"Alive." Gaunt nodded. "Surprisingly. Tenuous, but alive. A tough young lad."

"Shouldn't you be watching him, then?"

"He is in God's hands," Gaunt growled low. "And the last man who implied I shirked my duty is rotting at the bottom of a bog south of Novgorod." He wiped his bristling chin with a massive bear paw. "I've done what I can. The rest is up to God." He settled back. "But my brothers are still at the hospital, watching over him if truly that does concern you."

"Glad to hear it."

"You found Chalstain's body," Gaunt said. "Nils took you out to see it. You were waylaid upon your return. Ambushed. They should have killed you but didn't. What did they want? What was it you found besides the body?"

"Who says I found anything?"

"You're lying again."

"Oh?" I sat back. "How can you tell?"

"I can tell when you speak truth," Gaunt said. "It is as out of place on you as laughter in an abattoir. Two assassins tried to kill you, in the street, in broad daylight."

"Maybe they were just highwaymen."

"I think not. One of the two of you on the city watch? Both armed. Nay. Not highwaymen. And this business of the five? Another attempt on you tonight, through your own admission? What do they want? What is it you possess?"

"Maybe they're just jealous of my charm."

"You found something."

"Go fuck yourself."

"There's a price on your head set there by the Lord Bishop himself," Gaunt said "Gold. A parcel of arable land."

I was out of my seat, Yolanda drawn. "What?"

"Sizable." Gaunt ate another spoonful. "A man might retire on it alone. Comfortably."

"Why?"

"I know not." Gaunt shook his head. "I know only that His Eminence sent a warrant by emissary to the hospital yesterday, a warrant with your name on it. Dead or alive. He's issued them across the city, to both enemy and ally alike."

"May I reiterate, go fuck yourself."

"Play your games, Krait." He raised both of his paws outward, as though to lessen his threat. It did not, not even a little. "I care neither for gold nor His Eminence's decrees. But you found Chalstain. He's to be interred today, at noon."

"Oh? How nice for the grieving widow."

Gaunt rose, knuckles cracking, hands clenching into fists, a mountain set to avalanche. "A little respect for a good man might be in order."

"Never knew the guy." I gave no ground, stood eye to eye, or eye to sternum. "But me and my brother wouldn't be stuck three knuckles deep in this quagmire if that bastard had done his job. So a little respect from me might be a little too much to swallow."

"Well, open up," Gaunt snarled, pushing back the sleeve of his mail shirt.

"Gentlemen!" Brother Tomas stood suddenly

between us, his stick arms and hands wide apart like the referee of a bare-knuckle contest. "Might that not be a good place to, uh, investigate?" He turned to me, eyes begging. "Krait? Yes-yes? The funeral?"

We both froze, glaring at Brother Tomas.

"Well, shit, yeah," I admitted. "They tossing him into a plague pit? Or lighting him up?"

"Neither," Gaunt grumbled like far-flung thunder. "He's to be buried with full honors."

"Is the funeral being held on Mummer's Isle?" That might give me a chance to not only get back on the Isle, but also into the crypts. With a large contingent of men attending the ceremony, I could sneak on. Somehow. With Crowley Street most likely being watched, it was my sole option other than swimming and climbing. So, sneak on, get back into Old-Oath, open Cain Raachwald's tomb, see if he was even in it. And that just for starters. But I'd need an angle to get past the guards. A disguise. Monk would do nicely. I could procure a cowl and robe from the monastery, move with the procession, blend in, slide my way past the guards in all the furor.

"Nay," Gaunt answered, slaughtering my plans.

"Shit. Where then?"

"Saint Hagan's Cathedral. He's to be interred within the necropolis. Chalstain's father fought with the church over the decision, I'm told. Desires his son be entombed within Solemn Rock's crypt."

"Lord Taschgart?" I raised an eyebrow. "Heard he and Chalstain weren't on the best of terms."

Gaunt shrugged. "Taschgart's pleas made no dint in the Lord Bishop's plans."

"I'll need to attend," I said, reconfiguring my plans.

"I must advise against it," Gaunt warned.

"Oh?" I glanced up. "Why's that?"

"*Firstly*, I'm tasked with keeping the peace, and so having a lit fuse like you in the midst of so many powder kegs will only render my task more treacherous. *Secondly*, I would warn against it merely for the fact that the Lord

Bishop and Lord Raachwald are both to be in attendance."

Brother Tomas's spoon froze midway to his mouth. "Lord Raachwald's going to be in Saint Hagan's?" He made the sign of the cross and started mouthing a silent prayer.

"All the five families shall attend." Gaunt nodded. "More and more fuses jammed alongside the powder keg, all begging for burn."

"And they all came together and agreed on *you* to keep the peace?"

"Driven so far apart, rather. More like each man hates me, but hates me equally. Raachwald's steward, Inglestahd, and the Lord Bishop's legate, Father Paul, brokered the deal. The Brulerin boy acted, as well. An accord was reached, following a laborious process, I'm told."

"Hate," I said in awe, "driving people so far apart they come back together."

"Thirdly—"

"Jesus, there's a *thirdly*?"

"Aye. There is a second party that wishes to see you dead."

"Are you it?" I asked.

Gaunt ignored me. "I know not who, but they've spread the word. I gather it comes from the eastern bank of the river, but I am uncertain."

"Raachwald?"

"Likely. Your assassins are another possibility."

"How much is it for?"

"One hundred and fifty crowns."

I whistled low. "Maybe I should turn myself in? And why's the Lord Bishop want me? I'm working for him."

"How should I know? You're working for two men at cross purposes," Gaunt said. "Powerful men of little conscience." Gaunt regarded me with a cold glare. "Perhaps it is Chalstain's ledger they desire?"

"What ledger?" I asked smooth as a sabre.

Gaunt closed his eyes and seemed to be counting. He counted a long while before he spoke. "You found his body, his personal effects. It is assumed that you also have his ledger. There are many who wonder what is written within its pages."

"You one of them?"

"I am."

"And who else?"

"Everyone else. And they who are everyone else would not have cringed from the thought of you dead before. Now with the addition of this bounty?"

"Really? Jesus," I confided in Brother Tomas, "your friend's smart."

"You possess the ledger?" Gaunt asked.

"What business is it of yours?"

"You know my business."

"Fuck your business, and fuck you."

"You have it then?"

"I have *a* ledger. I don't know if it is *the* ledger. Hell, I don't know if the body was his."

"It bore his sigil on his chest."

"It bore no *head*," I retorted.

"I've also heard it through the streets," Gaunt said, "and if the streets know, everyone knows. And whether or not that is Chalstain's body or Chalstain's ledger, they're going to continue until they have it."

"Jesus Christ, are you serious?" I asked. "Tomas, is he serious?"

Brother Tomas gulped.

"Why don't you go off and protect your broken city?" I spat.

"Why don't you tell me what the ledger says? Perhaps I might offer help?"

"Why don't you fuck off?"

Gaunt turned to Brother Tomas. "Your friend can't read the ledger. He can't read it because it's written in code." He turned back to me. "I'm right aren't I?"

"A code?" Brother Tomas perked up. "Y-you mean a cipher?"

"That's why he came," Gaunt said. "He needs you to break it. Don't you, Krait?"

"Actually, I came for the soup." I slurped a spoonful. "Mmm... So good."

"I could take it from you if I desired."

"You sure about that?" I glared up willful, defiant, and fair certain he could, too.

"As sure as I am about anything." He leaned forward, face hidden in shadow. "This can go one of two ways, and neither of us is likely to enjoy the second."

I thought about it a moment and realized I didn't want to fight a titan in a room the size of an outhouse. So I pulled Chalstain's ledger out and slapped it on the table.

Brother Tomas quivered in excitement, fingers twittering alive, like a hive of bees, the malaise in his face momentarily suffused by ecstasy. "Is it Sir Myron's?"

"Probably," I said.

"M-May I?"

"You know him?" I asked.

"No."

"You?" I asked Gaunt

"I've had dealings." Gaunt nodded. "He fell not into the trap that befalls so many hunters-of-men. Becoming that which he hunted. A good man, solid, forthright, honorable. A reliable man. Your polar opposite."

"I'm reliable."

"For what?"

"Ask the whores at the Stone Ruin Ten."

Gaunt grumbled.

Brother Tomas hovered like a starving jackal set to descend on a carcass. "Please, may I?"

"Sure." I nodded, and Brother Tomas was already devouring it. "Only part of it's in cipher. The rest looks like it was scrawled by some lunatic who downed a fistful of bad mushrooms."

"Did you read it?" Gaunt asked.

I ignored him, as much as I could. "Can you break the cipher?"

Brother Tomas might have orgasmed at the word '*cipher*,' I don't know. I don't want to know. He was ripping through pages, whipping them right to left, his face suffused by a warm orange glow.

"A fan of ciphers?" I glanced at Gaunt, who shrugged.

"We use ciphers in many of our record keeping." Brother Tomas licked a finger, kept turning. "Shipping manifests. Sometimes even for amusement," he whispered gleefully, glancing around as though the abbot might be peering disapprovingly over his shoulder. "Creating ciphers for our brothers, breaking them, an exercise to hone the mind. So stimulating. So engrossing. So—"

"*Right.*" I knew monks used ciphers, secretive, weird fellows that they were, and with Stephan languishing in Lord Raachwald's dungeon, Brother Tomas was my only shot. "Think you can break it?"

Brother Tomas might not have heard me, for he was already in the process of decoding it. A pen and ink bottle had appeared on his desk alongside a roll of parchment. "May it?" He pointed at the lantern by my arm.

"No." I placed it on his table, doubling his light. He scribbled something down, then something else.

"That was—" I started.

"Shhhhh!"

"Right."

"Has your man turned up?" Gaunt asked.

"No," I lied. "Hoping he will soon. Hoping he's freed my brother and the three of us'll sally forth on our merry way til this shithole's a speck of nothing in the distance."

"You hope?" He rumbled. "Your man's name must be King David or Saint George for him to commit such deeds of valor. Of bravado. Breaking into Raachwald's keep. Killing his men. Burning his home. Riding off with his whore. And even so, the best men I've ever known languish forever in pagan dirt."

"Bravery's an illness easily cured."

"There is no bravery," Gaunt said. "There is only one's duty and allegiance to God. You either perform your duty, or you do not."

"Said with all the moral complexity of a five-year-old."

"I'm not the one sitting on his arse drinking wine and '*hoping*' for things to happen."

"Said the bloke charged with protecting the city who's presently sitting on his arse and sucking down soup."

Gaunt exploded from his seat, covering the distance between us in the blink of an eye. His hands clamped like vices round my wrist and throat, slamming me against the wall, stars exploding before my eyes. My legs kicked off the ground. Gaunt's eyes bulged mad, teeth grinding so hard they might crack. Brother Tomas was at Gaunt's side, trying to reason with him, placate him, but he might have reasoned with a distempered bear. "I told you what happened to the last man…" Fingers crushed my wrist and throat.

"Errrg, he lived…happily ever…after," I croaked or gurgled or maybe just thought inside my head. Brother Tomas pleaded beyond the buzz growing in my ears, the blurred lines consuming my vision. I drew the butcher blade and pressed it against Gaunt's crotch. I was close enough to get one solid thrust.

Gaunt's face twitched at the press of steel below. Then he laughed. *Laughed.* A grin spread across his wretched face, twisting scar and sinew. "I'm a monk, remember? I don't fucking use them!"

In that moment I knew I was going to die. I might take him with me; I might not. He'd be a ball short, maybe two, but apparently he didn't care. So I did the only thing I could. I dropped the knife. It rang out on the floor, a reverberating *ting.*

Brother Tomas kept yammering.

The gnarled tree root fingers, harder than stone, inched open, and I sucked in a rasp, my legs faltering as I collapsed against the wall, grasping raw at my throat. Brother Tomas was still talking, and even through the buzz, I could tell he wasn't making any sense.

"I…I came in peace," Gaunt whispered to himself,

staring at his monstrous hands, clenching, unclenching like beasts breathing, slowly, onerously.

I crumpled to the floor, knocking over piles of books.

Gaunt loomed, a monstrous shade. "This city is a house razed. I see its charred bones stark against the white of winter, huddled amidst the gale, skin blasted off in peels of cinder and ash. Yet it stands and shall continue to do so. It shall not fall. It cannot." He half-turned to Brother Tomas and blinked. "I'll...I'll bid good night to you, Brother Tomas."

"Good night, Brother John." Brother Tomas took Gaunt's hand. "And thank you. Thank you for the...the lovely visit."

Gaunt slid away into darkness.

"Despite his great strength, he can be so fragile in some ways." Brother Tomas shook his head slowly. "I've heard stories." He waggled a finger my way like some schoolmarm chastising a student. "You should tread more carefully around him."

"No shit," I croaked, rubbing my throat.

...Irene cannot sleep for worry. Nor can I. I have bade her quit herself to the more protected sanctuary my brother offers, but she refuses adamantly. A stubborn woman with a mind of her own, one of the many reasons I married her.
—Journal of Sir Myron Chalstain

Chapter 34.

I HAD MY APPOINTMENT at Saint Hagan's at noon, so before daybreak I headed through the streets, retracing my steps from last night's venture, back across the God-damned North Bridge upon which nothing good ever happened. At least to me. Tentatively, I set one toe on it then waited for the skies to open up, for the earth to rumble. Amazingly, no brigade of destrier-mounted God-sworn devils tried to mow me down. No crowd of starving city folk tried to trample me. No assassin squad waylaid me in the dark. I simply crossed the bridge, still freezing my arse off as usual, but thoroughly appreciating the mundanity of it.

Gaunt had guessed that I had Chalstain's ledger and, therefore, as he had said, others had probably guessed as well. Was that why the Lord Bishop had set a warrant on me? I'd reported to him. Sort of. I had lied about the ledger. Had he found out? He must have. But how? And what of the second bounty? Was that His Eminence, too, just utilizing other channels? Or was it someone else as Gaunt had guessed? The assassins? Somehow, I'd presumed the two that had ambushed me on the street and the five in the tavern were the same group. Now I wasn't even sure about that. Was one or both of them the Masada that Red Tom had mentioned? And who was Daniel, the man Casagrande had spoken of back at Abraham's money house? It seemed a fracture had occurred in the Quarter. Was Daniel the leader of this Masada, and had he been pressuring Abraham into joining? And using Casagrande to do so? Some deal had been at stake. That'd been plain. But what deal, I had no idea.

So through the streets, I walked, swift, purposeful, head down, making my way north again, following the same path I'd trod with Karl last night. Since there was a price on my head, I avoided the front gates. I drew my cloak over my shoulders as I approached the house with the tunnel. All was silent as I approached, as I paused in the alley and watched it for a spell, hunkered in the dark. Shuttered windows never moved, no lights glowing within. The sky was beginning to pink in the east, so under cover of failing dark, I made my way to the front door.

I knocked lightly. Waited.

Footsteps approached from the inside. Someone unlocked the door and opened it a crack. A cloaked man stared at me, a glint of steel below his face aimed my way, a crossbow bolt. "I know you, mister?"

"Naw." I shook my head. "I've a message for Daniel."

"Don't know no Daniel."

"Got a letter to deliver." I held up a folded piece of paper. A blob of wax sealed it shut. The letter was a farce but might hold up under scrutiny. I hoped it wouldn't have to.

His eyes narrowed. "Piss off."

"If that's what you want." I stepped back, hands up. "Got enough holes in me already. Ain't looking for new ones. But Red Tom's looking to sue for peace. Said it'd be," I screwed my eyes shut, "mutually beneficial."

The guard didn't say anything.

"So what's ole Red Tom do?" I asked. "What's he always do? The fucker sends me." The crossbow was still pointed directly at my heart. A tough shot even considering the distance. "Alright," I took two measured steps backward down the stairs, "I'll tell him '*no*.'"

"Shit." The guard lowered the crossbow, and the door swung open wide.

319

Temple Street was the main thoroughfare cutting through the heart of the Quarter, starting at the main square and moving north on through the money district, past the Quarter's main temple, and on into a barrage of manors and homes until it ended in warehouses and finally the docks. Only the North Sea lay beyond.

The sun was blaring red and low in the sky as I reached the manor house Karl had tracked the assassin to. In the dark of night, the street had held a sinister aura, long, congested, twin rows of infinite monstrosities leering down from on high, half aslumber. But in the light of day? Just two rows of large well-built houses fading off toward the sea. Mundane. Secure. The eight-foot wall surrounding the manor wasn't insurmountable by any means, just well-built, effective. As I took a sortie around it, getting a feel for it, seeing its four sides, I wondered where Blackbeard was right now. Was this his home? His base of operations? No. This was one of the biggest houses on the street, maybe the Quarter. Probably he was just some foot soldier running errands. This was his boss's manor. Daniel, this was *his* home.

Shit. Maybe.

I slid past a half-full corpse cart drawn by an emaciated mule, driven by a man who looked like he hadn't slept in a year. Black half-moons festered beneath his dead eyes as he plodded on, silent, tapping the mule on his ribbed side with a stick every few feet. The walking dead.

Waiting for him to pass, I slid back into the alley across from the manor. I couldn't just stand there in the street. Couldn't be slinking through alleyways in broad daylight. And trudging around lapping the manor all morning'd draw notice, too. I hadn't seen any guards in the manor, but they had to be there, and if they were any good, and it never paid to think otherwise, they'd be watching.

In lieu of hiding, I decided on the opposite. I'd make certain they'd see me. Make certain I'd be the first thing they'd see. I slung some dead monk's homespun cloak over mine and pulled the hood as far down over my face as possible. Down the road a piece, in front of the burned-out husk of a house, I hunkered on a set of stairs rising to nowhere and placed one of Brother Tomas's soup bowls out before me. Along with my new garb, I bore some dead monk's walking staff. It was thick oak, iron-shod, with a nice heft to it, which was essential, seeing as how I'd left Yolanda hidden back at the monastery. I still had my butcher blade and hatchets but felt naked without her. You don't name daggers, you don't name spears, you don't name halberds. You name swords.

"Oy," I mumbled, pounding the staff as some harried merchant hustled on by, his eyes wide, kindly offering me a wide berth as he heard the bells jingle, dangling from the tip of my staff. Something else I'd appropriated.

Leper, the best disguise ever. No one gives you a second glance. Hell, no one gives you a first. But they know you're there. They hear the bells and by rote their legs start tracing a half-mile circle round you, toss a coin if they're feeling particularly charitable. Certainly, no one'll talk to you let alone remember you. No one's going to strong-arm you cause no one wants to touch you, see you, feel the stink of your festering breath on their face.

Mobility's something of a problem. Lepers traditionally don't get anywhere in a hurry, but barring that, it's perfect. Unless they decide to kill you. And by '*they*' I mean everyone. That's the only time it's not perfect, and lepers are traditionally the only group as universally hated and scapegoated as the Jews. So passing time in Jewtown in leper guise might not actually be the sharpest play, might as well be wearing a bulls-eye on my chest, but it seemed lately I was anyways, so what the hell.

The shadows shortened as the sun rose, reflecting off fine glass windows, things of beauty, not just shuttered holes in walls. The street was clean, cleaner than the rest of the city, which admittedly was not a high set bar. Needless to say, there was no dearth of coin in the Quarter. Jews were forbidden from practicing most forms of work, which kept jobs open for good Christians. The one job not tacitly forbidden? Money lending. And with the fall of the Templar Knights a half a century before, along with their prodigious banking system, the Jews had fallen into that niche.

Which begged the question: who had the coin to buy out the totality of Lord Volkendorf's debts? Had it been someone from the Quarter? Who else had that kind of scratch? And who could afford to hire an entire mercenary crew of Genoese crossbowmen? Room them? Board them? Red Tom had said they were being stationed in the Quarter. Were they working for the Jews? For Daniel? If the Lord Bishop caught wind of that, it'd be trouble, bad trouble. And if it wasn't that, what the hell were they doing in the Quarter? Or was Red Tom full of shit?

Jesus.

The wind started picking up, swirling gusts of snow coruscating in glimmering ghost sheets down the way. The foot traffic was sparse, but anytime someone hurried by, I banged the butt of my staff on the ground, ringing the bells. Most hustled on, avoiding eye contact, pretending I didn't exist. But a few dropped a penny, nowhere near my bowl, but who was I to quibble? An hour or so later and this was actually working fairly well. Three pennies. I was halfway to considering a career change when I noticed movement beyond the manor gate. It opened inward smooth and silent.

I continued counting rocks in the street, watching out of the corner of my eye, banging my staff for good measure, bells tingling, calling out for alms until three hooded men exited the manor. The first two bore the watchful glare of bodyguards, each one moving cautious, aware, tense. Their gazes constantly shifted as they marched along, to open windows, to blind alleys, to me. I felt their gazes wash over me like a gust of cold air, a prickle of awareness tingling across the back of my neck, down my spine.

The third man emerging from the gate looked haggard, bent, worn. He moved like Methuselah, an old man sapped of strength and will. *Brittle*, a word that came to mind. Was this Daniel? This broken old man? As he paused, head down, hand at his brow, shaking, one of the bodyguards took him by the elbow, whispering something close in his ear. The old man glanced up, slow, measured, and nodded, clutching the bodyguard's shoulder and just leaning there, latched on like a drowning man to flotsam.

"Alms," I croaked, ringing my bell.

The old man turned, gathered himself, standing upright but bent still, as though some great weight burdened his shoulders. He swayed a bit before ambling on down the street in a fugue, aimless, the two guards steering him along. I watched them amble down Temple Street, south, and when they'd nearly disappeared in the distance, I clambered up, knees creaking, and followed, gaining speed, removing the bells from my staff, walking with purpose, becoming a monk. I wasn't afraid of losing them because I wasn't following them anymore because I knew where they were going, and I knew who they were. The old man was Abraham.

...past three months ten men have been murdered. Not a particularly high number for this city, however, these were all men of considerable means. Eight held substantial businesses throughout the city...
—Journal of Sir Myron Chalstain

Chapter 35.

THE SHOUTING DIED as swiftly as it had risen.

From across Saint Hagan's main aisle, the two men had come to blows, launching from their pews like eagles slamming into one another from on high, slashing, slamming, grappling, crashing. Men roared curses while fist thudded into flesh. Sir Myron Chalstain's coffin was knocked over, crashing, his corpse spilling halfway out, his helmeted head slamming against the marble floor. It rolled clanging into the altar. Lady Chalstain gazed numbly up at the stained glass depiction of the Lamb of God, a line of crimson rolling down from the corner of one eye.

I stood with cowled head bowed like all the other monks and priests, a veritable holy army, hands folded, penitent.

The two men fought, rolling across the smooth floor, gouging, grappling, fish-hooking. Teeth rained like hailstones, clicking on the stone floor as the Church-man gained the upper hand, hammering down blows, grunting, growling like an animal. Rocked, rattled, the Isle man drew a blade. Eyes wide on both sides, God's men and Isle men, all bristling, divided, set to explode.

Lord Eustace Hochmund stood above them all.

Despite the abounding hardships ruining Asylum, economic collapse, starvation, plague, Lord Hochmund had managed through sheer force of will and greed and foresight to remain repulsively obese. Inspirational, truly, *Song of Songs* inspirational. He stood at the pulpit, staring down, observing patiently, his pudgy fingers encrusted with rings as he drummed them. Bravely, he attempted to allay the murderous scrum by the indelible act of clearing his throat, loudly, *twice*. To no avail.

The other Isle Lords stood in the front row on the Isle half of the church: Lord Raachwald, stern, imperious; Lord Taschgart, tall and stately, his receding hairline of silver only seeming to make him all the more regal. He looked somehow familiar, though I knew I'd never set eyes on him before. Lord Brulerin, a youth of maybe eighteen, tall and straight, obnoxiously kempt and handsome, trying to hold back from aping the combatants' fisticuffs. The others restrained themselves more accordingly.

The melee ended with Gaunt's arrival, the wraith, hulking huge, silent, marching down the split, rising behind the two combatants like a perilous black sun across riotous horizon. Armed sergeants followed. Gaunt ignored the church-man. The sergeants descended on him.

The Isle man was another matter. He'd sundered the accord, bearing steel to the event. Gaunt seized him, grasping his wrist like a chicken's neck to be throttled. The snap didn't quell the cacophony. It was the man's shriek that did. All I saw behind the jostling bodies was Gaunt's other hand, steel-clad, descending toward the Isle man's face. Then a sickening rip, the sound of leather torn followed by a wet flapping squelch.

Gaunt simply turned and strode up the aisle as though on a jaunt for tea, only instead of carrying a tray, he was dragging a twenty-stone man whimpering along by the portion of his face still attached to skull. A reap of silence preceded Gaunt as his sergeants took station amidst the wake of red ruin. Opulent priests wrestled Chalstain's corpse back into its coffin. One knelt, cradling Chalstain's head like a homeless waif might his precious foot-ball, his eyes closed, lips trembling, mumbling, praying.

Lord Hochmund said nothing throughout the altercation but did clear his throat again when Gaunt hurled the man squealing out into the streets. The lord smiled wanly, humming as he waited for the priests to finish stuffing Chalstain back into his coffin with all the tenderness a pagan chief might cram burning rocks up a Christian's arsehole.

Lord Hochmund completed his eulogy then. Dryly. He sniffed, cleared his throat as he folded his parchment and stepped down from the pulpit as another, in an endless line of speakers, stepped forward and began droning on about something.

I wasn't listening.

I was watching Lord Hochmund. He strolled on a cloud of entitlement past the other lords, round the corner, toward the back. Strange for an Isle Lord to sit beneath his station. By rights, he should've been seated at the front, alongside the other three. Instead, he sat alongside his men. A magnanimous gesture? A man of the people? No. Strange only if you didn't know him.

I stepped from the rear of the church, lowering my cowl before passing in front of a pair of the Lord Bishop's men-at-arms, then slid through the crowd of standing monks and lesser clergy, making my way toward Lord Hochmund's seat, mumbling apologies and tossing signs of the cross about like they were going out of style.

I arrived just before Lord Hochmund. Stepping into the shadow of the headless statue of Saint Hagan, I waited.

"*Milord.*" I bowed as Lord Hochmund slid into his pew.

As one, his guards turned, twelve grim glares all told.

The lord slid in beside them, a short round man, dwarfed by his fighting men, a ball among sticks. "Brother?" He squinted me up and down, the twinkle of sadness in his eye melting instantaneously from his face like paint washed from a mummer's mask. My uncle's story of the three snakes played out in my mind. "*Brother* Krait. My, my, how droll." His voice was soft as steam. He sidestepped further into the pew, making room enough for me, and held out a hand. "Please."

I slid in, making the sign of the cross.

Lord Hochmund stared forward, observing the proceedings. "What is it you desire?"

"Alms for the poor?"

"Of course." He almost cracked a smirk. "I shall have it delivered to your monastery. Forthwith. Franciscan was it? Or Dominican? Your dress seems at odds with a variety of disciplines and disorders." He glanced past me to the exit at my right. "And now if that is all…?"

"Might I speak with you in private?"

The lord's captain leaned in, whispering quick, harsh.

"Impossible, I'm afraid." Lord Hochmund shook his head. "You see, I pay these gentlemen to protect me, and sadly, they cannot if I am off traipsing with you." He craned his short neck as another speaker took the pulpit. "Here will do."

I gripped the pew, "But—"

"Here *must* do." He chopped with his pudgy hand. "And tread carefully, *Brother* Krait. You're making my men nervous. Especially that crucifix." He glanced down at my walking staff. I'd tied a cross section to it and made a rather ostentatious crucifix out of it, and by *ostentatious* I meant shitty. But one pull of the string binding it together and it was walking staff once more. Or club.

"My Captain Abel here seems to think it more of the cudgel variety than crucifix. And he knows his business. I only do business with such men. I trust you'll remember that."

"Take it, then." I offered it. "To put your men at ease."

"Nonsense." He waved it off. "Never touch the stuff. And a word of advice, never allow men guarding your person to be at ease. Better they walk the razor's edge. It may lead to the occasional awkward moment from time to time, but…"

"And by awkward you mean?"

"The occasional overuse of force," Lord Hochmund whispered.

"Is there such a thing?"

He twittered. "Now, Krait, tell me," he pinched my monk's robe between two fingers and lifted it as though lifting a dead rat, "what abysmal circumstance has driven you against your indolent nature and forced you to take such *earthly* vows?" He released my robe and wiped his hand on a handkerchief. "You've not lost your manhood?"

"Some question I ever had it."

"Ah, I've missed you, old son." He grinned, showing the stubby yellow teeth that barely protruded through his thick pink gums. "Quite." He turned his attention back to the pulpit, serene, nonchalant, but I could tell he was uncomfortable, his eyes scanning the crowd. "It has been some time."

"How long?"

"Not long enough," he answered. "How is your father?"

"Still an asshole," I said, "and yours?"

"Still dead."

"Well, then, you win," I said.

"And your brother?"

"Which one?"

"The poor lad languishing in Raachwald's dungeon."

"You've heard then?"

"Hard not to. You seem to be in quite the predicament, stretched every which way, and with such a *sizable* price on your head. Tut, tut."

"Stephan's fine," I said as another speaker took the pulpit.

"Fine? I'm told Raachwald removed a finger."

"It was a hand."

"A hand, yes, forgive me. And yet here you stand, playing dress-up."

"I've always yearned for the simple life."

"Simple is not always tantamount to easy. Imagine the tedium, sitting there all day, copying texts, growing beets, turnips, what have you." He stifled a shiver. "Now, tell me, what brings you to Asylum City and incessantly to my very doorstep?"

"I came for the work."

"With the plague raging?"

"Gravedigging."

He smirked despite himself. "What is it you desire of me, old son?"

"I need to get onto Mummer's Isle."

"The same Isle which I share with my liege lord?" He shook his head. "My liege lord whose love for you is the very stuff of legend?"

"Since when is Raachwald *your* liege lord?"

"Since he has three times as many men as I." He loosened his collar with a finger. "Tough times for all. I fear I must clarify our previous proceedings."

"When you ignored me?"

"Ignore? Nay." Lord Hochmund shook his head slowly, apologetically, so I knew no apology would be forthcoming. "I would never ignore you, old son." He patted me tepidly on the hand. "I told you to '*piss off*.' There's a clear and patent difference."

"Maybe from your end."

"Many a man might have begged to be ignored by the occasional lord rather than wither beneath his vaunted attentions. Your brother is one such who comes to mind."

"Get me on."

"Whatever for?"

"Get me on, and I'll tell you."

"Why?"

"Thought I'd move into Coldspire. It's vacant. Roomy. Needs a drunk, threadbare lord to replace the old one."

"Well, you'd certainly fit the bill. But why should you require my assistance? You've already been traipsing around the rock, I'm told." He offered a sidelong glance. "And how did you get on? Hmmm? Now *that* would be something worth knowing. The Volkendorfs and Taschgarts both possess ways, I'm sure of it." He turned. "*Or* was it bribery?"

"How badly do you want to know?"

"Only moderately." He waved an offhand. "Though, if you did bribe someone, I should want to know whose guards. I trust they were not mine."

"Would it buy my boots landing on the Isle?"

"Only if you weren't in them." Again, he glanced past me toward the exit. "There exists an accord amongst the houses with regard to, ahem, visitors."

"I take it that accord includes me?"

"Oh, no." Lord Hochmund placed a hand on his chest. "Well, not you specifically. Just riff-raff *like* you."

"Might I remind you I am nobly born?"

"Remind me again what you've been doing for work as of late?" Lord Hochmund inquired innocently. "Caravan guarding for *Jews* was it?"

"I like to get paid."

"Ah, yes, *as generous as a Jew*, they're always saying," Lord Hochmund twittered. "It possesses a certain alliterative ring even if that ring is not simultaneously of truth."

"I have no idea of what you just said."

Lord Hochmund snickered. "In any event, I shan't help you. I'm sorry, truly, I am. I shan't sleep well tonight, I tell you. Verily."

"*Verily*?" I wanted to punch his fat face. "I *need* to get on the island."

"Dear me, and so here we go again." He twirled a finger. "Round and round."

"You sure you don't know?"

"I know Stephan's running out of time." Lord Hochmund nodded to himself. "What is it? A day til the big chop? I'm sorry. It's not funny. A sad tale, to be sure, but it is not worth my head to help you extricate your brother from Raachwald's dungeon."

"Didn't say I was going to break him out."

"Oh?" he said. "Then what?"

"You're a big bad lord."

"I'm big perhaps, but not so bad."

"How humble."

"Yes. I'm the most humble man there ever was, and ever shall, or ever could be."

"Never thought I'd see Lord Hochmund bow down

to Raachwald."

"You want my advice, Krait?" Lord Hochmund asked. "Look on the bright side. Your pious brother was practically born to be a martyr. He's probably salivating at the very chance. Tortured? Beheaded? Immortal fame through canonization? I almost envy him, greedy boy, having his cake and eating it, too. You, on the sinister hand, would make a terrible martyr."

"I have gold."

There came a rumbling from the crowd.

"Tsk. Tsk," Lord Hochmund said. "You have no gold, my dear hedge knight, or certainly not enough. The only gold you possess lies on the end of your neck. Best you leave Asylum today. Now. Best you keep it rather than I start reflecting overlong of my empty coffers." He turned to his men then nodded to the exit. "Gentlemen…"

"*She* has agreed to deal," I added.

"Eh?" Lord Hochmund held up a hand, ordering his men to halt. "*She*…? Am I to assume our previous negotiations have reopened?"

"Yeah. She mentioned you by name. Said you were the only one who could help, or would."

"Did she mention the sad ending to our previous negotiations?"

"A fluid situation. What was disadvantageous before is advantageous now."

He considered a moment, fingering his lip, then nodded. "For a price, but the same price I offered before. The price she was unwilling to pay."

"Done."

"You will take me to her?"

"No. I'll take her to you."

"Where?"

"Your keep."

"Nay," he said. "Let us conduct our dealings on the mainland until we've revealed our hands, eh? Away from prying eyes. Best, at any rate, for the lady to keep her distance." He rubbed his hands together. "When?"

"Tonight. Just after sundown."

"I shall have to scramble." He calculated, his lips pursed, brow furrowed. "Never a pretty sight. Where?"

"Outside the Gallows Eve Inn. Behind the stables."

"By the East Gates." Lord Hochmund nodded.

"And come alone." I glanced up.

A few things happened as the speaker finished his speech. One: the Lord Bishop rose from his seat and began shambling incrementally toward the pulpit. Two: Lord Hochmund was back on his feet, excusing himself, jostling past me, through me, out of the pew and to the exit. His men followed, near trampling me. And three: Lord Raachwald seized the pulpit ahead of the Lord Bishop.

His Eminence froze as soon as he realized he'd been cuckolded. In jittering fury, eyes afire, he seethed, the few teeth left in his liver-spotted head grinding as his miter hat tumbled from his head.

A chatter arose from the pews. Both sides.

Not good. Not good at all.

Lord Raachwald, tall and straight and horrible, stood like some pagan god incarnate as the sun shone through the colored windows behind, casting a halo of red and green and gold upon him in a nimbus of ethereal scintillation.

The chattering rose to a tumult.

"My boon fellows," Lord Raachwald rasped in that shifting-shale voice.

I couldn't hear what else he had to say because the tumult had risen to a cacophony, and because the Lord Bishop had unfrozen from his paralysis of hatred, and instead of a well-barbed argument, the Lord Bishop screeched like a mad harpy, his mumbled keen reverberating as he pointed a trembling finger at Lord Raachwald, "Kill him!"

...things connecting these men other than their odious business practices, as well as the fact that all were rumored to have incurred massive debt throughout the Quarter...
—*Journal of Sir Myron Chalstain*

Chapter 36.

COWARDS AND HEROES make the best compasses. In any situation. You want to roll the dice and die horribly or achieve passing fame? Follow the hero. You want the chance to live and flee another day? Follow the coward. In that moment, as the two halves of the church rose up as one, I chose Lord Hochmund, because in matters cowardly, he would unerringly point north. Thus, the seat on the side of the church, deferring his rights of status to wallow behind boot makers and shit-shovelers simply to be near an exit.

Out the door and down the stairs, Lord Hochmund pounded, trailed by his guards, one after another, a well-oiled-fleeing machine.

I followed suit, casting a parting glance toward the pulpit. Lord Raachwald was speaking but inaudible beneath the rising clamor, while crippling forward, the Lord Bishop smacked Lord Raachwald over the head with his crozier.

Then all hell broke loose.

Both sides of the church erupted into one melee, all but a blur as I tore out through the door, bounded down the first flight of stairs, skidding to a halt before a huge stained-glass window. Bearing his own severed head in hand, Saint Hagan fought a cadre of scimitar-wielding Mamelukes at the fall of Acre. He glared down at me in scintillating glory.

Another set of eyes glared as well.

Captain Thorne, a shadow in relief before Saint Hagan, stood on the landing below, four guards at his back. Our eyes met and recognition sparked, followed instantly by anger. "Hold!" He pointed a wicked flanged mace. "Sir Luther Slythe Krait, you are under arrest in the name of His Eminence, the Lord Bishop Judas-Peter."

Lord Hochmund and his line of men disappeared

down the stairs, swift as a centipede scurrying under a rock.

"Think you've bigger dragons to slay." I thumbed over my shoulder at the raucous din pouring past me, over me, through me.

A moment's decision was all it took before Captain Thorne barked, "Arnhold, lead them on," and the guards hauled up the stairs past me, mail jingling, steel gripped in their fists.

Captain Thorne, a glimmer of misgiving at having missed the slaughter by mere feet, clomped up the stairs toward me, using his mace as a walking stick. "I've been looking for you."

"Not too hard, I hope." He was eight steps down.

"You've been making friends." He paused, five steps.

"Captain, we both know that's a lie."

He brought the mace to his shoulder. Now, the mace is a crude weapon, crude compared to the sword, at least. Top-heavy. Ungainly. Unbalanced. But it has one advantage. A mace does not give a damn. It does not give a damn if you're naked, wearing a gambeson, boiled-leather armor, mail, or even new-fangled coat of plate. Where armor might turn a sword or deflect an axe, the mace'll continue on through, shattering whatever lies beneath. It's a crude weapon compared to the sword, but it occurred to me as Captain Thorne finished speaking that I didn't have a sword. I had a stick.

Footsteps clattered up the stairwell from below, more men, Captain Thorne's men.

Shit.

"I'm told you have something." Captain Thorne stood just out of reach, waiting on his men, the safe move, the smart move. "We both know what it is. I want it. Now drop that fucking stick."

"Afraid of a stick, Captain?" I tore the crucifix's cross-section clattering free.

"Men!" Captain Thorne shouted over the banister. "Up here. Step lively now."

Below, the footsteps pounded faster.

"I know how you feel," I said up to Saint Hagan, whipping up the shod end of my stick. The iron tip missed Captain Thorne's nose by an inch as he flinched, and I slid down a step, planting a boot-heel into his chest, knocking him backward down the stairs as three guards reached the landing. Captain Thorne barreled into them, knocking them over like pins. I made to leap the banister, but more guards were hauling up from below.

I froze. "Shit."

"Oy!" Captain Thorne roared, spittle flying. "Grab him!"

As Captain Thorne scrambled to his feet, I was charging downstairs, leaping onto the banister, hurling myself over the captain and his men, turning midair, chin tucked to shoulder, shod end of my staff leading as I shattered through Saint Hagan's severed head, the world a tempest of scintillating reds and greens and blues all tinkling in symphony as I fell through the air and landed, thudding, rolling down the rooftop. Flying buttresses vaulted up around me, lead tiles ripping free in a swathe. At roof's edge, I slapped a hand on a gargoyle's arm and stopped just shy of plummet, the avalanche of tile and glass cascading into open air, dropping onto the crowd below.

"Krait, you fucker!" Captain Thorne screamed, smashing out through the broken window. "Halt!"

I barely heard him as I clutched onto the gargoyle's outstretched arm, my feet dangling, gorge rising, before dropping ten feet down to a secondary roof, then another ten to the hard stone street. Bodies surged past me. Captain Thorne roared above. I was on my feet, slick-slide tearing along with the herd of bodies pouring out of the cathedral, vomiting forth from all exits, keeping my head down through the gates and into the street beyond, the labyrinth of alleyways and cross streets engulfing me.

I didn't look back until I was lost and could hear nothing but the buzz of blood pumping in my ears.

Chapter 37.

"YOU STILL ALIVE?" I poked Karl with a finger.

"Hrmm?" He rolled over, tearing the blankets off himself. "Say something about a funeral?" Karl licked his cracked lips, split like overcooked sausages. "How'd it go?"

"Well, it wasn't mine," I answered, "so that was good."

"Hrmmm." He hocked something foul into the bucket by the bed then collapsed back, pale as a dead fish. "Good. Me, too."

"Hey, you alright?" I poked him again.

Karl grunted something that was probably, "*Fuck off.*"

The door creaked open. "Leave him alone," Lady Narcissa ordered. "He needs his rest."

"Greetings, lady."

Lady Narcissa slid past bearing an armload of wood, furniture legs mostly, and dropped them atop a pile by the fire. She wiped her hands. "Move." She pushed past me, laid a hand on Karl's forehead, held it there. Her cheek was purple, nearly black, where I'd struck her. It did not make her less beautiful. "His fever is no worse. No better, either, but…" She brushed a length of midnight hair from her mouth then poured ale into Karl's mug. "Here." She pressed it to his lips, lifted. "Drink."

"Ale?" I was suddenly parched.

"Don't you touch it," she warned without looking. "Drink."

Karl coughed, sputtered.

"If he doesn't want it?" I offered.

Lady Narcissa lifted Karl's head again and poured more slowly, cursing beneath her breath as he gagged most

336

of it up again.

"You're drowning him," I observed, envious.

"Filthy cur." She stomped away.

Karl snored softly.

"I'm surprised you're still here," I said.

"Stoke the fire, would you?" Lady Narcissa emptied her rucksack, piece by piece, not looking at me. More wood. An empty bottle. A wedge of greenish cheese. "We had a deal."

I did as she bid, tossing a couple table legs into the fire. There was a substantial pile. It might last for days. I selected a long sturdy piece.

"Where are you going?" Lady Narcissa demanded.

"For some sound financial advice." I went to help myself to Karl's ale.

"Touch that, and I'll slit his throat the instant you walk out that door."

"And what if I slit yours first?"

"Then your brother's as good as dead."

"Might already be."

"With you as his only hope, I can but only agree."

"This isn't going well."

"Did you find him?" Lady Narcissa marched across the room and placed a wet cloth across Karl's forehead. Lips pursed, she pressed it into place. I glanced over to be sure she hadn't placed it over his nose and mouth.

"Yeah." I explained about the funeral and ensuing festivities. "Caught Hochmund inside. Before the row. Claims he'll help. Says he wants the same price as before. Didn't say what it was."

Lady Narcissa glared out the window, eyes hard, fevered, mad, before she stifled them dead.

"You alright with that?" I asked.

Her jaw muscles working, teeth grinding. "I do not have to like him. I do not have to be grateful. He is not helping me. He is helping himself. The fat slob."

"He's actually well groomed," I said. "More of a fat dandy, in all fairness."

"Ever the gentleman." Her voice was acid, eyes blazing. "Implying that which you lack the fortitude to come out and say plainly. I told you I'd accept his terms, and I shall."

"And those terms are?"

"None of your business."

Karl leaned over and threw up into the bucket. A lot.

Lady Narcissa crossed her arms. "Oh, just go ahead and die, already, would you?"

Karl rolled back over and died. Possibly.

"Bug up your arse?" I asked.

"Eustace. Him. All of them." Lady Narcissa stared into the fire, arms crossed, shaking her head slowly. "Vultures. Picking at a gleaned corpse. He rebuffed me once then acquiesces?"

"He claimed it was you who said no."

"You say you know the man, aye?" she challenged. "Then you must know what his word is worth." Her hand clenched into a fist. "He said no. When I was in need. Everyone... They all said no."

"All except Stephan." I tossed a couple more legs into the fire. "Look. I know none of this is ideal, but—"

"*Ideal?*"

"He'll get me onto Mummer's Isle."

"And you trust him?"

"What's the matter?" I asked. "Cold feet? This is what you wanted. You said we could trust him to be himself, and he's a greedy fuck, yeah? He wants to help."

"He wants Coldspire."

"It's the same thing," I said.

"Yes. It is the same thing, for that's what I am." She took a mouthful of ale, swallowed it. "Territory. Property. A means to an end. There is no loyalty. No chivalry. Right now there's some serf sitting in his dung-walled hovel eyeing the piss-mire across the way, ruminating on how it could someday be his. You all want what you have, and then you want more. And woe to whoever stands between you and more."

"What about your lover?" I asked. "You must have asked him for help."

She considered. "Once in a great while, a person has been known to surprise me. Once in a great while."

I snuck a sip of Karl's ale, unsure of what she meant.

"He did what I expected of him. They all did what I expected of them. Eustace's fear of confrontation is his greatest character flaw, matched only by his greed. And Emile?" She sniffed. "A proud old fool."

"I need to know something."

She glanced up through her haze. "What?"

"Do you think it possible that Raachwald killed your husband and murdered your sons? Did he set this all in motion?"

If I'd backhanded her again, she couldn't have been more stunned. "*What?*"

"You never saw Cain Raachwald's body."

"Is this another ill-attempt at humor?" She drew herself up, pointing a finger. "I warn you, your hand across my jaw will have gone over smoother."

I crossed my arms, waiting.

"Of course he's..." Lady Narcissa grabbed at the table to steady herself.

"You weren't at Cain's funeral," I said. "And Raachwald refused to allow me to investigate his corpse. Mary never saw Cain's body, either. The three who might have seen him..."

"You think he murdered his own son?" Lady Narcissa was trembling now. "I had not... Rumor told he was a bastard. But would he?" She fingered her lip. "Yes. Yes, he might. And if he did..." She looked up. "You believe he murdered my boys?" She swallowed. "His keep lies closest. He had the most to gain." Her fingernails dug into the table. "Say it."

I raised my hands. "Maybe. Or maybe Cain's still alive somewhere. Hidden."

"Which changes nothing."

"It's a theory. I've no proof."

"Why would he go through all of this?" she asked, as much to herself as to me. "Abduct your brother? Why force you to find the killer if it were *he*? Why the mummer's farce?"

"To make you more pliable," I answered. "If he played the gallant hero and you the grieved mother, maybe you'd acquiesce more readily to his desires? Make his plans move smoother. Did it work?"

Lady Narcissa touched her purpled cheek. "He'll murder his wife if he has not done so already and then force me to wed. In doing so, he shall claim Coldspire for his own, force me to bear his *spawn* to cement his claim." She stared me dead in the eye. "And then someday, he shall murder me."

"*Did it work?*" I demanded.

"Yes, *damn* you."

…because Irene's soul and her mind are lost, but her body remains behind. Death would prove a relief. In the end, I saved neither of them, failing in my triumvirate of duty: my duty as a father, as a husband, as a man.
—Journal of Sir Myron Chalstain

Chapter 38.

HUNCHED LIKE A hoary old raven, Abraham sat in his chair, hard at work as I closed the door behind me, carefully, taking a gander out into the street as I did so. Abraham didn't even bother glancing up as I slid through the partition. He merely raised his hand in my general direction, acknowledging my existence, bidding me wait, then scribbling on like a demon in a ledger so vast it must've weighed as much as a child. Five little stone-men now sat on his desk, their obsidian eyes staring expressionless in my direction.

"Hello…" I leaned forward and looked one in the eye.

"One moment." Abraham looked frail, enfeebled, like a man who hadn't eaten, who hadn't slept, a man who'd been sapped of twenty years of vitality overnight.

"What's it say?" I squinted. Lines were etched into the stone-man's forehead, a terrain of minute scars.

A pall lay over the room. Silent. Empty. Even the ever-present guards were absent. Abraham studiously ignored my question, his lips moving as he skimmed a page.

I took the opportunity to snatch one of the stone-men. Its form was the same as the rest, that of a man, but a man of immense proportions, wide shoulders, thick arms, and legs, all smooth. It regarded me dumbly, black eyes twinkling. No, not scars. A rune. A letter. Hebrew?

"Ahem."

I glanced up.

"There are seven characteristics of an uncultivated person." Abraham adjusted his glasses.

"Only seven?"

"There are seven *official* characteristics of an uncultivated person."

"Yeah? How many unofficial?"

"That I do not know. Yet, invariably, I seem to unearth new variants in your presence, and with alarming alacrity."

"*Alacrity.*" I nodded, impressed. "And what have I helped unearth today?"

"Snatching things off of someone's desk without permission."

"Well, one's not so bad."

"Dressing in the guise of something you're not." He clucked his tongue at the Jew-cloak thrown over my shoulders.

"Only way to get past the gate," I lied. "And two's still not so bad."

"I've counted six more beyond."

"Six?" I counted on my fingers. "Eight total?"

He nodded. Firmly.

"I'm sure I have my good points, too."

"You are sure. I, however, am not." He dipped his pen into an inkwell and began writing again. "I had thought I was clear when I told you your debt was voided, that I wished not to conduct further business with you, that I wished not to see you again, in any capacity." He glanced up. "Ever."

"Apologies." I set the stone-man back on the desk. "But what's it say?"

Teeth gleaming beneath curled lips, Abraham snatched the stone-man and for a moment, throttling it, I thought he might hurl it. His hand was trembling, but he slowed his breathing, set it back down, pushed it away. "You...you were saying?"

"Just wondering what the marks on its forehead say."

"Can you read Hebrew?"

"Would I ask if I could?"

"If you were trying to be clever."

"I'm not clever."

"I said '*trying to be.*' I did not say '*succeeding in being.*'"

"Well, I don't. Didn't. Wouldn't. I don't know what the hell I'm saying."

Abraham's eyes narrowed. "It's a letter. '*Emet.*' It means truth. Or reality. Or both, but truly neither."

"Well, that's as clear as dog piss. What're they for? The stone-men?"

"They are symbols." Abraham rubbed his head, gazing about his desk. He seemed taken aback that there were so many. "Symbols of my innumerable failures."

"Five's not so innumerable."

"What is it you want?" he said. "Your debt is erased. You are free. Go. Go! Do not come back." He deflated, spent. "Can I be more clear than that?"

"The vault's open," I observed. "And where're your guards?"

"They're...it's *Shabbat.* A day of rest. Our day of rest."

"Looks like you could do with some yourself."

"Sir Luther, I have no money to lend you," he pleaded. "No time to spend bothering my fellow countrymen on your behalf, no patience left in answering your incessant questions. I have difficulties of my own that require my full attention."

"I believe you, Abe. It wasn't merely for my benefit, though." I patted my chest. "My bothering you, that is."

"Stephan," Abraham nodded, "of course. How fares he?"

"Alive. But it's not threatening long-term status."

"Ahem." He shifted uncomfortably in his seat. "Things have been rather hectic here as of late. I meant not to belittle your travails. I have been rude. Forgive me. Lack of manners, another trait of the uncultivated person."

"If you're looking to identify more traits, I met this dancer in Novgorod who can pick up a silver penny with—"

"Please!" He stopped me with his raised hand. "That won't be necessary, now, or ever. Please, if you are able to speak to your brother before the…give him my regards. He is a good man if ever I have met one. He shall remain in my thoughts and prayers until the end of my days." Pale lips pursed, he nodded, stood, offering his hand. "Good luck, Sir Luther."

I took his hand. "You alright?" He was still trembling.

"I…I could not sleep last night."

"Lot of that going around." I released his hand. "Any particular reason?"

"It is a private affair." He closed his eyes, pinched the bridge of his nose and collapsed back into his chair. "Some of what we spoke of previously. I wouldn't think to burden you."

"Men tried to kill me last night. Why was yours so bad?"

Abraham froze. I could almost hear gears turning in his head as he thought, calculated, weighed. "I could not sleep."

"You already said that."

"Yes, I…my son, my boy was attacked last night." Abraham's head fell, his eyes glistening full to tear. "By a mob. Stabbed." Unconsciously, he pulled a finger across his throat. "Forgive me. He died. He is dead. Yes." He shook his head in grim revelation. "Saying it aloud, gives it weight, hideous weight. My *son* is dead." His hand crept like a spider up his chest, clutching. "I should be there, Lord, my wife. I should, but I just could not bear it. I thought I would die. I wished it. Seeing him like…" The room was empty of people, empty of sound, empty of air. "I should return." Abraham flinched as the front door burst open.

I turned as four men piled in. Blackbeard at the fore. Behind stalked a lanky bastard, pox-scarred face, a shirt of boiled leather covering his chest, another of the assassins from last night. Blackbeard bore a wicked axe, Pox, a dinted sword. Two others strode behind, the guards, Baldy and Locks, short-bladed swords in their fists. The four fanned out.

Silence.

Money house, a bad place to be ambushed. Tough to get in. Tough to get out. There'd be no half-rotted wattle and daub walls to kick through, no boards to pry free, only clean, square stone walls as thick as my legs're long. I could hear the frown in Abraham's voice as I vaulted his desk, kicking books and stone-men flying, beakers breaking as I shouldered past him, practically knocking him over, putting the desk between me and the four.

"What is this nonsense?" Abraham gathered himself. "Ezekiel? This is a place of business. Not of…" he glared back at me an instant, choking on what he was about to say.

I yearned for Yolanda as I raised my walking staff before me. Blackbeard and Pox started forward, stepping through the partition.

I backed up through the labyrinth of desks, toward the rear door, kicking a chair from my path, tripping over something and landing on my arse. I said nothing but scrambled to my feet instantly, back toward the wall, staff in hand—and something else. It was as hard as a rock, pointy, smooth, cool. One of the stone-men. I knew it without looking. Beneath my fingers, I could feel its shape, its weight.

Backward, I slid, eyes on the four, til I hit the back door, found the knob, twisted. Locked. I mule-kicked it, fast and low and hard. It didn't budge. "Shit." I slid along the wall to my left as Baldy and Locks vaulted the partition at either side of the room. I stopped along the middle of the wall, the open vault a chasm yawning behind.

"Enough!" Abraham shouted, his one arm held out in a vain attempt to corral the armed men. "I will not have this here!"

The four froze.

"Out of the way, Rabbi," Blackbeard spoke softly, a note of apology in his voice, and then it was gone as his gaze fell to me. "Plague pit's begging for this one."

Abraham stared down his nose as though he were a teacher and the four but naughty students. "This is not the way of our people."

"It's the way of *all* people, Rabbi," Blackbeard said. "Now step aside. Won't ask again."

Abraham shook his head, unmoved.

"He's the one killed Isaac." Pox pointed his blade at me.

Abraham stiffened as though struck. He did not turn. "Is that true?"

I watched all four simultaneously, tried to anyways, fanned out in a semicircle amidst the riot of tables and chairs. Only Abraham held them back, and only on Blackbeard's say.

"Was it you?" Abraham smote his desk with the palm of his hand, turning, eyes ablaze, the tired and haggard burned clean free, leaving only anger, hate.

I licked my lips, swallowed, nodded.

"Say the words, Krait." Abraham clutched his own throat. "I want to hear *you* say them."

"Yeah, Abe." I twitched a nod. "It's true."

"Why?" Abraham hissed. "*Why?!*"

"He was with a squad sent to kill me."

"Enough," Blackbeard snarled.

"With those two." I pointed at Blackbeard and Pox. "I barely escaped. I didn't recognize him. Isaac—"

"Do not speak his name!" Abraham roared.

"I didn't know him." I straightened. "I'm sorry, Abe. Truly."

"This is true?" Abraham, this man whose son I had slaughtered, stood like a bulwark between me and Blackbeard. "Ezekiel?"

Blackbeard's dead eyes never left mine. "He's lying, Rabbi," he said as he gently but firmly forced Abraham aside.

"And yet now he lies dead?" Abraham said. "You brought my son in on your schemes? Amidst all the death this plague has wrought and still you seek more? All this insanity? You and you're damned *Sicarii*."

Blackbeard lowered his hand, moved forward, his

men following suit.

"You'll wreak death upon us all," Abraham hissed.

"Talk to Daniel," Blackbeard said. He wasn't rushing things. I had nowhere to go. "It was his say. And Isaac volunteered. Brave lad." He pointed at me with his axe. "Kill this fucker."

"Aye." Pox slid forward through chairs and desks, slick as an eel round river rock. Baldy and Locks took the corners. They'd all come at me at once. It wouldn't be stage fighting where the bad guys attack the hero one at a time, and there was no hero here, except, maybe, for Abraham.

Blackbeard started forward.

Abraham clutched at Blackbeard's shoulder. "Violence begets—"

Blackbeard shoved him back, tripping over a chair and to the floor.

"Krait! Surrender to them," Abraham screamed. "I'll see you're justly treated."

"Justly treated'd mean a noose," I said.

"Aye," Blackbeard deadpanned, hurling a chair underhanded at me.

I sidestepped it as it broke against the wall; Pox lunged at me simultaneously, sword point aimed at my face. I batted it aside and thrust out my staff, hoping Pox'd overcommit, but he didn't. Quick as a fox he'd lunged and shot back out of range, blade cocked and ready again. Just testing the waters.

"Please," Abraham begged.

No one listened.

The noose tightened as Locks and Baldy edged toward me from opposing sides.

I shuffle-stepped left to match Pox as Blackbeard slid to my right. Stepping back again, heel touching the wall, I whipped the stone-man at Blackbeard. He ducked, and it shattered against a post. All four were close now, a half-moon steel trap closing in, all around, no ground to give, no ground to take. As soon as I committed to an attack at any one of them, I'd sprout steel out my back.

"Lovely," I grumbled.

Pox lunged forward again, flicking the tip of his blade toward my face, not committing again, distracting me as Blackbeard stepped in swinging. I slapped Pox's blade aside then pivoted, my staff whipping back, out of the way of the falling axe, the tip thudding off Blackbeard's thick shoulder. Armor. Shit.

Footsteps clomped, and Pox lunged again. I parried and slid back into the protected confines of the vault just before Baldy and Locks converged.

The vault walls offered immediate security. They couldn't flank me, yeah, couldn't all fit through the door at once, but I was fucked long term. Short term, too.

The wicks of two old ceramic lamps sputtered swirls of smoke, casting a quiver of light and shadow. Shelves gaped empty floor to ceiling, no coin, no jewelry, no nothing. Lockboxes yawned open, empty, one after the other. Blackbeard and Pox stepped in front of the door, Blackbeard's wide shoulders eating up most of its width.

The vault door squealed as it began to close.

Diving forward, I tore one of the hatchets from my belt and drove it edge forth under the door, wedging it in; then I sprung up and kicked it in more and set my foot against it. Metal screeched, scraped, ripping apart the floor. The door stopped moving a foot shy of closed.

It bought me a moment.

"Krait!" Blackbeard barked. "Get your yellow carcass out here and fight like a fucking man."

"You come in," I bellowed. When he didn't, I laughed, a taunting laugh, a haughty laugh, a bullshit laugh. We both knew I was screwed.

Pox started forward, blade leading, but Blackbeard's grabbed him by the shoulder. "No. Ain't losing another." He turned. "Simon, go get the fucking crossbow. It's on my roan outside." Blackbeard raised his axe. "Sit your arse down, Rabbi."

Footsteps stomped.

I snatched up an oil lamp.

A door slammed.

"Enough!" Abraham screamed.

I couldn't see him for the jammed door. Then suddenly Abraham was on Blackbeard's back, clawing at his axe, the two careening, slamming into desks, casting shadow demons weird and wicked, writhing across walls, until Blackbeard hurled him over his shoulder onto a desk the instant a ceramic lamp shattered against his side. A spray of oil and ceramic shard—*Whompf!*—and Blackbeard burst into flame.

Orange licking up his side, he lurched up screaming, knocking into Pox, tripping and lighting Abraham's desk on fire. Flame ripped across the piled tomes like some ravening beast released from its cage. I hurled the second oil lamp, smashing it across the wood floor, a wave of liquid flame spreading out toward Blackbeard and Pox's feet. In a gout, flame reared up, coiling, scrambling, swarming up a column and clawing across the ceiling in all directions. Pox tore Blackbeard aside, stripping the blazing cloak from his body, flames crackling around both.

Locks stood hunched, hacking, as I burst from the vault, crouched, scrambling through the heavy black smoke, choking thick already. Pox beat at the flames roaring off Blackbeard. Felled by the smoke and heat, on hands and knees, I clawed like a crippled dog through the maze, holding my breath and crawling over the partition the instant I slammed into it, continuing on past for the front door. Black smoke banked down the walls as Baldy burst back in through the front door, crossbow in hand; I smashed him in the face as hard as I could, dropping him.

"Help!" Abraham choked from somewhere behind, in the charnel black.

The misty cool of night kissed my face, and for an instant, I knew heaven in all its glories. But instead of blessed flight, I took a deep cool breath and turned, dropping low and stumbling back to the partition, flames roiling across it. Someone slammed into me, past me, making for the door. I dropped to my belly, could see desk and chair legs, then him, Abraham, splayed out on the floor, bleeding from the head. Covered in char, I scuttled forward as the smoke slithered down, the stifling black crushing down nearly to the floor. Abraham moaned, face blackened by soot, just staring numbly at the shadow flames rippling like a hellish water surface above. Each breath burned. I latched onto Abraham's arm and dragged him as best I could toward the front door that was suddenly so very far away.

Chapter 39.

"SAINTS BE PRAISED." Lady Narcissa stood before the glowing hearth, arms crossed, a look of annihilating disdain souring her lovely face, "you brought a dead, half-incinerated Jew."

I grimaced up from the floor where Abraham and I'd collapsed in a huffing, hacking heap, coughing black shit from our lungs. "Thought he might grant us three wishes," I managed.

On the floor, mouth gaping like a fish, Abraham lay, his hair scorched, his glasses bent, broken, but somehow still perched on his nose. I'd dragged him, sputtering, shivering, half-burned and fully broken through the streets back to our safe house.

"Hmm?" The Lady Narcissa loomed over us. "Oh, no." She nudged Abraham with a prim toe. "He's alive."

I struggled to my feet, char-black water puddled beneath me. Lady Narcissa ghosted back as though I bore the plague, drawing her robe snugly about her. I dragged Abraham across the room, wrestled him up, plunked him into a chair by the fire.

"Wine?" I eyed Lady Narcissa.

"For him?" she asked. "Or you?"

"Both," I answered, glancing over at the bed and the lump that lay within. "How's Karl?"

"He's not snoring anymore."

Not bolstered overwhelmingly by the report, I limped over to Karl, still passed out, white as a ghost. Leaning over him, I listened, watched, poked him. No response. He was breathing, shallow, short. That was something. I drew the blankets back, checking the bandages on his leg. They were clean, and they were new. I glanced at

Lady Narcissa. She glared back defiantly, a cup of wine in hand. I sauntered up to her, snatched it, drained it.

"Thanks," I said, holding it out for more.

Go fuck yourself, her look clearly conveyed.

"Yeah." I nodded my head toward Abraham. "Him, too."

"You both have arms," she said, staring past me. "Well, *you* do at any rate."

I shouldered past her, snatched the wine bottle, poured, offering a silent prayer before slugging it back. Into a chair by the fire, I collapsed, wiping my mouth with the back of my hand, took another drink, filled it again. I held it out to Abraham who ignored me, consumed by a hacking fit, so I pounded it back.

"There's not much left," Lady Narcissa warned.

"We'll have to rectify that forthwith."

She nodded at Abraham. "Who is he?"

Abraham struggled to his feet, still hacking, then collapsed back into the chair, fist covering his mouth, a line of black drool attached to his chin near wobbling to the floor.

"Jesus Christ," Lady Narcissa muttered.

"No," I said. "Different Jew entirely."

Abraham kept right on hacking.

"He'll be alright," I lied.

"Did he have *two* arms when you found him?" Lady Narcissa asked.

I just gave her a look.

Abraham's coughing finally subsided. "P-Please, water."

"Do we have water?" I asked Lady Narcissa. "And more importantly, do people actually drink it?"

Lady Narcissa was up already, striding across the room, a washing bowl held out before her. She set it down on the table next to Abraham, offering him a washcloth as well.

"My thanks, lady," Abraham said, taking the washcloth.

"You're welcome. Let me get you some wine." She sauntered over to me, snatched the glass from my hand, offering a demon's dare of a glare. "Here." She presented it to him.

"Eh?" Abraham took the glass without looking at it and drank. Copiously. "My thanks again."

"You're welcome," she said.

Abraham glanced up. "Forgive me, my lady. My poor appearance. My poorer manners. Abraham. My name is Abraham Ben-Ari." A coughing fit seized him again as he fought to stand and bow, failing at both endeavors. Lady Narcissa eased him back into the chair. "I have been through...it has been a trying night, a trying day, a trying *everything*."

"No forgiveness is necessary." Lady Narcissa waved him off. "By all appearances, you have nearly met your death, not to mention you've been forced into the company of Krait for what must seem a decidedly interminable period of time."

Abraham wiped his eyes, cleaned his face, dried it with the towel. "And again, for your kindness, my lady, I thank you. And you are...?"

"Lady Narcissa Volkendorf." She offered a bow, smooth, shallow, precise.

I stood. "I hate to break up this love-fest, but I need some answers."

"You." Abraham turned to me, eyes awake with anger. "*Why?*"

"Why *what?*"

"Why do you hate us so?"

"I don't hate you any more than I hate everyone else," I grumbled.

"I pray you derive little solace from that statement."

"No, I derive solace from this." I drained the last of the wine straight from the bottle then belched, just for emphasis.

"I am leaving." Abraham clambered unsteadily to his feet.

"Abe," I warned.

"You'll have to stop me." He staggered for the door.

"I'll have to stop you." I nodded in total agreement, intercepting him as he reached the door. The door opened a crack, thudding to a halt against my outstretched hand. Whistling wind snaked in tendrils of biting cold. We stood eye to. He yanked on the door. With a growl, I slammed it shut and took hold of him, snatching him two-handed, grappling him into an arm-bar, forcing him around, over, gasping, grunting. I marched him stumbling on tiptoe across the room and thrust him back into his chair.

"Mother of Mercy, Krait..." Lady Narcissa looked appalled.

I warned her off with a glare. "Take a deep breath, Abe."

He flexed his hand open and closed. "I must go."

"No."

"I have to see my wife, my son. Please, my people."

"No dice." I crossed my arms, unmoved.

"I'm a prisoner, then?"

"Until you tell me what I need to know," I said. "*Everything* I need. Then, and only then, are you free to leave."

"I'll say nothing more to you."

"Abe, I like you. But you'll sing."

"*Torture?*" He spat. "Nothing you can do would shock me."

"Lady Narcissa," I turned, "it just dawned on me. You've been left in the dark. Abe here's the source concerning your late husband's miraculous, posthumous financial recovery."

Lady Narcissa turned, swiveling slowly, eyes frigid, empty, predatory, a pair of cat's eyes locked on an injured mouse. I could almost see her tail flipping as she studied him in a new light.

"Do you know *who* your husband owed?" I asked.

"As I said, I was privy not to personage," she said woodenly, "only sums."

"Well, Abe claims all your debts to the Quarter are square."

She drew herself up. "Impossible."

"Abe...?" I turned. "Care to shed some light?"

"My lady, I own—"

Lady Narcissa raised a hand, cutting him off. "I have heard of you. Your house. Did you lend to my husband?"

Abraham nodded. "A considerable sum."

"That's news to me," I said.

"And from how many others did he borrow?" Lady Narcissa asked.

"All of the major houses," Abraham admitted. "Many of the lesser."

"Yet you claim these debts have been paid off?" Lady Narcissa asked. "By whom?"

Abraham shook his head. "I do not know."

Lady Narcissa's eyes narrowed, dagger-sharp. "How can you *not* know?"

"Forgive me, my lady," Abraham pleaded. "Your husband's record of repaying debt was...spotty at best. I personally attempted to collect payment, beg payment, even in portions, and was rebuffed at every turn."

Lady Narcissa offered only a curt nod.

"Who bought the debt off you then?" I asked.

"From me?" Abraham shook his head. "No one."

"But you said it was square."

"No." Abraham raised a finger. "I said it was *settled*, the greater portion. Some of the smaller houses yet hold marks. Yet for weeks, a man has stalked the Quarter, offering pennies on the pound to purchase your husband's debt. Many, nay *most*, jumped at the offer. I, however, was not one of them. It was obvious the business practice was not *on the level*, as you might say." He turned to Lady Narcissa. "I redacted your husband's debts from my books months ago, both the principle and the interest. I knew I would never see payment, let alone return, and so I wiped my hands of it, to be done with any further involvement."

"That was big of you, Abe," I said.

Abraham looked at me as though he'd just drunk a glass of sour milk.

"So who is this man purchasing the debt?" Lady Narcissa asked.

"As I said, I don't know." Abraham shook his head. "All the transactions were conducted through an agent."

"And this agent?" I considered. "You've no idea who he represented?"

Abraham shook his head. "None."

"And you thought not to ask?" Lady Narcissa asked coldly.

"I made inquiries, my lady, of course, but this agent refused to relinquish any information concerning whom he represented. None of my countrymen were privy, either. We are, after all, but Jews."

"Casagrande." I snapped my fingers.

"Mister Casagrande, yes." Abraham nodded.

Lady Narcissa looked up. "You know the man?"

"Yeah. A mercenary. A shit. A rat-bastard murderer for hire. Take your pick. Is it true he and his men've been stationed in the Quarter for over a month?"

"I have heard so, yes," Abraham ventured. "But I could not ascertain it for truth."

"An entire mercenary company stationed in the Quarter?" Lady Narcissa asked. "Who could afford the coin?"

"Not many, my lady," Abraham answered.

"So you claim, yet all of Asylum's money is locked up in the Quarter," Lady Narcissa snarled. "It was one of you. But who? Who could afford to buy all the debt? Which one thinks to wrest Coldspire from me?"

"I—" Abe started.

"Yours is the biggest lending house." Lady Narcissa cut him off. "Well positioned for such a venture. I could let it be known that your house was conspiring to revolt against the powers that be."

"You motivated yet?" I asked Abraham, but he didn't hear me.

"Lady, what proof—?"

"*Proof?*" Lady Narcissa scoffed. "What but my word would be required?"

"Krait," Abraham glanced at me, "tell her she is mistaken."

"Is she?"

"Krait," Abraham pleaded.

"You know something," I pressed.

"I tell you, I know nothing."

"Tell me about the Masada," I said.

Abraham froze at that, blanching; then he began diminishing visibly, as though eaten away from within. "Very well," he murmured. "There is a story all Jewish boys learn of when they are young. Staunch parents frown upon them hearing it at too young an age, yet they whisper it amongst themselves." Abraham rubbed the bridge of his nose. "It is a tale of destruction. A tale of rebellion, a tale of war, and such tales can have but one end. This is the tale of the Masada.

"On the eastern edge of the Judean Desert, rising a thousand feet into the sky, there stands an ancient Roman fortress. Unassailable from any direction. Impenetrable, or so the Romans thought.

"In the year 73, or so writes Josephus, a rebellion burst up amongst the Jews. It began for the reason most rebellions do. Inequity between ruler and ruled, and it was just. It lasted months, years, long years, protracted years. It was dark, and it was deadly, as wars are. Murders in the night. Murders in the light. Murders…" He let out a sigh. "Under the full might of the Roman war machine, though, the rebellion flagged. Men lost hope. The Jewish people were on the verge of breaking, but amongst those resisting there emerged a small cadre of men who believed the Jews could still achieve victory. Trained. Formidable. Ruthless. A group with no barriers, no limitations, no code but utter destruction of the enemy, they had been reined in by the rebellion leaders, for those men in power feared them. These men called themselves the *Sicarii*."

"You said something about them to Blackbeard," I said. "What's it mean?"

"*Dagger-men*." Abraham glanced at me. "These dagger-men were able to evade the Masada's defenses and slay the Roman garrison to a man. Then they took it for their own. But, of course, the Romans could not stand for that, would not stand for that. They laid siege to the Masada, but it held, for months it held. But give the Romans time, give them men, give them resources, and the Romans possessed all these things, and it becomes a matter of simple mathematics. The Romans breached it, broke it, stormed it, and within discovered a thousand men, women, and children dead. All of them. The *Sicarii* had committed suicide and murdered their own families rather than be taken alive."

"This," Abraham shook his head, "is a story that *inspires* the youth of my people. Can you understand that? For I cannot. I...perhaps there is a certain pride in defiance, just defiance. But defiance that ends in such tragedy?"

"Nice history lesson, Abe, but how's it all pertain to Asylum?"

"Yes." He took a sip of wine. "A year ago things were bad for my people." Abraham sniffed. "As though there were some other status quo. Things are always bad, were always, but last year, things grew worse, and worse rapidly. Fiscally, even, we as a people were shattered."

"Impossible," Lady Narcissa scoffed.

"What did you see in my vault?" Abraham asked me.

"Nothing," I answered. "It was empty."

"Precisely." Abraham nodded. "And our money is our only...it is all we have, besides one another. Over the past two years, we lent out coin to various Asylum nobles and received no return. It seemed a concerted effort to break us, and it was working. And do you believe the Lord Bishop forewent levying his draconian taxes upon us even when we received no return? Do you think he would offer us a special dispensation when the Quarter could not pay? No, he did not, and in its stead, he placed liens on all of our properties, our businesses, our possessions. They became *his*. We had argued that the Isle Lords had bled us dry and that he should turn his gaze in their direction.

"Alas, our pleas fell on deaf ears. Oh, eventually he did as we begged, but by then, it was too late." Abraham turned to Lady Volkendorf. "Your husband must have heard rumor of our grievances and took umbrage. There was rumor of the five lords set to ride into the Quarter, of imminent slaughter, of holocaust, of erasure of all debt. We were on our own.

"An emergency council was convened. I took part in this council, as did most of the landed men of the Quarter. It was a debacle, as most meetings are between powerful men with disparate views. Pride, anger, wrath, always they impede the path to truth. Whoever speaks the loudest speaks the truest, and the truth was that we as a people were in dire straits. Some counseled running, some surrender. Others cautioned erasure of all debts, just starting over, and some, mostly the younger, counseled war."

"What did you counsel?" I asked.

Abraham adjusted his glasses. "Erasure of all debt. It would happen anyways, was happening, one way or another. We would need to find a way to persevere, to regroup, to recover, three of my people's great strengths throughout the epochs. That was my counsel. Alas, my voice was small and fell on deaf ears.

"It was futile, a deadlock, hot words by hot heads were exchanged, enemies made, blood feuds sworn. The council shattered into factions, and no progress seemed possible. Indeed, the old discounted the young as brash and stupid. The young accused the old of weakness and torpor. Truth barbed with lie and its reverse were cast from both sides. Then, one of the younger men rose amongst those counseling war, and he began speaking of the Masada. Yes. An intelligent young man, quiet, forceful, well-reasoned, I can do his words no justice. As he stood there amidst the council, he said he saw himself within those bleak fortress walls, within the Masada, high above the swirling sands, hot sun beating on his brow, the Judean Desert to one side, the Dead Sea to the other. The army of the centurions he saw climbing like locust swarms from all sides. Trapped, he said, left with nowhere to run, and he said he would not run, and he would not surrender.

"Before he finished speaking, others, too, saw themselves within the Masada. And they saw their choices dwindling, shriveling like fruit too long on the vine. The majority now counseled war, and they called themselves the Masada, and those who bore weapons in the fight, and spilled blood, came to name themselves the *Sicarii*." He scowled. "Infantile."

"Did you agree with them?" I asked.

"What?" Abraham stiffened. "No. I pleaded with them, sued for peace through appeasement and failing that, relocation. 'How many must die?' I screamed. But my protest again fell on deaf ears."

"Daniel was this leader?" I asked.

Abraham closed his eyes. "Yes. Daniel said that so much horror and destruction had been wrought upon our people already that 'they can do no more harm to us than has already been done.' And they believed him."

"You can always squeeze more blood from that stone."

"Youth. Naiveté." Abraham shook his head. "Nonetheless, the Masada preached war, and the *Sicarii* waged it, a silent war, a war in the back alleys, a war in the streets, a war of dark ships paddling softly through the sea, taking by unawares. Stealing. Killing. Burning. Whatever could be done was." He glanced at Lady Narcissa. "Your husband, my lady, forgive me, had little regard for us in the best of times, and in the worst?"

Lady Narcissa stood there, stock-still, arms crossed, listening frowning. "Go on with your story, Abraham Ben-Ari. Finish it."

"Lord Volkendorf aimed to shatter us. In the cold dark of autumn, he and his men stormed the Quarter. How many were killed in the streets? I don't know. Hundreds? Dozens, certainly. But the *Sicarii* retaliated."

Lady Narcissa spoke, her voice a whisper, "I remember that night, the night he and his men came back beaten, broken, the night I saw something within my husband's eye I'd not seen before." She swallowed. "Fear."

Abraham stared at her.

"You're proud of them," I said.

Slowly, Abraham turned toward me. "I am ashamed that a part of me is and ashamed that a part of me isn't. Does that make any sense?"

"Yeah, Abe," I said, "perfect sense."

"Did these dagger men kill my sons?" Lady Narcissa demanded.

"I do not know, my lady," Abraham said.

"They wanted my husband dead!" she spat.

"Lady, near as I can tell, *you* wanted your husband dead," Abraham countered. "Forgive me, but I shall not stand here and indict my people. They acted in self-defense, for survival."

"You had a hand in murdering my sons." Lady Narcissa rose up.

"Wait." I interceded, raising a hand. "He didn't. These *Sicarii* did."

"He's a liar," Lady Narcissa pressed.

"Abe is many things," I broke in. "Liar's not one of them."

"But he was part of it."

"Sounds greyer than that."

"He admitted guilt!" she said.

"He cautioned *against* killing."

"Yes. Precisely. *They* had a council." She pointed at Abraham. "*He* was in attendance."

"Every community has councils, Lady—"

"But he knew of it, the crime, in advance, and if not the crime, he knew the men who would commit it. He knows who did it, these *Sicarii*, even now, and he did *nothing*, has done *nothing*. He's harbored them, abetting them through his curtain of silence. What more is there? Even now he has offered nothing of true value."

"Well, shit." I glanced at Abraham. "She does have a point, Abe. Might as well skip to the end. I need names. Addresses. Dates. Descriptions. I'll need a story. They stormed a fucking castle in the middle of a blizzard? I want to know how. Raachwald'll want to know how. And what of the bloodletting? The witchcraft? The injuries?"

"I…I don't know, not any of it," Abraham muttered numbly. "I think it some sort of sick ruse to muddy the waters."

Lady Narcissa started forward, murder in her eye, that blade back in hand.

"Right." I snatched her by the wrist. "Enough." I dug the knife from her fist. "Relax." Then to Abraham, "I need to know. Which means *you'll* need to find out." I cast the knife aside.

"Me? I shall not bear false witness."

"Good, cause I'm only interested in truth." I shoved Lady Narcissa behind me. "You'd better come around to the fact that you have to ask some serious questions and get some serious answers from some serious people. Cause if you don't, those same questions are going to be asked of those same people and their families and their friends, only they're going to be asked as hot pincers pull flesh off of bone."

Abraham just gawped.

"That's no threat, Abe. It's fact. You know it. I need to bring Raachwald something that doesn't equate to him hacking the lungs from my back. Yeah? That means a story that holds water." I kept an eye on the lady. "And heads. I want Blackbeard. I want Pox. I want all those bloody-bastards who tried to kill me. And I want the guy who started all this. Daniel. Those three. Those three to start with."

Abraham opened his mouth to speak, but I cut him off. "This is not negotiable, Abe. Heads." I chopped my hand into my palm. "I need them. Your people need them."

"Thou shall *not* kill." Abraham gathered himself up, his chin quivering. "You cannot answer murder with murder and call it justice."

"Just watch me. An eye for an eye, *lex talionis*. But you feel free to call it whatever you will."

"I call it scapegoating."

"And what of *my* children?" Lady Narcissa hissed. "My sons?"

Abraham turned white, froze. "They would not have murdered children."

"You just admitted it!" Lady Narcissa hissed. "These *Sicarii!* You claimed there were no limits to what they would do! They killed them! And here you stand—"

"You twist my words!"

Lady Narcissa snarled, "The blood-libel—"

"Blood libel?" He cut her off. "Fah! You people will believe anything, but especially the worst. Forgive my rudeness, my lady, but the blood libel is a tale spun by small-minded men of ignorance and overwhelming prejudice. Used whenever they require the appearance of propriety and just cause for mass murder. There is no such thing. Eaters of men?" He closed his eyes, throwing up his hand. "Fah!"

"He defends them!" Lady Narcissa pointed. "And how is it he knows of their actions? Why is that? Because he is one of them!"

Abraham stood tall, his eyes meeting mine. "If you believe that, then take my head now." He eased himself down to his knees, leaning forward, offering his pate. "Take it, Krait, it's yours. I shall go to my son, but before you strike me down, see within your heart—"

"Whoa! Would you two shut your bloody traps!" I snarled. "See within your heart? *Jesus Christ.* Are we lovelorn teenage girls?" I held up my hands. "Alright. This is what's going to happen. Abe, you're going to walk out that door."

Abraham blinked in astonishment.

Lady Narcissa reared back like a coiled serpent.

"But first," I said, "I need names and descriptions. For starters. And I need to meet this Daniel."

"I cannot—"

"You can, and you will." I cut him off again. "I know you're too damned straight-laced to take part in a rebellion. I know that. And I believe you cautioned against it. But you do know who these *Sicarii* are, yeah?"

"I will not—"

"You will. Simply because if you don't, you're culpable. You and your people. The whole Quarter. You're all *culpable*. A good word. Know what it means?"

"It means you're a monster."

"It means I'm a realist."

"You wouldn't—"

"Enough. I may not want to, but I would. I'd have to, just to save my own neck. And you know how fond I am of it. Not to mention Stephan's." I thumbed over my shoulder. "And even if I *wouldn't*, you know she *would*. Hell, she might no matter what I say."

Abraham's eyes fell on Lady Narcissa. "If she is to condemn my people regardless, then there is nothing to gain. If they are simply to be slaughtered no matter—"

"Your people *won't* be slaughtered." I cut him off. "Will they, lady? Justice is the desire here, yeah? *Not* a body count? *Not* a fucking holocaust? You want the men who did this. And only them. Tell *him* that. Convince him."

Lady Narcissa said nothing.

"Tell him that, or this goes no further," I said. "You want the killers' heads? This is the only way to get them. You savvy that, lady?"

Eyes wide, glimmering before the fire, she nodded. Once.

Chapter 40.

ABRAHAM WAS GONE. I had the names I needed. The descriptions. The locations. Now I only needed heads and more time. Lady Narcissa stood just outside the door, waiting, staring at the snow falling, orange embers glistening in the plague firelight. I shook Karl gently by the shoulder.

"Hey, shithead," I whispered.

Karl stiffened, cracked an eye, nodded. "You going?" he rumbled softly from somewhere deep. He looked bad.

"Yeah." I thumbed towards the door. "You coming?"

"Nar, just…just gonna lie here a piece. Let you do the heavy lifting…for once. We got a plan?"

"*We?*" I said. "Well, someone needs to lie in bed all day with his feet up, complaining about chickenshit bullshit and bleeding all over the place, drinking wine, being an asshole."

"Well, seeing as I got that covered…"

"Damn," I said, "and here I was hoping I'd fill those shoes."

"Been filling them for years. Just tell me you got something in mind."

"I got something." I told him the broad strokes.

"If it comes to it." Karl coughed, struggling to raise a hand. "Odin's eye. I mean, you actually find these fuckers and heel 'em proper, you think the Cyclops'll keep his word? Think he'll let Stephan go? Think he'll just forego hurling you off some cliff? Cause I don't."

"I think a cliff side plummet's a little too impersonal compared to what Raachwald's got in mind. But, we've got

365

no choice. Or, rather we've got a choice. We can say 'Fuck you, Stephan,' and then beat feet." I glanced sidelong at him. Shrugged. "It's a choice. Even if it's a mouth full of wet shit to swallow. Besides, Raachwald's a lord, Karl. He doesn't have to keep his word to anyone he thinks is beneath him."

"That include you?"

"I'd imagine it includes Jesus Christ and King Arthur and the signers of the Magna Carta."

Karl tried to move, failed. "Think you got a grip on it all?"

"No. Not even a little. But I've an idea. There are still holes. Who exactly did the killing? These *Sicarii*? They don't fit the description. A giant killer Jew? They make more sense, maybe, but not enough. And what of Lord Volkendorf? How could a lord become afraid of these *Sicarii*? Sure, they're mean fuckers, but so what? There are mean fuckers everywhere. And then there's Raachwald. The best positioned for it, the most to gain, the most gained. And his boy, Cain? I still have yet to see inside his coffin. Jesus. Did I say holes? A God-damned rats' nest full of them, but then they're always there. Gaping. Legion. Even in the aftermath."

"Yar." Karl glanced over at Lady Narcissa. "Don't trust her."

"I don't."

"And Hochmund? He'd sell his mother to Libyan slavers for pork pie."

"Pork pie is delicious," I admitted.

"Yar."

"Well," I said, "if I'm not back by tomorrow or the next day…"

"Yar, be seeing you, lad, this side or the next," Karl muttered, laying his head back, closing his eyes, his face grey, chest rising, then falling.

"Yeah." I leaned forward and whispered in his ear then closed his eyes with my hand. "See you around, too, you gnarly old bastard." I stood up, made the sign of the cross, for what good it would do, then strode out the door and past the lady.

Lady Narcissa turned to me. "How is he?"

"He's dead." I didn't look back.

...my home smolders, a charnel ruin. It matters little now.

—*Journal of Sir Myron Chalstain*

Chapter 41.

TOGETHER, we huddled in the mounting twilight. The shadows grew long and wide, rippling incrementally across uneven earth, distorting, sliding sideways longer and longer until they all merged into one. The windows of the Gallows Eve Tavern were as dark as smoke, opaque, but music leaked out through them, through the walls, in lyrical wafts, ebbing and flowing amber soft. Somber. A horse whinnied inside the stables. Beneath her hood, Lady Narcissa's violet eyes twitched each time the scuff of boots sounded past the alley's maw.

"I..." Lady Narcissa cleared her throat, "I am sorry for your friend."

I said nothing in return.

"He...he was a brutish oaf, but staid, able," she managed, "and he did not force himself upon me as I had feared when first we met."

"Well, that's about the nicest thing anyone's ever said about Karl."

She almost looked at me. Almost. Instead, she nodded, long and slow, drawing her cloak ever tighter about herself, fingers worrying the frayed edges. She was nervous, that was all, or a good actress. Maybe both. Probably both.

"Nerves?" Hell, I was afraid, too.

"No." She pursed her lips. "Yes. We're forced to stand out here, behind a slag heap in God-knows-where. Waiting for the least trustworthy man in the kingdom to come to our rescue."

I gave her a sidelong glance. "You said we could trust him."

"Bravado, sheer, upon my part." She pulled a loose strand of hair from her mouth. "Eustace possesses more coin than the other lords. They may listen to him. And he is not without a certain level of cunning and commensurate influence. Even so, the man's a pig. You know him, do you not?"

"Did I disagree with you?" I pulled out Karl's flask, took a sip, offered it.

She took it, sniffed, frowned, but sipped it delicately. "Liquid courage?"

"Nay." I thumped my chest. "I'm too strong-willed to succumb."

Footsteps approached from the east, gravel and grit crunching under boot, the rustle of mail, the clank and clatter of weapons. I was on my feet, waiting, hand wrapped around Yolanda's hilt. Ready. A round shade, flanked by two taller ones, waddled from the last vestiges of dying light.

"I told you to come alone," I said.

Lord Hochmund pulled his hood back. "Trifles." He winked, promptly dismissing my existence forthwith, and dropped nimbly to one knee before Lady Narcissa like Sir Galahad on May Day. To his heart, he laid a splayed hand, glittering in gold. He gave pause when he noticed the bruise on her cheek, but he carried on. "My Lady Narcissa, even ensnarled in cloth of homespun, you are a vision of ethereal radiance." His eyes gleamed. "What say you?"

Lady Narcissa curtsied low, offering her delicate hand. Lord Hochmund snatched it like a lifeline and kissed it delicately with those pudgy lips. "My answer is yes, dear Eustace," Lady Narcissa answered, rising with practiced grace.

Lord Hochmund beamed, dabbing his forehead with a kerchief as he removed a ring from within his coat. "This ring was forged by my grandfather's grandfather in Outremer. Antioch. The second crusade. They say a sliver of one of the nails of the true cross was alloyed into the gold. A beautiful setting. Classical. Look." He pointed. "The diamond hails from the Far East, along the Silk Road." It was the biggest diamond I'd ever seen. "Magnificent and yet still it does you no justice."

"I've not seen its equal," Lady Narcissa whispered in

awe.

"May I, my lady?" Lord Hochmund asked.

Her gaze locked onto his, she nodded.

Swallowing, licking his lips, Lord Hochmund slid the golden band onto Lady Narcissa's finger. "As though forged for your very hand," he said. With hand to thigh, he levered himself up and brushed off his knee. He leaned in, sliding his hand around to the back of her neck, and kissed her softly. It was like a fairy tale, a shitty, awful fairy tale. "Ahem…" Lord Hochmund drew back, taking her in at arm's length. "Does it hurt?" He caressed her bruised cheek with the back of his hand.

"As much as might be expected." She glanced reproachfully over her shoulder.

At me.

Lord Hochmund nodded sagely, mirroring her disgusted glare, though a smirk shimmered through for the briefest of instants, a desert mirage, and then was gone. He turned to one of his men and nodded.

Beneath my cloak, I gripped my hatchet and butcher blade tight, forcing my breathing to slow.

Lord Hochmund's guard withdrew a tabard from under his cloak and held it out. It was the tabard of House Hochmund, a red fox on field of orange. "Don it with pride." Another guard handed me a helm. "My men are guarding the bridge currently, but one never knows whose eye may be turned toward the Bastard." He raised a hand to his heart. "Apologies. A crude jape, but then, crude is not always tantamount to ineffective."

While I pulled the tabard over my head, Lord Hochmund took Lady Narcissa's hand in his, guiding her down the alleyway as though in promenade. He leaned into her, whispering close. *Conspirators*, a word that came to mind.

Lord Hochmund's guards stepped together, blocking me.

"Hochmund…" I growled.

Lord Hochmund stopped and turned. "Forgive me, Krait. Come along. Let him pass, gentlemen. We've nuptials to attend."

I shouldered roughly through the two.

"…and so you must act the part of the new servant," Lord Hochmund finished saying as I arrived by his sides.

"As *my lord* wishes," Lady Narcissa answered, her eyes aglow. Lord, she *was* good.

"Oh, I do like that," Lord Hochmund twittered. "I do, indeed, *my dear*."

Lady Narcissa offered a half smile, a smoldering half smile that spoke volumes in that curl at the corner of her mouth, in the hunger within her eyes. "And I *that*, my lord."

Jesus.

"Oh, yes, indeed," Lord Hochmund said. "Of course, in reality, it is I who am *your* servant. Try your best not to be so radiantly lovely, my dear, if such a thing is indeed possible. Every eye in the city shall turn our way. Here. Allow me." He swept his fingers through her hair, brushing it back, letting it collapse in sweeping arcs through his fingers. "Two feet of liquid midnight."

"You've the soul of a poet," she exclaimed.

I groaned inwardly as he tucked her hair beneath her hood.

"Yes," Lord Hochmund murmured, stepping back, arms crossed, entranced. "Very…very good, indeed. Now keep those twin amethysts down, my lady. The ethereal light of your essence radiates through like indigo moons." He kissed her fingertips then paused, and on tiptoe, added a chaste peck on her cheek.

Donning my helm while trying not to puke, I tied my cloak as they strode off, voices low, guards trailing, keen-eyed, alert, and ever at my back. Lord Hochmund and Lady Narcissa spoke too low to hear, and a cannonball of doubt lodged itself somewhere in the pit of my stomach. The two of them chuckled at some shared joke, Lord Hochmund patting the back of her hand.

The cannonball swelled.

* * * *

We passed Brother Tomas's Franciscan monastery. Lord Hochmund waddled along beside me now, jubilantly regaling me with the epic saga of how he had dodged the vice-like pincer attack of plague by hiding within his castle store room and eating his way through half-a-ton of dried meal and other various goods. I was duly impressed.

"You don't appear to have missed many meals," I agreed.

"I even managed to invent some new ones."

"A pioneer."

"I prefer the term genius," Lord Hochmund shrugged, "but to each his own."

Lady Narcissa strode behind, head down, cloaked, the obedient servant. The guards came next. We'd entrained a few more en route. There were eight now, four marching in close formation, the others spread out, ferreting the alleys ahead for trouble.

"But you came out for Chalstain's funeral," I said.

He nodded. "An occupational hazard."

"For a *funeral?*"

"Sir Myron was a friend, a good friend."

"Funny. You two seemed to have little in common."

"We had one thing." He waved a glittering hand. "Besides, his funeral was the toast of the town. Admittedly, the toast was stale, weevil-ridden, and neither buttered nor sprinkled with cinnamon, but in these times one must persevere. I could not in good conscience pass up the chance."

"To what?"

"To what?" he scoffed. "To witness a gathering between the Lord Bishop and Lord Raachwald, of course. Two men at each other's throats come together under guise of honoring the dead? There is no finer spectacle upon God's earth than a war you wish no part in."

"I thought all of you Isle Lords were involved?"

"We do our part."

"I noticed you left early."

"I noticed you followed." Lord Hochmund smirked.

"One does best not to become embroiled in drama of the stage. Enjoy it from a distance, as it was meant to be." He shivered. "Though beware, once the players leap from the stage the time for departure has long since fled. I've never been one for audience participation."

"Nor I."

The Morgrave River sluiced past below, chunks of ice piling up in the middle as they lodged against one another, quivering, rattling around until they were either ground into nothing or shat out like yesterday's dinner. Mummer's Isle loomed above.

Lord Hochmund turned back to Lady Narcissa. "My dear, I implore you. I have a safe house near the bridge. My men shall escort you. I would prefer you not accompany us onto the Isle, for your own safety."

"Eustace," she glared from beneath her hood, "I am coming on. That was the keystone of our bargain."

"Lord Raachwald has taken Coldspire, my dear." He licked his lips like a reptile. "There it is. Forgive me. He ordered a cadre of his men into the keep yesterday. I met with Emile and the boy, and we lodged an official protest, but it did little to dissuade him, of course, and so I must insist, if you are to come, you must remain at my keep. You shan't visit Coldspire, not until after our business is concluded, yes?"

"Of course." Lady Narcissa nodded, though I could tell she was seething.

"There, there." Lord Hochmund patted her hand. "It shall be ours soon enough. And forgive me, but it would be best if you walk again behind." The Bastard's Bridge lay ahead. "And Krait, you by my side. Those are the Brulerin guards at the near end. Mine hold the far," he said. "They're a lazy bunch, these Brulerins. They shan't notice you, and if they do, they shan't care. It is the lady. We must ensure none of them recognizes her."

I reseated my helm, pulling the nasal guard lower, and slid into formation beside Lord Hochmund. The Brulerin guards wouldn't recognize me, but there was a fair chance that on an Isle this small all the fighting men would know or at least know of each other. A new guard might raise an eyebrow or two, but certainly, they'd all recognize Lady Narcissa.

Two guards stood at the Bastard Bridge turnpike, both armed with spears and shields. One strode out smartly to meet us.

"Oy, Captain," the Brulerin guard said as Lord Hochmund's Captain Abel marched forth. A manly handshake was exchanged, followed by conversation in low tones.

I glanced sidewise at Lord Hochmund as he chewed nonchalantly on a strip of dried beef. I watched the Brulerin guard's eyes and waited as he and Captain Abel jawed on. I couldn't hear about what. Beyond, on the far side of the bridge, a thin wisp of smoke roiled up from the guard shack's chimney.

The bridge spanned some fifty yards, the wind howling as it ripped through the expanse.

Captain Abel guffawed at something the Brulerin guard said then pounded him on the shoulder. The Brulerin guard stepped aside, waved us on. Captain Abel remained, talking as three of his men strode past, followed by us.

"Tally ho," Lord Hochmund offered a limp salute in passing.

Slowing my pace, I matched him stride for stride, Lady Narcissa and the remaining guards following.

"You and she had a fine discussion," I muttered out of the corner of my mouth, "back at the Gallows."

"She insisted." He shrugged. "She's insistent."

"I prefer the term harridan."

"Oooh, *harridan*, a good word. What's it mean?"

"It means she's a stone-cold bitch."

"Ah, how nice to sully a lady's character and yet still sound so *literate*." He nodded approvingly as he strolled, slow, measured, feet clunking on the wooden slats.

"We all have our strong points," I admitted.

"Aye. And she certainly has hers."

"There've been worse looking brides," I conceded. "Easy on the eyes, but the ears? Voice like a cat being tickled with a bone-saw. Might make a short life seem decidedly long."

"I'll not argue the point." Lord Hochmund smirked. "Though, you've felt only the steel point of her personality, as is often the case with persons under duress. And she has been under duress, old son, make no mistake about it. No doubt a lesser person would have folded, broke, shattered, yet she tarries on, climbing back up, rung by rung. A determined woman. Besides, she has other attributes, not the least of which is her wonderful husband."

"Wonderful?" I flinched. "You?"

"Me? Nay. I'm merely the betrothed. I refer to her *previous* husband, both rich and dead. What happier combination of possibilities exist?"

"I heard he was poor."

"Poor? My, my, my, oh no. No no no."

"Debt," I insisted. "Massive."

"Pfaw, *coin*," he scoffed. "What is coin? The man owned a castle. *The* castle." He glanced up at Coldspire, the stone keep perched precariously hundreds of feet above, piercing the twilit sky. "The abode of kings of old, dear Krait. My ancestors. Her ancestors."

"Family trees should have a few branches," I said.

"Nay," he ignored me, "coin means little. Coin can always be made, had, taken." He shook his head. "But *stone*, stone is strength. Stone is power. Stone is as close to permanence as this world dares offer, and one does not simply lose a hereditary keep because of a debt to some Jews." He raised a hand to cover his snickering jackal mouth. "He had land. He had time. He had opportunity. What he had little of was patience or sense."

"Now he has neither."

"And now *she* does."

"And you're the new husband."

"One must strike while the iron is hot, as they say."

"What's Raachwald going to say?"

Lord Hochmund's eyes flickered toward the bridge's far end, his pupils wide. That cannonball in my gut feeling struck again. Suddenly. Swelling. Eight guards stood at the far end of the bridge. They wore the green tabards of House Raachwald. Haefgrim towered amongst them. I stopped, turned, stared out over the water as it rolled on north toward the endless sea, "So, exactly how much did you sell me out for?"

"Coin was not transacted." Lord Hochmund adjusted his collar, a sour frown on his face.

I was on him then, dagger drawn, point digging into his neck as I hurled him smashing against the parapet. Lord Hochmund's guards reacted in slow motion, all turning inward, surrounding me in a circle of steel. I twisted the collar of his cloak, letting him feel the gusting winds whistle, the long black of the abyss swallowing at his back.

"Please…" Lord Hochmund raised a hand to halt his men. "Don't do anything stupid or rash."

"What?" I hissed in close. "Like trust you?"

"Touché." Lord Hochmund croaked. "You're making my men nervous. And nervous men with sharp implements are renown for neither restraint nor decision-making prowess. Agreed? Good lord, you truly did not foresee this?"

"I believed you to be a man of honor." The lie was so worm-riddled I nearly laughed myself.

"Good lord, Krait," Lord Hochmund snorted, nearly impaling himself on my dagger. "Appealing to *my* sense of honor? Hire a blind beggar to paint your portrait next time, you'll achieve sounder results."

"We had a deal."

"And I think it fair to say it lies sundered," Lord Hochmund said. "I've given my men specific orders to carry out in the event of my demise." His glance twitched to the left, and one of Lord Hochmund's guards pushed into view, the Lady Narcissa held before him, a dagger to her side.

"You're using *her* for leverage?" I gasped. "Against *me*?"

Lord Hochmund cleared his throat. "I think she'll suffice considering your brother's entanglement, and I've instructed my good Captain Abel that if such a situation presented itself, he was to have the Lady's throat slit and hurled bodily into yon river. You have approximately a count of *five*…"

At that, Lady Narcissa's hand flashed, and she was surging, struggling as three of Lord Hochmund's guards grappled her, grasping her by the arms. She seethed and sneered in their collective grasp, was brought to bear, a swathe of blood smeared across her face as Captain Abel tore a knife from her grasp. "You snake!" she snarled. One of Lord Hochmund's guards leaned crippling against the parapet, ashen, clutching at his groin as he slid to the ground, hissing through gritted teeth. The men forced Lady Narcissa against the parapet, near strangling her as she kicked and thrashed and snarled like a rabid wolverine.

Lord Hochmund cast a look my way. "*One*, old son…"

"Now *two*…"

"*Three*…"

"*Four*…"

"*Fuck.*" I lowered the knife and shoved Lord Hochmund away from the parapet. A spear point was introduced to my gut and another to my side. The other guards moved in, each taking hold of one of my arms. Another snatched Yolanda, the butcher blade, my hatchet, a trio of daggers.

"Tut, tut." Lord Hochmund raised one finger to Lady Narcissa. "Manners, my dear."

Lady Narcissa's eyes blazed.

"Now settle down," Lord Hochmund said as though calming a spooked horse. "Lord Raachwald just wants to talk."

"Yeah?" I said, skeptical.

"Krait," he glanced over, "are you a praying man?"

The giant and his men pounded close.

"You said Raachwald just wants to talk."

377

"Oh, I meant to me." Lord Hochmund scratching his cheek. "You, though, I was under the distinct impression he most certainly wishes to kill. He mentioned slow, specifically. I think he's not yet surmounted his loss over the demise of his sons."

"I got that same impression." I nodded toward Lady Narcissa, struggling still, a hand clamped round her throat. "And what about her?"

"I imagine he wants to do something entirely different to her."

"Yeah."

"And what about you? Lord of Coldspire? All your dreams?"

"All my *dreams*?" He scoffed. "Am I five? I choose my moments, old son. I choose them well."

"And this isn't one of them?"

"This isn't one of them," he echoed in full agreement. "I am sorry, if that holds any weight. The situation was dire. You must understand that?"

"Yeah, I understand," I said. "Hell, I *over*stand."

"Then tell me quickly," Lord Hochmund whispered close. "Why risk your life to get back on this cursed rock?"

I just stared at him for an instant as Haefgrim loomed. What the hell did it matter now? "I wanted to know if Cain Raachwald's funeral was open casket."

"Oh, you're a *ghoul*," he said, recoiling, suppressing a shiver. "Ahem. I attended, and it was closed."

"Did you see the body?" I asked. "At any point? Ever?"

Lord Hochmund shook his head then thought about it a moment. His eyes opened wider, slowly, realization dawning. "Was he truly—?"

"Don't know." I cut him short. "I can't find anyone who's seen him. So Cain might still be alive. And if he is, Raachwald's the murderer. How'd that sit with the rest of the Isle Lords?"

"Not well, not well, indeed. But it might not matter,

given our present state as a disparate collective." Lord Hochmund smiled sorrowfully, patting me on the shoulder as he waddled past, offering his arm to Lady Narcissa, still restrained. Lord Hochmund glanced to Haefgrim, just outside the ring of Lord Hochmund's own. "It is me, or it is him," Lord Hochmund muttered low. "Your previous ruse, I assume it a ruse, might benefit from your acquiescence here? Remember, you've been rescued from abduction, yes? I leave you to decide. Quickly."

Lady Narcissa ceased struggling, mastering herself. Her breathing came harsh, her breast rising and falling, steam pouring free in gouts from between those perfect lips. Her glare of hatred fled, though, and she nodded. "Forgive me."

"Nothing to forgive, my lady." Lord Hochmund glanced at his men, nodded warily, and they released her. "T'was but a moment of hysteria amidst the furor."

She took his arm, gathering herself, stifling her hate.

I stood still, unmoving, spear points pressed to my flesh.

Lady Narcissa's eyes were blank, dead.

"Apparently you're not going to a wedding," I said.

"Hush now," Lord Hochmund warned. "She is, or rather, she can attend one wedding and one funeral, or simply two funerals."

"You'll want this back." Lady Narcissa smiled as she removed Lord Hochmund's ancestral ring from her finger and tossed it casually over her shoulder, glittering as it fell into the river. "Oops."

"No—" Lord Hochmund lunged, his eyes bulging, and I thought for an instant he might leap after it, but he didn't. Alas. He just stared down, shoulders slumped in despair.

Lady Narcissa strode through Lord Hochmund's men to Haefgrim's side, towering silent beneath that demon helm. He bowed. Then both strode down the bridge.

I stared at the rushing water far below, considering my limited options.

Lord Hochmund swallowed as though clearing a sour taste from his mouth. "I know what you're thinking, Krait," he began, "we're very much alike, you and I. You're not quite as intelligent as I, and I'm not quite as handsome as you, and though neither of us represents the pinnacle of our respective strengths, we are both more than aware of that sad fact. We've no illusions. Yet, we survive and we survive *because* of that, because we are *honest* liars, because we possess the courage to levy sheer cowardice even before the full light of day. Many can be bullied into bravery but, nay, not we few." He followed my glare down to the rushing water. "I leave it to you, but neither one of us, I think, has the fortitude to forge such a leap. Mayhap if instant death were certain, but, mayhap it's not. Sharp pointed rocks shatter bone, and the water is so very cold, and so very dark, and so very deep."

"What is our way, then?"

"To tarry on, just a little longer, and see what happens." He shrugged. "The wind is not blowing your way now, but who can say which way it shall continue to blow?"

"What'd you sell me out for?" I asked as a guard stepped behind me.

"Nothing of worth," Lord Hochmund sighed, "merely my life." He nodded to the guard and everything went black.

...of money-houses on Lender's Row. I have stalked the Quarter's streets, observing them, following them. My questions they have ignored politely, feigned ignorance of; some even claimed illiteracy of my tongue. They hide and scurry away, and I give chase. But in the darkness, they continue to gather...

—*Journal of Sir Myron Chalstain*

Chapter 42.

I OPENED MY EYES to darkness. "What...?" A dull white throb tolled like a bell in my head, behind my eyes, pounding, subsiding, striking again with each movement. How long was I out? Hours? Days? I had no idea. I hadn't pissed myself but could feel the urge to. Hours, then.

"Are you alright?" A voice, breathless, hoarse, outside my cell.

My what? Shit. Stone walls. Bars. A dungeon. Somewhere. My hands were bound before me, numb, useless.

"Uhhh...no?" I wiped something wet from my face. Drool? No. Thick. Gritty. I could taste iron, so blood. A single flame flickered on a withered stalk of candle set in a sconce beyond the barred window in my cell door. Grunting, groaning, I pushed myself up off the cold floor and slunk across, a chain rasping with each shuffled step. Fetters encircled my ankle, its far end fixed to the wall. Shit. I peered out the window.

A hunched wraith mirrored me from a cell across the way. "I thought you were dead," the wraith wheezed. Stephan, he sounded sick, beyond sick.

"No, not yet—" Clamping a hand over my mouth, I stifled a gout of vomit, the sour burn, and swallowed it. "Could use a drink." I looked around. Seemed unlikely. "Where are we?"

"Coldspire."

A frigid breeze whistled softly through the tunnel. I

shivered, staring at the fluttering flame casting horrors across stone. "We're how many feet below ground, and there's *still* a fucking draft."

"An engineering marvel." Stephan shambled a bit. His skin and face were revenant-blue, gaunt and clammy looking. His eyes were voids set in his face, a death's head. My baby brother. He held up a palsied hand wrapped in bands of soiled linen and gripped the bars of his cell door. Each breath seemed a labor.

"How are you?"

"Getting along," Stephan answered. "And you? You're shivering."

"It's cold."

"And Karl?"

"Doing about as good as us. Probably see him right after Raachwald cuts off our heads. Or, at least, I will. I imagine slightly different aspects of the afterlife for you and me."

"What's happened?"

"Since I last saw you?" I shifted, trying to move my numb fingers. I couldn't. "Not much."

I told him everything that had happened since last I'd seen him. I told him of my meetings with Abraham. The ensuing battle. Our discussion afterwards about the Masada, the *Sicarii*, Casagrande, my thoughts concerning Lord Raachwald and his son. The prices set on my head. He stood hunched there in the dark, looking like Grim Death himself, pressed quietly at the bars, taking it all in, listening, not interrupting, just calculating while dying by degrees.

"I don't know," Stephan said. "This business with Raachwald's son? It just doesn't sit well with me."

"Me, either. None of it does."

"And what's Casagrande doing in Asylum?" Stephan asked. "In the Quarter? I'm sorry. There are too many holes still. It just doesn't make any sense. Everything. All of it. Abraham. The Jews."

"Volkendorf was setting up for another incursion," I explained. "He was going to ride in. Ride in and slaughter them all. He'd tried it once and failed. But he was gathering forces, or trying to anyways."

"To erase all his debts?"

"Seems so," I said. "Fine way to do business. So, the Jews got wind of it or figured it was coming again anyway. So these *Sicarii*, they struck first."

"No, not their motive," Stephan said. "That, I understand. Strike first. Kill Volkendorf before he kills you. Makes sense."

"Cut the head off the snake," I said.

"Precisely. But again, their motive I understand. There are men who would do it. There are always men who would do it. Men who would do *anything*. But are there men who *could* do it? Men who during the heart of a winter blizzard could scale the heights of Mummer's Isle? Break through the defenses of a keep and kill seven knights? Could these *Sicarii* accomplish that?"

"There's at least one secret way onto the Isle," I offered. "The tunnel from Crowley Street. I've heard rumor of another."

"Yes, but Lady Mary claimed the killer broke in through the front gates, the portcullis, and then through a reinforced door. You said you saw all three. Broken. Sundered. And she claimed it was one man."

"Yeah, a giant, a Jewish giant?" I offered dubiously.

"Here." Stephan snaked a hand out through the bars and held something up. "Look."

"What is it?" I squinted. "One of the rocks?"

"Yes and no. It's not rock. It's clay. Hard as rock. They're little bits of clay. Fired clay? Dried clay? I think."

"Clay…?" Something tickled at the back my mind.

"So, it was something someone brought in," Stephan said. "A weapon?"

"Of clay?" I thought about it. "I've heard of clay vessels of pitch, of Greek Fire?"

"But no evidence of fire?"

"No. None."

"Cannon?"

"I've never heard of clay cannonballs."

"A shield, then," Stephan offered, "or armor?"

"No. Dinnerware, perhaps. A plate?"

"No. It's too thick. This means something."

"Yeah. Been trying to wrap my head around it." I took a breath, fighting down nausea. "The clay shards scattered on the floors. The injuries. Both the same. It's like one of Karl's gods snatched them up, crushed them in hand then tore them limb from limb. Literally. Parts were missing at both sites, too."

"*Land of Goshen…*"

"I thought that perhaps two murderers…?" I winced.

"Hmm? That would require a great deal of coordination." Stephan crossed himself. "It's improbable, I suppose, but not impossible. It would explain the differing methods. Yet, Abraham claimed these *Sicarii* would not kill children."

"Men are men." I shrugged. "Some kill children. Some do worse. And Abraham's biased, more than a little."

Stephan nodded. "A hired man, then?"

"Maybe."

"Even still, would these *Sicarii* be so nihilistic as to murder a lord's brood in a way that would, under scrutiny, be construed to have been perpetrated by Jews?" Stephan held up a hand. "What would be the point? The blood libel business is rot, obviously, but many accept it as truth, and those that don't never speak out about it. We've both seen the aftermath of such accusations."

"What's nihilistic mean?"

"Lou," Stephan warned. "Would these men, so bent on striking their foe in retribution condemn their whole community? Their own families? To what conceivable purpose? It was as though the killer placed a sign on the corpses that said '*Jews perpetrated this act*.' If they meant to kill the boys, then why not just kill them as they killed the men? Why leave a breadcrumb trail leading back to the Quarter?"

"What if the two murderers acted independently?"

"A coincidence, you mean?" Stephan scoffed.

"Yeah, I know," I ceded, scrapping the idea. "So, we have two murder scenes. One with clues pointing directly at the Jews. The other one pointing at…someone else."

"Which do we believe?" Stephan asked.

"Both. Neither. Shit, I don't know."

"Who benefitted from the murders?" Stephan asked.

"Who didn't? Volkendorf was unusually unpopular, even for a lord." I started counting on my fingers. "Raachwald. Lady Narcissa. The Lord Bishop. The other three houses. Everyone's moving up. Losing an enemy. Hell, the Quarter as a whole benefitted, in the short run, anyways. Seems everybody but you and me, brother."

Neither of us said anything for a long while.

Stephan's chain rustled.

"What is it?" I asked.

"Just," he began, "promise me if you get another chance, you'll take it. You'll run, escape, scrape and crawl to get back home, somehow. See the kids. See Helen. And for the love of all that's holy, try to make amends. Honestly try."

"Right," I scoffed. "Door's two inches thick. Level. Solid." I kicked the bottom. Ouch. "I'll get right on it."

"Shhhh…" Stephan clutched at the bars, his fingers as brittle as bird bones. "Someone's coming."

A door slammed up the tunnel, hinges squealing, and footsteps clomped down the hall. A slender black shadow blocked the meager candle.

"Sir Luther Slythe Krait," the Grinner licked his lips, his sallow eyes glaring, "Lord Raachwald humbly requests your presence at his wedding feast."

...there exists a small but highly skilled cadre of armed men in the Quarter.

—Journal of Sir Myron Chalstain

Chapter 43.

MEN HUSTLED to and fro, sheaves of crossbow bolts cradled in arm, spears, axes, swords, implements of destruction all rattling, all clanging. Chain mail rustled. Coat-of-plate clacked and scraped. A stack of kegs stood in the corner. Gunpowder. Weapon racks filled the hall. The endless line of men rolled past in and out the great hall door, the same great hall door that had been burst in a month past, the same great hall that'd been littered with broken blades and shards of clay and anointed with dead men's blood.

The shattered door and line of men were the first things I saw when they yanked the burlap sack rasping off my head, the stink of onions and dirt still clinging to me. The second? The Gallows Lord. Still as a statue, leaning over a table cluttered with maps, wine, weapons. Daggers were stuck point down at a map's four corners. Crude stone icons as numerous and tactically placed as chess pieces. My mouth watered, stomach yawned. Yolanda, sheathed, lay across the table. Lord Raachwald reached for a dagger, gripped it, stabbed it down, his eyes on me throughout.

Old Inglestahd stood by Lord Raachwald's side, bombasting feverishly of troop strengths, hammering at the map with his thick forefinger. "Here and here," he said belatedly, glaring up from beneath wiry white eyebrows. He slid another map over the first.

"My lords." I bowed as best I could, hands bound still before me, legs shaky beneath, "forgive my appearance. The day has been...unkind."

All heads turned as Lady Narcissa emerged from the far darkness, a silent banshee cloaked in white, gliding softly forward, taking station by Lord Raachwald's side. She didn't so much as glance at me as he drew an arm about her, leaned toward her, whispered something in her ear, his lips curling back, revealing sharp canine teeth. Lady Narcissa listened, wide-eyed, and nodded.

I waited for him to finish. "My lord, I—"

Lord Raachwald raised a hand. I swallowed. "A fine blade, Krait." Withdrawing Yolanda scraping from her scabbard, he studied her blade, the swirl-patterned steel glinting like falling stars in the half-light of flickering torch. "Not the blade of a caravan guard."

"I'll not deny it," I said.

Men continued filing past, bearing implements of destruction. Haefgrim strode in, heavy boots clomping, a swathe splitting open wherever he strode.

"I do not recognize its maker's mark." Lord Raachwald held Yolanda point-out from his one eye, gauging her lean, scouring for imperfection. He would find none. "Where did you obtain it?"

"*Her,*" I corrected. "Prester John himself granted her to me."

"Hrrrrm?" Old Inglestahd sputtered in surprise.

Lord Raachwald, for his part, said nothing. His gaze fell on something behind me, Haefgrim, sauntering forth, looming like the shadow in the valley of death.

"She's crucible steel," I said.

"As of the dragon men of old?" Lord Raachwald nodded to one of his men, hauling a small barrel. "Arnulf, I want the pitch in two wagons. At the Brulerin Bridge forthwith. Pass the word."

"Aye, my lord." The man staggered on under his burden.

Lord Raachwald turned back. "Continue."

"As you said, not unlike the steel of the dragon men of old," I babbled on headlong, afraid that as soon as I ceased talking, he'd see me dead. "The good steel, the Ulfbert. Not that brittle peat-bog shit. She's of modern design, though, of course." I gazed at Yolanda, taking her in from point to pommel, continuing my tour. "As you can see, she bears patterned swirls similar to Damascus steel.

Indestructible, or so they claim. You can fold her over near in half, and she won't break. The hilt is pitted." I pointed with bound hands. "It was my uncle's."

"I'll require a lineage upon the blade."

"Certainly," I said. "Pen and parchment and you'll have it." And that is how a true lord appropriates your property, magnanimously, while simultaneously requesting you do more work on his behalf. "My lord, as I've said—"

"Was this the blade with which you *murdered* my two eldest sons?" Lord Raachwald asked, still staring at Yolanda.

And there it was, the reason Lord Raachwald hated me. I'd killed his two sons, years past, near a decade. My spine stiffened and asshole puckered as I heard a sudden *SHIIIINNNNG* behind me. Haefgrim drawing that damnable falchion. I didn't turn. Didn't dare. Better to be taken in the neck than the face. I wouldn't even feel it if it was the neck. I hoped. A sensation of falling maybe? The face, though, there's just something about a heavy slice of steel lodging in your face, *KA-CHUNG*, and it just sits there quivering like an axe in a tree trunk, and you're not *quite* dead.

An instant passed.

Then another…

"Well?" Lord Raachwald demanded.

"No, Lord Raachwald." I'd killed Kraile Raachwald during the wars, at Crecy, in the first wave that charged up our hill and actually made it through the arrow storm. A dagger through the eye slit. His older brother Arrold I'd bested in single combat nearly a year later to the day. We'd fought at sundown on a hill above a marsh outside of Calais. It had been a close thing. "Both were with different blades. Both long gone."

"And is that the hand you used to strike my wife?" He turned to Lady Narcissa, brushed her hair back, revealing the bruise.

Lady Narcissa's eyes veritably glistened, quivering as she glared at me. With glee? Triumph? Or fear? "I shall bear this as a mark of honor, my lord." She took his hand in hers.

"Tis but a whisper, a dead echo of the travails I have endured."

"You claimed no knowledge of the abduction," Lord Raachwald turned to me, "no part in its act." I said nothing; there was nothing to say. "And yet when you found the lady under guard by your fiend, this man who murdered my men, who burned my home, and he is your man, is he not?"

"*Was*, my lord."

"You swore to bring me his head."

"A crossbow bolt to the leg," I said. "It festered. He's dead."

"You think me a fool?" Lord Raachwald turned sidelong in question to Lady Narcissa.

"Yes, he was dying." She nodded.

I kept my breath even, slow, balanced on razor's edge.

"And so justice cannot be dealt *him*." He took Lady Narcissa's hand to his lips, offering a granite kiss. "Yet, when you found my lady in this murderer's possession, this fiend, you did nothing." He took a slurp of red wine. "Nothing? Nay, not nothing. You kept her prisoner, did you not? Against *her* will. And you failed to bring her to me. Against *mine*. You failed in this task. You failed to hold your word by conspiring with my enemy. You failed. You failed. You FAILED!" He slammed his fist on the table, daggers and axes jumping with each declaration of my failure.

I could hear Lord Raachwald's men freeze, the clink of steel weapons, the rustle of mail, the stomp of boot on stone, all gone. A cold wind ripped howling through the shattered front door, slamming it in dangling pieces against the wall, a clattered rhythm, the beat of death's disparate drums.

Lord Raachwald turned slow, smooth, deliberate, his piercing gaze lighting on his new bride. "I would know what other injustices were visited upon you, my lady."

"I—" Lady Narcissa clutched at her throat.

"This is my hall now, and I am lord. It is my court,

and it is one of law. I bid you speak."

"Of course, my lord." Lady Narcissa bowed her head. "Forgive me. It is only that the ordeal was…"

Lord Raachwald laid a stone hand on her far shoulder and drew her in suffocating close, whispering again, lips working. Lady Narcissa stiffened, nodded, whispering back in near silence. Lord Raachwald cleared his throat then straightened. "I shall bid you speak of what you have gleaned during your capture. No more."

She held his gaze, glistening, proud. "I shall say only that I have learned that not all knights are worthy of their station." She cast me a sidelong glare. "Not all hold firm reign over their baser, *animal* instincts. Not all knights are above commingling with the lesser aspects of civilization, nor becoming embroiled in their poisonous schemes. I was present at a discussion…"

"Go on, my lady." Lord Raachwald's eye gleamed with a vile light.

Lady Narcissa clutched at her chest.

"Who was party to it?"

Lady Narcissa nodded, reluctantly, placing a hand on Lord Raachwald's shoulder as she gathered herself. "Krait and a Jew."

"And what was the Jew's name?"

"Abraham Ben-Ari, a moneylender of some repute."

Lord Raachwald nodded. "I know of this man."

"Oh, my lord." Her fingernails dug into the table. "Forgive me. To bear the burden of being the one to tell you." She bit her lower lip. "It was the Jews that murdered my husband, my sons, and your own son." My stomach dropped as she passed her death sentence. "This man Abraham confessed as much. He spoke of a council called the Masada. He indicted all the landed men of the Quarter. And within this council, there lay an inner sanctum. A cabal called the *Sicarii*. Their leader is an outlaw named Daniel." She wiped her eye. "These *Sicarii* murdered our sons."

Lord Raachwald worried a dagger free of the table. The corner of his mouth might have twitched, a cold fleeting grin. "The Jews…" His breath was a bellows as he inhaled and exhaled through flaring nostrils. "A conspiracy."

Lady Narcissa gathered herself. "Forgive me, my lord."

"And the blood libel, lady?" Old Inglestahd asked.

Lady Narcissa nodded. "There were whispers of it, aye."

"My lord." Old Inglestahd rose up.

Lord Raachwald raised a hand to silence him. "It is grave news you bear, my lady," he said, "but I pray that with the casting off of it, some burden from your soul is cast off as well. I pray that some manner of peace might take root when the guilty are razed and harsh justice dealt."

Lady Narcissa bowed her head.

"Excuse me, my lord. My lady." Old Inglestahd leaned forward and coughed roughly. "But might the lady expound on the methods used in the crime itself? Since when have Jews the strength to tear iron? And smash oak? Crush bone? Tear knights limb from limb? A trial must be held, my lord, affidavits drawn, inquiries made and answered, confessions signed. Aye. Accusations can be made, but they must be supported by evidence, witnesses, the law, even though they be but Jews."

Lord Raachwald's withering glare fell on Old Inglestahd, but the old badger did not wilt. "Is the lady's word not evidence enough?" Lord Raachwald hissed softly.

Old Inglestahd gave pause.

"My lord," I said, "some of—"

Slam! A fist hammered me in the kidney, wilting my legs beneath me, dropping me crumpled, breathless. Gasping. Rasping. Reaching. I sucked in a stifled croak as Haefgrim clutched a fistful of my hair and proceeded to grind my face into the jagged floor. He bore his full weight down on my skull. I couldn't breathe, couldn't move, couldn't anything. My teeth scraped against stone.

Old Inglestahd cleared his throat. "And what of Sir Luther's claims? He should be heard, for the record. The law states—"

"Bring him here," Lord Raachwald commanded, and I was hauled by the collar like a side of beef to my dead feet, dangling, and slammed against a wall. I fought to stand on wobbling legs, failed, contorting over like some palsied cripple.

"My lady, tell me again what you told me earlier," Lord Raachwald said.

"It was my distinct impression that Krait owed a great debt to this Abraham Ben-Ari," Lady Narcissa said. "Through business dealings of some kind or other. Furthermore, it seems this debt was erased, *somehow*, under opaque circumstances."

Lord Raachwald's eye slid to mine. "Do you owe this Jew money?"

"Rrrrg…no." I pawed at the wall, numb fingers scrabbling at the joints, for purchase, to stand on my own. I couldn't. I could only watch as the Grinner slunk into the great hall from outside.

"Milord," the Grinner said, "the men are ready."

Lord Raachwald glowered. "And the others?"

"They await at the Brulerin Bridge."

"Very well…" Lord Raachwald said. "See the men ready. I shall arrive forthwith." Then to me, "You were in league with this Jew?"

"In league? I, no—"

"You labored in his employ?"

"Yeah. I worked for him."

"So you *were* in league with him."

"I guarded wagons, for shit's sake," I said. "You should know. You stole my whole fucking—"

"And you have no outstanding debts?" he continued calmly, icily.

"No." I found my legs, finally, right where I'd left them, and stood, hunched, nearly doubled over, sucking wind, fighting back the urge to puke.

"But this shipment you lost?" Lord Raachwald inquired. "How was it you accounted for its loss?"

"Are you fucking kidding me?" I gazed toward the

heavens, saw only Lord Volkendorf frozen in glass staring down. "I didn't. Couldn't."

"Yet you claim you are *not* in this Jew's debt. Explain."

"He felt it prudent to wipe clean the loss and sever any future dealings with me."

"And you consider that *no* debt?"

"Fuck yourself," I said because I knew I was.

"Nay, you owe him more than coin." Lord Raachwald leered forth, his grey cragged head huge, cyclops eye glowering, terrible. "You have sold a piece of your shriveled soul to a Jew for the price of a handful of shorn sheep. And know this, you serpent-tongued devil, whilst you languish below, becoming allies with the dark, awaiting the blood-eagle talons, I shall kill them. I shall kill them all."

...I am certain. The Lady Narcissa was aware of her husband's debt, though I remain uncertain as to whether she was privy to the full extent of the principal as well as the massive usury...

—*Journal of Sir Myron Chalstain*

Chapter 44.

ACROSS THE TUNNEL, within his cell, Stephan snored, a soft gurgle rattling with each labored exhalation. Chains clinked as he shifted. At least he was still alive. I stared out the window, listening to the thud of feet pounding far above, reverberating through the rock like thunderheads on a far horizon. Then I went and lay down, closing my eyes, trying to sleep. What the hell else was there to do? The skittering of rodent nails clicking on stone kept me company. Lord Raachwald's diatribe on the finer aspects of dungeon living rang in my mind. Sleep didn't take, so I lay there, shivering in the dark.

"*Krait,*" hissed a voice.

"Huh?" I lurched to my feet, groggy, half-awake, skull pounding in fits. Eyes straining, I peered out the window.

"*Krait—*"

A woman's voice. From beyond the tunnel door. Followed by the sound of a key sliding into lock, a sweet sound, it turning, growing sweeter still. The tunnel door opened, groaning like an old ghost. Bearing a hooded lantern, a cloaked figure stepped into the hallway and flitted from door to door, peering into one cell after another.

"Lady Mary," I hissed, dangling numb fingers through the bars. "Here."

Lady Mary turned, pale, wide-eyed as she hustled over, a huge jangling key-ring clutched in her small fist. She tried the first key. It didn't work. She muttered beneath her breath, tried another, then another. I forced my face against the bars, practically ripping my eyeballs out of socket trying to see out.

Another key. Another key. Another *wrong* key.

"*C'mon,*" I hissed.

She swallowed. Three more keys and one finally worked, metal teeth shearing past tumblers, turning, clunking with a finality that nearly made me piss my pants in ragged delight. I shouldered the door open the instant the lock clicked. "My ankle." I hpped on one foot, fetters jangling. The fifth key unlocked them.

Lady Mary was at Stephan's cell next, trying a key. It didn't work. Jesus. Neither did the next.

"Eh?" came Stephan's voice, groggy. "Who...?"

"Lady Mary and your brother," she whispered, tongue between lips as she inserted another, tried it, was stymied. "*Judas Priest...*"

"Narcissa's maid." I hovered over her shoulder, shoving my bound hands practically in her face. "A blade?"

"Watch it." Lady Mary withdrew a small blade from her cloak and sawed away my bonds.

"Jesus." I nearly collapsed as blood rushed back to my corpse hands.

"Leave me." Stephan wobbled like a newborn colt, arms shaking as he pressed himself up then collapsed. He coughed, and I could hear the fluid in his lungs, the infection, the death creeping. "I'm a dead man."

"Like hell you are," I said knowing full well he wasn't wrong.

Lady Mary tried another key.

"No, it's...it's not this." Stephan shook his crippled stump. "They're going to *execute* me. Tomorrow. Or," he stared off a moment in a fugue, "was it...?"

"Shut your mouth."

"There's...there's no time." Stephan oozed to the door, crawled up it. "Go. *Please.* Both of you."

"Fuck you, you little prick!" I growled. "When's the guard change?"

"Now," Lady Mary hissed, working. "They'll be here any moment."

"Go." Stephan pleaded. "I'll only slow you down— *ulp!*"

Thrusting my hand between the bars, I grabbed his throat. Numb tingles buzzed through my hand with each phlegm-rattling breath.

"Do it," Stephan hissed, his eyes wide, black, unfocused. "Then go." His gaze shifted. "Thank you, my lady. Forgive me the hardships I've undoubtedly caused you."

Lady Mary cursed, shook her head without looking up, focused still on the lock.

I growled, released him, pushing him back. "Give me those." I snatched the keys from Lady Mary, dropping them with a metallic clatter. "Idiot," I muttered to myself, bending, snatching them back up with cramped claws.

Lady Mary glared me up and down.

"Jesus—" We turned at the same instant; footsteps and voices echoed from beyond the tunnel door, the clatter of steel.

"We have to go," Lady Mary said. "When they find the guard…"

I snatched her hooked hand, feeling wet on it, rubbing the thick, viscous black between my fingers.

Lady Mary looked down, away, "I…"

"Go." Stephan pointed a skeletal claw outside the bars.

"Fucking martyrs." I shoved the key ring back into Lady Mary's hand. "Weapons?" She held up the small knife. "Anything else?" She shook her head. "Did the guard have one?"

"I…I don't know."

My eyes focused on the iron hook. "That thing come off?"

She glared at me.

"*Fuck.*" I tore down the tunnel, took a left then a right and found a small chamber with a desk and overturned chair. Behind the desk, on the floor, lay a guard, corpse white, splayed out, leg propped up on the fallen chair, a

396

black pool of midnight stagnant beneath him. Behind him, a stairwell spiraling up into stone. Voices echoed from above, light and shadow bouncing, flickering, black and orange triangles growing and receding with each step. A truncheon leaned against the desk. I had it in hand a moment later.

The footsteps drew closer.

Voices. Guards. Two.

I dragged the corpse against the left wall. Flexing my hands open and closed, I slid to the right corner and crouched down a moment before the first guard stepped in. Then the second.

As the first caught the corpse and froze, I rose and smashed the truncheon across the back of the second's head, *CRACK,* dropping him like a stone and continuing on through, whipping out on my backswing at the first, clipping across his bared teeth.

"Blackguard!" His head whipped back instinctively, blade gleaming half-drawn from its scabbard as he stumbled back, my foot driving heel-first into him, catching him in the gut, driving him against the wall. He crashed, head smashing, but the wall caught him and held him upright. He ripped his sword free, but two-handed, truncheon hurtling, crescent-arced, I smashed him again. No glancing blow this time. Solid. The bones in his forearm shattered in half, his blade clattering to the floor.

He raised his other hand to fend off.

I broke that one, too.

Then I broke the rest of him.

* * * *

Stumbling, barrel-assing after Lady Mary, naught more than a swinging lantern ahead, we hauled through rock-hewn catacomb vaults, natural caverns, claustrophobic passageways. I ducked beneath an overhang, lurched through a tight passage, and froze, nearly dropping a nut as I clutched at the uneven wall. Gale winds ripped past. Staggering against the biting cold, I stared out over a void overlooking the dark waters of the Morgrave, churning hundreds of feet below.

"Over here." Lady Mary beckoned.

I nodded, following the uneven path, about three feet wide, sheer rock face to my right, a drop into nothingness to my left. Crabwise, I edged along, back pressed to the wall, my left arm clutching Stephan's waist, my right holding his arm draped across my shoulders. Like lugging a corpse.

I glanced back at the way we'd come, nothing but a crevice in the rock face. Then onward. Nothing visible but the western half of the city across the river, a dark tumorous mass ripping into darker night, pockmarked by points of quavering light, church steeples jabbing at the sky like teeth, and roaring plague fire burning bright.

"In here." Lady Mary ducked into a fissure in the rock.

"Jesus." I nearly collapsed as I made the tunnel.

Stephan did.

"Krait," Lady Mary knelt by Stephan's side, "this will kill him."

"There are worse ways to die," I grunted, catching my breath, leaning against the wall. "Sorry. You saved our arses. I know that. I suppose we should thank you." I took another breath, slowing the pounding in my ears. "So, thank you. For me. For him." I bent over, grabbing my brother. "Come on. Up." I tugged on his arm, half-heartedly. "Bad place to stop."

"We..." Stephan crouched, raising his crippled right arm, nothing but a stump at the wrist. "We must stop him, Lou."

"By 'we' you mean 'me,' yeah?"

Lady Mary drew a wineskin from within her cloak, knelt, and held it to his lips. "Drink." She upended it.

"My thanks." Stephan stared at her hook hand.

"Thank me by fulfilling your vow." Lady Mary covered her hook.

I scoffed, pulling my brother to his feet then

snatching the wine, taking a swig.

"Excuse me?" Lady Mary asked.

"Fulfilling my vow?" I glared. "To who? The mad lord bent on murdering me and a city's worth of Jews? Or his loving wife who sold me out?" I looked at Stephan. "We don't owe her. At worst, we're square. Even. Hell, if Raachwald wasn't consumed with genocide, we'd both be blood-eagled across—"

"What choice did she have?" Lady Mary's tone withered.

"She could have *not* sold me out."

"You're referring to that mummer's farce up there?" Lady Mary asked. "I saw. You think she had any choice? You think for a moment if she said anything he didn't like, she would still draw breath? Ask where his former wife is, why don't you? Poof." She snapped her fingers beneath my nose. "She has one '*missing*,' like all the rest. My good lady steps a razor's edge. One misstep and she falls, and even should she not, still she bleeds."

"'*Good*' is a bit strong," I deadpanned, "but just because she didn't like the options didn't mean she had no choice."

Lady Mary rolled her eyes. "We don't have time for this. Lord. You want to get out of here? You want to stop Lord Raachwald? She told me if you bring her justice—the heads she desires—she'll see Lord Raachwald halts his invasion. She *vowed* it."

"Is her word supposed to mean something?"

"Don't you see?" Stephan clutched at my shirt. "She did what she had to stay alive."

"You think Abe and his people'll give two shits about that when Raachwald comes calling? I didn't trust her *before*. You think I'd trust her now?"

"She claimed you would say that," Lady Mary said.

"Yeah," I shook with fury, "and what hell else did she say?"

"She said that Cain Raachwald's tomb lies empty."

Chapter 45.

GARBLED VOICES and shouts careened, echoing off hot gouts of air blasting from within the monastery's great hall. The clash of steel, the stomp of boot, the shudder of tables moving, dinnerware crashing to the floor, shattering. Roars. Screams. The ring of steel on steel.

I clawed my way through a mass of broken chairs tossed haphazardly down the middle of the hallway. A harsh glow blared like molten sunshine beyond the double doors, growing stronger, hotter, as I neared the dead feast. A war axe leaned against the wall, bent at the haft, cracked, broken, bloodied. Armored carcasses lay splayed out across the floor. No tabards called out their house, their affiliations, the nameless dead.

I crept closer, sweating, truncheon in hand.

Cupping a hand against the glare, I peered in, and *they* stared back, the three great blazing eyes roaring like the furnaces of hell. The three hearths, once desolate and cold, were now overladen with dead monks stacked like cordwood, immolating five high. Some were sat up, some bent back, others knurled inward like dead leaves as the fire ate at their bones, nude skulls staring down from on high, bright hellish white blackening fast before the hammer clash of a melee song. Six avatars black as ash stood in bas-relief before the rippling red gouts, six avatars of shadow dancing before the rip-roar of crackling flame, the burst of cooked bone.

His back to the flames, a shade, a giant, pivoted behind his shield. It was Gaunt; it had to be, his hand rearing back, a sundered blade clutched in his gauntleted fist. The other five harassed and harried him like wolves might a wounded bear, nipping, stabbing, jabbing with lightning strikes. Four fought up front, spread out, leaping tables, casting aside chairs. Blades drawn, whipping, they licked out, driving Gaunt back, back, back through the maze of great tables, toward the blaze. One warrior hung back, a loaded crossbow brought to bear, waiting for a clean shot.

As steel clashed and men swore, I waded through the labyrinth, keeping low, stalking up behind the crossbowman. He was focused, and not on me. Two-fisted swinging, I shattered my truncheon across the back of his neck. The fucker dropped, crossbow releasing, the bolt chip-skittering across the floor, sparking the trail of a dying star. But no one noticed. No one but Gaunt and the silent jury of hellfire monks. Clash and clang. Sword on shield. Spark and crack. Hissing garbled swears and taunts from the four. Gaunt, though, fought on silent, ceding ground, always ceding, never gaining, until the demon flames licked his heels, poured out over his shoulders, his back, and he could cede no more.

But I'd reloaded the crossbow, and I fired it, point blank at the nearest of the four.

"*Gah!*" he screamed, the bolt feathers just visible, sticking out of his right flank. He dropped to a knee, contorting awkwardly before I smashed him in the head with the crossbow stock then hurled it at another as he turned to his comrade's cry. The solid oak drilled him in the face.

My onslaught split the remaining warriors' awareness, and Gaunt took advantage. Full. Lashing out, he drove forth from the fire, hurling his sundered blade at one, sending him ducking. Then Gaunt pivoted, latching onto the blade of the other with his free hand, yanking, drawing the man in a half step as Gaunt's shield, like an executioner's axe falling, descended in a great arc, glancing off the man's head. He staggered aside, crumbling, broken, half-catching himself on a table as his comrade lunged back in, burying his blade into Gaunt's side.

Still silent, Gaunt swung his adversary's stolen sword, reversed, hilt first, burying a quillon into his foe's face. The man stood there an instant, a look of dumbfounded disbelief on his face. Then he fell. Gaunt hefted his shield two-handed, bringing it down on the man's head, crushing it.

"Krait…" Gaunt turned toward me, blood streaking down his arm. He marched with purpose, the blade sticking out of his side, awkward, like some vestigial appendage. He snatched a huge war-mace from off a table and ripped his helm from his head. It clattered to the floor steaming with cooked blood.

"The ledger." I snatched up a blade, leveling it before me. "Did he decipher it?"

"Aye." Flame roared at Gaunt's back.

"Where is he?" I stepped back.

"There." Gaunt pointed toward the shadows.

Bound spread-eagled across a table, Brother Tomas lay, flickering orange cascading over him in waves as the holocaust roiled behind. The ripple of flames seemed almost to give him life, movement, but it was illusion. A spear stood from the center of his chest, aimed toward the heavens.

"Who were they?" I swallowed.

"I don't know." Gaunt staggered out from behind a table. "Armed men. Trained men, for certain. Isle men? God-men? Mercenaries?" Blood trickled from his flank, down his leg. "I might ask you."

"How the hell should I know?"

His anger permeated the room like a caustic fume, a thing palpable, pressing outward, threatening to crack the mortar, dislodge the walls, bring down the roof. The funk shifted a mite then, and I could tell he meant to kill me.

"You have a question, Krait?" He stepped forward, devouring distance.

"You don't like me very much, do you, Gaunt?"

Gaunt ignored me. "How did they know to come here?"

"I need it."

"How did they know to come *here* for that damned book?"

"Think." I took an involuntary step back.

"Everyone knows about it. I was followed. Ambushed. You said yourself everyone knew about me. Hell, maybe it was *you* they trailed."

"Death trails you now, Krait," Gaunt said. "High time it caught up."

"Tomas chose to help me." I retreated another step.

"Brother Tomas was an innocent."

"And innocents die. That's life. But he *chose* to help me."

"They were torturing him when I arrived." Gaunt stomped the head of a corpse, shattering skull. "You know that? No. You're aware only of yourself." Drool coursed slick down his chin. "And they knew their craft. And I tell you this. *You* would have broken. *You* would have sung whatever tune they desired. And I say this," he put a hand to a table, steadying himself, "so too would have I. So, too, would have *anyone*." His voice faltered. "But that scraggling little pipsqueak of a man would not break. For you," he slammed a table with his fist, "*FOR YOU!*"

I glanced at the spear, upright in Brother Tomas's chest.

"The spear was mine."

"A mercy, then."

"Aye. Allow me to offer you the same." Gaunt raised his war mace high. "You scab of a man. Wandering through lives with a disregard for the carnage riding riot in your wake."

I was running out of room. "Tomas didn't die for me, Gaunt. He would have, but he didn't. He died for what I'm doing. He died because I'm the only one in the bloody city doing anything about the murder of three kids.

"You claimed this city is your charge to protect," I continued. "Well, guess what? You're a fucking failure. Raachwald's amassing an army to raze the Quarter. Tonight. He aims to kill everyone. *Everyone*. And just maybe there's something in that ledger that'll solve this rotten puzzle. Something that'll stop him. Or don't you care because they're Jews?"

"Do not attempt to convince me you do."

"I suppose like the Lord Bishop, they're your own personal piggy bank, too. Is that it? Coin? Oh, tell me it's not. I thought you the blood-thirstiest of berserkers. Tell me you're not at heart just some bean counter like the rest. Berserkers at least warrant respect."

Gaunt loomed, mace poised high, two-fisted for a killing stroke.

"Raachwald's attacking *tonight*," I spat. "Hell, maybe *now*. So tell me where the ledger is, and let me do what I can," I adjusted my grip on my blade, "or come on and kill me if you can."

...I had always remanded such fantastic stories to the realm of myth and legend...

—Journal of Sir Myron Chalstain

Chapter 46.

OVER MY HEAD, arms wobbling, I slid the mail shirt, holding the sleeve ends, letting go of the rest, an icy river of rippling steel cascading over my head, chest, and arms, settling in a ringing, rustling skein. I gathered the best weapons I could from amongst the nameless dead. A longsword. Daggers. I took the crossbow. Lady Mary scoured the great hall for bolts. Through coughs and sputters, Stephan blazed through Brother Tomas's translation of Chalstain's ledger.

"Where are you going?" Lady Mary asked.

"Don't know," I glanced over, "Stephan?"

Stephan held up his stump as he huddled by the flames, a blanket wrapped around his sparse frame, shivering despite the heat, Chalstain's ledger held close to his face, the immolating dead reading over his shoulder.

"What are you going to do?" Lady Mary found another bolt.

"No idea." I buckled the sword belt around my waist, cinched it tight.

"Shouldn't you have a...a plan?"

"Probably."

"Well?"

"Stephan, ideas?" I asked.

"You're going to find Abraham," Stephan said without glancing up. "Find him. Warn him. His people."

"The Lord Bishop's got soldiers guarding the Quarter," I said.

"Yes, but they're not expecting a full-blown invasion," Stephan countered. "You said you got a glimpse at Raachwald's maps?"

I closed my eyes. "Yeah. A frontal assault, right

through the gates. All his men. Meat and potatoes."

"That's something," Stephan said. "You'll need the heads, too, of course, of these *Sicarii*. Get them. Deliver them to Raachwald."

"I'm an assassin now?"

"Call it judge, jury, and executioner, like in the old days." Stephan looked up, cheeks sunken, skin grey, but eyes clear with defined purpose. "And when you offer the heads to Raachwald, you must do so in a public forum. Make sure witnesses are present. His men, Lady Narcissa, as many as possible. Force him to honor his word."

"You truly believe he'll call this off for *three* fucking heads?"

"If you don't believe it, why are you donning mail?" Stephan asked.

"Not huge fan of getting stabbed." I stuffed a pair of daggers into my belt. "And I think maybe we should just lay low. Find a bolt hole."

"Raachwald'll call this off if he gets the heads," Stephan said. "We have to believe that. And we hold Narcissa to her word that she'll fight to that end. Lady Mary? Her word is true?"

Lady Mary looked away, saying nothing.

"Lady?" Stephan raised an eyebrow before I could.

"You think there's a prayer in hell she'll honor it?" I pressed.

"Will it matter?" Lady Mary ran a hand through her uneven brown hair. "I don't know. But yes, she'll keep her word. She'll try, for Michael and Gilbert, for them, but that's only half of the bargain. Lord Raachwald?"

"Lotta links in this flimsy chain," I muttered. "The axe…"

Lady Mary picked it up, tossed it across the table; I caught it on the fly.

"It doesn't matter." Stephan rose, eyes blazing, the audience of skulls glaring from the flames. "That rests on him, on *his* conscience, *his* soul."

"You think he's got either?"

Stephan ignored me. "Justice is at stake, yes, but more importantly, lives. We must do whatever we can to stop him."

"And if we fail?" I asked.

"Failure's your bread and butter," Stephan said, "and you choose *now* to fear it?"

"Ouch."

"The Quarter needs fighting men," Stephan said. "More. As many as possible."

"What of Brother Gaunt?" Lady Mary asked.

"I warned him of the attack," I said, stuffing bolts into the quiver.

"But what'll he do?" Lady Mary asked.

"Probably get killed, if he's not dead already," I said. "And he has no alliances with any of the lords. I don't know how many he can muster. Not enough, that's for damn sure. But he *is* mustering." I glanced at Lady Mary. "Your husband was a warrior. How many's Gaunt got?"

"Before the plague struck?" Lady Mary fingered her lip. "Twenty heavy cavalry. Twenty at most, I should think. And about that of foot soldiers."

"Forty, then." I nodded. He had in the realm of fifteen men at the funeral. Five on the bridge. The plague had hit them just like everyone else. "A third of that, then, on a good day. And cavalry's actually footmen if they're manning a wall. So twelve or fifteen against ten times that. Shit. But they're closer. Will muster faster. Disciplined bastards, I'll say that. But we still need more."

"Who has more?" Stephan asked. "Who has more and hates Raachwald?"

"The Lord Bishop," Lady Mary answered.

"Good. Yes." Stephan nodded. "You must warn him, Lou. He's the only one."

"Yeah, but…"

"But what?" Lady Mary asked.

"The Lord Bishop swore out a writ for my arrest. For my head."

"I did not take you for a coward, Sir Luther," Lady

Mary said.

"*Really?*" I said. "Where've you been?"

"You must warn him," Stephan pressed.

"No, I've a better idea." I slung the quiver over my shoulder and fixed Lady Mary a glare. "*You* go. You warn him." She made to protest but I bulled on through. "No, you're his *enemy's* enemy. Which makes you his friend. Sort of. Maybe. Look. He hates Raachwald. You hate Raachwald. He'll listen to you."

"Lord Raachwald allowed me to live." Lady Mary shrunk away.

"After he tortured you, yeah?" I said. "After he took your hand. You owe that shit no loyalty."

"Maybe I'm just afraid..."

"I didn't take you for a cowardess."

"Touché." Lady Mary shook her head, feeling the sharp tip of her hook with soft pink fingers. "A truth, and a hard one at that." She closed her eyes, nodded. "I shall go. For what good it shall do."

"Might do some," I said. "Hell, might do some bad. Most things're that way. Now, who else has men?"

"The Jews," Lady Mary said. "The *Sicarii.*"

"Yes," Stephan said, "and they're already in the Quarter."

"Jesus." I checked the edge on my new blade. It would do. "So, I'm supposed to warn the *Sicarii and* bring Raachwald three of their heads? That'll go over like a wet fart at the altar."

Stephan waved his hand. "Just warn Abraham. He'll warn the *Sicarii.* He'll have to."

Scanning the dead one last time, I toed one of the carcass's heads towards the light of the hearth. He didn't look so much like a bastard dead; he just looked like some fella who'd laid himself out for a snooze. I glanced over at Brother Tomas, strewn out across the table. "Why not just use three of *these* heads?"

"Because you gave your word to Lady Narcissa you'd bring her the *actual* murderers." Stephan shook his head, disgusted. "And even if you were to break your word, and you won't, we don't know who these men are. What if *Raachwald* is the one who hired them?"

"No," Lady Mary glanced over the faces of the dead, "they're not any of his."

"You'd know." I considered. "But maybe he hired some new men? Mercs or hedge knights? Or hired some on the sly?"

"No." Lady Mary shook her head. "Something this important?" She followed my gaze to Brother Tomas. "Assassination? He'd have sent Haefgrim. Or Slade. One of the named men to head the squad."

"They were fighting men." I scanned the carnage. Gaunt knew his business. Sure as shit. "Well-armed. Trained."

"But not Raachwald's," Stephan said. "Whose then?"

"I'd recognize at least one, most likely, were they with one of the other Isle Lord's men," Lady Mary said.

"You know the Lord Bishop's men?" I hoped.

"No." Lady Mary shook her head. "Not many."

"Then they're the Lord Bishop's," I offered. "They were coming after me. The bounty."

"Their skin is dark." Stephan squinted from one corpse to another. "All dark hair. Olive complexions. Mediterranean looking. Jews?"

"Or Dagos."

"The Genoans?" Stephan said.

"So how do you tell a Dago from a Jew?" I asked. "Sounds like a bad joke. It probably is, somewhere. Somehow. What's the punchline?"

Stephan and I just looked at each other.

"You could, ah..." Lady Mary held a crossbow bolt pointed up.

"Ah, *what?*"

"Well, if they're Jews, they'll be..." She made a chopping motion across the head of the bolt.

"Huh?"

"*What in heaven's breadth?*" She rolled her eyes.

"Circumcised," Stephan exclaimed. "That's part of their covenant. If they're not cut, they're Casagrande's Genoans."

"Yeah," I muttered. Obvious. Idiot. I waited a moment for either Stephan or Lady Mary to show some initiative. When neither did, I sighed, drew a dagger, knelt by one of the dead, slit a trench in his pants and took a gander. He wasn't a Jew. I checked the rest of them. "All *not* Jews."

"The Genoans, then," Stephan said. "Casagrande's men."

"Yeah, best we quit this place," I said. "The sooner the better. Won't be beneficial to our long-term health to be here when he comes calling on his men."

"But who's he working for?" Stephan asked.

"That's the big question," I said. "The answer? Still don't know. Not for sure. He was putting pressure on Abe, though, to buy up his share of the Volkendorf debt. Abe says he was trawling the Quarter, buying it all up. Pennies on the pound. Amassing a negative fortune in Coldspire debt."

"So he's *not* working for the Jews?" Lady Mary asked.

"No. Not Abe, anyways," I said, "but there's the split in the Quarter. The hawks and the doves. Maybe Casagrande's working for the *Sicarii*? But why would he want the ledger?"

"He doesn't." Stephan shook his head. "Whoever he's working for wants it. Because it says something about *them*. Evidence. They want it destroyed."

"What the hell's in that God-damned thing, anyways?" I asked.

Stephan snapped it shut. "You're not going to believe it."

Chapter 47.

THE JEWISH QUARTER lay silent except for the pounding of the surf ten blocks to the north. It was a ghost town this late. This early. The air sat dead, heavy, the houses all dark, morose, gothic, looming up and over like slumbering beasts. They'd wake soon enough. Gaunt hadn't arrived, which was bad. But neither had Lord Raachwald.

The gates to the Quarter sat wide open, and the Lord Bishop's men were conspicuously absent. For the first time in the past week. So, the Lord Bishop had recalled them. When, though? And why? Or had His Eminence gotten wind of the invasion and was setting a trap? There were no soldiers nearby, so no trap, just an open invitation to slaughter. Maybe Lady Mary could convince the Lord Bishop to get the guards back? Them and the rest of his men.

I moved on into the Quarter but had no idea where Abraham was. I checked his house. The front door to his home was burst off its hinges, the dark inside so silent, so still, so pervasive, I could tell no one was within.

I checked anyways.

No one, nothing, but palpable darkness lay within.

I checked his money-house next. It sat right where I'd left it, the roof collapsed, the rest burned nearly to the ground, crumbling stone walls jagged, wood supports black and reaching, invisible but for the void of stars they cast upwards. I stared at the smoking remains.

Where the hell had he gone?

What the hell was he doing?

Had he been taken?

Had he lied to me? Was he actually *with* the *Sicarii*?

And if so, where? I checked the three addresses he'd given me. They didn't exist.

Shit.

I meandered through the streets, aimless, lost.

I could do a door-to-door search. Might only take me a month and a half, and that was if the *Sicarii* didn't kill me on first sight. Same thing for warning them. Would anyone listen to the half-mad ramblings of some haggard Christian fool traipsing around in the dead of night? They'd probably throw me into the asylum. I'd be sitting right there next to Chalstain's widow, mewling, drooling, weeping crimson tears. Besides, there were half a thousand houses in the quarter, not to mention temples, shops, money-houses, warehouses, a whorehouse—

I froze, nearly staggered, my mind working for once, finally, drawing lines, making intersections, connecting people, events, Chalstain's ledger. Then I tore off running.

...cut the legs out from under me. I possess no powers now, no influence, no place of refuge. I cannot fathom it...

—*Journal of Sir Myron Chalstain*

Chapter 48.

I COULD SMELL her from across the room. Drunk. Wasted. Slathered across a chair, the goddess of drek and Bacchanalian despair, all lolled out, a bottle poised in one hand, red-gold hair disheveled in twisted ringlets plastered across her face. An eye cracked open, and I swore I heard the sound of rusty hinges creaking.

"Hey." Her hair wafted up in front of her face as she spoke. She smeared it aside, her arm slapping like a dead eel back down onto the armrest. A table by her side was littered with bottles, some empty, some not.

"I told you not to come back here," I said.

She smirked, waved a hand, muttered something.

"You need to leave." I strode over, snagged a bottle, shook it. Empty. Shit. "Now."

She didn't move.

"Where's the boy?" I tried another. Empty, too.

"Who...?"

"Girard." I found one with some slosh, yanked the stopper. "He still here?"

"Our boy?"

"What?" I took a drink. It was wine, cheap wine, glorious wine, and it didn't stand a chance.

"*Our boy...*" She laughed without mirth. "You called him that when you...when you left last time."

"I suppose I did."

"Well, that was so much horseshit." Lorelai struggled up in her chair. "I knew it was horseshit when you said it. So did you." She pulled at the collar of her blouse. "It doesn't matter. He comes and goes. I haven't...haven't seen him much." She reached for another bottle, toppling

413

others over in the process. "Damn."

A crust of bread and some crumbs on a plate lay next to the bottle graveyard. "Who brought you the bread and the wine?"

"Sakes alive." She fumbled for a bottle, seized it, and hurled it. "Fuck you!"

I ducked it. Barely. "Been awake much?"

"I don't need advice from you."

"Fair enough, let's go." Tossing aside the bottle, I grabbed her by the arm, pulling her out of the chair.

She tore slithering from my grasp, staggered back, arms flailing, nearly falling. I caught her, steadied her. "Let. Me. Go." She jabbed an accusatory finger into my face. "You have no idea. Everyone…everyone dying. Sick. Everyone killing. Everyone dead." She sobbed into her hands as she melted to the floor. "Everyone."

"You're wrong."

"Just leave me alone. Ow!" she shrieked as I grabbed her by the elbow. "You're hurting me." Wildly, she cast a slap at my face, missing wide, drunk-wide. I let her go; she oozed bonelessly back to the sanctuary of her chair. "I know why you're here, so get on with it."

"Get up. Now. We're leaving."

She stuck out her tongue, the petulant child. "Fuck off."

I glanced up at the ceiling. Someone was upstairs. "Girard?" Dagger in hand, I stepped softly to the bottom of the stairwell. "That you?"

After a moment, a voice came from the top. "Sir…Sir Luther?"

"Yeah." I took a long breath; it was him. "It's me. Come on down here, kid."

Girard crept down the stairs like a deer setting hoof into an open field, wide-eyed, set to bolt.

"Get your things," I said. "You're leaving."

Girard's eyes went wide in question to Lorelai. "Where?"

"Don't listen to him." Lorelai flopped a hand.

"Listen to me, boy," I said softly. "I came to say goodbye."

"Fuck your goodbyes," Lorelai said.

"Apologies." I squared up on her. "I know it. I've never been any good with goodbyes. Or hellos. Hell, or with anything in between."

"He's come to kill me," Lorelai moaned.

"She's drunk," I said.

"Don't mean she's wrong," Girard whispered, half hid behind the banister.

I paused, straightened, nodded. "Yeah. It doesn't. But I'm not going to."

"How do I know that?"

"You don't. That's just how it works."

"Why's she think you're gonna kill her?" He pointed with his chin at Lorelai. "Huh? Why's she think that?"

"She thinks that because she betrayed me to some men who want me dead. She tried to set me up. Get me killed. Twice. She thinks that because she believes she knows me pretty well. And up until this moment, she didn't know if I knew. Isn't that right, Lorelai?"

"Don't leave," she pleaded to Girard.

"Know any good bolt-holes in your old neighborhood," I asked Girard. "Clean? Dry, preferably? Away from the Quarter? But close enough to stagger to?" I snatched another glance out the window. Still no soldiers marching up the road.

"I could find one," he said softly.

"Might be a tall order?" I said.

"I'll manage."

"Good. You're gonna take Lorelai to the nearest."

"Alright."

"Good. Go upstairs. Get your shit and get out. And don't ever come back here." Outside the back window, I could see the old Roman wall abutting the back of the house, separating it from the Quarter. Wouldn't pay to be this close. Not tonight. "Take the alley, not the street. Work your way west for four houses. Wait for us there." Girard stood perched at the bottom stair, his eyes flitting back and forth between me and Lorelai, questioning, hesitating, torn.

"Men are coming to burn the Quarter," I said. "They mean to kill everyone inside. And killing like that won't be contained by walls. It'll spill over. It'll drown you both in hellfire, or worse, if you stay. Go get your things. Please. And hers, too. And be quick."

"Fuck." Lorelai grabbed at the last stoppered bottle, missed twice, got a good hold. She worked the stopper free then huffed down deep into her chair, catching her breath. Then she took another drink.

"May I?" I snatched the bottle away. It was heavy, full.

She scowled up at me. "That's the last—"

I took a pull, wine sloshing out the sides of my mouth as I struggled to maintain, glugging it down, swallowing, guzzling, emptying it. "Ah…" Wiping my mouth, I pounded it back on the table. "You ready now?"

She snatched it, shook it, upended it. "You shit!" Lorelai struggled to pull herself from the chair. "Why'd you come?"

"You can read, yeah?" I nodded to myself. "Kept the books for your husband, maybe? I'd wondered about the Crowley Street note."

She recoiled. "You *are* going to kill me."

"Did you fuck Devon?"

"Who?"

"Come on, Lorelai. Devon. Ezekiel. Blackbeard. Whatever his name is. The man that came to kill me. The man you helped. The *Jew* you helped."

"Jealous?"

"No."

She shrugged, settled back. "It's what I do."

"You didn't tell me he was a Jew."

"I didn't know."

"How could you not?" I let it sink in. "You sold me out. They came to you, and they offered you coin. I won't ask how much. Don't know if I could take it. But you did."

She sat frozen as a spooked rabbit.

"Don't look down. Look at me." She did, glistening eyes quivering. "You'll find no monster. No Galahad. Just something bent and broken and in between. I don't blame you for taking their money. What am I to you? A mark. John. I know it. You owe me nothing." I raised a hand. "Maybe there was a moment where you weighed who I was against the coin. I can see that now, thinking back. You tried to tell me…" I ran a hand through my hair. "I don't know. I'm sure of which side the scales fell. Well, you were right. I am scum. I do deserve to die. Most men are and do, you look close enough."

"I didn't have a choice."

"No. You did. You always have a choice."

"I changed my mind." She sobbed. "In the end. I stayed with you, didn't I? I could have cut and run."

"Yeah." I nodded. "You could have. Would have been the smart move."

"Seems I never make the smart move."

"You and me both, lady."

Girard pounded down the stairs.

"Got what you need, lad?" I asked over my shoulder.

He nodded.

"Good. Here. Catch." I tossed him a sheathed dagger, and he caught it on the fly. "Smartly done, lad. You'll need to watch her. You up to it?"

Girard studied the dagger. "What are you going to do?"

"Go wait where I told you. Stay clear of the main roads."

He nodded but still didn't go.

"Go on," Lorelai hissed. "Get out of here. Piss off."

Girard looked me in the eye. "She gonna be alright?"

"I don't know," I said.

Girard nodded once then slid out the back door, closing it behind.

"You need to go," I said, "but first, I need to know about Blackbeard and his men. Jews. You knew, and when I asked, you said you didn't. Probably still riding the fence at that point, yeah? Didn't want to throw in with me all the way. But couldn't bring yourself to be party to murder. It was more than some might have done. But I need to know. And I need to know now."

"Know *what?*" she spat.

"Anything. Anything at all."

"No, I…nothing. We just drank and…"

"And they never said anything to you?"

"No. I wasn't a partner to them. I was just a thing." She closed her eyes. "I'm always just…"

"A place. A name. A business. An address. A building. Neighborhood. Anything?"

She shook her head.

I drew a dagger.

Her eyes widened, but she scoffed. "Do it then." She rose in her chair, chin up, defiant. "I'm ready. Been ready."

"I ain't gonna kill you, Lorelai."

She made to sit up, scream, but I covered her mouth, clamping a hand over it, forcing her sinking into her chair. "Him, though…?" I glanced to the door Girard had just exited.

She struggled.

I held her down. "You know I'd do it, yeah?"

Panicked, she blinked, said something, muffled, struggled, twitching a nod as tears coursed down her cheeks, my hand.

My dagger point rested just under her breastbone. "Tell me."

"I…" she swallowed, looked away, "one of them…give me a drink, please. I need a drink."

"One of them *what?*"

"One of them mentioned a…a temple. A warehouse."

"There are half a dozen temples in the Quarter.

Warehouses, too."

"They're both by the sea," she moaned. "Something about a wall, a temple wall falling in. Collapsing. And the sea reclaiming it. Flooded, I think. I don't know. That's all I know. I...I think they might have something to do with that. Some place where they go. And they said something about a *sick...sick*—"

"*Sicarii*," I said softly, rising, turning.

…money and power and the promises of fissure the landscape, but who is it that pulls the puppet's strings?

—Journal of Sir Myron Chalstain

Chapter 49.

I SLID BACK through the gates of the Quarter moments after I'd left Lorelai's. Still shy three heads. Still no guards manning the gates. Gaunt hadn't shown. Nor Lord Raachwald, thankfully. I stood there a moment, staring at row upon row of peaked edifices, shades trailing off toward the sea, everyone still sleeping, the iron and oak gates gaping wide.

Off to the south, caught on a fell wind, I could just hear the pounding of hooves on cobblestone. The march of footsteps. Far off. Just not far enough.

Shit.

I chose the door of the first house I could sprint to and started banging on it. Like a lunatic. It took a moment, but a man finally poked his head out a second-floor window.

"Is it a fire?" the man called.

"Soon enough."

"What are you saying, man?" He turned to someone unseen, "No love, just some madman. Now see here, I'll call the watch, you blackguard."

"Look. I'm a friend of Abraham Ben-Ari." Sort of. I raised my hands. "Lord Raachwald's coming to raze the Quarter. Tonight. Now. *Right now.* Listen, do you hear me?" The man sputtered. A second head appeared at the window, a woman. "Did you hear me? Lady? Lady, listen to me. The Lord Bishop's men are gone, and the gate lies open. Unmanned. And Lord Raachwald's coming. He's coming to raze your house, and he's going to do it with you in it. The same for all your family, your friends, everyone you know."

Both man and woman stared silent from the window.

"I have to go," I said. "I'm leaving it to you to warn

your people, yeah? YEAH?"

I didn't wait for an answer; I just tore off, vaulting down their steps and up the street, north along Lender's Row, running past silent monstrosities, toward the sound of waves pounding against the fallen walls of a dying temple.

* * * *

It was an ancient temple being consumed by the sea, gnawed inch by inch, stone by stone, year by year, by surf and by gale. The Temple of Moses. Once, it'd been a magnificent structure, one of the largest buildings in Asylum, barring the largest churches, but the sea had forced its way in, years, maybe decades ago, and the people had abandoned it. A series of walls, breakwaters, had been built out into the harbor to stave off the sea but had all failed, incrementally, beneath the pounding blows, the chew of salt and cold. Give anything enough time and it'll fail, the one certainty in this world.

Like some titanic leviathan beached on the shore, the temple sat, the collapsed northern wall yawning open, jagged like some tooth-filled grimace. The leviathan lay silent, unmoving but for the echo of waves reverberating deep within its maw. A slick of salt and rime whitened the precision-cut stone. Barnacles and dried sea foam. Clinging seaweed. Glistening slime.

I crept into the courtyard, toward the temple's front doors. Through a broken window, I caught a glimpse of a dim flicker within the inner sanctum but could make nothing out. I couldn't tell if the light were some torch flame quavering or some trick of the moonlight reflecting off water or glass.

Across a wide mall, waves rolling up halfway through it, lay the warehouse.

I'd check it after. If there was an after.

I circled west around the temple, sliding close along it, the loaded crossbow cradled in my arms as I ducked windows, starting at noises, making my way toward the fallen wall and the sea that had claimed it. Waves pounded on hewn stone, echoing, rebounding within, growing louder as I crept on. The leaded roof above was sagging, virtually unsupported, one haphazard pillar of disjointed stone reaching up, tenuous, but still touching.

I swallowed.

A mountain of rock and scree lay tumbled before me.

I slipped the bolt from the crossbow and discharged the string. Wouldn't do to shoot myself scaling the damned mound.

Around stone blocks as wide as I was tall, I clawed up the lower jaw of the leviathan, through jagged rubble teeth, all piled amidst the rolling waves, the sagging roof leering above. Achieving the summit, pressed into a crevice, I paused for a moment, listening to the waves boom, flinching at the cold spray of salt, reaching me even up here. Beneath it all, voices seemed to echo from within. Low. Furtive.

I poked my head up just enough.

Within the infinite black, I could make nothing out. Were the voices real? Imagined? Or just tricks of the dead air and space? But the cyclopean moon chose that moment to cut through cloud and for an instant shone brilliant, a caustic white glare illuminating the sea in a shimmer of molten silver shivering off into the infinity of the north. The blade of silver cut a swathe through the leviathan's maw. Three white faces glared up. Sucking in a hiss, I didn't move, didn't blink, didn't anything but pray I wasn't seen. The pale faces looked down again, the moonlight fading and dying as cloud churned past, the shroud of night settling once more.

I took a breath.

Staying low, trying not to offer my outline against the night sky, I scaled down the slope, slithering headfirst lizard-wise through crevices, squeezing beneath a felled obelisk, into the temple, the surf roiling below. At the bottom, a wide tidal pool lay between me and the sagging flagstone floor on the far side.

Leaning back against a jag of broken stone, I unslung the crossbow from my shoulder and placed it down between my legs. Setting the stock against my stomach and grimacing, I pulled the thick string back with two hands, wincing as I set it behind the catch.

The pound of waves and hiss of foam stifled any noises.

I hoped.

Placing a bolt between my teeth, I rolled over onto all fours, stifling a groan as I sunk my arm to the elbow in the brine, barnacles rough against my palm, cold biting to the quick, to the bone. A deep breath then before crawling on hand and knee into the pool, feeling the brush of spiny sea creatures with chitinous beaks and tentacled feelers palpating soft and wormlike past. The crossbow. I held it above the water, trying not to get the string wet, weaken its draw, doing my damnedest as waves rolled in through a channel, buffeting me from behind, the chop deadened by the stone but not killed outright. Grit and sand and sharp rock scoured past under hand and foot until replaced by the smooth ocean-washed stone of the rising floor.

Wincing at every wave, gasping at the merciless cold, breathless and shivering, I reached the far side, dragged my numb carcass up, out. Behind an ancient altar, I collapsed, rolled onto my back, stared up at the ceiling. I opened and closed my hands, trying to pump life back into them.

A soft orange light flickered in waving tendrils across the ceiling.

When I could feel my hands, I rolled over, crawled along the edge of the pool and slid behind a massive stone column.

I peered around.

Two men hunkered by a shielded fire, one warming his hands, rubbing them over the flames, the other pacing like a wolf. A third sat nearby on the floor, his head down. He was bound by ropes to a stone statue, manlike and tall, so tall its face was lost in shadow. Echoes of what Stephan had read to me tolled like a death knell in my mind. The bound man glanced up, staring in my direction, head wobbling. His face swollen, black and blue, Abraham glared at me, one eye a red slit which he surely could see nothing from.

On my knees, frozen, I held my breath until he lowered his gaze.

Of the other two, I recognized one, Pox, Blackbeard's swordsman. *Shit.* Blackbeard's very able swordsman. A bandage was wound around his head, a blade sheathed at his hip. The other man was armed, too, a wicked spear at his shoulder as he paced back and forth, up and down the room with a pronounced limp, his orange cloak rippling in spasmodic waves as he vaulted along like he had no joint in his right leg, no knee, but moving with precision, as though he'd been at it some time.

Pox knelt in close to Abraham, brandishing a lantern, laying one hand on the back of the old man's neck, talking close, familiar, gesticulating with his free hand. Shrugging, he pulled a blanket up over Abraham's shoulders, worrying it tight around his neck, tucking it in with care.

"You need not do this," Abraham said.

"We do, Rabbi," Pox said, his voice carrying, distorted. "Daniel's making the calls now, and he doesn't want you swaying the Masada."

"Boys," Abraham pleaded. "Don't do this."

"We aren't boys."

"But can you not see?" Abraham implored. "They must hear! They must heed. I warn you, this shall prove a black mark upon your soul. A holocaust is coming! I swear it."

"There's nothing to be done now, Rabbi. I'm sorry." Pox patted Abraham on the shoulder then turned back to the flames. "And I'm sorry about the ropes." Pox rubbed his hands over the heat of the flames. "Truly, I am."

Abraham lowered his head again.

Behind the column, I loaded the crossbow, took a deep breath, rose. I stepped around the monolith and into the light. The only of the three facing me, Abraham's eyes went wide an instant before I squeezed the trigger—"No!"

he screamed—as Pox whipped around, springing up from his crouch, blade already drawn. The bolt took him in the chest, burying itself deep, knocking him off his feet.

Instantly, the Limper turned, wide eyes blazing, spear leveled and charging, vaulting the fire. Sneering, I hurled the crossbow at him. The Limper parried it aside with the shaft of his spear, embers exploding as it landed within the flames. The Limper didn't break stride, lunging at me with a thrust to my chest—

"Krait!" Abraham screamed.

Pivoting from the spear's path, ripping my sword free, I caught the haft on my blade, binding onto it, steel biting into wood and forcing the spear-point down. Away. The Limper retreated a step, retracting his strike and thrusting again. But I held the bind, keeping my weapon to his, gauging without thought, slipping it past to the other side as I slid in, snaking a foot around his maimed leg and dropping my shoulder, staggering him back. Short-blading my sword and following, I threw a roundhouse punch, quillon leading, catching him in the face, punching teeth down his throat, rocking his head back, an arc of blood streaming.

I turned as Pox forced himself woodenly to his feet, using his blade for leverage, struggling, grimacing, grasping at the feathers sprouted in his chest. Pale, haggard, he spat a mouthful of blood as he trudged forward, his blade tip squealing across stone behind.

"Abe, tell him to stop," I said.

Abraham just stared, hang-jawed.

"Abe," I hissed, "tell him he's a dead man. Make it easy."

"Fuck." Pox stared down at his chest. "*Fuck!*" He collapsed to one knee, staring me in the eye, all hatred and wroth. Steadying himself with one hand, red drool dangling limp from his chin, eyes blazing with a dying light, he pushed to his feet again, sword raised, roaring an oath. Forward he staggered, a clockwork man driven by warped gears.

He made a cut—

I stepped forward and to an angle, dodging his clumsy swing and cut back-handed. A crippled shriek as he lurched, eyes open wide. The pristine weightlessness of my blade sliced through the cold air, a rooted strike, my hips driving the action, my shoulders squaring, arms like ropes, relaxed, their only purpose connection, my hands guiding, angling, levering forward at the last, edge whistling through Pox's neck as though it were nothing.

"What is it that you don't understand about, *thou shall not kill?*" Abraham fought against his bonds.

I shrugged, huffing, catching my breath as I peered around the silent temple. "Are there any more?"

"What...?" Abraham's eyes bulged. "Is *two* not enough? I've known those men since they were children. I stood for both of them at their bar-mitzvahs, watched them grow, become men. I guided them."

"And you did a real bang-up job, Abe."

"Make a joke, then," he spat. "That's all you're good for. Men lie dead, scattered like chaff, and you make jokes. Who'll laugh over your corpse, Krait?"

"Whoever's there, I'd hazard."

"Well, I'm sure there are more than a few with that thought in mind."

"Good. Let's talk more about them," I said. "Where are they right now?"

Abraham clamped shut.

"How about a touch of gratitude, yeah?" I asked.

"They were *not* going to kill me."

"Says you."

"They were merely holding me. Holding me prisoner for a time. And I didn't want to be set free. I just want to speak to the council. I can sway them." He recoiled in horror as I bent down, snatching up Pox's head by a fistful of hair. "What are you doing?"

I sauntered over to the Limper, knelt, placing Pox's head on the floor. I wiped my sword on the Limper's cloak then took it off him. I drew a dagger.

"Is...is he dead?" Abraham hissed. "Release me

and maybe—"

"These two were both *Sicarii*, yeah?"

Abraham looked away, swollen jaw clamped.

"Then you know what I'm doing." I went to work.

"Oh, my Lord," Abraham looked away.

When I'd completed my grisly task, I wrapped the two heads in the Limper's yellow cloak and stood, tucking the end of my makeshift bag through my belt. "A necessary price. And they *are* guilty of murder, I might add."

"Since when in your lexicon is armed men killing armed men murder?"

"How about the three children?"

Abraham grimaced. "They were not responsible for them."

"You lied to me once, Abe."

"They were not—"

"Then *who* was?" I cut him off.

Abraham glowered.

"Right," I spat. "What the hell's that mean, anyways? They weren't responsible? How do you know? You believe the men that beat you and tied you up are saints? That they have some sort of code? *Expedience*, that's their code. You know something? You were a man who spoke truth. Once upon a time, anyways. So what is the truth?"

"The truth shall be the death of us."

"Now there you go again, getting all cryptic. Care to expound?"

"You wouldn't—"

"Then tell me!"

Abraham froze, taken aback. "I'm talking about old magic, Krait. Older than Solomon, older than Moses. I'm talking of the magic of *shedim*, of the dark lady, of Lilith…" He closed his mouth, trembling.

"I'm here trying to save you and yours." I knelt in front of him. "So you owe me. Get it? You owe me a story. You owe me a head. You owe me, you owe me, you owe me." I patted the makeshift bag at my hip. "Here's the start. I'm looking for the finish."

"No," Abraham said. "Enough. Enough blood."

"It's never enough."

"Then take *my* head," Abraham pleaded. "Do it. Come on, brave knight. Do what you always do. What you're made to do."

"Fucking martyrs," I grumbled. "I'm done with you all. I'm not going to kill you, Abe. And it's not truth that's going to kill you. Hidden or otherwise. You were right, a holocaust is coming. And Lord Raachwald's bearing the torch. He's coming to burn, and he's coming to kill. And he's not going to stop til he's done."

"I'm surprised you're not riding with him."

"Now who's spouting jokes?" I shook my head. "No, wait. You're right. It'd be the smart move. But then, I don't usually go in for the smart move. But you know that already." I drew my blade, the same blade I'd used to cut off the Limper's head, the same blade I'd used to threaten Lorelai, the same blade I'd used to murder his son. "What's the last trait of an uncultivated person?"

Abraham recoiled, eyes locked on the blade.

"Not acknowledging truth when confronted by it," I said. "Raachwald's coming, Abe. Now, look into my eyes. You see any jokes? Any lies? Any schemes?"

"No," Abraham swallowed, "I see only death."

"Good." I slit his bonds, stood, yanked him to his feet. "Then you finally do see the truth."

I am being hunted…
—Journal of Sir Myron Chalstain

Chapter 50.

THE WAREHOUSE loomed above, squat, wide, immense. Left and right, its brick walls disappeared into oblivion. To the south beyond, a light was beginning to glow amidst the Quarter.

"Move." I shouldered past Abraham, pulling the ring of keys I'd snatched off Pox. The fourth key unlocked the door. It swung back to reveal nothing but impenetrable night, a yawning chasm thick with the scent of dried pine and ages-old dust, and something else. Decay. Death.

"I need to know what happened." I glanced sidelong. "I need to know about *it*."

Abraham sucked in a hiss. "*It?*"

"You're a shit liar, Abe," I said. "The stone-man, the *thing*. Whatever the hell it is your people set free. I need to know what it is."

Abraham stiffened.

"In." I shoved him through the door. "Your people. Your *Sicarii*. It was Chalstain who unraveled the threads. In his madness. My brother who wove it back together. The pieces of clay. The impossible injuries. The smashed portcullis and gates. Stephan told me what it was. I told him he was crazy, but…"

"Very well." Abraham beckoned, the darkness within cutting him in twain like some aspect of Hel. "This way."

"Yeah." I tailed him in, liquid abyss cloying like oil. I stifled a shudder. The sole comfort I could muster was my grip on my blade. Pox's lantern. The sound of the ocean muffled a few feet in and only the pounding shock of surf could be felt, softly beneath my feet, through aur, a rhythmic reverberation like the footsteps of some titan striding afar.

"Once there was a city." Abraham shuffled on

ahead through a corridor of stacked crates. "Forget its name. Its name is unimportant. Know only it is gone, its people scattered like ash to the four winds. In this city that is no more, there dwelt both Christian and Jew. The Jews were treated as most were treated, in that time as in this, which is to say poorly. The bad times began with drought and, as bad times are wont to do, began to fester."

We meandered through the labyrinth of crates, five, ten, twenty feet high, continuing on seemingly forever. Support columns rose amidst the twisting corridors like massive tree trunks in some dismal forest, canopies lost in the dead night above. Stagnant air pressed in, the reek of death growing stronger.

"With time, the drought became famine and Famine is never long without, for his two siblings Pestilence and Death invariably arrive soon after, each one exacting their pound of flesh."

"Thoughts turned ever to the why of it all, and for men of dark mind, and darker purpose, invariably came the *who*? Who has done this? Who has laid us so low? Who is responsible? And these men searched for a reason, and when they found none, they concocted one." Abraham took a deep breath, his shoulders rising, falling. "It is an old tale, a tale retold through the ages, a tale with only one conceivable conclusion."

Sweat beaded across my forehead as we stalked along like rats through a warren, scuttling through chases and corridors, past dead ends and *cul de sacs*, following along the path, turning and twisting onward through Hades.

"Except, that in this time, the conclusion was different." Abraham turned back, his eyes glimmering. "These Jews who owned no weapons, who had no training, and had not numbers, possessed but two things: faith and knowledge. Our faith was as solid as stone, our knowledge as ancient and deep as the sea. And these two things that we possessed had come together through the ages in the form of our stories, and a story can be a powerful thing."

He started back onward with a sigh. "One of those

stories was that of the golem, a thing shaped by man, formed of mud, of stone, of any unloving material. *Unloving?* Forgive me, I meant to say *unliving*." He waved a hand. "This thing, this golem, it was said man might breathe life into, through eldritch rite and ritual, a pale shadow of how Jehovah breathed life into man, but a life nonetheless."

I was breathing through my mouth now, the reek of death so strong.

"Intimately," Abraham continued, "one man knew of his people's history, the stories of the cities of Chelm and of Prague and of Slaughtertree, the story of Adam and of Lilith. This man, this one *foolish* man, thought he might..." Abraham cleared his throat. "You see, he possessed tomes no one else possessed, tomes that had been ancient when Cain wandered the wastelands of Nod, tomes entrusted to him from an infinite line of men, men of will, men of wisdom. Good men. And so this man, privy to this secret knowledge, sought to build a golem to save his people. You see, he believed himself one of these men of will and wisdom, one of these *good* men. Such thoughts did not afflict him long." Abraham trod on, picking his way past a stack of lumber, his breath coming in rasps. "*Hubris*, destructive pride, are you familiar with it?"

"My meat and potatoes, Abe."

"To build something whose sole purpose is destruction and yet believe it might be harnessed?" He rubbed the bridge of his nose. "The height of hubris. But this fool built it, nonetheless.

"In the beginning, this thing of destruction, this thing of stone, of clay, of sorrow and red ruin *could* be harnessed, *could* be directed, and it did destroy his enemies. A warrior beyond all measure, indestructible, unstoppable, a thing of the Old Testament." Abraham stepped into a wide-open area, free of boxes and crates, an area so wide I couldn't see the far side. "It annihilated the Christian folk, exterminating them, man, woman, and child." Abraham stood there in the pressing dark, sobbing gently. "But then it did not cease. For when it had destroyed *them*, it did the same to *us*."

"How did you stop it?"

Abraham looked away. "At great cost."

"Your arm?"

"*This?*" He held up his ruined stump. "This is nothing."

"And for all that, still you raised another."

"No." Abraham shook his head. "I possess many faults, Sir Luther, hubris being chief amongst them, but stupidity is not one. I vowed never again to raise another, and my vow remains intact."

"Then who?"

"I should have destroyed them." Abraham pursed his lips. "My tomes, you see? They had been entrusted to me long ago, and I should have, but I did not. Could not. Their historical value was beyond priceless, and so I kept them under lock and key, kept them secret, kept them safe." He sighed. "I had claimed before that I am not a stupid man, but I fear I must revisit that sentiment, for the height of stupidity is to allow oneself to befall the same troubles over and again. Hubris. Pride. Again." Head downcast, he nodded to himself, weeping and pointed up. "They were stolen."

"Mother of God..." A figure loomed above, a huge silhouette nigh on par with the dark, some twenty, twenty-five feet tall. An abomination of stone and rock metastasized into something only peripherally manlike. I saw why they had called it the monk. Its misshapen head was wide, angular, reminiscent of a monk's cowl, white eyes gleaming, caught in the lantern light, its shoulders nearly as wide as it was tall. Arms as thick as a horse's torso hung down, one huge hand on a ludicrously long arm stretched out across the floor. An immense version of the clay sculptures infesting Abraham's desk.

I stepped back.

"A monstrosity." Abraham nodded in confirmation.

It was not made entirely of clay, of stone. A circular shield lay plastered into its head, a sword, too, molded to its form, a monstrous riot of smooth and jag. Other shapes, only hinted at for the dark, cobbled together its repellent form.

The golem stared down at us dumbly when a voice barked out from beyond the circle of light. "Abraham!"

I drew my sword.

"These are the men you seek," Abraham said quietly.

"Lay your steel on the ground, you cunt." Another voice. Blackbeard.

Turning around, steel and flame in hand, squinting into the geometric shadows, I made out a gallery of silhouettes amongst the stacks.

"Ezekiel bade you lay your weapon on the ground," the speaker stepped into the circle of light, a dark blue cloak cast over his narrow shoulders, "and you have not." His arms were thin as the blade of his dagger, his nose hooked like an eagle's beak, beneath fierce eyes. "I advise you to do so."

"I'd appreciate knowing who I'm surrendering to."

"Forgive my rudeness." His empty hand went to his chest in mock apology. "My name is Daniel." He offered a nodded-semi bow, holding his hand out to the shadow gallery behind. "We are the *Sicarii*, as Abraham said." Seven men edged from the dark, Blackbeard at the fore, a crossbow cradled in his hands leveled my way. Bandages swathed his neck, his arm, parts of his face. His beard was singed clean away on half his chin, a haunted look in his eyes. The other six looked hunted, war-weary. One bled from the head. Another held his arm in a makeshift sling. Four crossbows stared me down straight.

"I came to warn you." I tossed my blade aside. "Lord Raachwald's planning a massacre. Tonight."

"You're too late." Daniel's eyes were dead as he spoke. I could tell that in his mind's eye he was watching me die. Wordlessly, Blackbeard stepped forward as another man emerged from behind, stripping me of the rest of my weapons, one by one, and finally the lantern. "The Cyclops has already taken the gates, the square. He burns his way north."

"Yet you're all here?" I said.

"Is the ledger on him?" Daniel asked.

"No." Blackbeard aimed the crossbow directly at my face. "Where?"

"Fuck off," I said.

Blackbeard glanced to Daniel, asking the question I didn't want answered.

"Abraham's had your ear." Daniel smacked the flat of his blade against his palm then pointed with it, a fox grin toothy behind the steel. He stepped up onto a crate. "And perhaps before tonight, he might have had mine. But not now, and not ever again."

A staircase of stacked boxes lead up to the golem's head.

"Tell me, Krait," Daniel asked, "are all your holy men lying hypocrites?"

"Mostly," I answered.

"And do you know how your *Men of God* treat us?" His footsteps echoed hollow, one by one, as he strode up the staircase. "We who garner their gold? Outstripped only by the amount of ill will garnered. Yes. We strip the populace of its coin, but on *his* behalf. The Lord Bishop. Yet it is *we* who are reviled."

"Good deal for him," I said.

"And do you know *why* your people hate us?" He had almost reached the top.

"My people never *need* a reason."

Blackbeard adjusted his grip on the crossbow. Swallowed. He stood just out of reach, eyes focused, unblinking, begging for the word, his fingers white, tense.

"Nice piece." I glanced at his crossbow. "Genoese?"

"Daniel…" Blackbeard warned. More men emerged from the darkness. Twelve now, at least. "Please."

"We've lost already, have we not?" Daniel stepped atop an obelisk of precariously stacked crate, the golem's monstrous head looming beyond. "Tell me some good might come of it, and I'll do as you ask. Will it change anything?"

Daniel held something white and square in his hand, a slip of folded parchment. "Will it?"

"No," Blackbeard barely choked out.

"Then vengeance is all we have left." Daniel laid an open hand upon the golem's forehead, "Open, *Mentsh*," and where there was no mouth before in the malformed expanse, a ragged crack appeared, stone rumbling as a jagged beak parted. "You must finish what was started."

"No!" Abraham lunged. "Look at it, just *look*!"

To the shoulder, Daniel reached his long arm into the jagged maw then withdrew it, his hand emerging empty. He placed a palm on the monstrous thing's dented forehead. "Close now, *Mentsh*, and go. Do your good work."

"Stop!" Abraham wailed as men wrestled him back. "Please!"

The golem turned, the sound of an earthquake, of millstones grinding, boulders cracking, shifting, splitting, and as it took one ponderous step then another, pebbles raining down, clattering, it clomped off, driven by powerful, stumpy legs. Each step boomed. A huge set of doors rolled open, sideways, parting the distant dark, followed by a fresh inrush of sea air, sea air tainted by the scream of woman and child, the roar of man, the score of steel on steel, the char of flame and burnt flesh.

Eyes wide, I pointed toward the golem, "No!" I screamed.

Blackbeard turned—and I bolted in the opposite direction.

"*Alive*!" Daniel screamed behind. "Heel the fucker alive!"

I darted back into the labyrinth. Crossbow bolts *thunked*, splintering wood as I tore left then right then left, slamming shoulder first into wood, trip-trampling over falling boxes as boots clomped after.

"Krait!" Blackbeard roared.

Engulfed by the maze, I hurtled on, blind, hauling through passages, past crates piled twice as high as I was tall. I kept running. My only reference point came from behind, the stomp of feet and grunt of men running, tripping, slamming into thin-shelled wood.

The warehouse was endless.

Blackbeard's voice boomed. Barking orders. They were to either side of me, gaining, outstripping me in parallel passages, a half moon, calling out, herding me on like some questing beast as I tripped, got up, stumbled along.

I rounded a turn and froze. Shit. A dead end of timber stacked ten-feet high blocked my path. The briefest of pauses, then I was moving again. Up. I leapt, latching on with fingertips, nails ripping, splinters biting as I scrambled up. Reaching the top in spastic disorder, I could just make out the far side of the warehouse, the double doors twenty-feet high, as the golem ducked out ponderously.

"Shut the bloody doors!" Blackbeard roared somewhere behind.

I leapt from one crate to another, nimble as a drunk bear, careening over a four-foot path ten feet below then scrambled up another five and down the other side, freezing as someone glared up from below.

"He's here!" he screamed.

I kicked a box down into his face.

Blackbeard was invisible off toward the double doors, calling out his men. In the half-glow of hidden lanterns, the maze was illuminated from below, the hell city of Dis, chock full of ranting devils.

The massive cargo doors began rumbling shut.

But I wasn't headed that way.

I hopped another chasm and continued on. The door we'd entered was near. A slight breeze blew in offering me strength. Hope. I hopped another chasm. Close. Closer.

I was two chasms from the door, in midair, when a bone-crushing vise cinched round my ankle. I grunted, snatched a glimpse of a black beard followed by the glimmer of steel as I fell head over heels, slamming upside down, back first, into a crate wall, splintering it before landing face-first amid an avalanche of falling goods.

...I can sense it. I have snatched glimpses of it. It is no man.

—*Journal of Sir Myron Chalstain*

Chapter 51.

COLD. FREEZING. I came to, bound to a great stone jutting up from the rocky shore, lodged not far from the break of the open ocean. Harsh hemp rope bit into my wrists, my ankles, my chest. An orange glow lit the horizon, outlined by building silhouettes.

The Quarter was burning.

In the distance, carried on fell winds, came the shouts of men, the clash of steel, the clomp of hooves. Ash fell like snow, wafting, whirling like dust devils. The night sky thundered with cannon fire, reverberating waves of sound slamming into me, over me, through me. Pebbles danced. I turned my head, the ropes rasping. Daniel sat on an ancient piling, his eyes wide, visage haggard as he sharpened his long knife in measured strokes.

"What's happened?" I asked, my head pounding.

"The *Sicarii* ambushed Raachwald." Abraham sat slumped on a rock by the rolling surf. "Near the square. They are fighting, and they are losing."

Daniel turned, cold embers in his eyes flaring to fire.

"Where's the golem?" I asked.

"It is no golem, it is a *shedim*." Abraham glared at Daniel. "A thing of darkness, a demon, and it has gone mad."

Daniel stopped sharpening. "I control it yet."

"Where it is?" I asked.

"I sent it on an errand to fetch His Eminence." Daniel pointed with his dagger off to the southwest, a horrid grin stretching across his face. "A first of many tasks tonight."

"What?" Abraham's jaw dropped. "You'd kill the one man who keeps the wolves at bay?"

"Wolves at bay? Even now as a holocaust rages? Are

you blind? Deaf?"

"And who is it that shall step into his shoes?" Abraham hissed. "Raachwald? Someone worse? The devil you know, Daniel. Have you heard the expression? Do you not ken its meaning?"

Daniel shook his head slowly, disgust contorting his visage.

"You're a fool," Abraham sneered.

"I've done nothing you've not, so spare me your words, old man."

"You've killed us all."

"Coward."

"So we're all up shit's creek, yeah?" I said.

Blade gripped shaking in his fist, murder in his eyes, Daniel strode forth. Grit and sand crunched underfoot.

"Do not kill him." Abraham stepped in his path.

"Why?" Daniel spat. "The man's trash. Offal. Nothing."

"I beg you not to kill him for what it shall do to you, not him," Abraham said.

"Thanks, Abe," I muttered.

"You're no murderer," Abraham pleaded, clutching at Daniel's shoulder. "You were supposed to learn from my mistakes. You were supposed to be better than me. Please."

"Unhand me, Abraham," Daniel said.

"Do not call me that." Abraham clutched tighter.

"It's your name."

"I am your father." Abraham straightened, rising, eye to eye with his son. "And I know my own son. He is still in there. Somewhere. Thick-headed and mule-stubborn as always, but he is in there. He can hear me, I know it, and he will do the right thing, in the end, in the now, *you* will do the right thing."

Daniel lowered his blade, staring out over the flames leaping across rooftops. "And what is the right thing, *father*? Fight and we die. And if we don't? What difference is there?"

"I…I don't know anymore, son." Abraham

nodded toward me. "But not this, never this."

"*You* don't know?" Daniel sneered, incredulous. "And yet here you stand offering counsel? Bah!" He tore free from his father's clutch. "Counsel from a man who consorts with the murderer of his own son? I can't understand you. I won't." His teeth gleamed. "Think of Isaac. No. Don't look away. Think of him cold and alone in that box in the ground." Abraham was weeping. "Now look at Krait and tell me he doesn't deserve death." He brandished the blade. "Tell me in your heart you believe that."

Abraham fell to his knees. "No…"

"Hey, shithead," I craned my neck, "you're the one that pushed Isaac out the fucking window. Then you blame the ground for the bloody result? Well, I was the fucking ground. I admit that, and I regret it. But I didn't know who he was. You did. You're the one who sent him to his death."

"Fifteen years old." Daniel fingered his blade, testing its edge.

"I'm sorry, Abe." I strained to look. "I know that's shit. So let me do something to balance the scales. Let me go. I'll bring the heads to Raachwald. I'll finish the deal."

"Shut your filthy trap," Daniel rasped.

"There's a chance—"

"You think Raachwald will just call off his attack?" Daniel asked. "Just turn around? Leave? Order the fire to cease its burn?"

"He promised." I knew how empty those words sounded even as they came out. "His keep is called Old—"

"No. His keep is called Coldspire, and he has won his game," Daniel nodded to himself as though coming to some decision, "or so he believes."

"Isn't it worth a chance?" I cried. "However small?"

"One thing is certain." He loomed over me. "No matter what happens, you will not walk out of here alive. I want you to see the hell you've wrought before you die."

"The Quarter's burning down around you. Your family's out there somewhere in the cold dark night and the only thing that's going to warm them's the firestorm." I shook my head. "And you're here wasting vengeance on me?"

"Truth be told, killing you won't garner much." Daniel knelt by my side. "It won't bring Isaac back. It won't balance the horror of tonight. And as far as the ledger?" He shrugged. "A small matter now. But it will be a reckoning, of sorts. The life of one *murderer* to balance that of my brother."

"Murderer? Take a look in a mirror, you skinny little shit."

Daniel frowned. Retracted. He didn't like being called a murderer.

"You hold me responsible for your brother's death?" I asked. "I'm as responsible as you are for the Volkendorfs."

"No," Daniel said, "there's no comparison. We put down a rabid beast. A rabid beast who was a scourge to our people. You—"

"You had more than one put down if I remember correctly."

"They've been killing Jews for decades, centuries, eons," Daniel spat. "Murder. Genocide. And Volkendorf was plotting, did they not tell you that? It was time to fight back. High time." He laid the blade across my throat. "Something…something had to be done."

"And you murdered children in the process?" I swallowed.

"Bite your tongue. You're the only child murderer here."

"I know three ghosts who might tell different."

"Bah! Raachwald slew them."

"His own son?" I challenged.

"The boy was a bastard, and a man such as he could hold such a creature only in contempt."

"You know that for a fact?" I asked. "Cause I know for a fact that Raachwald didn't. I read Chalstain's ledger."

Daniel waved a hand. "One of his hirelings, then."

"No."

"You're a liar," he seethed.

"Yeah."

"The golem did not kill them. I did not kill them."

"Someone did, though," I said, thinking, trying to work it out. "Someone who knew the golem was going to attack. Someone who knew your plan. *Who* was it?"

Daniel paused, the blade still resting against my throat, his eyes growing wide with recognition, wider with realization.

"There it is," I said. "You know who it was, now, don't you?" I turned to Abraham. "Gears are turning. A second murderer. That very night? Amidst the storm? How could he get onto the island? How did he know?" I swallowed. "Because he'd been dealing with you, Daniel. He knew the golem was attacking that night because you told him. He trailed it in and committed the murders after it attacked. Hell, maybe during. And he left two clues afterward. One pointing at you and yours, the other at Raachwald. He fucked you over."

Daniel's lip curled back.

"Please, let him go, Daniel," Abraham pleaded.

Daniel cocked his head in question, birdlike, as though he didn't quite understand what had been said. "What kind of man are you, father?"

"You're no murderer," Abraham pleaded.

"I am tonight."

I could feel his hand quivering through the blade, the near nothingness of the edge biting at my Adam's apple.

"He could help us," Abraham begged.

"No. And even if he could, I would not have it. I'd rather we were all dead. All of us."

"Who else knew of the golem?" I hissed. "Who is this man to take the Lord Bishop's place? The one who knew? The one directing Alonzo Casagrande? Who bade you murder Chalstain? It's him, don't you see? He's *not* your ally."

"True, Krait," Daniel said as he leaned close, "but then, neither are you."

Chapter 52.

THE BLADE RESTED against my Adam's apple. I could just barely feel it, so thin and sharp, almost nothing, biting into my flesh without any pressure, holding itself there seemingly of its own accord. Then Daniel's hand tensed. I closed my eyes, inhaling reflexively, waiting for it, the quick nick, the rip, slicing me open like a slaughtered pig, spilling me across sand and stone. The surf slammed the shore, rhythmic, regular. I waited, breath held, thinking of my wife, my sons, my choices, a fucking cliché.

And nothing happened.

I cracked an eyelid.

I'd thought it the pounding of the surf, the quiver of the ground transmitted through the rock and into my back, but it wasn't. It was footsteps. Giant footsteps. *Its* footsteps.

Daniel gawked up as the stones around shivered into a dance. "What…?"

Amid the thuds of stone on stone and wave pounding against rock, there was something else. Screams. Muted. Muffled. A cacophony of weeping song, a dirge of pain, of agony, of terror, all crying, all broken, all mindless.

It was awful, a new kind of awful.

Thoom… Thoom… Thoom…

The golem came, a titan of scripture old, twice as tall as it had been in the warehouse, at least. It lumbered past the fallen temple, gripping a cornice with a great three-fingered hand, crushing stone, sending an avalanche tumbling to the earth. The roof and walls of the ancient edifice's leviathan maw bit downward, groaning, failing, devouring itself. The golem slathered its fistful of rock across a gaping chasm in its chest, filling it.

Daniel staggered back. "Father…"

"Madness…" Abraham gibbered.

"You're not wrong," I murmured.

Malice poured off the golem in a choking fume. One of its eyes was a white skull, the other twinkling cold as a dead star. It glared down. Something about it was different and *worse*, infinitely so, and not only for being bigger. It strode on like some warped, crippled thing, its long arm scraping along the ground behind like some misshapen tail. The screams grew louder as light from the burning city caught it, and I wished again for the darkness.

"What have you done?" Abraham gasped.

The golem's surface, its skin, cracked and uneven, protruded at angles not fit to describe. Smoking debris, the hafts and blades of weapons jagged out like hellish quills amid patches of steel and stone, and amidst this riot hung bodies. Man. Woman. Child. Appendages stripped of flesh, burnt black, dangled limp. Others, slathered bodily in, plastered whole, still moved, fingers twitching, hands grasping. Riddled flesh twitched feebly. Faces frozen mid-scream peered out from its arms, its legs, its chest. Mouths gaped fishlike, struggling for breath, emitting warbled moans, a sound I'd never heard before and hoped never to again.

The demon, for Abraham had been correct, it was no golem anymore, lifted its massive arm and within its grasp, against the night sky, hanged a man by a single leg. The glint of his eyes caught the light. His thin arms clawed meekly, in futility, pawing at empty air. Alive. Still. Then the demon slammed him down onto the rocky shore, smacking him flat as a dead mackerel.

"The Lord Bishop?" Abraham muttered.

Dust settled. His Eminence Judas Peter's once immaculate robe of office was soiled brown and black and red. It was torn, ripped, fouled. His palsied hand twitched on the ground like a white spider, tremulous, followed by his shivered whimper.

"*Jesus Christ*," I whispered as the demon stepped forward without hesitation, no moment of pause, of poise, of impending doom, and crushed the Lord Bishop. It laid its entire weight into him, twisting its elephantine foot the way a man might smother the dying embers of a campfire. The Lord Bishop's decrepit form resisted for not even the whisper of an instant but it seemed somehow longer. His brittle bones popped and crackled like flames as he squealed, so high-pitched, so intense it snuffed out instantaneously.

"*Jesus... Fucking... Christ!*" I writhed against my bonds.

"You must destroy it," Abraham muttered.

"I..." Daniel gasped, turning to the sea.

The demon snatched Daniel up quicker than it ought to have been able, engulfing him in stone and clay and grasping flesh. His bones crunched audibly amidst his screams. His blade, twinkling in the moonlight, fell like a star as the nightmare smashed him into itself, smearing his carcass across its chest, slathering him into itself, into nothingness.

"*Abe,*" I hissed.

Abraham collapsed to his knees.

"*Abe!*" I roared. "Grab the fucking dagger!"

Abraham blinked down, casting his numb gaze about like maybe he'd dropped something.

"By your left foot!"

Abe nodded dumbly, stooped, picked it up, looking at it as though he had no conceivable idea of what it was or how to work it.

"Cut the fucking ropes!" I hissed, spit flying, as the monstrosity turned, eclipsing everything behind. Crushed faces stared down as the ropes began to fall, Abraham sawing furiously, pulling, weeping, muttering in tongues.

"Hurry!" I whined, practically leaping from the stone as the demon trod toward us, its nubby head glaring, skull eye tracking us as I nearly tore Abraham's remaining arm from its socket dragging him along. "Come on!"

"No!" Digging in his heels, Abraham tore from my grasp, turning toward the monstrosity, the tidal wave of cemetery dirt and stone, of bone and corpse, of drek and ruin.

"Run!" I yelled.

"No," Abraham said calmly, his son's blade dropping from his nerveless palm, clattering to the rocky shore as he stepped away from me, toward it, waving his lone arm. "Save them, Krait."

My own brother hath betrayed me...

—Journal of Sir Myron Chalstain

Chapter 53.

I BOLTED WILD round the corner of the warehouse, tripping, righting myself, skidding to a halt. A horse reared, whinnying, screaming in terror, its hooves flecking mud past my face.

"Whoa!" roared the knight astride it, his arms flailing then clutching, crushing his steed's neck. As twin hooves crashed down, sparking across stone, the knight lost his seat, flying head over heels as his squad of crossbowmen dove aside.

Grunting, mad-eyed, I dropped my shoulder and bulled through them, hurtling bodies, splitting the sea of yellow-tabarded crossbowmen. I might have felt the barbs of steel bolts sprouting in my back had the demon not clambered around the warehouse—through the warehouse—in that very instant. My blessed savior. Fists swinging like wrecking mauls, hacking through stone, smashing brick and mortar, rock tumbling after it in an avalanche, the screams of the squad joined those of the damned as they threw down their weapons and scattered.

Only the terror-driven steed possessed the speed and wherewithal to match my cowardice, the horse galloping hard, gaining, hooves clobbering behind as I sprinted south toward the orange gleam. From the corner of my eye, the horse drew even, outstripping me. I snatched onto its saddle with one hand, hopping, fighting to maintain grip as it poured on, nearly dislocating my shoulder as I made a leap of faith, of hope, of blind desperation, dodging steel-shod hooves, landing arse-up halfway across the saddle. The horse kept on galloping. I dared not glance behind, nor forward, just clung there fighting, cursing, to slide one foot to a stirrup, somehow finally managing it, then levering up, kicking my other over, gaining my seat, grabbing the saddle, reaching for the whipping reins. I snatched them and risked a glance behind.

The demon clambered on, slamming into a house, collapsing it into ruin as it hounded me from the cold dark of the shore and into the unholy conflagrations of hell. Men screamed as the demon trod on them, over them, through them. I yanked the reins, shouting, forcing the horse down another street, a tighter one, then took a left and continued on, hoping to shake the monstrosity. A gout of flame roared across our path, bursting from a burning house, rolling over us as we pounded on.

Flames leapt from roof to roof, holocaust claws rending the sky, caustic wind howling like fiends, burning my flesh like dragon's breath.

Hooves clomped like the beat of a hundred drums. Choking spume churned through the cramped road, wave after wave, clear as mid-day one instant then gone the next. Nothing but smoke and char coating my tongue, my throat. Hacking, coughing, retching, I tore on the reins, forcing the horse down a dark alleyway and out onto Temple Street.

"Shit!"

Bolts zipped through the air, a swarm of wasps stinging past.

We tore on south towards the clamor of battle, waves of concussive heat slamming us. Bands of warriors, killers, madmen, roamed the streets. Armed men. Fleeing men. Fighting men. Women and children limped along in huddled clusters, lost, eyes wide with fear at the pound of hooves, the clash of steel, the cacophony of chaos and murder.

My world was blinks of the eye. Glimpses. Impressions. I tore past Blackbeard, axe gleaming in hand as he stood with his back to a burning alleyway, fighting off the concerted attacks of three of Lord Raachwald's warriors.

White tabards blackened by soot and blood and holy cruciform came next, a squad of Gaunt's men-at-arms, God's monsters, axe or mace or maul in hand, shields and weapons swinging, hacking, them all silent but for one, helmetless, spouting orders, pointing, driving before him another troop of yellow-tabarded crossbowmen, all scattering, stumbling in disarray, some fifteen men and less by the step, a wake of limb and corpse breadcrumb-trailing through the nightmare.

My horse leapt the trail pretty as a picture.

I didn't look back.

Alonzo Casagrande, tabarded in yellow, lay around the next bend, small, quick, a long thin dago-blade, little more than a spike, dripping in his fist, a mad gleam in his eye as he thrust it into the eye socket of some poor struggling sod. The blade slid twisting in slowly, almost gently, disappearing in its entirety, a grand finale, a mad magician's baleful prestige. Casagrande giggled impishly as the man fell limp, weeping tears of blood. His eyes aglow, Casagrande rose and tipped an imaginary cap as I blazed past.

His men aimed their crossbows—

I crouched against my steed's neck as a shower of bolts zipped past, around, one striking me like a fist to the kidney. The horse screamed—awful—bolts *thunking* into its haunches and neck, but it fought on, foaming mad. Rounding a corner, I was nearly thrown, my legs and arms clutching, burning, the horse screaming, the conflagrated building before me spouting smoke and flame, erupting into a hail of brick and mortar. Like some Hadean birth, the demon ripped through it, emerging as though from some rock womb, a massive three-fingered hand clawing free of its stone caul, all aflame as the monstrosity stumbled and slammed shoulder-first into the money-house across the street.

It rose, righted itself, turned.

Galloping, I stared back in awe, terror, horror.

Casagrande and half of his squad bolted, the other half obliterated beneath the crush of avalanche. The demon reached out, hellfire raging across it, brickwork and mortar, flaming detritus of lumber and corpse clinging to it, becoming it.

Over a pile of bodies stacked five high, we leapt,

pouring into the Quarter's open square and skidding to a halt. "Jesus Christ."

The whole world was aflame, buildings, edifices lining the square, all blazing. Salvation lay only through the gates to the south, a horde of folk fighting mad to escape.

"Kill him!" Lord Taschgart roared, perched atop a toppled monument, pointing at me. His sky blue eyes riveted onto me until he looked beyond, dropping his sword. "Mother of God…"

The demon trudged into the square. Its gaze met Lord Taschgart's. He broke and ran.

I didn't blame him.

"Yah!" I whipped the reins, kicked the horse's flanks.

It was Gaunt I glimpsed next, one man amongst many, against many. Surrounded by Raachwald men, Brulerin men, Taschgart men, he towered above them, standing alone, a huge war-mace gripped two-fisted swinging. He roared. He challenged. Men of the Isle fell with each swing, shorn of life and limb. They pressed around him then froze, gawking north as a peal split the air. It was Lord Taschgart, screaming, caught up in a smoldering three-fingered death-grip, crushed writhing, burning alive, dying, then suddenly not.

Gaunt stood alone then. His foes as one fled before him, scrambling over one another, trampling comrade and brother.

Gaunt did not flee.

He tore his ruined helm free and cast it aside.

I pounded toward him as he marched toward me— no, not toward me, toward *it*. Heaving that horrid mace to his shoulder, he strode forth, eyes shimmering aglow, a glow of madness-born war-lust, a light of desperation, of insane glee, of messianic consummation, his voice booming hollow like some forlorn god of war extolling the onrush of swift death. "Yes!" he roared. "*YES!*"

Like a dagger-thrust to the heart, my steed plunged into the packed crowd, hammering aside bodies and running them down. Some dove aside, some stumbled, some didn't as we pounded into them, over them, through them, crushing limb and body, bounding over wagon and corpse. I smashed heels to flanks, screaming my bloody head off and snapping the reins until snorting red foam poured from my steed's nostrils and the bastard just fucking died beneath me, collapsing to a bloody mess and flipping me face-first across the street.

A forest of legs slashed past, bodies falling, flailing, feet kicking, stomping. I caught the blank stare of a little girl dragged past, drained hollow by terror, a ragged doll of bound cloth hugged in her arms, stuffing leaching out through its belly like entrails. And all throughout, gargantuan footsteps shook the earth behind.

…and so bereft of refuge I wander the city an outlaw…

—Journal of Sir Myron Chalstain

Chapter 54.

KNIFING MY WAY through gaps and holes in the throng, forcing myself forward, I fought on through, sliding, swearing, slashing my way south. Always south. The gates rose ahead, but the space between lay glutted by riot.

"Move, you fuckers!" I screamed.

A body slammed into me, spinning me round.

The song of steel rang out as someone unsheathed a sword. I saw the tabard of a red fox on orange. He slammed me aside with his shield, and I stumbled, arms wheeling, caught another same tabard then two more, side by side, a wedged phalanx moving with the crowd, no, *through* the crowd. I shoved bodies aside, hurling them, smashing them and dove in behind the phalanx, joining it, clamping a hand on the rotund bloke's shoulder in its midst. I screamed in his ear and drew his own dagger from its scabbard, and held its point to his flank.

"Are you fucking kidding me?" Lord Hochmund's eyes nearly burst in disbelief. "You'd be doing me a favor!" His voice was lost below the dirge of collective terror. "Put your backs into it!" Lord Hochmund dropped his shoulder into Captain Abel's back and shoved onward like the Greek hoplites of old. "*PUSH!*"

I dropped his dagger and followed suit.

Lord Hochmund grunted then snarled and pushed, and we were through the gates and out of the Quarter. The press lessened, liquid for a few blocks, then re-solidified, the phalanx stopping dead. Underfoot was paved in corpse, each step a snapping pop as bone broke.

The North Bridge rose before us.

"Are you fuckers daft?" Spittle flew from Lord Hochmund's mouth. "We've one shot at this!" He dropped his shoulder, bulling on to no effect. The bridge was jammed solid with bodies. The far side of the river, the western half of the city, was burning, flames licking the night sky. "Push your fuckers!" Saint Hagan's was burning, *so* was the bridge. "Push, you dandies!"

"The bridge is on fire!" I pointed.

Lord Hochmund swore, "South, then!" as he grabbed Captain Abel. "Make for the Isle!"

A sudden crack, like lightning, split the night. I glanced back at the shades behind, lost in the crush of body and blind animal panic. The hellfire demon crashed through the gates, the ground trembling, embers glowing, swirling like snowflakes amidst a storm. They swept up into the sky orange and yellow and red as it strode, its eyes the sole thing not engulfed in flame, nothing now but twin holes of stark emptiness bored straight through its core of ash.

The press of bodies, frozen, fractured, fissured, let loose.

"Move!" Lord Hochmund bulled onward.

"Push!" I wailed.

Captain Abel tripped ahead. I caught him, somehow, dragging him along and hauling him back up to his feet, barely, as I took the fore.

Mummer's Isle rose like a fist in the glimmer of hellfire burning. Bodies glommed in, crushing us, hurtling us onward. One of the shield men disappeared. Lord Hochmund's big head smashed me in the chin, and I nearly bit off my tongue as I stiff-armed him back. Another guard disappeared, trampled, cut off, I don't know.

We scrambled along the Morgrave within a river ourselves, a river of flesh, a river of screams, a river of sorrow, three lost amidst many, flotsam borne along the mad current, swept along, pushing, running, staggering—I couldn't say which.

Then the Brulerin Bridge rose ahead, Mummer's Isle across it, and high atop its cliffs another battle raged.

...snatching fitful sleep where I may. I dine upon scraps, refuse, Saints preserve me, I've dined upon...

—Journal of Sir Myron Chalstain

Chapter 55.

ACROSS THE BRIDGE, atop Mummer's Isle, men of the church fought men of the Isle, a riot of close combat, of murder, scattered across the wandering cliff trail up. Blades sang. Bodies rained like hail, arms flailing, plummeting, screaming like sheep as they caterwauled off the footpath, smashing into stone below.

I forced my way across the bridge amid the crushing hail of flesh and iron. There was nowhere else to go. Hundreds surged along with me.

"Shatter them!" Lord Raachwald roared above, his fell voice carrying. Steel clashed against steel. He and the Isle men fought up the trail, held at the summit by the men of the church. Swarms of bolts rained down.

Lord Raachwald forged through the clamor, cutting down men, tireless, emotionless, a cold-blooded killing machine. Weapons glanced off as he strode forth seemingly invincible, ducking blows, shunting them off with a raise of his iron gauntlets. Through the riot of bodies, he strode purposeful, raising Yolanda, stabbing her through the neck of some soldier, beheading another. He turned matter-of-factly, pointing, ordering his men. Men tabarded in every Isle color jumped to his command, surging onward, suicidal, upward.

A wave of heat struck as I set foot on the path. Behind, someone had fired the bridge. Refugee and soldier alike fought up the trail, I amongst them.

Halfway up, I turned. "Jesus Christ…"

A riot of cries pierced the air from below, the sound of a thousand harpies' keens. Trapped between the rampaging demon and the burning bridge, the tide of bodies below, inhuman silhouettes against the blare of raging flame, surged forth, lurching toward the bridge, the chasm. Driven forth, the herd stormed *en masse* over the parapet, arms and legs flailing, the inhuman shades reclaiming their humanity in that last instant, their faces illuminated by hellfire as they poured over into infinity.

"Move it, Krait!" Lord Hochmund and Captain Abel shouldered past me.

I gave chase, stumbling to the summit. Church and Isle men lay in a corpse tangle across the flat cliff top.

Azure-Mist, the Brulerin keep, rose before me, and before it stood two lines of some fifty-odd men, all Isle men, grim silent men, colors mangled together, longbows and crossbows in hand, the fear of God in their eyes.

I swallowed.

City folk tore haphazard past through the lines. Lord Raachwald stood before the Isle Men, the wind blowing his white hair, madness in his eye. "*Release!*"

I ducked reflexively as twenty-five archers unleashed steel-tipped missiles screaming through the night. Their feathers singed across my upraised arm. Not a single missile missed its mark and not a single one made a shit's worth of difference.

The demon strode on.

"Second line, ready!" Lord Raachwald roared. "Aim!"

The second squad, tabarded in Raachwald green, stepped forth.

"*Release!*" Lord Raachwald glared down. "First line!"

For an instant, the demon paused before the burning bridge, as though considering, then stepped upon it, an instantaneous squeal of protest quivering into abject failure. The burning bridge crumbled as though constructed of bird bones. The demon plummeted into the abyss, disappearing below, the world beneath shuddering, quaking, followed by the hiss of some titanic serpent as the demon's fire quenched. An impenetrable mist billowed up, suffused beneath by an orange glow.

Men and women cried out.

"Make ready, you fuckers!" Lord Raachwald roared. "Anything in your life ever been that easy?" His gaze locked onto me as he spoke, lit by an unholy glow. Haefgrim and the Grinner slunk out of the gathering mist, marshalling at Lord Raachwald's shoulder.

I turned to run, froze. Shit. Run where? People continued spilling up the trail, scrabbling, falling, kissing the ground.

"Heel him," Lord Raachwald rasped.

His two lieutenants started toward me.

"I think you've bigger fish to fry." I nodded at the glowing mist rising.

Haefgrim stepped forward and belted me in the jaw, dropping me to my knees.

"Lord Hochmund," Lord Raachwald said, "many thanks."

Dazed, drooling, I glanced at Lord Hochmund, his eyes wide, a deer staring down the business end of a bolt, and for the sliver of an instant, he begged my forgiveness. Then he blinked, and it was gone, his mask back up. "A pleasure, my lord."

"I know who killed your son," I grunted from on all fours.

"Haefgrim..." Lord Raachwald blew snot out one nostril.

Haefgrim kicked me in the ribs.

Sputtering. Gravel in my mouth, my ears rang.

"Across that rock," Lord Raachwald ordered.

I fought to stand, to fight, to struggle, but my arms weren't working, legs either, as Haefgrim snatched me by a fistful of hair and dragged me kicking to the cliff side. He lifted me bodily, and for a moment, I thought he was going to hurl me into infinity. Instead, he slammed me chest first onto a rock jutting up at the precipice. A rib cracked, my knees screamed. He snatched one of my arms, twisting it up, back, behind, a sliver shy of snapping. "Slade," Lord Raachwald commanded. The Grinner oozed in, grabbing my other arm, torqueing it out wide.

"Fuck!"

Lord Raachwald drew that black axe from his belt, its beard pronounced, sharpened at the fore and back of the blade, made for chopping in and prying back, cutting through bone.

"I found the killers." I tongued gravel from my mouth. "There was more than one!"

Lord Raachwald loomed over me. The cold steel beard of his axe slid into the collar of my mail shirt, snaking in cold as an eel, then ripped back, up, popping riveted links. Again, ripping back and up, cutting a metal gash down my back, chain links ringing, singing out in a soft sorrow dirge across stone. The Grinner and Haefgrim gripped my slit mail and tore either half outward, rasping across my back.

Gasping at the cold, I stared into the chasm, waiting, wanting, praying like the bloody hypocrite I am. Lord Raachwald set one heavy boot on my back and leaned in, lips close to my ear, just breathing, having his moment. "Black magic, Krait," he whispered, "black magic from the Quarter." Spitting aside, he raised the axe, not high, for these would be precision cuts, just enough to cut through my ribs at the spine. Not kill me. Not right away, at least.

"It wasn't them," I hissed. "They didn't kill Cain."

"Who then?"

"My Lord," Old Inglestahd appeared, bulling his way through the press, "Coldspire's been taken!"

"*What?*" Lord Raachwald straightened. "*Who?*"

"The Church. The Taschgarts."

"Emile Taschgart is dead," Lord Raachwald growled.

"Both banners fly—"

"It's *Father Paul Innocent,*" I gasped. "He's a Taschgart. The last. The *heir.*"

"The eunuch priest?" Lord Raachwald wiped his chin. "How many men?"

"I know not, my lord."

I opened my mouth to say something wholly inconsequential when there was a crash, a thunder, an elongated ripple that shook the rock beneath our feet. The men released me, trying to maintain their footing. I clung to the rock as men trembled to their knees.

Lord Raachwald, still afoot, peered over the precipice, unperturbed. "It is coming."

"No shit." I licked my lips.

It ghosted up from the chasm, just a noise, muted at first, muffled by the fog, and it was terrible. It was the sound of a man tortured nearly to death, a man pushed past his limits, a man broken to the extent that he could no longer feel pain, could no longer assess reality, a man no longer human. Then it changed. Something awoke within. Something shook that man and forced his eyes open, forced his heart to beat faster and stronger, forced his mind to understand the horror around him. And those screams grew. They grew along with the orange glimmer rising through the mists below. They grew along with the wet *slap* and *thwack* as though someone was slapping a ton of fresh-killed carcass against cliff.

"Raachwald," I scanned the squads, "arrows won't cut it."

Lord Raachwald ignored me. "Bind him." A knife was at my throat as my hands were bound before me. "He goes where I go."

"Do you have a cannon?" I yelled.

And for once, Lord Raachwald acknowledged me without the hatred, the vengeance, the lord's eye view. "The whelp has cannon." Lord Raachwald thumbed over his shoulder to Azure-Mist's high walls. From high atop the battlements, framed by night sky, Lady Narcissa stood watching, wrapped in her ermine fur.

"Brulerin's coming," someone yelled.

"Not fast enough," I said.

But even as I said it, I heard the creak and clatter of wheels, the stomp and chomp of boots on rock. Lead by the Brulerin youth, a squad of men hove into view, dragging a cannon, followed by three more. A handcart followed, then two more, each full of powder and stone shot.

The wails rose along with the glow from the mists, intensifying like sunrise from the gorge as the thing below scaled the cliffs.

"Load those monstrosities!" Lord Raachwald yelled.

The tall young lord lead his men swiftly, dropping his own shoulder to the end of a cannon to aid in turning. They spun it swiftly, as precise as automatons, aiming the fire-belching end toward the precipice, his other men following suit. I couldn't hear his words but knew Lord Brulerin was directing his men with concise orders, and the men were responding, loading the cannon like they must have a thousand times. "Fine work." He took a length of slow-match, smoking, in his hand. "On my word," he looked each of his men in the eye, "no one else's."

"Aye, my lord!"

Lord Brulerin's eyes flickered toward me an instant. He nodded, eyes filled with fear, but with steel, too. To possess such poise at a young age? I hated him instantly.

"Roll those abominations to the edge!" Lord Raachwald bellowed.

"Hold." Lord Brulerin raised a hand, calmly stifling the order. He said something to his men, raising a hand as he knelt, sighting along one of the gun barrels. "We hold here."

"It's coming, you whelp," Lord Raachwald growled.

"We hold, you wraith."

"Coward!" someone yelled.

"We hold." Lord Brulerin glanced up from the cannon at Lord Raachwald. "Why don't you go claim your prize?"

"An assault on Coldspire?" Lord Raachwald seethed. "Ladders. Grapples. Men, how many?"

"There's another way." Lord Brulerin pulled a chain from within his mail shirt. A key dangled. He cast it at Lord Raachwald's feet. "A secret way. Through my wine cellar. Take the catacombs."

Lord Raachwald stared with his dead eye. "You're to guide us then."

"Nay." Lord Brulerin adjusted the cannon's aim,

nudging it as he sited along its barrel. "I'm a mite busy."

"On your feet, whelp!" Lord Raachwald roared.

"Ask your beloved bride," Lord Brulerin blew on the end of the slow-match, ember glowing, readied by the cannon's touch hole, "she knows the way."

...in blood I scrawl verses of madness in the dark.

—*Journal of Sir Myron Chalstain*

Chapter 56.

DANK, FREEZING, we stood in the stairwell, huddled against the wall. Lord Raachwald strode past, following Lady Narcissa up to the landing. Haefgrim and Old Inglestahd trailed, close weapons and torches jutting from their fists as they spearheaded the last vestiges of Lord Raachwald's men. Twenty men, maybe. Twenty spent men.

Lady Narcissa stopped atop the landing, at the same door Lady Mary and I had days ago.

"Beyond lies the great hall." Lady Narcissa clutched her collar, fingers working, worrying the fabric.

Muffled sounds of footsteps were muted beyond the thick wood.

Lord Raachwald turned, "Should Krait escape..." he left the rest unsaid, merely pointing with that axe at the yellow-eyed bastard.

Eyes flashing, Slade licked his lips, "Aye," tightening his grip on the fistful of my hair, wheedling the tip of his dagger into my flank unconsciously, or consciously.

I was shivering.

"On my command." Lord Raachwald hissed like a serpent, his voice wending past his men trailing down into the spiraling dark. Mail rustled softly. Lord Raachwald waited the space of three breaths then lowered his shoulder into the door. He disappeared through, followed by Haefgrim, Old Inglestahd, and then the rest, one after the other, a pack of wolves loping toward fresh kill.

A count of ten I made in my head before shouts lit out. The sound of hacking, steel thunking into flesh, gurgling. Someone screamed. Shadows cavorted, men grunting, blades rasping. It was over in a flash, nothing but the reverberation of steel ringing into silence, the hacking smacks of cold iron into immobile flesh.

"Move." Slade prodded me on.

Scattered, broken, four church-men and five Taschgarts lay dead across the floor. Only two of Lord Raachwald's held that distinction. The rest stood huffing in a circle, their blood up, unquelled, still hungry, ravenous, waiting for orders, begging for orders, begging for orders that would unleash them for more slaughter.

Lord Volkendorf's stained glass effigy stared down, emotionless in his disapproval.

"Up." That was all Lord Raachwald said as he set his booted foot on a dead church-man's head, holding it down as he pried his axe free, levering up the handle. Then up the stairs, he loped.

His men followed.

The Grinner shoved me past a pair of cannon, a pyramid of stacked powder kegs, and into the stairwell.

Upstairs and through hallways, Lord Raachwald led his assault, quick, sudden, rapacious, driving the scattered remnants of the church and Taschgart back and up, always up, until only the door to the keep's acropolis lay between him and foe. The heavy door was locked. Wind howled outside.

"Those behind lie dead." Old Inglestahd emerged from a hallway, wiping blood from his forehead. Haefgrim loomed by his side.

"Open it." Lord Raachwald stepped aside.

Haefgrim shouldered past, ducking a rafter, snatching a battle axe from one of the men. Setting his feet, he started hewing into the door. Teeth gritted, grunting, savage, he swung. Wood chips flying, he murdered it, hacking til it was naught but kindling dangling from scarred hinges.

"Parley!" A voice commanded from beyond.

Lord Raachwald held up a hand and edged forward, keeping to the wall.

"I would discuss terms." It was Father Paul. "I would discuss terms with you, Lord Raachwald. Only you."

"I am here!" Lord Raachwald bellowed back.

"In the open," Father Paul shouted.

"As you wish," Lord Raachwald snarled, grabbing a fistful of my hair and nearly hurling me through the doorway, using me as a human shield.

"Fucking bastard," I cried, thrust stumbling forth. Six men, six I could see, crouched behind a waist-high wall of barrels and block and tackle set by the far side of the acropolis. "Don't shoot!"

"Hold!" Father Paul rose from behind the barrels, his sky blue eyes wide, wary, the loaded crossbow cradled in his hands rising along with him. He looked like his father, Emile Taschgart. I could see that now. "Sir Luther?"

The acropolis of Coldspire stood silent, a jagged finger of stone perched eagle-eyed above the burning city. The air reeked of smoke and ash, suffused by the taste of gunpowder and burnt flesh. Cannon fire erupted from the south then on a fell wind came the screams of men.

Footsteps. Footsteps came next, slow, measured, massive. The keep shivered beneath my feet.

The church-men rose from behind the wall of barrels, seven men all told. Captain Thorne stood amongst them, a pair of crossbow bolts flanking him aimed my way.

Craning my neck, I looked out, searching, could see nothing.

But it was coming.

"Still trying to fix things, Father?" I asked.

"My men?" Father Paul asked.

"Dead," Lord Raachwald rasped from behind.

Father Paul stared off over the dark river cutting through the heart of the city. "An expected risk."

"It is coming," Old Inglestahd warned.

"He's the one had Cain killed," I hissed behind.

I saw it the instant I spoke the words, Father Paul's eyes widening, lips moving, "*Loose!*" as Lord Raachwald bull-rushed me onward, crossbow bolts firing. Lord Raachwald's men howled like depraved wolves as they poured out *en masse*. A bolt ripped past my shoulder as I stumbled forward, Lord Raachwald hurdling me, Yolanda shining in his fist as he took a bolt to the chest. Still, he kicked through the barrels, bringing Yolanda down on a guard, shattering through his blade and into him.

Captain Thorne leapt the barrels only to meet Haefgrim, that falchion of his slinging down like murder incarnate, smashing Thorne's guard down. Sparks flying. Again. And Again. And again. Breaking him. Hammering him down into nothing.

The others fell quickly, Lord Raachwald continuing his onslaught, the Grinner stabbing and smashing, hacking like a madman, Old Inglestahd roaring a blood oath as his war-hammer shattered a helm and skull within.

And then it was over.

Father Paul stood, back to the chasm, shorn of his church robes, clutched in one hand, snapping in the wind. One by one his fingers opened and the gale took them. Upon his chest lay the Taschgart family sigil, the red phoenix rising. His crossbow was spent. He dropped it. "They would have followed me. They all would have…"

An orange glow rose behind like the morning sun.

A forest of legs surrounded me, grim faces above staring in awe as weapons were raised, the men silent, shaken, but not one broke.

Flames leapt into the sky as a huge three-fingered paw latched onto the parapet, fingers thicker than a man's chest pulling mortared stone apart like a child might a castle of sand. Coldspire groaned, shifting underfoot, shuddering as the demon hauled itself up. Flames poured up and over in a whirlwind firestorm.

"Mother of God…" Father Paul collapsed to one knee.

The numb lifeless eyes of the demon loomed above. Its great burning hand reached out, snatching Father Paul up as a man might a flipped coin. Immolating in white fire, Father Paul screamed as the demon's hand closed, wilting inward like the petals of a dying flower.

The hellfire demon stared down at the charred thing in its hand, abyssal-eyes watching without feeling, without

464

sense, without humanity. Father Paul's charred carcass shriveled, crisping to a crippled cinder. Waves of flame whipped alive, incensed, across its body as wind tore past, feeding it. The corpse demon looked down at me and Lord Raachwald, as though considering.

"Attack!" Lord Raachwald raised Yolanda overhead.

Orange light shimmered off drawn steel, and the corpse-demon struck, swiping its long arm, backhanding, through the mass of men. Heat and flame ripped overhead as I ducked, rolled, scrambled. The men scattered, screamed, flailed, were hurled flaming into infinity.

I was running, running for the door, for the stairs, for my life. Haefgrim stood in my path, a barrel of gunpowder hoisted over his head. Somehow. I ducked as he charged, hurling it at the demon. An explosion followed, a shockwave kicking like a mule, knocking me breathless across the rooftop. Flames erupted. Timber cracked. The demon stumbled, one of its legs blown off, its flailing arm obliterating the stairwell, pulverizing stone and man alike as it sank through the roof like it was mud.

Coldspire shivered, seized.

Another explosion rocked me sprawling against the parapet. I gasped. Stones dislodged. A tangle of legs and arms flailed around me as I fought to stand, scrabbling at the parapet, fighting through the daze. Lord Raachwald, next to me, smoking, rose, too. I looked up, saw the block and tackle crane looming above as the floor gave way, collapsing like an inverted wave. Scrambling up, I knocked the brake open and leapt, grabbing the rope as it tumbled free and fell weightless into abyss.

And as I fell, the demon fell, too, disappearing through the rooftop above.

The rope tore to a halt, yanking me up like a fish on a hook, burning my hands, dislocating my shoulder with a sucking pop. I felt no pain, only a dim wrongness. The burning city swirled before me, stars rotating above. I dangled for an instant, watching the world collapse when an explosion tore out in all directions below.

Blown sideways, I landed caterwauling across a slanted roof, bouncing, rolling, sliding as tiles shattered, rock and body avalanching. Hitting the ground, I broke loose a tooth, rose and was on my feet, scrambling. I clawed my way past the ancient obelisk and stumbled out the sundered gates. Turning, I nearly collapsed, grabbing onto something, someone, to maintain my footing.

The Isle rumbled.

Inwardly, awkwardly, inexorably, Coldspire collapsed, what was left of it, nothing more now than a skeletal ring-wall aimed jagged and hollow as a broken bottle at the sky, glowing windows glaring like eyes, charred stone and timber falling piece by piece into a blaze that Hell itself might envy.

...should anyone find this book, if the thing does not destroy it, if I should be...

—*Journal of Sir Myron Chalstain*

Chapter 57.

"TELL ME, KRAIT," Lady Narcissa stood by my side, watching her ancestral home burn, "are they all dead?"

I glanced at her, sidelong. "You still have that blade?" I held out my bound hands.

A look of reluctance, of consternation, glimmered in her eye as she drew her knife, clutched in a death-grip, her knuckles white, hand shaking ever so slightly. Inhaling sharp then exhaling slow, measured, her hand steadied, and she sawed at my bonds.

A section of tower collapsed, sending spark and ember bursting skyward, a flock of luminescent angels soaring.

"Lady, I..." The world went grey, buzzing to a haze. I sat on a fallen pillar. Drooled. Swallowed. After a moment, my vision cleared. "You have my thanks."

Lady Narcissa took a seat and waited, watching.

"They're dead." I followed her gaze to the fire. "The ones that killed your boys, all of them."

"You are certain?"

"Yeah."

Lady Narcissa smoothed out her skirts, saying nothing. Then she rose, ashen, and strode off in a fugue. She was beautiful, more so even than when first I set eyes on her, when she was clean and fresh and something new. Her cold arrogance was gone, along with the haughtiness, replaced by a drawn sadness heavier than all the sundered stones of Coldspire.

A crowd was gathering to watch Coldspire burn. Nobles, ladies, paupers, merchants, Jews. Lord Brulerin stood in their midst, soot-stained, powder burnt, but still whole. Lord Hochmund lazed on a rock, sipping wine, staring at the flames. It was something to see, the object of so many dreams, so many machinations all going up in ash. Fighting men, tabards of every color, milled about, interspersed amongst the masses, engrossed by the flames raging above, only the black obelisk still intact, still erect, still unmoved.

Out of the peal of blaring bright, two silhouettes emerged, striding from the shattered keep, nothing but shades at first, mirages rippling in blur, solidifying into focus with each step. Lord Raachwald. It was him, limping, purposeful. Haefgrim strode by his side, tall, unbent, unbroken.

"Jesus... Fucking... Christ." I rose to slink off through the crowd when I felt a prick at my back.

"Miss me, Krait?" It was Slade, charred black with soot, only his yellow eyes and jackal grin giving clue to his identity.

"Not especially," I deadpanned.

"The demon is slain!" Lord Raachwald stopped amidst the throng.

A moment of silence, then as one, man, woman, and child, hands raised, weapons aloft, metal clashing against metal, they cheered. Lord Hochmund, off to the side, shook his head slowly, raised his bottle in salute then downed a mouthful.

Lord Raachwald continued through the crowd, arms embracing him, patting him on the back, congratulating, thanking, praising. I could feel his gaze, though, could see hands edge towards weapons.

"Bring him here," Lord Raachwald demanded as the Lady Narcissa, all crystalline beauty, intercepted him, entwining her hand through his arm. She kissed him, his glare at me black murder even then. A cheer rose even as the Isle men around me turned as one, a thicket of weapons brought to bear, blades angled toward my throat from on all quarters.

The cheer rotted from within to without and died.

Those unarmed melted back, away.

"Pyotr." Lady Narcissa pulled Lord Raachwald's face toward her, holding it there a moment, whispering to him, mouth working. What she said, I couldn't hear. But he shook his head, lips curling back in a sneer, and pushed her away, firmly, inexorably. Then he came limping toward me, a hobbled thing, a lame thing, a terrible thing.

He parted the thicket of steel encircling me.

"Never enough for you, is it?" I said.

"Enough of what?" Lord Raachwald said.

"Enough of anything," I said. "Everything." But no one heard me, or if any did, none cared. Shaking my head, I turned. The haze of smoke split and the whole of Asylum lay bare before me, half burning in the dark of the new dawn. An awful kind of beauty.

"*Justice!*" Lord Raachwald announced, his voice a clarion call echoing far and long. A broken bolt shaft protruded still from his armored chest. "Tonight, the demon that slew my son, and so many others, has met its fate." He pointed back at me. "Yet tonight, there is more justice to mete out. This man," he aimed Yolanda's tip a hairsbreadth from my throat, "Sir Luther Slythe Krait is a murderer as well. He, too, must pay. The old way. Tonight. *Now.*"

"The old way?" I swatted aside Yolanda's razor tip. "I've *not* been tried. *Not* been convicted. *Not* found guilty of *any* crime."

"I'll hack the bones bloody from your back," Lord Raachwald rasped low, black spit coursing down his chin.

"Is that justice?" I hollered. "If I'm to be executed tonight, try me first. Gather a judge. Assemble a jury. There's plenty folk here." I turned in a slow circle, grim faces all around. "Or grant me trial by combat as was custom. As was law. As was the *old way.*"

Slade sniffed, adjusting his grip on the blade in my side, hand quivering in anticipation.

Lord Raachwald's glare degenerated from black murder to something beyond, something broken, something barren and cold and dead as a tundra sun. "So be it."

"My blade!" I yelled.

"Nay. *Mine*." Lord Raachwald steadied himself with Yolanda, using her as a crutch. His leg was broken. Something was bent, wrong. "*Yours* should you prove your innocence." He cleared his throat, hacking. "Haefgrim!"

A cheer arose as Haefgrim strode forward, raising that heavy-bladed falchion, tendrils of smoke still hissing, still twirling off his charred armor like something spawned of hell.

I backed up a step, but the Grinner prodded me forth.

Lord Hochmund's Captain Abel stepped in Haefgrim's path, his hand on his own sword. "Give the man a moment," Captain Abel glared towards Lord Raachwald, "and heel your devil." Captain Abel was tall, taller than me, but still shy of the giant by a head and a half.

Haefgrim offered Lord Raachwald a questioning glance.

Lord Raachwald nodded then fixed his glare on Slade. Without a word, Slade melted into the crowd. His gaze still locked on the giant, Captain Abel slid back, breaching the circle of steel surrounding me. "Give him some room, men," he ordered. "Give him a moment."

Lord Hochmund watched from the flickering shadows, sipping at his bottle.

Captain Abel nodded. "My lord, he could do with a taste."

Taken aback mid-gulp, Lord Hochmund took a moment to recover then shrugged, wrestling himself to his feet.

"Why?" I asked Captain Abel.

"You saved me back there when I fell," Captain Abel answered. "Could have left me." He nodded to himself. "Suppose it just seems like the right thing to do, is all."

"Not a recipe for a long life, Captain." I flexed my fingers, wincing.

"I am no cook, sir." Captain Abel pursed his lips in concern down at my hands.

"They'll do," I said. "Go stand by your lord. That's the recipe, eh Eustace?"

Lord Hochmund arrived by my side, laying a hand on my shoulder, steadying himself. "Cheers." He raised the bottle.

"Wouldn't perchance be poison?" I deadpanned.

"Sorry to disappoint you yet again, old son," Lord Hochmund replied, shoving the bottle in my face.

I snatched it. Cranking back my head, I took a long pull. A glorious pull. Wine eked in drizzles from my lips, down my cheeks, my neck. I took another. Jesus. Guzzling more. If only I could have drunk from that bottle for the rest of my life. As it was, it might be a close thing.

"It's time." Captain Abel looked over his shoulder.

The mob's rumble grew.

I lowered the bottle, wiped my chin. "Any advice?"

"Run?" Lord Hochmund offered.

I took another pull. "Yeah."

"You're in no shape, man," Captain Abel said grimly, appraising me. "He'll murder you."

"That *is* how these things work." I raised an eyebrow. "*You* want to fight him?"

His gaping-wide mouth, offering only silence, answered for him.

"Don't blame you." I cast an eye Lord Hochmund's way. "How about you? Any grand gestures?"

"I did just share my wine," he sniffed.

I smirked and handed him the bottle. "Fair enough."

Lord Hochmund wiped its mouth with his sleeve. "Give my best to your uncle."

"I'll give my best to Haefgrim."

"Sir Luther, I'd be remiss—" Captain Abel gripped my shoulder.

But I pulled out of his grasp and marched away, shouldering past bodies, rubbing my wrists, opening and closing my fingers, flexing feeling back into my hands. The pain of the day, the week, the month, all dulled as warmth spread through me. A circle formed in the mob, faces orange in the roaring light of the dying keep.

I entered the circle.

Haefgrim stood on the far side and strode forth just shy of its center, that falchion perched, two-handed, at his shoulder. I waited, empty-handed. Captain Abel materialized, pressing his own sword into my hands. "Take it," he smacked me on the back, "and good luck."

"Right." By rote, I felt the sword's grip, testing its heft, gauging its balance. It wasn't Yolanda, not even close, but it was a damn sight better than nothing.

"Justice be done!" Lord Raachwald bellowed, breaking me from my reverie.

The grim giant stood silent.

The crowd swayed as crowds do, antsy, impatient, men moving from foot to foot, fidgeting, salivating, a ravenous thing alive.

"*You fucking snake!*" someone called out.

"*Worm!*" screamed another.

A hailstorm of insult rained down. I ignored them. Focusing. I'd heard it all before, by a whole bunch of fuckers wearing dirt right now. I spat and strode toward the center, pausing ten paces from the giant. Lady Narcissa stood by Lord Raachwald's side. The wind lifted her midnight hair in streamed tresses, and she gazed into my eyes with those violet amethysts. I could read nothing within their gleam.

"Hey." I looked Haefgrim in the eye. "*Fuck you.*"

Haefgrim nodded. His shoulders rose as he took a deep breath, steam pouring in a gout from the ventail of his iron helm. The giant was a foot taller than me, wider, and I suppressed the despair spreading like cancer through my gut, threatening to metastasize, to cripple my heart, my head, my soul. I tested the edge of Captain Abel's sword, breathing slow, breathing the bad feeling out with each exhale, trying to, at least. Steel was the lone cure now, and even the best might not succeed. Hell, even if my name were *Arthur* and my blade *Excalibur*, I'd have given my chances one in a thousand. And sadly, my name was Krait and my blade was probably *Dennis* or *Mervyn* or something.

I raised it nonetheless, mirroring Haefgrim, taking it up two-handed in the high guard, to the sinister side. Most fight from the right. A left-hander's something different, something odd. An advantage. Maybe.

Haefgrim stepped to his left, angling to my right.

Moving, too, I circled opposite, keeping just out of reach. Distance, he hadn't closed it yet, was waiting, watching, gauging. The look of boredom had burned clear from his eyes.

I had his attention.

And he mine.

"Murderer!"

I focused, watching Haefgrim move, step, flow, biding my time, focusing on my breath. Slow… Slow… Slow, *damn it!*

The crowd distorted back as we moved, flowing behind, around, beyond, evaporating as the cliff side materialized, revealing a sheer drop to my back. Death ground. Shit.

The wind whipped.

Without warning, Haefgrim stepped in and swung, whipping that falchion in an arc intended to split me from shoulder to hip. It came strong, it came quick for such a big man, for such an unwieldy weapon. The air vibrated as the blade buzzed past, but I was quick, too, quicker, as I pivoted just out of the arc of his strike, swinging at the same time, a master-cut from the high guard, the edge of my blade smashing his armored forearm as it whipped down, biting, cracking, sparking off his gauntlet.

Haefgrim offered no tell, no grunt, no reaction, only continued onslaught, hacking again, grunting, a reverse cut slung up off his initial cut. But I already had that quarter of my body closed off by the downward swing of my blade. I raised the hilt of my blade, turning over my hands, keeping the point virtually in place, taking the brunt of his strike angled on my blade, sliding from point of impact to the strong, lock-stopping dead against the quillons as I drove in.

Armor's reactionary. Invent a new weapon and someone'll build armor to nullify it. Well, the armor hasn't been made that can stop the point of a bastard-sword backed by ten stone of downward force. A coat of plate over mail and a gambeson, maybe. Haefgrim wore mail. My point snicked through it like it wasn't even there, into his left thigh, followed by my shoulder slamming into his chest, knocking him off kilter.

Twisting my blade, I continued moving in, invading his space, eating his ground, not to do more damage—which I certainly did—but to gain my strong side again. I drove forward, in, tight, striving continually, relentlessly. A big opponent's strong in close, but he's stronger from afar. Nothing worse than him reaching you but you can't him. So be where you can damn well reach him.

And I was.

Haefgrim hobbled back, spinning in place, me driving him counterclockwise, propelled by my blade lodged through his thigh, my quillons locking his blade down. He was bigger than me, twice as strong, a whole lot meaner and tougher and it all meant shit so long as I kept moving forward and in a circle. He couldn't draw his falchion away, or I'd drive my blade all the way through him, fillet his leg, open it completely. He couldn't stop. Couldn't find his root. Each time he tried, my momentum ate the distance, reinforcing the lock, pushing him off balance, sawing sinew and flesh, using his thigh bone as a lever, blood pumping black in spurts.

Haefgrim let go of his falchion with one hand and smashed me across the face with an elbow.

Stars exploded.

"*Fuck!*" I saw God, Death, Odin Stormcrow waiting patiently. But I held on, dropping my weight, ducking a second swing, a third, pressing in. Relentlessly. His fourth blow glanced across my head. I half-circled into him, shuffle-stepping, my shoulder in the pit of his stomach, forcing him back as I hooked one leg round his good one, tripping him crashing to the ground. My blade tore arcs of black as I jump-stepped back, keeping my blade in the low guard, parrying Haefgrim's swing.

Haefgrim was down, on his arse, cliff to his back, dying. But a swipe from that falchion'd still cut me in twain. He fought up to one knee, slinging another cut wild at my legs, desperate, trying to back me up, force open some space. Instead, I jump-stepped in, taking the ringing blow on the strong of my blade as I drove the point down, stabbing into his midsection quick as lightning then retreated out of reach.

Gasping, mad, growling, he tore his helm free, casting it soaring over the cliff. His eyes were round, black, mirroring the round blackness pumping out fast beneath him. Sweat glistened like scale as his bare head steamed. Blood ran black from his lips, staining his tangle of beard.

"Falchion's a piss-poor weapon for a duel," I grunted because it was. On the battlefield, it's durable, reliable, lethal. Not particularly versatile, but it doesn't have to be. It only has to chop. But really, it can *only* chop. And chopping's not good enough in a duel. Not against a fair opponent. And I was that, seemingly, at least.

Haefgrim grunted something that sounded like accord. He said it wearily, slurringly, like he knew what was coming. Hacking a spray of blood, he hissed, forcing himself up as I stepped in and with a flick of my wrists split his head clean in two down to his chin. I stared into those eyes for an instant, two disparate holes separated by crimson. Then he toppled forth like a hewn oak.

I collapsed to a knee, huffing, spent.

Around me, the mob murmured, pressed in close, uneasy. Lord Raachwald stood at its forefront.

"My blade," I gasped, holding out a shaking hand.

"*You*—" Lord Raachwald launched himself forward, madness in his eye, teeth gritted like a steel trap, reaching, clawing, scrabbling for my throat with one hand, Yolanda, gleaming, drawn back for a telling blow in his other.

I didn't flinch, didn't move, didn't react. I couldn't. But Lord Brulerin and Captain Abel and others closed in, ensnaring him like a cast net, grappling him kicking and roaring back. Snarling, slavering, a rabid beast, Lord Raachwald fought an arm free and raised Yolanda—

"*Your oath*!" I rose.

Lord Raachwald froze amidst the tangle of bodies restraining him, and then the madness vacated. He opened his hand, relinquishing Yolanda, letting her drop ringing to the ground.

Someone bore her to me. I know not who.

I took her with grunted thanks.

I did not remain long after.

Chapter 58.

I DREW BACK my hood and took a seat at the table hidden away in the corner. Stephan pursed his lips in consternation as I reached across for the wine, poured myself a cup, took a slug.

It was late.

The *Kraken's Arm* was quiet, most of its patrons having gone, though a few were laid out across chairs pushed together into makeshift benches, snoring, drooling, mumbling in slumber. Long kraken arms stretched sinuously from floor to ceiling, support columns hacked ragged to that likeness. Red embers, tickled into motion by an updraft, glowed in the hearth along with a few sputtering lamps. The patter of raindrops against the roof was continuous, monotonous, hypnotizing.

"How's yer lady-friend?" Karl settled back, one eye on the door, taking a pull on his ale. Color had returned to his face.

"Which one?" I asked.

"The one that hates you."

"You'll need to be more specific."

"The whore."

"How is she, Lou?" Stephan had filled out since his stay in Lord Raachwald's dungeon. He was still gaunt, still pallid, but healthier. Not healthy, per say, but *healthier*. A stiff breeze might *not* knock him flat on his arse. His shorn stump was wrapped neatly in white linen.

"She didn't want to see me." I took another sip.

"Can't blame her," Karl said.

"She was dealt a rough hand, brother," Stephan added.

"Aren't we all." I rapped the table with my knuckles. "I asked Nils to drop in on her from time to time."

"Har, tough, job, that." Karl slapped the table. "Coming and going." He guffawed like an obnoxious mule, worse probably.

One of the drunks raised his head, stared over at us, beyond us, wavering dazed, then blacked back out.

"She'll be alright," Stephan said.

"She's drinking herself to death." I raised my cup of wine. "Cheers."

"You find out *anything*?" Karl asked. "Anything useful?"

"No." I drained my cup. "I cased Goathead top to bottom. The Point. The waterfront. A no-go, all around. No one remembers a kid's body washing up. It was the bad time, the start of it all. Plague. War. Hell, sometimes they just don't. But it fits. Still."

Karl glared at us in succession. "Huh?"

"Lady Narcissa said that Cain Raachwald's tomb was empty," I explained.

"So…" Karl scratched his beard, "The boy weren't killed?"

"Oh, he was," Stephan explained. "We know it wasn't Lord Raachwald who killed the Volkendorf boys, so it's almost certain Cain was killed, too. It seems likely the assassin hurled Cain Raachwald's corpse out the window and into the river." Stephan quieted a moment, stifling a shudder. "To sow discord, muddy the waters, point the finger at Lord Raachwald rather than the true perpetrator."

"Good thing it didn't work," Karl grumbled into his ale.

"Yeah," I said.

"So," Karl's eyes screwed shut, "how was it they was all entangled?"

"Who?" Stephan asked.

"All of them." Karl opened his eyes. "Everything."

"*Everything*?" I echoed, trying to wrap my head around it all. And failing.

"Well, Lou did some digging." Stephan worried the bandages on his stump. "Father Paul was the key. Obviously. He was born the youngest son of the Taschgart's, and being the youngest, he had no hope of inheriting the family keep or lands let alone Coldspire, so his father offered him to the church. More prospects there.

"He began his God-work as an oblate in some monastery on the Danube. Eventually, he took vows as a priest and spent his life rising through the ranks, moving up, always up. He was named bishop of Worms ten years ago. And five years later, he was sent back here and given a small congregation on the Point. Saint Cuthbert's."

"Which is strange," I interjected. "A bishop being demoted. He had prospects. Clout. Momentum. And they send him back here and to a shitty little church at that?"

"He must have requested it," Stephan said. "Seed he'd sown since his departure come at last to fruition. He'd been lying in wait, biding his time, patient, and on his return, it seems none were aware of his familial connection. It'd been decades." He waved his hand. "Oh, Chalstain knew, and his father, his family, of course, but it wasn't common knowledge."

"An ace in the hole," I said.

"I wonder whether the Lord Bishop knew, though I think not," Stephan said. "And Father Paul harbored ambitions, and as before, through the years, through the changes in power, from the Volkendorfs to the English to the Church, he rose and he rose."

"Crafty bastard, eh?" Karl grumbled. "Ruthless, too, having his own kin murdered."

"Yeah." I nodded. "He was born to the Isle, so he *had* to have it, whatever the cost. They all do. It was bred into them. Him. So he did what he had to get it. Which, it turned out, in the end, was a lot."

"Hrrmmm, so what about the Jews?" Karl asked. "What's their connection?"

"I'd thought initially it was *them* buying up all of the Volkendorf debt," I said. "The Masada or *Sicarii*. Figured them for the only ones with the coin and balls to attempt it, let alone achieve it, but I forgot about the church. Somehow. Forgot all the money the Quarter scratches together gets taxed to hell and back, and all those taxes end up in church coffers. So Father Paul consolidated the lion's share of the

Volkendorfs' debts."

"Con...sola...date?" Karl worked out the word.

"*Jesus Christ*," I muttered, "should we act it out with finger puppets?"

Stephan leaned in. "Father Paul bought up all the Volkendorf debt, using church funds on the sly. He wanted to seize control of Coldspire, and he did so, on parchment, at least. The Jews didn't squawk. They were getting red off their ledgers, and besides, they didn't know what was going on. Most of them, that is." He glanced over at the door. "And the Lord Bishop was none too popular in the Quarter, anyways, with his draconian taxes and liens on I don't know how many properties." Stephan took a sip. "These clandestine interactions must have somehow brought Father Paul into direct contact with Daniel, and they forged some form of bond. Alliance. It blossomed from there. Follow?"

"*Blossom*?" Karl grunted. "Strange pick of word."

"At some point, Father Paul found out that Daniel was unleashing the golem to murder Lord Volkendorf," Stephan went on. "Maybe Daniel trusted him, or maybe he let something slip. I don't know. In any case, he sent Casagrande that night to eliminate any and all of the possible Coldspire successors, sowing discord, fear and raising himself up in the line. The Lord and Lady Volkendorf, plus three heirs, all in one shot. But Lady Narcissa was *indisposed* that night, as she said, and so she lived.

"It all proceeded as smooth as clockwork until then." Stephan set a few of the pieces of clay onto the table. "The golem killed Volkendorf and everyone standing in between while Casagrande took the Taschgart tunnel onto the Isle, made his way into Coldspire, waited for the golem to strike, then did his red-work. And in the aftermath, while everyone was blaming each other, killing, starving and dying of plague, Father Paul, as ever, was biding his time, patient as a spider, spinning webs and crawling upwards."

"Audacious plan," I admitted. "With the Lord Bishop dead, Father Paul was next in line there. So he'd have had half of the city right there. Then when he took

Coldspire? He'd have united Asylum under himself."

"Fucker," Karl spat. "What about Casagrande? How'd you *know* it was him?"

"I'm smart." I tapped my temple.

"Like shit you are."

"Well," I said, taken aback but moving on, "he's always done red-work for hire. We know that. But it was the way he did it. His *modus operandi.*" I sat back, waiting for either to be impressed by my diction. Then I stopped waiting. "A real sick bastard." I tried not to see the two Volkendorf boys' faces in my mind's eye, took a long breath, finished my wine, poured some more. "The Volkendorf boys had both had their throats slit, but there was something else, too. Both had puncture wounds in the corner of one of their eyes. Small holes, nearly unnoticeable."

"Dago blade?" Karl wrapped his thick fingers around his cup, squeezing.

"Yeah. He shanked the kids before carving southern smiles. And then he did Lady Chalstain but didn't finish her. Maybe didn't want to draw attention? Maybe he figured it'd be crueler? Maybe someone interrupted him? Don't know. But it happened there, at Saint Edna's. Father Paul was probably worried she knew something. Was worried she'd jaw on in the wrong ears. Spill something. Attract attention."

"But how'd you ken it was *him*?" Karl asked.

"Saw him skull-fuck some poor sod the night of the demon."

Stephan turned pale, paler. "We should be leaving."

"I'm still drinking," I said.

"No, I mean Asylum. We should leave it. Tonight. Now."

"I said, 'I'm still drinking.'" I poured more. "Besides, weather's holding raw. Roads're shit. No one's moving still, and *he's* watching them. Like a hawk. Raachwald. Got a squad west at Dunmire's heap and all along the east and south roads." I held up two fingers. "Two weeks and we slide out real nice and quiet-like. Dark of the moon." We'd been pulling a vagabond tour of Asylum the past few weeks, never spending a night in the same place, sleeping under bridges, in burnt-out foundations, abandoned buildings. Never showing face to the light of day. "Or, I've had my eye on a boat might suit us?"

"Theft?" Stephan frowned.

"Blessing of the plague," I countered. "Owners're dead."

"You're certain?"

"*Sure*," I lied.

Karl chuffed a laugh, took a pull of ale.

Stephan glanced over his shoulder. "I don't like it here."

"Who does?" I sat back, eyes on the door. *Footsteps?* I reached under the table, waited, no, eased back. "Hell, Raachwald wants me dead as much as you. Shit. More." I smacked Karl's arm with the back of my hand. "Care to weigh in?"

"Nar." A ragged grin spread wide and wicked as pestilence. "I'm dead, remember? Ain't nobody gives a shit about me no more."

"You're saying there was a time someone did?" I eyeballed him, skeptical.

"Lou, you're absolutely *certain* it's Raachwald wearing the mantle of power?" Stephan asked.

"Yeah, until Narcissa decides to shank him in his sleep," I said. "Abe says the taxes are going to one of Raachwald's men now. Taxes, protection money, same difference. And Nils says that yellow-eyed fucker's commanding the city guard. Slade. Says he's been recruiting. Gaining numbers. Holding the gates. Hunting dissenters. Brought the Fool's Hand, the whole waterfront, in line and he's working the eastern gangs now.

"The church's broken, too. No one's got the scratch to fill the Lord Bishop's shoes. And anyone tries, he's gonna wish he hadn't. Raachwald ain't taking chances. And he ain't shy about making martyrs." I shrugged. "Most of the church's soldiers are dead, anyways. No one now but priests and nuns. My question, though, is *why* hasn't Raachwald come forward? He's got the power. No one's fixed to oppose him. Why all the shadow business? Why not some blatant display of power? A proclamation? A coronation? Something?"

"Coldspire's a smoking ruin," Karl said.

"True, but they're already rebuilding. And it's his." Stephan fingered his lower lip, nodding. "As soon as Raachwald declares himself Lord of Asylum, the church and king are going to hear of it, and neither's going to be pleased. They'll send soldiers. Armies. So right now, the city's in shambles. Chaos. Mayhem. Infrastructure shot. Raachwald wants it that way. No one outside knows what's going on. But word'll leak out once the roads open. I suppose Raachwald'll declare then." Stephan glared down at his stump. "Someone needs to stop him."

"Why?" I asked.

"He's a killer. A madman. A—"

"Yeah?" I shrugged. "A decisive one, though."

"And that makes a difference?"

"Sure. He pulled the whole Isle together. The Five Houses. Ancestral enemies. United them all. Well, four anyways."

"To raze the Quarter," Stephan said.

"And he was successful, too." I sat back, hands up. "What? He was. And he's more popular than ever. He felled that…that thing. There's not many that could have done that."

"*Rose of Sharon,* you're defending him?"

"No. I'm speaking truth. The one thing's got nothing to do with the other. He razed the Quarter. Yeah. Hell, he also fought off a surprise attack by the Lord Bishop. Halfway through the Quarter, Teutonics and Jews fighting him in the north. Street fighting. Hard going. And then the Lord Bishop's men come ambushing him from the south. Battling on *two* fronts. With that nightmare marauding. And Raachwald *won*. He led the charge. He's a fucking hero to most."

Stephan muttered, shaking his head, scowling at the

dank surroundings. "We shouldn't have come here. We should have stayed where we were. Out of sight."

"I told you, we've business here tonight," I said.

"What sort of business?"

"Needlepoint."

"Judas Priest."

"I'm doing this for you."

"For me?"

"You gave Narcissa your word that *all* the killers would see justice."

"Justice?" Stephan cleared his throat. His cough still hadn't left him, not entirely. He sat silently for a moment, considering. "Casagrande?"

"Yeah."

"You lied to her, then?"

"A little. Yeah. Had to."

"He's still alive?"

"I intend to rectify that."

"How?" Stephan adjusted himself. "When?"

I glanced over at the door. *Footsteps?* They were quick, light. Yeah. *Her.*

"Fucker's a dead man, lad." Karl slapped Stephan on the back with a *thud*. "Just, he don't know it yet."

Stephan had barely recovered from the blow when the front door creaked open, a raw wind gushing in. A shadow scurried in from the wet and cold, sliding through the maze of tables. "Quickly." Lady Mary pulled back the hood of her cloak, her eyes wide, her shorn hair plastered wet across her face. "He's right behind."

I reached under the table for the crossbow.

She gave me a warning look, glanced at Karl and then Stephan. She offered a curt nod. Stephan nodded then looked down.

"You're certain?" I asked.

"Aye." She brushed back her wet hair. "I did what you bade."

"Ask and you shall receive, little brother," I said, mussing Stephan's hair.

Lady Mary sat down, grabbing a wine cup, her big eyes wide over its rim. Winking, I pulled my hood up, watching the door out of the corner of my eye.

Karl leaned forward, grinning ear to ear, a wolf slavering at the promise of sheep.

The front door flung open, banging against the wall, wind whistling as three men hustled in one after another, shaking water from their cloaks, scanning the room as they headed for the bar. The last one closed the door behind.

In the gloom, I could see the dago's meticulously trimmed mustache, his pony-tail tied behind his head as he pulled back his hood. He scanned the room, his hunter's eyes sliding to us, lost in shadow, then past. A pair of gleaming hilts glinted at either hip from under his cloak. He stood at the bar an instant later, jawing up the bartender, looking over his shoulder, this way and that, speaking low, one hand gesticulating like dagos do.

I sipped my wine, blending in with the rest of the shit in the place. A strength of mine. I laid three fingers down on the table, catching Karl's eye.

"Three," Karl grunted.

"You can count that high?" I nodded, impressed.

Stephan pounded back a drink. Fast. Hard.

"Just doing what we do best, little brother."

"He's a bad man." Lady Mary snatched a glimpse at the bar.

"Sure as shit, he is, and then some." I watched Casagrande as he leaned against the bar, taking a tentative sip of wine, his predator gaze riveted to the door, hand to the pommel of one of those dago blades. "Bad men do bad things, little brother," I pushed up from the table, "watch and learn."

ABOUT THE AUTHOR

Kevin Wright studied writing at the University of Massachusetts in Lowell and fully utilized his bachelor's degree by working first as a produce clerk and later as an emergency medical technician and firefighter. His mother is thrilled.

For decades now he has studied a variety of martial arts but steadfastly remains not-tough in any way shape or form. He just likes to pay money to get beat up, apparently.

Kevin Wright peaked intellectually in the seventh grade. Some of his favorite authors and influences are George R.R. Martin, H.P. Lovecraft, Lloyd Alexander, Neil Gaiman, Joe Abercrombie, and Joseph Heller.

Made in United States
North Haven, CT
07 October 2021

10200527R00288